Praise for the Oak

"A tender account of unconditional love and the deeper joy that results from overcoming the odds, Lang's latest is recommended for all collections."
Library Journal

"Lang has written a novel that's close to her heart, in which a mother's love for her child knows no boundaries. This book is heart-wrenching but heart-warming at the same time."
Romantic Times BOOKreviews, **4-star review**

"Beautifully touching and completely absorbing, this bittersweet novel will entertain and educate."
Compulsivereader.com

"Maureen Lang's novel *The Oak Leaves* is a work both masterful and deeply touching. weaving together modern medicine and Irish history, *The Oak Leaves* is a lush and moving tapestry of love, fear, and faith."
Christianbookpreviews.com

"Drawing from her own life experience, Maureen Lang invites us to experience the honest disappointments and glorious discoveries that come from mothering a son others may see as 'different,' yet God sees only as His beloved child."
Liz Curtis Higgs, best-selling author of *Thorn in My Heart*

"I couldn't put this book down. Vivid, compelling and deeply moving, with issues that touch the soul, *The Oak Leaves* was a story that lingered in my heart, and made me ask, just how much am I willing to accept from the Lord? . . . Every moment you spend with this book is worth it."
Susan May Warren, award-winning author of *Reclaiming Nick*

"Maureen Lang's *The Oak Leaves* is a beautiful, beautiful story of the many kinds of love and their divine author. I feel privileged to be one of the first to read it."
Lyn Cote, author of *The Women of Ivy Manor*

On
Sparrow Hill

MAUREEN LANG

TYNDALE HOUSE PUBLISHERS, INC.
CAROL STREAM, ILLINOIS

Visit Tyndale's exciting Web site at www.tyndale.com

Check out the latest about Maureen Lang at www.maureenlang.com

TYNDALE and Tyndale's quill logo are registered trademarks of Tyndale House Publishers, Inc.

On Sparrow Hill

Designed by Beth Sparkman

Edited by Kathryn S. Olson

Published in association with the literary agency of WordServe Literary Group, Ltd., 10152 S. Knoll Circle, Highlands Ranch, CO 80130.

Scripture quotations are taken from the *Holy Bible,* King James Version.

Scripture quotations are taken from the *Holy Bible,* New International Version®. NIV®. Copyright © 1973, 1978, 1984 by International Bible Society. Used by permission of Zondervan. All rights reserved.

Library of Congress Cataloging-in-Publication Data

Lang, Maureen.
   On sparrow hill / Maureen Lang.
     p. cm.
   Sequel to: The oak leaves.
   ISBN-13: 978-1-4143-1346-7 (pbk.)
   ISBN-10: 1-4143-1346-2 (pbk.)
   I. Title.
   PS3612.A554O6 2008
   813'.6--dc22
2007030031

Printed in the United States of America

14   13   12   11   10   09   08
 7   6   5   4   3   2   1

Dedicated with gratitude to teachers and therapists
who work with special-needs kids.
You embody true servanthood.

Nature has some perfections to show that she is the image of God, and some defects to show that she is only His image.

BLAISE PASCAL

ACKNOWLEDGMENTS

This book would not have happened except for my agent, Greg Johnson. I am deeply grateful you didn't listen to my first ambivalent reaction to the idea of a sequel to *The Oak Leaves*. I would have missed a huge blessing!

I would also like to thank Jim Powell, commercial manager to Holdenby House near Northampton, England. Without your help, my Rebecca would have had little to do on her day job. I am sincerely grateful you didn't mind my frequent, question-riddled e-mails. Thank you!

Also thanks to Christine Nelson, my English friend and encourager who helped me step out of my American way of thinking and into the skin of my very British characters.

As always, I'm grateful to those who are sharing this journey with me, for their encouragement and inspiration. A special thanks to Sherri Gallagher for her friendship and help.

I cannot end this without another thank-you to Stephanie Broene, Karen Watson, and of course Kathy Olson at Tyndale. Your support and enthusiasm add to the joy of writing, but your professionalism and insight allow this work to exceed my abilities.

My dear Berrie's life can be summed up by hope and worship, along with a fair share of suffering to keep her fixed on eternity. Enclosed are the letters she sent to me so long ago, when we were both young and had much to learn.

—Cosima Escott Hamilton

1

Hollinworth Hall, Northamptonshire, England

Rebecca Seabrooke didn't have to open the letter in her palm to know its contents: the annual employment offer from England's National Trust. More money than she would ever see at the private historical home at which she now worked. More prestige. Perhaps even a choice of locations, since so many of the country's national home treasures were owned by the Trust.

She really must e-mail her father and ask him to stop wasting postage on such offers. Despite what at least one Hollinworth thought of the work she did here, Rebecca was convinced the Hall was as much a treasure as any other property listed in the Trust's considerable inventory.

Brushing aside the letter, she turned her attention to her busy calendar. With her education staff manager on temporary family leave, Rebecca found herself taking charge of house-and-garden tours in between meetings with business associates and brides wanting to schedule the manor for banquets and weddings.

But none of that took precedence in Rebecca's mind today, for today the owner of Hollinworth Hall would return to the private quarters he kept in the north wing. And she'd only learned of his impending arrival this morning.

Nonetheless she'd already asked Helen to make sure his rooms had been aired and cleaned. Fresh flowers from Rebecca's favorite garden brightened every alcove, and even now Helen was baking his favorite bread. Rebecca could smell the fragrant herbs all the way up in her second-floor office. Given his mother's recent quote in a local newspaper about closing the Hall to visitors, Rebecca knew she had a fight on her hands, and the son, the legal owner of the Hall, might very well be the rope in this tug-of-war.

Thankfully she'd outgrown the adolescent crush on him she'd once suffered. Her father had pointed him out as the son of the family he formerly worked for, and when she was twelve and he thirteen, she thought Quentin Hollinworth the most sophisticated and handsome male alive. He was still handsome—she knew that despite seeing him only once or twice a year—but growing up had taught her a few things, one lesson being that classes didn't mix well, even in today's all but egalitarian England. Though he wasn't dating the daughter of an earl anymore, there was still his mother. She was proof enough the classes should mix only when both parties wanted to be in the same one.

Rebecca had far too much work to be dwelling on such irrelevant things. Directing her attention back to her computer screen, she pulled up her e-mail. The first one she noticed was from a college friend about meeting at a club in London this weekend, another event Rebecca would be sure to skip. She skimmed the content, part of her admiring the busy city life her friends had chosen, part of her knowing she'd followed the right path in staying out here in the country.

Before long, her gaze returned to the window, hearing the crunch of gravel beneath a car. Quentin Hollinworth had arrived. She imagined the estate caretakers, Helen and William Risdon, going out to greet him, welcoming him home.

Unwillingly she glanced at the bottom drawer of her desk, where she kept the newspaper society pages she couldn't seem to resist. It was silly of her to have kept so many clippings, except that it all pertained to the family connected to the estate she ran. Keeping a scrapbook of their lives was part of her job as steward of their legacy. Preservation was more patriotic than personal. In that drawer was Quentin Hollinworth's recent history, from his political work to his not-so-private breakup with Caroline Norleigh. Rebecca couldn't think of Quentin without remembering all of that.

She returned to her e-mail, reading a message from a teacher who had visited recently and was thanking Rebecca for bringing their Victorian heritage to life for the two dozen children she'd guided that day. These were Rebecca's favorite notes—ones that proved her work made a difference. If the Featherby were awarded, she could spend more effort in attracting such groups. They didn't pay as well as business banquets or weddings, but to Rebecca, educating children was far more important.

"Good afternoon, Rebecca."

Quentin Hollinworth looked tall and strong even with a massive doorway behind him. His broad shoulders filled out a casual, somewhat crumpled, beige linen suit, a stark contrast to his dark hair.

"Welcome home." She quickly averted her gaze and shifted the chair closer to her desk. Her battlement, safe behind the mahogany. It had been nearly three months since she had spoken to him. He trusted her so thoroughly with the running of the Hall that he almost never checked in. If she was to have her way, though, that must change. She alone couldn't prove the value of the Hall in its current public state. She would need his help.

"I see you've single-handedly held down the roof."

"Hardly single-handedly." Rebecca thought of William and Helen, who lived in the estate home on the grounds and supervised most household needs. And the education staff members who came on tour days to create an authentic Victorian atmosphere. Not to forget the many maids and repairmen going in

3

and out, the land agent who oversaw the crops, nor the head gardener, who lived in the village but spent most of his waking moments making sure Hollinworth Hall lived up to its reputation as one of the finest garden spots in the United Kingdom.

"Without you," Quentin said as he neared the desk, "I'm sure the place would fall to ruin, no matter how big a staff."

"And how is your mother, Quentin?" Rebecca didn't really want to know, unless Lady Elise Hollinworth had something to do with his visit. To close the Hall to the public? "She's well, I hope?"

"Yes, she is well," he replied. "At the cottage for the summer."

Rebecca nodded. Despite the cozy term for the Hollinworth estate inherited from his mother's aristocratic side of the family, the so-called cottage was anything but quaint. Less than fifteen kilometers away, the sprawling mansion surrounded by fifteen hundred acres of meadow, lakes, and woods was the center of Hollinworth country social life.

"The tour season is off to a healthy start," Rebecca said. "We've received several calls for visits here before the next holiday."

"The schedule is in your hands, Rebecca. I plan to be here rather than at the cottage most of the summer."

Here? For the summer? To assess whether or not to keep the Hall open? "I'll be sure no one gets in your way." How calm her voice sounded despite the blood pumping madly through her veins. "Guests still have access only to the usual spots, of course, depending on the event." Myriad thoughts clashed with her effort to keep the conversation going. If he *were* here to evaluate the merit of keeping the Hall open, she must convince him—the sooner, the better. If he closed the Hall to the public, it wasn't just a matter of losing a job she loved. Failing a dream came at a much higher price.

Taking a seat opposite her, Quentin appeared at complete ease. "I've no doubt you'll keep me well protected."

She caught his eye, then looked away. Protecting him from the general public was part of her job. "Yes, between me and a good security system, Quentin, that should be manageable."

He said nothing, and Rebecca wasn't sure what he was thinking. She might have known of Quentin Hollinworth since she was a child, but in reality he was no more than an acquaintance. Her grandfather had been the last in a long line of valets to Quentin's male forebears, most of whom had been Hamiltons and members of the peerage. By the time Rebecca's father was of an age to take up the position, valets had long since fallen out of vogue. So her father had taken on the role of houseman and resided in the very estate home William and Helen now occupied. Her father had stayed only long enough tofinish his graduate work in Victorian studies. When he decided to leave employment of the Hamilton/Hollinworth family—a Seabrooke tradition for no less than twelve generations—Quentin's father might have been put out. Yet he'd revealed neither disappointment nor frustration over having to hire someone entirely new to the family to oversee household workings. Quite like the fine English gentlemen he'd been. Setbacks were to be expected; it was how one handled them that proved the true character of a man.

"We're being considered for a Featherby Education Award," Rebecca said finally. Her finest weapon, another award to prove that the preservation of historical English life should be valued not ignored, forgotten, sold, or kept hidden in the private lives of the elite.

"Yes, so I've heard. I received the notification at my London flat. It's entirely due to you, Rebecca. Congratulations."

She managed a steady smile. "We haven't won yet."

"As they say, it's an honor to be nominated." He caught her shifting gaze. "Actually, Rebecca, that was one of the reasons I planned to stay the summer. I thought I might lend a hand, talk to the judges, be immediately available if you need to consult about anything."

Relief, surprise, and pleasure melted through her. He supported her effort to win the Featherby? If he wanted the Featherby, he couldn't support his mother's idea to close the very function that won the nomination to begin with. "That would be lovely. I was considering going through the vault again. Perhaps we can re-create new attire for the staff." She turned to the monitor on her computer. "I have the vault's inventory here. If you have the time you might take a look at it."

He shook his head. "Helen tells me you've taken tours every day this week and have been working yourself silly. Can I have tea brought up for you?"

For a single moment she remembered her old crush, especially when she caught his eye as he waited for her answer. She shook her head. Now was certainly not the time to fall back into *that* old habit. "No, you go ahead. I'll check my e-mail, catch up on a few things here."

Quentin stood, nearing the door as she eyed message headers on her e-mail. An unfamiliar subject caught her eye.

"Quentin," she said slowly, clicking on the note, "have you heard of a place called West World Genealogy?"

He stopped and turned to her. "No, I don't think so. Why?"

"I've an e-mail from them with your name in the header. Shall I read it?"

He nodded.

"'Dear Mr. Hollinworth, an American family desires to make contact with English cousins such as yourself. In our research we have determined the lineage to be accurate. They have in their possession a journal belonging to Cosima Escott Hamilton, of whom you descend, which you might find of great sentimental interest.'" Rebecca looked at Quentin. "Are you familiar with a journal by Cosima Hamilton?"

Quentin shook his head.

"Nor am I." She looked again at the screen, noting the attachment. "There is a pedigree here. Would you like to see it?"

Without a word, Quentin rounded the desk. When he leaned over her, Rebecca could smell the faint trace of soap, the same pine scent he always used. The same brand Helen kept stocked in every bathroom in the Hall.

"The ancestry is correct," he said. "At least I think it is, from what I recall of those portraits hanging in the gallery. You probably know better than I; you write the tour scripts full of my family history."

"These names are right, even as far back as the first viscount. Some names I don't recognize, though—Grayson, Martin. I suppose that's the American side. We don't have many records of families outside the direct line."

"A shame we're all such snobs," he said with a grin. "What do you think then? It's legitimate?"

She nodded. "The list includes Cosima Hamilton's four children. I wonder if there is more family history that I don't know about."

"I doubt that," Quentin said, and she smiled at his assured tone—one of complete and utter trust that she knew more than she actually did.

"I will contact them first if you like. Just to make sure it's valid."

"You're my champion, Rebecca. Protecting me again."

She studied the names even as she wondered why he'd used that word again. A reference to protecting him shouldn't contain an undertone of disdain; she was paid to do that very thing—by Quentin himself. "I doubt this could be a hoax. They have too much of the correct lineage."

"I've an idea," said Quentin, leaning forward, "Since you claim not to need tea, why don't we go down to the vault now?

I can't imagine Americans having the *original* journal belonging to one of my grandmothers."

"Kipp Hamilton might have owned it. He was Cosima's son, and he went to America." She eyed him. "It would be fun to have a look, though."

Quentin went to the door, holding it open. "To the vault?"

Nearly three hours later, Rebecca tucked an annoying strand of hair behind her ear. She should have it cut to shoulder length or at least go upstairs and find a hair band to pull it away from her face.

"Ready for some dinner at last?" Quentin asked from another corner.

Perhaps she'd sighed aloud when she had only meant to complain to herself about her irksome hair. "In a bit."

He neared her, his long white sleeves covered in black butler's wraps, his dark hair uncharacteristically unkempt from sifting through crates and boxes for the last few hours. "I'm not for throwing in," he said, "just taking a break."

She stood away from the box she'd been hunched over, feeling the pull of an oddly used muscle. "I hope you know I realize how ridiculous this is. I *should* know everything in this vault. Wouldn't Cosima have left something here if she was prone to journaling?"

"Maybe she wrote only one journal and gave it to the child who went off to America as you said earlier. In any case, not being certain about what's in this vault isn't your fault, Rebecca. If anyone is to blame, it's I." He lifted a hand to take in their tall surroundings. "This is all mine and yet I've no idea what's here."

Rebecca glanced around the high-ceilinged room. Part of a 1920s renovation, it was a veritable bank vault of security with its steel walls, complete darkness when closed off, and more recently, a regulated temperature. "When your father hired me three years ago, one of the pledges I made was to update the inventory system." She saw items she knew were catalogued. "I honestly cannot fathom how I could not know as much about Cosima Hamilton as another branch of your family—one not even English!"

Quentin's gentle laugh echoed off the high metal.

"I've never seen you so perturbed, Rebecca," he said. "I like it."

"Like . . . what?"

"Seeing you as frustrated as the rest of us when looking for something."

She raised a brow. "The rest of us?"

He nodded, leaning over to shut the curved lid on the trunk of china she'd been searching. "The rest of humanity, Rebecca. I've always thought nothing could irritate you and you were therefore set apart."

"Never irritated? Perhaps that's because you've not been home when the goats manage their way beyond the gate and rummage one of the gardens, or a nervous bride changes her banquet menu a dozen times, or a corporate manager expects a two-hundred-year-old hall to easily accommodate his electrical needs for an online presentation."

"Perhaps I'll be fortunate enough to witness something along those lines this summer."

She returned his smile. "And may I say I hope not?"

"I'll ring for dinner to be served on the veranda."

Rebecca watched him walk to the telephone mounted just inside the vault door. The exchange line was a precautionary measure, since the vault locked from the outside. Turning back to the last trunk, Rebecca listened to Quentin's voice as he directed Helen. A light dinner. On the veranda. For both of them.

She focused on the task before her. The latches on each side of this last trunk were stiff, but she managed to free them without marring the receptacle. Inside, a quilted dustcover protected the trunk's contents.

This trunk was one of two they had found only a short time ago, hidden from view behind a large Chippendale chiffonier. The first of the two trunks had contained nothing more than a set of china. She'd recognized the pattern immediately; while a popular nineteenth-century style and the number of settings plentiful, it wasn't particularly noteworthy except that it was Irish. It would be disappointing indeed if this second trunk contained only more of the same.

Instead of dishware, she found two small pouches, a set of books tied together with a leather strap, and a wooden box.

Rebecca heard Quentin approach from behind.

"Perhaps we've reached the end of the rainbow," she said, taking up one of the leather-bound books.

But they proved to be Victorian novels, not journals. One was *Vanity Fair* by Thackeray, and the other, *John Halifax, Gentleman* by Craik. No pot of gold here, even if the latter was one of Rebecca's favorite classics. Each looked like a first edition and was probably worth something, particularly the Thackeray novel with the author's original illustrations.

"Let's see what's in these pouches," Quentin said. He pulled the string on one, tumbling a handful of polished stones into his palm. "Nice specimens."

"Perhaps some should go into the science hut," she said. "I'll have a look at them later to see what kind of stones they are."

She pulled the box from the bottom of the chest. It was made of smooth wood, stained and varnished to a sheen, capped at the corners with dark metal brackets. On the lid were words burned into the wood in meticulous calligraphy: *Everything that is done in the world is done by hope.*

"Isn't that something Luther said?"

Rebecca nodded, tracing a finger over the letters, unable to resist touching them. "It's lovely, isn't it?"

"Let's see what's inside," he said.

She rocked the lid loose. It was stuck tight from years of disuse. At last it came free, squeaking as she lifted it.

"Papers," she said. "Letters, with a note on the top."

"Does it say whose they are?"

Rebecca shook her head, reading bold words written at the top of the yellowed sheet of paper. "'For I reckon that the sufferings of this present time are not worthy to be compared with the glory which shall be revealed in us.'" She looked at Quentin. "That's from St. Paul's letter to the Romans."

"Does it say anything else?"

She read the rest of the note. "'My dear Berrie's life can be summed up by hope and worship, along with a fair share of suffering to keep her fixed on eternity. Enclosed are the letters she sent to me so long ago, when we were both young and had much to learn.'"

"Hope, worship, and suffering," Quentin said grimly. He looked from the box to Rebecca, holding her gaze. "The life of a Hamilton—and a Hollinworth. At least my father's. Maybe mine, to some extent."

She wanted to dwell on his observation, discuss the suffering he'd been through since the loss of his brother and father when their small plane went down in a fog, ask countless questions to fathom if it had turned him bitter or soft toward worship. But old fears stood in the way. Too personal, don't pry. And yet . . . the look in his eye . . . Perhaps he wanted her to.

No sooner had she identified such a look than it disappeared. "Let's take this with us to the veranda, shall we?" he said. "Have a peek over dinner, before it gets too dark outside?"

She nodded, following him from the vault.

Minutes later Rebecca sat with the box on her lap. The sun

set to the west, and the scent of a 150-year-old rose garden wafted on the air to mingle with the enticing smell of potted chicken, herb bread, and almond tarts.

Despite having been tucked away in an environmentally regulated vault, the words were fading, particularly along the creases. But they were still legible.

"It's exciting, isn't it?" she asked. "A portion of your family's history is here, perhaps something you don't yet know about."

Quentin shrugged. "I confess I'll be interested in contacting this American relative who inspired our search. Beyond that I haven't nearly the fascination for the past that you—and the American, I presume—have. Read one."

Rebecca obeyed. The letter on top was addressed in a neat, feminine script.

To Cosima Hamilton

"Not *from* your great-great-great-grandmother. *To* her. To Cosima." Rebecca realized she'd reverently whispered only after the words left her mouth.

"From Berrie, I assume from the note," he said. "That would be Beryl, from the portrait next to the one of Cosima and Peter Hamilton."

Untying the ribbon, Rebecca gently opened the fragile envelope. Whatever wax had once sealed it had long since dried, leaving behind a faint blue shade. She glanced down the page. "It goes into some detail."

"Let me," he said, setting aside his cup. "It's the only way I can prove I'm not bored by the topic, historical though it is, and at the same time give you a chance to eat."

Rebecca put the letter into his outstretched hand, took a bite of the creamy chicken, then pushed it away and settled back in her chair.

She knew exactly what Beryl Hamilton had looked like. Berrie was forever young in Rebecca's mind and lovely, too. She had dark hair like her brother Peter's, though she didn't have his dark brown eyes. Rather, Berrie had unimaginably blue ones that somehow survived in Quentin today.

Rebecca had no trouble picturing what it was like on the day Berrie Hamilton had written that letter. . . .

2

Loving greetings from Berrie, April 6, 1852

My dear Cosima,

Do you recall I once feared that I should find myself before the judgment seat of God with an unlit lamp? There I might have stood, ordained with some talent— surely I had one: I convinced myself of that—and yet not having used that with which I had been blessed.

But I have begun to fear I am ill-equipped to answer what God has called me to do. My life, to date, simply has not paved a way for me to serve but rather to be served, to my shame. I was raised to think I should be wife and mother, yet in such a role would I have served even a family? Had I the faintest idea what true servanthood really is?

Besides those shortcomings, even if I were qualified for this role, there are many things beyond my control. Despite these two years of planning, studying, and *preparation, I have now reached the point where others must make the final decisions. Let me list some of the outsiders I now find myself beholden to: First, various inspectors, surveyors, clerks, and officers of health must approve of all I have done. Second, I must rely upon the long-lasting generosity of donors. Third, and perhaps most importantly, I must establish—then maintain—the trust of parents bringing their children here.*

And another thing I shall need, as taught to me already by your dear brother Royboy: I need physical perseverance as never before to answer this calling.

Yesterday was a prime example of my ineptitude. The day began with such promise, yet before the sun was very high I proved the depth of my incompetence. . . .

Berrie breathed in the lavender-scented air and turned around to assess the distance traveled. She'd made it all the way up the hill today.

Just a week before that had been impossible, with her pampered lungs and muscles as untried as a baby's. Mrs. Cotgrave, with her hefty bosom and at least a score of added years, was in better condition than Berrie.

From atop the hill, Berrie saw Escott Manor. No less than eight chimneys dotted the roof, and perhaps this winter each one would be in use, after the students arrived. The thought quickened her heartbeat, and this time such a pulse had nothing to do with exertion.

It was almost breakfast time, and Berrie's day would begin with Royboy. His wavy blond hair and smiling hazel eyes that reminded Berrie of a Van Dyck portrait. Her sister-in-law, Cosima Hamilton, was right that though her brother might be chronologically sixteen, he was in mind and behavior no more than three.

When she returned to the manor, Berrie found him already up and dressed, thanks to Decla. The woman was a wonder-worker, and Berrie thanked her at least a half dozen times a day for staying behind when she could easily have gone with Mrs. Escott to England. In what had undoubtedly been a difficult decision, Decla had remained to work with those who needed the skills of someone with her experience. No one would have missed her more than Royboy, of course, even if he didn't have the words to express such a thing.

"Good morning, miss," said Decla as Berrie took a seat opposite Royboy in the dining room. Decla oversaw Royboy's table habits, something she used to do in the kitchen. Upon transference of Escott Manor into Berrie's hands for the school, everyone used the dining room. The banquet hall that had once served the brother of a duke—and before that, landed Irish gentry— would soon be filled with students and their caregivers. No lines here between servants and those they served, since those served would average in competency from Royboy to . . . Berrie had no idea. Yet.

"Good morning."

"Greet Miss Hamilton, Royboy," Decla encouraged.

Without looking up from his plate, Royboy said, "How do you do."

"I'm very well, Royboy. And how are you today?"

"Now say, 'Very well, thank you,'" Decla modeled.

"Thank you," Royboy echoed the last two words as he took a bite of bread too large before Decla could stop him. The bread fell out of his mouth as he spoke, but he caught it on his lap and stuffed it back inside. Then he repeated, "Thank you."

That was a satisfactory effort as far as Berrie was concerned. In fact she was quite pleased. "I'll have a bit to eat, too, Royboy," said Berrie, "and then we'll be off to our very first lesson. Would you like that?"

He didn't answer or look her way. His lack of response was something Berrie was adjusting to. It wasn't as if he were ignoring her, Cosima had explained. No, quite the contrary. Royboy took in everything. He acknowledged almost nothing.

Berrie ate a light breakfast, finished her tea, then invited Royboy to come with her. This was to be a lesson for her as well as him. Royboy, in many ways, would be her teacher. For the past two years, Berrie had read essays from doctors who worked with the infirm in both France and England. She'd corresponded with other teachers before making the decision to come to Ireland. Indeed, that was how she'd found the wonderful Mrs. Cotgrave. Through letters from those who worked in such schools in England.

But here was the real learning. With Royboy. And for Berrie it began today. At the very least, by the time they accepted their first paid student, Berrie intended to have grown in experience.

They made their way upstairs to a classroom. It had once been a small parlor, still lovely with its green silk wallpaper, complementary green curtains pulled aside into bronze holdbacks. The occasional tables and knickknacks had been removed and sold, replaced instead by one functional table and a few sturdy chairs.

"Come and sit, Royboy," Berrie said with the singsong tone Cosima had told her Royboy loved.

Royboy sat without having to be told twice. Surely this was where they both belonged! She pulled another chair closer to his, taking up the small stack of watercolor drawings she had placed in the room last night. Berrie had spent hours creating various drawings, representing images captured from outdoor nature to familiar household items. Vivid shades marked each picture, with large letters identifying such things as trees and leaves, birds and butterflies, lamps, furniture, and windows.

"How do you like this, Royboy?" Berrie handed him a drawing of a brilliant fritillary butterfly, wings extended, orange and black drawn as near the likeness of the insect as she'd witnessed alternately floating and resting along the edge of the manor garden. "Can you say *butterfly*?"

Royboy accepted the colorful drawing, mumbled something that might have been *butterfly*, then held the sheet closer to his face.

Raising it above his head, Royboy's gaze soon left the picture as he placed both hands toward the center of the upper edge, easily tearing it in two.

Berrie, heart racing and sinking at the same time, leaned toward the drawing. He held it beyond her reach to tear another portion, crinkling the triangular shape and stuffing it quickly into his mouth.

"No, Royboy! You mustn't eat it." She did then what came naturally and tried to retrieve the crumpled paper from between his teeth. Such strong teeth, she learned as they clamped down on her fingers. "Oh! Ouch! Oh . . ."

3

Rebecca leaned forward, taking the letter from Quentin's out-stretched hand.

"You might be able to use some of the information in there for your tour scripts," he said, taking a bite of what was surely by now cold chicken. "We have my American relatives to thank for that."

"Should I contact them, then?"

"Of course. My family could use a bit of expansion, I think."

Rebecca nodded, though she doubted his mother would think so.

"Invite them here, if they intend coming over some time."

Rebecca eyed him. Strangers? Not that she was in accord with his mother's line of thinking, that anyone worth knowing was already in their circle. But Americans, if she were to general-ize, were among the boldest visitors to the Hall. In speech, cloth-ing, and behavior.

"For a tour, at least," he said softly.

"Of course," she said. That much she could handle.

She soon took the letters back to her office, where she sent an e-mail to the genealogy service inviting direct contact with the American cousins.

Perhaps she should have said something to Quentin, asked

him about his mother's public comment to privatize the Hall. Perhaps, if Rebecca had an inkling of suspicion that was his intention, she might have.

Instead she kept silent, preferring to put off the battle if one was to be had. The Featherby would cement the value of the work she did here, if Quentin did lean toward his mother's way of thinking. This particular award's emphasis was exactly where Rebecca's efforts glowed: reaching the youth to show them first-hand how this country—their country—had lived in its glory days.

Surely even Quentin's mother could be convinced of the importance of that.

Rebecca picked up another letter. If this correspondence added to the Hollinworth family's noble history, Rebecca was just the one to make sure everyone knew about it.

4

Have you any guess, Cosima, how much paperwork accompanies opening this school? Mr. Truebody, the justice of the peace whom I mentioned in my last letter, is excruciatingly exacting. Not only must our documents be submitted in a timely manner, but if any flaw is found—and by that I mean anything from a misspelled word to the smallest smudge—it is sent back to be completely redone. Not fixed, mind you. Begun again and submitted without evidence of any error.

Your father's library has become my office, though what books were left behind have been sold for quite a nice profit. I am assured by Mrs. Cotgrave that the volumes are better off in the hands of those who will read them instead of worrying over pages being torn, bindings being ripped.

Your father's large desk is littered with no less than fifty sheets of paper, various forms of one sort or another. How can such a simple idea as to help those born less fortunate create such a mass of documentation?

*I have no idea what I would do without Mrs.
Cotgrave. I beg you to keep her in your prayers, because
I am quite certain without her our school would be a
miserable failure already!*

"Legal sanction, lunacy commission, certificates of insanity, reception orders, election applicants . . . Oh! I think we shall be blockaded by ordinance and procedure before we accept our first student."

Mrs. Cotgrave smiled serenely from behind her own pile of paperwork. "Never fret, Miss Berrie. Soon we'll have a staff in place, but if you're to run things, you need to know what's what. Don't you?"

Berrie nodded, albeit with uncertainty. "I do have a brain; I've just never pressed it very hard. Not with anything like this, at any rate."

Mrs. Cotgrave patted Berrie's hand. "You've a good brain, and before long you'll know more about this than I do, I daresay."

Mrs. Cotgrave explained the uses of the forms in front of them. The clerk they would soon hire would record each student's personal information and distribute it to various places, among them Mr. Truebody, the officers of health and board of guardians in Cork, and finally the Lunacy Commission in London, to which they all answered. Berrie's mind spun before long, even as some of Mrs. Cotgrave's knowledge surely sank in. There might be duplication in answering to various inspectors, surveyors, commissioners, board members, doctors, and right up to members of Parliament itself, but the way Mrs. Cotgrave explained things, the pieces seemed to fit. While certain powers must be respected, the underlying goal was the same: to help and protect the children who needed so much.

Daisy, one of the housemaids they'd hired, entered the room after a brief tap.

"A lady arrived just now. She says her name is Miss Katie MacFarland and that she has business with you, Miss Hamilton."

Berrie exchanged a glance with Mrs. Cotgrave, who appeared every bit as surprised by the announcement as Berrie herself. The governing and medical boards were comprised of men, so it couldn't be one of them. And though they did plan to have female teachers, attendants, and one nurse, those slots had been filled; they weren't searching for any more.

"Perhaps she's here to name a candidate for residency," Mrs. Cotgrave suggested.

Berrie nodded, although Mrs. Cotgrave had said this sort of thing was to be handled through the mounds of paperwork they were sending out, not in person.

"Show her in, Daisy," Berrie instructed.

A moment later a woman entered the room, dressed meticulously in white lace and green broadcloth with a small felt hat sitting smartly atop perfectly coiffed hair, a yellow scarf tied at the back. Her features were more plain than pretty, though no single aspect could be called offensive. Rather, her eyes and mouth were on the small side, her forehead on the large. Only the scarf altered her perfect attire, for although every other detail of the lady appeared well attended, the scarf was off-center and askew.

She said nothing upon her entrance. Instead, she stepped close to the desk behind which both Berrie and Mrs. Cotgrave sat. Without making eye contact with either of them, she held out an envelope somewhere in between.

"This is my introduction," the woman said. "It will tell you all about me, it will. Once you've read it, you'll see I may be of great help to you and your students alike."

"I'm afraid we've hired all the help we need, Miss . . . ," Berrie said.

25

"Read the letter, if you please."

The young woman spoke with the familiar cadence so common in Ireland, though not like a servant. No, her enunciation certainly matched the finery she wore. Berrie opened the envelope, unfolding the single sheet she found inside. She held it at an angle so Mrs. Cotgrave might see it as well.

I am Katie MacFarland, twenty years, two months, three days
of age. I am strong and hardworking, and will never tell a lie.
I have come to help you with your school, since I am strong and
hardworking and will never tell a lie. You will have children in
your school for me to take care of and teach. I can teach them
for most of the day and also after dark since I require little sleep.
I also do not eat much, so I will create little expense. I have
brought my own clothes. I will be of great value because I am
strong and hardworking and will never tell a lie.

The letter, though neat and without error, appeared to have been written by a child.

Berrie placed the letter on the desk in front of her, standing and going to the library window. From there she saw the lane leading up to the manor house, but it was empty all the way to the road down below.

Surely the young lady hadn't come alone. Any girl her age and from the kind of house that matched her clothing and ability to write would have a carriage and chaperone. More than that, even if this girl had broken all rules of etiquette and set out alone, how could she have found her way to them unattended? From her stiff demeanor and lack of eye contact, and from the words on the page, Berrie guessed the girl would be better off a student than a member of the staff.

"How did you arrive, Miss MacFarland?" Berrie asked.

The young woman stared straight ahead like a soldier at

attention rather than one of three women chatting in a room. "My name is Katie, and I walked."

"From your home?"

"No, from my carriage."

"And where is your carriage now?" Berrie looked out the window again, unable to see directly in front of the portico. Perhaps the vehicle was out of her line of vision. "Still waiting outside?"

"I was let out at the bottom of the lane, and I walked up the hill. I like to walk; it's good for breathing." She took a deep, clear breath as if to demonstrate.

Berrie returned to her seat and spoke quietly to Mrs. Cotgrave. "I haven't the faintest idea what to do. Have you?"

"I'll see if Daisy glimpsed the carriage," she whispered, "or if she has any other information about the girl. If we don't know where to return her to, I don't see any option but to keep her, at least until we find out where she belongs."

"Without paperwork?"

Mrs. Cotgrave grinned, apparently pleased that Berrie had been indoctrinated to the importance of various documents. "We can only do our best for the girl. I'm not sure she'll be able to tell us much to be of any help."

Even with the pronouncement, Berrie could see Mrs. Cotgrave had her reservations about letting her stay. Nonetheless, the older woman left the room to start her search.

Berrie offered Katie a chair opposite.

"How far have you come, Miss MacFarland?"

Katie glanced at Berrie while coming to rest rigidly on the edge of the chair. Eye contact lasted no longer than a moment as the young woman stared somewhere over Berrie's shoulder. "I am to be called Katie. Even Sophy, my maid, calls me Katie. My sister says servants should call me 'Miss MacFarland,' but since that is what they call her, how shall I know whom they are addressing if we are called by the same name?"

"What about Miss Katie?"

"The name in our Bible on the family record says 'Katie,' not 'Miss Katie.' I don't know why anyone should call me by anything else. I don't call servants 'miss' or 'mister.' I don't see why they should call me anything other than my name."

"So you have a sister. What is her name?" Berrie shifted closer to place herself in Katie's line of vision. Katie's gaze floated higher.

"Her name is Miss MacFarland. That's what everyone calls her except my brother and I. My brother calls her by her Christian name. I don't call her anything. I haven't used her name in six years, five months, and eight days. I'll not say the name of someone who doesn't like me."

"Your sister—Miss MacFarland—doesn't like you?"

There, a brief moment of eye contact. "She does not. She says I am quite annoying. When you say *quite*, that means something more than simply annoying. She means that I am more than annoying. I have always annoyed her, although I don't know how or why. And so I promised myself to never say her name, not ever. If you meet her, you may call her Miss MacFarland and that will be enough."

"But I thought it was your sister who brought you here."

"Yes, she did."

"Yet you didn't speak to her?"

"I did talk to her, although she doesn't like it when I talk. I can see she thinks what I say is quite annoying."

"How long was the carriage ride, Miss MacFarland?"

"That is my sister's name. My name is Katie."

Berrie silently chided herself. She really must learn to communicate better; obviously the person she spoke to was more important than rules of etiquette.

"Was it a long carriage ride to get here, Katie?"

"Yes, I do say so. It was even farther than Dublin. My brother took me to Dublin once. He goes there often, and one day he asked if I would like to see it and I said yes. So we went."

Berrie assumed, then, the MacFarland family lived to the north or perhaps the northwest. That might narrow it down, though not by much.

"Was your brother with you today?"

"No indeed, only my sister." Now Katie's gaze flitted around the room, taking in the surroundings. The room was nearly empty except for curtains, four chairs, the desk, and all the paperwork on top of it. The settee, extra lamps, and most of the books were gone, leaving behind only a few volumes pertaining to botany that might prove helpful to the staff. Shelves that had once housed a variety of published sermons, novels, and first editions of philosophy and history now waited for the storage of files on various students yet to come.

"My sister told me you needed me," Katie continued, "and I agree it would be very nice to work instead of staying at home. My sister does not work, although she has many friends who keep her busy. My brother works. Since my father died, my brother has to do all of his own work as well as Papa's. It was sad when my father died because I cannot talk to him anymore, but I know he is in heaven even though my brother says he is no longer sure there is a heaven. I reminded him Papa and Mama both told us there is a heaven, so I know that's where they are. You cannot see heaven or God or Jesus, so this is harder to believe than some things. There are many things we cannot see that are real. Like wind. It can nearly make me tumble over if I stand on the cliffs behind my home, but I cannot see the wind—only the things it moves."

Berrie listened to Katie, trying her best to keep up with all of the shifts in topic, knowing she needed to find out more about the young woman to be of any help at all.

"There are cliffs near your home, Katie? What town do you live in?"

"There are cliffs by the water. I mustn't go into the water because my clothes would become too heavy to get out of the water. Then I would drown. Wind is made of air, which you also cannot see. We all need air in order to breathe. I would not be able to breathe if I were under the water."

Cliffs and water. That could be almost any Irish coast from what little she knew of the island. "And what is the name of the town in which you live?"

"I live in a big house . . . by the cliffs."

Berrie sighed, wishing she'd been the one to search for information with Daisy. Perhaps Mrs. Cotgrave would be more successful with Katie. "What is your brother's name, Katie?"

"Simon."

"And what kind of work does he do?"

"He tells people how to make boats. And he fights the English."

"Fights the English?" Berrie frowned, imagining all sorts of ways an Irishman might fight her English countrymen. "Is he a soldier?"

"No."

Just then the door opened again. Berrie gratefully acknowledged Mrs. Cotgrave with a nod, but the older woman shrugged and lifted her hands.

Katie watched Mrs. Cotgrave walk around the table and retake her seat beside Berrie. Then Katie returned her gaze toward Berrie's general direction. "When shall I begin teaching the wee ones?"

"We haven't actually accepted any students yet, Katie, so there are no teachers here just now except Mrs. Cotgrave and myself." Berrie motioned to the paperwork in front of her. "All of these papers must be read and completed before we can begin accepting students for our residential program."

"So will I begin work tomorrow, then, instead of today?"

"I'm afraid it will be a bit longer than that. Perhaps we should get in touch with your sister or your brother and have them take you home for the time being."

Katie's eyes widened to small blue circles, and she looked at Berrie for the longest moment yet before staring once again beyond Berrie's shoulder. "But I came to work here. I cannot go home. My sister has a new beau, and she doesn't want me to annoy him the way I annoy her. She said if I live here everyone will be happier, until she gets her beau to kiss her, and then they'll be married like Mama and Papa. Besides that, if I go home, I'll not be able to leave again if my brother returns first."

"Where is your brother?"

"In Dublin. My sister brought me here while he is away so Simon could not say no. He thinks only boys and men prefer working, and if a woman must work, she should do so at home with the wee ones at her feet."

Berrie frowned. If Katie's brother truly was a man who fought the English and believed women only good for working at home and having babies, then he most assuredly would not approve of his sister being at a school run by an Englishwoman who intended to make this school her life's mission.

"Tell me, Katie," Mrs. Cotgrave said slowly, "I wonder if you have anything that might tell us where you live? Perhaps in a pocket of your cloak?"

The girl shook her head.

"Your pockets are empty, then?" Berrie asked. It would have been a fine idea for Katie's family to tuck in identification—if they wanted to make sure she'd find her way home.

Katie put her hands in her pockets, pulling them inside out. They were indeed empty.

"I fear we have a dilemma," Mrs. Cotgrave said. "If you are to live here and work with the other students, we will need to fill out paperwork such as this." She motioned to one of the stacks in front of her. "We need signatures of two people giving permission for you to live here."

Katie looked between the two women, as if a third face between them could receive her gaze. "What does that mean?"

"That we must speak to your sister *and* your brother," Berrie said. "Can you tell us how we may contact them?"

Katie's wide forehead crinkled in a frown. "I came to work. Here."

"And perhaps that shall still work out," Mrs. Cotgrave said gently. "But until the students arrive, there isn't much to be done, is there? We can summon you back, when the time is right."

Katie still looked at the absent third face. "Do you have paperwork too? For both of you to work here?"

Berrie glanced at Mrs. Cotgrave, who seemed amused and perhaps a bit impressed by the question.

Mrs. Cotgrave nodded. "We do have paperwork, Katie. Miss Hamilton has papers stating she may manage things here, and I have papers stating my prior experience."

"And I have papers, too, that I gave you just a moment ago."

"Yes, but your papers aren't signed by anyone, Katie," Berrie said. "They must be signed by the proper authorities."

Katie's shoulders slumped, and her eyes dwindled from meager circles to unhappy slits.

"How can we help you find your way home, Katie?" Mrs. Cotgrave asked.

"I cannot go home. My sister doesn't want me there until after she gets married."

"Surely they'll welcome you back," Mrs. Cotgrave said.

"And there is the possibility you can return to us after we have the proper papers," Berrie added.

Katie looked up again, her brows high. "With two signatures, you say? My sister's and my own? I can sign my name: K-A-T-I-E."

"We must have two signatures," Mrs. Cotgrave confirmed. "But neither can be yours. They must be signed by someone else who promises to let you come back to live with them after your stay here is finished."

"Finished? But I thought I should work here forever, be very useful until I go to heaven like Mama and Papa."

Mrs. Cotgrave stood. "You shall stay here the rest of today, Katie. But as soon as we find your brother and sister, you must go home until we can acquire the signatures."

Berrie stood as well and eventually so did Katie. What had her sister been thinking? How could she have simply dropped her here without knowing what would become of her?

Berrie opened the door, only to see Daisy standing there, poised to knock. Perhaps she had news.

"Yes, Daisy?" Berrie asked.

"I . . . um . . . yes, miss. I came to see if I'll be making up a room for the new girl, or if you need me regardin' her."

"Yes, as a matter of fact, we do. I'd like you to send Duff to tell Mr. Truebody about this girl. Her name is Katie MacFarland, and we must learn where she lives in order to send her home."

"Yes, miss."

"And in the meantime," Berrie said to Katie, turning back to her, "we'll have a nice evening meal, and then we'll let you see where you'll be staying tonight, all right?"

Even as Berrie led the way to the kitchen, she wondered what might happen once Katie was reunited with her brother. Berrie could only hope the sister would take responsibility for her actions. An English-hating brother might be too eager to look elsewhere for blame—perhaps even at Berrie's door.

5

"Helen said you received a note from my American cousin," Quentin said as he peeked around the door to Rebecca's office. "She's already coming to England?"

"Yes, that's right," Rebecca replied. "Actually your American relative will be spending time in Ireland but hopes to visit here as well. I'd like you to read the note. It contains something of a mystery, or at least something they seem to want to share only with you."

He laughed lightly and she welcomed the sound. She'd heard him laugh too rarely since losing his father and brother.

"They obviously don't know you're more than an employee," he said as he took a seat. "What sort of mystery?"

While she could easily prove she was nothing more than an employee to him, at least based on the number of conversations they'd shared in the past three years, she decided it was best to ignore the comment.

"I've printed the e-mail for you," she said, handing him the page. "You'll see the note refers to something that started generations ago. I can't imagine what she means."

Quentin scanned the page, then read aloud:

"'Dear Miss Seabrooke,

My name is Dana Martin Walker, and I'm so pleased to have been given your e-mail address through West World Genealogy. My sister, Talie, and I recently contacted the genealogy service in regard to our English cousins for several reasons.

First, I'll be spending time in Ireland with my husband, who will be working for three months as a consulting architect in County Kilkenny. It's my hope to visit England within a few weeks.

Second, I hope to learn more about the various branches of my family. I descend from Kipp Hamilton, who was the youngest son of Peter and Cosima Hamilton. When Kipp came to America, he brought with him Cosima's journal, which has been passed down through our branch of the family. My sister and I have transcribed it into an electronic file to share with our cousins here. We'd be pleased to forward this file to the Hollinworth family if they are not already acquainted with Cosima and Peter's history.'

"I'd like to see it," Quentin interjected, "and I imagine you would too. We might do the same for them with the letters written to Cosima."

Rebecca nodded. "I can transcribe them if you wish," she volunteered. "I'd enjoy it."

He returned to reciting the e-mail printout.

"'There is much to be learned from Cosima's journal— things that have had repercussions in our family even to this day, which my English cousins might be interested in learning.'"

Quentin looked up from the page. "What could have repercussions from so long ago?"

Rebecca shrugged. "I've no clue. It's my guess she's hesitant to share it with me instead of someone in the direct line."

He finished reading the note.

> "'Please let me know if you would like me to send an electronic copy of Cosima's journal so my English cousin(s) might read it. In the meantime, I'll keep you posted on specifics of when I'll be in England.
>
> And by the way, I noticed your name. There is a loyal valet briefly mentioned in Cosima's journal by the name of Claude Seabrooke who once worked for the Hamilton family. Isn't that quite a coincidence?
>
> Sincerely,
> *Dana Martin Walker*
> *Cosima Escott Hamilton's great-great-great-granddaughter'"*

Quentin grinned. "Coincidence, indeed! Now we really must read the journal, if both our forebears are in it."

"I thoroughly believe history can teach us all sorts of things," Rebecca admitted. "But the word she used—*repercussions* . . . How could a 150-year-old journal have repercussions today?"

"Hard to imagine." He set down the note and tapped his forehead. "Perhaps my American cousin is crackers."

While that was conceivable, she doubted it. Rebecca couldn't help trying to imagine—and possibly forestall—any undesirable consequences of connecting with someone claiming to be a distant family member. The original note had come to *her*, after all. If anything unpleasant happened as a result, Lady Elise was sure to find out.

More importantly, Rebecca simply had no wish to be responsible for any thorny thing entering Quentin's life.

"I'll send a response and copy you on the e-mail," Quentin said. "I suppose it would be nice to have the letters transcribed before she gets here. If she gets here. Will you need help? We can hire someone to work on it if your schedule is bogged."

Rebecca shook her head. She was too eager to read the letters herself. "No, my education manager is due back tomorrow. That'll free up much of my time. I imagine you'll want to read the letters too. Would you care to read them now or after I've transcribed them?"

"After, I think. The handwriting was clear enough, but I think minimal handling of the old pages best, don't you? My guess is you'll want to return them to safekeeping in the vault."

She nodded. "I'll print out each letter as I finish, then. I've begun the first already."

"You might print a copy for my mother as well. She's always been proud to be married into the Hamilton line. I think she'd appreciate knowing more."

"Of course," Rebecca said, although she had always thought Lady Elise must believe her position as the sister to the Earl of Eastwater brought the Hollinworth family greater prestige, since the Hamilton line had lost its title along with the Hamilton name. "Shall I e-mail them, or will you be taking them to her?"

"She'll be coming round for dinner on Thursday. We can tell her what we're about then."

We? Rebecca wanted to question just what part she would play in telling his mother but wasn't sure how to word it without sounding either surprised or, worse, horrified. In all the years Rebecca had known the Hollinworths, she doubted she'd been noticed by Lady Elise.

"This is Tuesday; I don't think I'll be able to transcribe many of the letters by Thursday."

"We'll just tell Mum about them. You'll join us at dinner, then? Eight o'clock?"

Confusion, eagerness, and dread collided over the prospect of sharing dinner with Quentin . . . *and* his mother. Rebecca was nothing more than a staff member, granddaughter to a valet. She was to sit at the same table with Lady Elise, an Endicott daughter, sister to an earl? From what Rebecca knew of Elise's social life, she seldom had a quiet little family meal. Since her husband and older son had died, she lived almost constantly with an entourage of other society people who shared the same interests—and disinterests. What prompted Quentin to suggest such an astonishing notion as inviting Rebecca to the same table?

She must have taken too long to reply, or perhaps trepidation appeared on her face. Quentin's gaze was fixed on her. "Rebecca? Would you rather not share dinner with me and my mother?"

"No, no. It isn't a question of what I'd like. I'm just rather surprised. I've been connected to your family all my life, Quentin. Only not socially."

"Hmm . . . Extraordinary yet true." He lifted teasing brows. "I pledge my best behavior, and I shall tell my mother to do the same. Perhaps, just for the evening, my social circle will be good enough for yours?"

She tried to laugh, but it sounded rather hollow, forced as it certainly was. "I think it's rather the other way around, don't you?"

He leaned forward from across her desk, resting his elbows on her shining mahogany. "Rebecca." He spoke her name gently, pausing so long afterward she wondered if that was all he meant to say. When she was a child, either parent or tutor only had to say her name to communicate praise or reprimand. Just now she had no idea what Quentin meant if he left it at that.

If he had planned to expound, perhaps he changed his mind. He sat back, glanced toward the window, then looked at her again. "I'd like to tell my mother not only about the letters but about the Featherby nomination. You should be there for that. You deserve her gratitude at the very least. Maybe," he added with a grin, "you might find I'm not as dull as you think if we spend some time together."

Dull? For a moment she was a child again, wishing his company would never end. Nothing dull about that, even as she reminded herself such a silly reaction needed to be left where it belonged: as a memory of a childhood crush.

Still, she couldn't ignore her interest in sharing dinner with him, even if it came with his mother's company. "Very well, Quentin. I'll be available."

He left her office after that, abruptly it seemed. Rebecca stared at the door he closed behind him. Thursday.

She'd best get to work on the letters if she was to be able to speak of them with any authority whatsoever.

6

Have you ever had a notion, Cosima, so mixed of doom and intrigue that you are not sure which route to hope for? That was how I felt the day we showed Katie to her room. On the one hand, there was in her eyes such a guileless sweetness, a purity of hope, that she had found a place to give meaning to her life. How well I understood that! And yet on the other, I felt as though to keep her and expect her to work as she hoped would be looked upon as the vilest usage of another human being. At the very least, I was convinced that was how her brother would have looked upon it, had he only known where she was.

After providing Katie with dinner, Berrie asked Daisy to bring upstairs whatever belongings Katie had arrived with. When Berrie saw the housemaid carrying what appeared to be two weighty satchels, Berrie marveled that Katie had carried them by herself all the way up the steep lane. No doubt the girl was in better condition than even Mrs. Cotgrave.

"After we show you your room, Katie," Berrie said on the way upstairs, "would it be all right if Mrs. Cotgrave and I looked in your belongings to see if we might find something to help us look for your sister and your brother?" At the girl's hesitation, Berrie added, "We must find your relatives for the signatures, so you'll be able to work here when the time is right."

Katie nodded at last, just as Daisy set aside the bags to open a bedroom door. The rooms on this, the middle of the three stories, had been redesigned with living quarters on one end and schoolrooms on the other. Berrie and Mrs. Cotgrave each had a room on the far end, with two others yet to be occupied. They anticipated one room to be used by visiting family members, those who wanted to see how their child fit in before leaving them in Berrie's care. The empty room they stood in now was to be used by two staff members: a teacher who had requested live-in accommodations and a round-the-clock nurse, required by the Lunacy Commission, which had assigned them status as a hospital rather than a school. Students and their attendants would occupy what had become dormitories on the uppermost floor.

Daisy moved the satchels to a spot on the floor at the foot of one of the beds in the room. Instead of leaving, Daisy curtsied in front of Berrie. "I'd be happy to unpack the bags, if you please."

Katie stepped closer before Berrie could answer. "I'm to show Miss Hamilton what I've brought." She turned to Berrie. "You can be sure I'll not trouble you for uniforms or the like. I've another pair of shoes as well, and slippers, too. Those are at the bottom with my underthings in this bag." She pushed that one aside, lifting the other one onto the bed and opening it. "I'll not show you my underthings, because no one is to see such things except the person wearing them . . . and her maid, of course. I did not bring Sophy, my maid. My sister wouldn't let me. I brought my favorite dresses, though they have buttons. I told my sister I don't know how I shall button my dresses in the back without Sophy. I was able to tie my own scarf today when it came free in the wind, but as I cannot see behind me, I don't know if it is straight. Sophy would know, but I couldn't bring her. My sister wouldn't let me."

As she talked, Katie withdrew several neatly folded cotton day gowns, a more festive gown of green organdy with many flounces and yet another of brown tarlatan. Two more formal gowns were rigidly folded and would need to be hung to let go of the creases. A day gown of sturdy gingham looked more practical, and another of warm merino was obviously made for colder weather.

Berrie frowned. Whoever packed this bag obviously intended its wearer to stay through the summer and on into autumn, or perhaps even winter, judging by the variety of material suitable for different seasons.

"My other bag," Katie said after laying out the last dress, "besides the petticoats, has another hat like the one I'm wearing but made of straw. And I have gloves, a shawl, and my shoes." She turned to Berrie, once again choosing to look beyond Berrie's shoulder until she seemed to notice her surroundings for the first time. "This is my room?"

"Yes, for tonight."

"If you were to take the furniture from this room it would be perfectly symmetrical," Katie said. "The door is directly in the middle and there are two windows evenly placed, thus." She pointed to the tall windows with identical yellow curtains dangling in gentle waves to the wooden floor.

"Yes, I see what you mean," Berrie said.

"But of course the furniture is too distracting to notice the symmetry, with the beds on one side and the cabinets on the other." She glanced toward Berrie, then to the windows before speaking again. "Your face, Miss Hamilton, is also symmetrical. If you could fold it like a piece of paper, it would match." Her glance flitted in Mrs. Cotgrave's direction. "Yours, Mrs. Cotgrave, is not. You have a mole beneath your left eye and your mouth sags to one corner and your left eyebrow is higher than your right. You could train yourself to hold your brows at the same level, but that wouldn't eliminate the corner of your mouth being different or the mole. Therefore you cannot have a symmetrical face anyway, so I don't recommend wasting effort with your brows."

Berrie exchanged a look with Mrs. Cotgrave, though it appeared neither one of them had a response to Katie's observations. Berrie took a step toward the chiffonier. "Daisy will help put your things in here, Katie. For the time being, this room is all yours."

Katie nodded and Daisy was already opening the chiffonier door. Berrie scanned the room to make sure there was nothing that could be tampered with that might hurt either the occupant or the room. She was surprised to see that the bedside lamps had been taken out. Daisy? Thankfully it was well lit by the afternoon sun. Gas lamps must be used sooner or later but for the moment wouldn't be missed.

Berrie quietly asked Daisy to see if there might be some item among Katie's belongings to suggest the whereabouts of her home. Daisy nodded; then Berrie closed the door, following Mrs. Cotgrave down the hall.

"Would you care to check on her in a bit, or shall I?" Berrie asked.

"I don't mind." Mrs. Cotgrave gently laughed. "Symmetry, indeed. I daresay, I haven't been insulted with such a fine vocabulary in quite some time."

Berrie looped her arm through Mrs. Cotgrave's as they made their way down the hall. "Do you suppose she might be of help? She seems well in control."

"Oh, she's an odd one, that's for certain. She has an excellent manner of speech, though. I've seen her kind before. If we keep to a schedule, as we plan to anyway, she might set a good example for those who struggle with rules and language."

"But we don't know if she'll stay," Berrie reminded her. "Even without someone funding her, she said her brother doesn't know she's here. From what I gather, he might not approve. Her sister shipped her off without telling him or anyone else, not even Katie's maid."

Mrs. Cotgrave glanced back toward the closed door. "Poor dear." She smiled sadly. "But then it's true those with the mind of a child often don't see the harm hurled their way. God bless them."

7

Thursday came quickly for Rebecca. Between her daily duties overseeing the Hall, writing a new script to accompany the refurbished wardrobe for the women demonstrating a Victorian afternoon tea, and filling out preliminary paperwork for the Featherby, she only had time to transcribe a few letters from Quentin's forebears.

Tonight his mother was to arrive for dinner. Rebecca had watched Helen dither about what to serve Lady Elise since being informed of the visit two days ago. Should Helen serve shepherd's pie? Ploughman's soup was her specialty, but she thought it too provincial and the weather not nearly cold enough. Despite that being her husband's favorite, William agreed, having been infected by Helen's distress. The last word Rebecca heard of the main course was something about a traditional London broil or perhaps roast lamb. The only item not in doubt was trifle for dessert. Helen was known throughout the village for them.

Helen had also called in an unusual number of housemaids in the last two days, lending an undercurrent of anxiety that added to Rebecca's unease. Everywhere she turned someone was scrubbing what already appeared clean, polishing what already gleamed, straightening what already hung properly. Featherby judges couldn't possibly inspire more angst.

Although Quentin had been home these past few days,

Rebecca saw almost nothing of him. That was by her design. She filled her days with work and spent her evenings cloistered in her suite. There was something decidedly different in having Quentin under the same roof. Something she would rather ignore.

Today there was no hiding, despite a stronger wish than ever to do just that. Rebecca had watched Elise Hollinworth from afar for years. Knowing her family's history of serving the Hollinworths, Rebecca paid attention when the Hollinworth family was in the news. Lady Elise Hollinworth was noted least often, and that seemed intentional. She was, Rebecca had learned, a private person who chose to live in a rather public social circle. Perhaps her parties weren't much different from other society events, and yet Lady Elise's held the added challenge of knowing reporters were especially unwanted. She'd once had one arrested for trespassing, while another had been dunked in the pool, camera and all. After that it became a challenge to see what the boldest society reporter could get away with at an Elise Hollinworth party.

Tonight, however, would not pose a problem, with only the two Hollinworths and Rebecca in attendance. The only one on edge tonight would be Rebecca herself; she was quite sure of that. And possibly Helen Risdon over her lamb selection.

Rebecca was ready far too early, dressed in a simple black dress adorned by a single pearl dangling from a braided gold chain. Her hair, looking nearly as black as her dress and set loose down her back, had surprisingly obeyed today, so the curls for the most part stayed out of her line of vision. However she had no intention of going downstairs any sooner than she was expected.

So she went to her office and clicked on her e-mail, seeing a note from Quentin's American cousin. Rebecca noticed immediately it wasn't directed to her but rather to Quentin. Perhaps there wasn't a secret to be heard only by Quentin, after all.

Dear Mr. Hollinworth – or may I call you Quentin, since we're cousins, after all?

I was so pleased to get your note and very eager to tell you my husband, my daughter, and I will be in Ireland for three months starting next week. We hope to visit you in England by the end of this month.

In your note, you expressed an interest in reading Cosima's journal. As far as I know, the one my sister has is the original, although it wouldn't surprise me if Cosima made copies for her other children as well (for the healthy ones at least). I'm attaching our e-file of the text, which my sister and I transcribed.

Once you've read that I'll be happy to talk to you about Royboy and the others in our family and how the genetic condition Cosima called a "curse" survived through these 150 years. From the ancestry report collected by West World, I'm guessing only Mary and Kipp were affected and that your branch of the family was spared. Praise God for that!

Rebecca read that portion again, wondering what it could possibly mean. She noted the attachment and for a moment entirely forgot she was due downstairs any moment. Much as she would like to read it now, she only had time to finish the e-mail.

In any case, I'll let you and your commercial manager (hello, Rebecca!) know once I arrive in Ireland and have a firm date for my visit to England. It's very nice, isn't it, to find someone who shares the same blood but has lived an ocean apart? How small and connected the world seems right now.

Looking forward to meeting you,
Dana Martin Walker

Rebecca smiled, though she wasn't a relation at all. What was it about family, even one so distant, that could create an instant link?

No more stalling; it was time to join Quentin and his mother.

Helen had chosen to serve dinner in the garden room. A hundred years ago it had been an aviary, but the family's interest in birds must have waned during one war or another, and birds were no longer purchased. A single blue and gold macaw remained, believed to be over fifty years old. Robert Hollinworth had always been its primary caregiver, and when he died the bird had stopped eating for days. Quentin claimed himself a poor substitute for his father, though their voices and stature were similar. It wasn't long before the bird seemed bonded to Quentin.

Rebecca met Quentin and his mother in the hall just outside the room.

"Mum," Quentin said, smiling Rebecca's way and extending a hand to her elbow, "do you recall Rebecca Seabrooke? She's cleared her schedule and will be joining us this evening."

Lady Elise was perhaps a hair's breadth taller than Rebecca. Whereas Rebecca was dark, Lady Elise was light. Her skin, unlike Rebecca's more olive complexion, was like powdered ivory. Her hair was a mix of blonde and white, impossible to tell if the white was partner to gray or added by design. Features, probably lovely when young, had sharpened with age. Her nose and chin pointed rather downward; her eyes seemed pulled the other direction. With attention to detail Lady Elise was still a distinctive woman, exquisitely dressed in an ice blue suit and expertly made up to take years from her face.

She was politely smiling with a bit of what looked like suspicious caution, mixed with a tinge of curiosity. Even so, it was a smile, and because of that, Rebecca felt sure the older woman had no idea who she was.

"I expected us to dine alone, Quentin, but tell me more about this woman in front of me."

Rebecca extended her hand, which Elise shook with just the right amount of firmness. "It's a pleasure to see you, Mrs. Hollinworth, although I must admit the advantage of knowing a bit about you and your family—at least, the Hollinworth side."

One brow lifted and Rebecca was reminded of a photograph she'd seen of Lady Elise during a rare visit to a public restaurant. The place had closed within six months, and Elise's face had encapsulated the reason. Rebecca was left wondering if almost no one liked the food or if Lady Elise had placed the germ of distaste in prospective diners before they'd taken their first bite.

"And how is it you know about the Hollinworths, Miss . . . it is Miss?"

"Yes, but please call me Rebecca. Your husband hired me as the Hall's commercial manager three years ago, so I've become quite familiar with the family's lineage."

"How interesting." She turned her blue gaze on her son, her pulled-up eyes narrowing slightly. "We're dining with the staff, Quentin?"

He laughed so easily Rebecca would have found some comfort in it if she could feel anything through the tenterhooks jabbing her. "No, we're dining with Rebecca, who happens to be the daughter of one of Father's friends."

That was, of course, another way to put it. Hardly the way Elise would interpret the relationship if she had all of the facts. Rebecca's gaze lingered on Quentin a moment longer. She hadn't known he was aware of the friendship between her father and his.

"So you knew my husband, Rebecca?" *Glacial*—that was the only word Rebecca could use to describe the tone.

"Yes. Or, rather, no. Not well."

"And your father is . . . ?"

"James Seabrooke."

Lady Elise appeared to ponder the name a moment, then shook her head briefly. "No, I don't believe I've met a James Seabrooke, and I assure you I knew all of my husband's friends. Are you certain your father knew my husband?"

Quentin laughed again. Rebecca wished she could join in, wished she wanted to.

"Father introduced me to James Seabrooke years ago, Mum."

She wondered if he was deliberately keeping hidden the fact that one member of the Seabrooke family or another had been employed by the Hollinworths for generations.

"Was her father from London?"

Lady Elise eyed Rebecca as she asked the question of her son, as though Rebecca were an exhibit being pondered instead of a dinner guest.

"Yes, James works for the Trust."

"Oh, well, why didn't you say so?" Elise asked, then stepped into the garden room. Bright and airy, the room was decorated in snowy white, which seemed the perfect accompaniment to Lady Elise's frosty blue suit. A pristine, padded wicker couch with matching wicker table and chairs gave the room an outdoor look, especially overlooking the rose garden. Upon their entry the macaw let out a screech. "I don't know why Helen told us to come in here with that awful bird. I've always detested that thing."

Quentin approached the huge gilt cage that housed the macaw, reaching inside to take a nut from its bowl to hand-feed it. "How can you say that, Mum? Father loved him, and he loved Father." Quentin grinned. "You could even say he's been a member of the family longer than either of us."

"I'm well aware of how long that bird has been around. However, when I married your father, there was nothing in the vows about tending to that creature." Lady Elise neared the table next to the windows. It was spread with spotless linen, adorned with nineteenth-century Wedgwood, eighteenth-century silverware, and fresh white orchids. "Does she expect us to eat the entire meal in here? I won't have it, Quentin."

"Oh, come now, Mum, it'll be fine. You can see the roses from here, and I know you like them. Would you care for some iced tea?" Quentin walked toward the tea trolley set off to the side. "I believe Helen said it's orange mint. How about you, Rebecca?"

She accepted the offer immediately. Elise declined.

"So tell me, Rebecca," Elise said, "why are you working as a commercial manager out here in the country? You should be in London, where all the other young people live."

"I like it here," Rebecca said, hating the meek tone but unable to take it back and replace it with something more robust. She cleared her throat and made another attempt. "I'm interested in history, and I like working with others to preserve it." Better, though still not herself.

Elise neared the table, the tip of one long finger grazing an orchid petal. "Some things are worthy to be preserved, although you must admit there is a plethora of Victorian homes available to schools and tourists. We don't really need this hall on a public list." She picked up a knife and inspected it, then replaced it. "Do you know, if the aristocracy isn't concerned enough to have families—and large ones—the English aristocracy will die that much sooner?"

Rebecca nodded. Only life titles had been given since the 1960s—none that would be passed on through the generations. One might attribute it to any number of things: politics, a goal for universal democracy, simple modernized thinking. Somehow Rebecca didn't think Elise would find any of those arguments compelling.

Rebecca slid her thumb along the cool glass in her hand, avoiding eye contact with either Lady Elise or Quentin.

"Since you are the commercial manager for this estate," Elise said, "how is the market for selling such a place as this?"

The glass nearly slipped from her hands. Elise wanted not simply to close the Hall to visitors—she wanted to *sell* it? It might not be home to her anymore, but it once was, when her boys were young. When her husband was alive, he spent much of the year here. The same home had housed Hollinworths, and Hamiltons before them, for two hundred years. Rebecca could think of nothing to say.

"Mum is daring me to sell or donate the place to the Trust," Quentin said, pouring himself a glass of iced tea. "But if you knew her better, you would see the ploy behind the suggestion. She wants the Hall to be either home or museum, not both. She's archaically old-fashioned. I intend to keep things as they are, at least for the time being."

A wave of relief rushed through Rebecca, one that had nothing to do with whether or not she kept a job she loved. If Lady Elise was so old-fashioned, couldn't she see history would lose a vital connection with today if it were owned by anyone else, even the Trust?

"Drafty in the winter, hot in the summer," Elise said. "And since it's open to the public on more days than ever, it's hardly a home and certainly no place to raise children."

"Why not? At least they'd have a thorough education on the running of a Victorian estate. Thanks to Rebecca, who made sure it won a Sandford Award and has just been nominated for a Featherby as well."

"How nice," said Elise, staring out one of the mullioned windows. "Sounds as if the Trust would be happy to have this place."

So much for an offer of thanks for Rebecca's part in distinguishing the Hall with educational awards.

Soon Helen and her husband came in with trays, a full five-course dinner beneath rounded silver domes. Quentin led his mother to the table, where the three of them took their seats.

"Just a moment," Elise said once the dinner was served and the husband and wife headed for the door. They both turned expectantly.

"Yes, ma'am?" Helen asked. "Can I get you anything else?"

"No." Her narrow gaze could have pierced steel. "Was it your idea or my son's to serve our dinner in here?"

"It was mine, Mum," said Quentin before Helen could answer. "I want the bird to know I'm home, so I've been having my meals in here."

One brow rose over Lady Elise's eyes in what looked like exasperated acceptance.

"Anything else, ma'am?" Helen's back, as well as her tone, seemed a bit stiffer than it had before.

Good for her. At least she isn't cowering.

Elise turned back to the table, effectively discharging them from the room. Rebecca caught the grin Quentin sent Helen's way, a simple gesture that softened the board she had made of her shoulders.

"There is a bit of other news," Quentin said as they began eating.

Rebecca paused before taking up her fork. Evidently there was no blessing to be said over this meal. Silently, quickly, she sent up a word of thanks.

"Other news?" Elise asked. "What news have you given me already that this should qualify as 'other'?"

"About the Featherby, Mum," said Quentin. Amazingly, his tone was light, forgiving.

"Oh, that," she murmured dismissively. "What other news, then?"

"We've heard from an American branch of the family. Direct descendants of Cosima and Peter Hamilton."

She waved a hand in front of her face at the names. "We? Whom do you mean when you say 'we've' heard?"

"The e-mail first went to the Hall's business address," Rebecca said, "but it was for the Hollinworth family: you and Quentin."

Elise's fork stopped midway as she scrutinized Rebecca. "Strangers are trying to contact my son through the Hall? Yet another reason to sell off this place and remove ourselves from being such easy targets."

"But they're authentically related, Mum. They've traced their family back to ours. Well, Father's line anyway. I'll be eager to meet them."

"Meet them? Why? Are you planning a trip to the US?"

"No, they're actually coming here. I assume they'll want to see the Hall, since this was where Cosima and Peter Hamilton lived and reared their children."

"Surely you're not having perfect strangers come here, Quentin?"

"No, not exactly strangers."

"The whole idea is positively frightening. Americans, no less."

"They have a journal," Rebecca offered quietly, thinking even that probably wouldn't change Elise's mind. But Rebecca was in this with Quentin and didn't want him fighting alone. "A journal belonging to Quentin's great-great-great-grandmother."

"I'm sure they do." Her tone indicated she didn't believe a word.

"Have you checked your e-mail today, Quentin?" Rebecca asked. A slight shift in the topic might ease the tension. "Dana sent the text of Cosima's journal."

He shook his head, smiling. "No, not yet. I'll look for it tonight. So you've seen it?"

"Only that it was attached. I didn't have time to open it."

"This is all so fascinating," Elise cut in, "but I assume you both know you could be fooled by a family of con artists wanting heaven knows what."

"Clever con artists, if so," Quentin said, winking Rebecca's way.

Maybe Rebecca was beginning to adjust to Elise's abrasive personality. Or maybe that wink, like the grin he'd aimed Helen's way, was enough to abolish whatever discomfort Rebecca still felt. She smiled.

"They've offered quite an extensive pedigree," she told Elise. Even her voice sounded like her own again. "I don't really see how it could be false. I've verified what I could with public records, birth and marriage certificates. It all appears legitimate."

Elise eyed Rebecca. "How resourceful of you."

"Besides, they don't want anything, Mum. Just to see the Hall, and they can do that by making an appointment for a tour anyway. And something else. When we heard about the journal, Rebecca and I looked through the vault and found letters from Cosima and Peter's generation that we'd like to share with these cousins of mine."

The corners of Elise's mouth went up as she looked at her son, but it wasn't what Rebecca could call a smile. "It's nice if you want to investigate Hollinworth history, Quentin. Keep it within the family, though. I don't want any tabloid memoirs released of my family or your father's."

"Sharing a few letters with distant cousins isn't making much of a public debut, Mum." He took another sip of his iced tea, and Rebecca respected his demeanor. Rebecca could learn something from him, if only when dealing with difficult clients booking the Hall. "We *are* keeping it in the family, after all."

Lady Elise sighed. "I don't like the sound of these so-called cousins. Just don't make me say 'I told you so' when these people try to cheat you out of this house or some of the funds it generates. I'd rather sell it than lose anything to frauds."

8

Mr. Truebody was not to be found, having gone to Dublin for reasons his clerk would not disclose. You might recall I have some slight reservations about Mr. Truebody, but they are insignificant in comparison to my opinion of Mr. Flegge, the local constable to whom Duff decided to go after finding Mr. Truebody absent. If you had stood in the blue room with me, Cosima, you would have seen the condescending look upon his face as clearly as I did. I could not imagine which he thought less of: a school for the infirm run by women or one of the infirm apparently having been abandoned.

"I've not a clue as to what you expect me to do, miss," said the constable, holding his hat in his hand. Mr. Flegge was neither ugly nor comely, rather somewhere in between, with thinning hair, only a slight paunch, and a chin that had grown soft in middle age. "I cannot very well leave me duties behind to go searching all Ireland for the girl's family, can I now?"

"Surely something can be done," Berrie said. "From what she's said, her brother will be very concerned about her."

"Then it's fair to assume he'll be searching for her. Perhaps he'll be contacting me office and I'll show him to yer door straightway; of that you can be sure."

Berrie sighed, knowing that unless she hired someone to search for Katie's family, the task would not be done. But every bit of the funds she'd been allocated—either by donation or from her father and brother Peter—were tied up in getting things started. Even the sale of items left behind in Escott Manor that wouldn't or couldn't be used by their school left little money beside.

As Berrie wished the constable good day and he took his leave, myriad thoughts crossed her mind. She must do *something*. Post a notice in one of the newspapers? It was worth a try since clearly Katie's family was literate, though it might not do much good if her family was from a rural area where newsprint circulation was limited. Perhaps she could spare Duff for a few days; he was reliable, hardworking, and honest—bright, too, for one so young. He showed such promise she planned to name him senior attendant once the children started arriving. She had been planning to send him out on a mission anyway. Perhaps he could accomplish two tasks in one outing.

One way or another, she would find Katie's family. She must.

9

Rebecca rubbed her eyes, trying to banish the sting of fatigue. Glancing at the desk clock in her office, she realized she'd been reading Cosima's journal far longer than she expected. It was nearly two in the morning.

But Cosima's story had captivated her. Was Dana also affected by the Kennesey curse? Had she too given birth to a "cursed" child? She said she'd be bringing her husband *and* daughter.

Rebecca had known Cosima Hamilton only through her portrait and her somewhat limited legacy: decorating themes that no generation since hers had seen fit to drastically alter; a storybook she'd written for her children full of Irish rhymes and tales; a few recipes. So far, Berrie's letters hadn't revealed much more about Cosima.

Perhaps it was just as well Elise Hollinworth had shown no interest in either the American cousins or whatever correspondence they sent ahead. Learning the Hamilton line had been tainted by a curse wouldn't be something Lady Elise would bring up in any of her circles.

Rebecca felt she really ought to go to her room and sleep. After Quentin's mother had left just past ten, Rebecca had excused herself despite Quentin's invitation to share a cup of tea. Herbal, he'd promised, without caffeine. But she had an appointment with a bride-to-be the following morning, and those oftentimes went on forever. She'd gone to her room, changed from the black dress into a soft T-shirt and cotton shorts to sleep in, then promptly found herself too wide-awake to sleep. So she'd headed to her office.

Even now, after several hours of diversion, the questions returned. Had she been a fool to decline extending an evening alone with Quentin? And why had he asked, anyway? Only being polite? Maybe she'd imagined the look in his eye, one that said he'd like to be with her.

But now she really must go to bed. A glass of milk would help.

To her surprise, she spotted a light already on as she neared the kitchen. She quickened her step. Surely Helen wasn't still there, fretting over the meal she'd served? Though Elise Hollinworth hadn't liked the setting, she'd spoken nary a word against the food. Helen should have been glad for that, considering Elise obviously didn't hesitate to say a negative word if one popped into her mind.

Rebecca stopped abruptly, nearly slipping on the cool kitchen tile. Not Helen at all. There, at the wide wooden table where Rebecca had watched Helen prepare meals and shared plenty, sat Quentin.

"I saw the light," Rebecca said by way of explanation for her hastened entry. "I worried Helen might still be here and something might be wrong."

If there had been any fatigue on his face when she'd first spotted him, it was gone now. He looked her over with a smile, and even though the slow glance was welcoming, she wondered if she should hurry back to her suite, at the very least to change her clothes. Although she wore less at the beach, this was hardly the right attire to be sitting with her employer—particularly one who'd once invaded many of her waking thoughts. And some dreams as well.

He seemed to jerk his gaze from her. He held up loose, printed pages and cleared his throat. "I printed out Cosima's journal. Fascinating. You should read it." He paused, momentarily staring at her again, then turned back to the pages, flipping through them. "But I seem to have left the first section in my room."

Rebecca took a seat, wishing she'd thought to put on a robe. She noticed he wore the same clothes he'd been in earlier, and she wistfully wondered why women's evening wear couldn't be as comfortable as men's obviously was. She wouldn't have had to change at all.

"I've read the e-file," she admitted. "I was so eager to finish I'll have to read it again more thoroughly, but I just now finished the last word."

Quentin looked at her squarely, a frown on his handsome face. "I thought you needed a good night's rest for an early appointment?"

A blush made her divert her gaze. "Yes, I do have an early appointment. I found I couldn't sleep after all." She looked at him again. "I intended only to read a few pages, but I feel like I know Cosima, if only through her portrait, and wanted to learn more about her."

"What do you suppose Dana Walker meant when she referred to the curse that affected Cosima? She said she has a daughter. I wonder if she's like Cosima's daughter, Mary. Or Royboy."

"I wondered the same. I imagine we'll find out, since Dana will be here before long." Rebecca looked at the pages, wondering how far he'd read. "I'll leave you to finish, then."

She started to rise just as he reached across the table, his palm landing gently on her wrist. The touch stalled everything but her pulse. "You cannot see the kitchen light from either your office or your bedroom suite, Rebecca. You must have come down here for some other reason."

"I wanted some milk, actually. To help me sleep."

He hadn't removed his hand. She told herself to withdraw but found herself still immobile. Outwardly, at least. Inwardly her heart darted from one corner of her chest to the other.

Quentin drew back. He stood, going to a cupboard and extracting a glass. "I made some chamomile tea—although I won't offer you that since you didn't want any earlier." She watched as he went to the large refrigerator and poured milk for her. He glanced at her. "I'm telling myself it was the tea, not the company, that you refused. Would you like it warmed?"

Rebecca shook her head and he handed her the glass, her fingers brushing his as she accepted it. She might have come for warmed milk, but she had no idea what to do with the time it would take to warm. So she took a sip of it cold, knowing without a doubt she would have to bring the glass back to her room if she was to get much milk past her suddenly constricting throat.

"Tell me, Rebecca," Quentin said as he sat again. His tone was so intimate she had to set aside the glass altogether, freeing untrustworthy hands. She pulled them beneath the table to her lap. "Do you wake in the morning devising ways to avoid me, or are you truly as overworked as it appears? If so, I believe you need an assistant."

She managed a smile. "No, I'm not overworked at all."

"Oh." He sounded disappointed. "Then it's the other option."

That she was avoiding him? Instantly she knew she couldn't deny it; it was true. Not that she could explain why. Being busy was certainly one reason. Leftover insecurities from a childhood crush was another.

She only hoped he didn't ask—

"Why?"

She attempted to brush away his question with a perplexed shake of her head, reemploying one hand to take another drink of the milk. Better to trust an unsteady grip to hide trembling lips than to admit the whole truth.

"Rebecca? Are you going to answer my question?"

She put down the milk, touching fingertips to lips, but that tremulous stroke did little to still her nervousness.

This was ridiculous. She'd felt like a child once already today, in Lady Elise's company.

"No, Quentin, I'll not answer your question." She was pleased to hear the firmness behind her voice.

"Then you realize I'm left to draw my own conclusions? That the reason you've chosen to avoid me can only be personal? Either you don't like me, Rebecca . . . or you like me very much. So much that it's made you uncomfortable around me. For what reason, I cannot guess, since I like you, too. Very much."

She pushed her chair from the table. This was really too much. "I'm sorry you've had to imagine such guesses, Quentin. It's very late, though, and I think . . ."

He stood just as she did, stepping around the corner of the table and taking one of her hands. He felt warm in comparison to the cool glass. Before she could think or breathe or arm herself with a defense, his mouth descended on hers, and there she stood, kissing him back, letting her arms go round his shoulders and marveling how broad they were, how strong he felt. How close he held her, how wonderful it was. Old dreams were one thing, but reality was altogether finer in every way.

When he lifted his lips from hers, he didn't let go. Instead he put a hand into the curls of her hair, gently inviting her head to the firmness of his chest. She wondered if his heart thumped as erratically as her own, but with her ear pressed nearby she found his beat was steady, strong like the rest of him.

"I didn't know how else to stop you from running away," he whispered.

"Seems to have been effective," she said, much to her own dismay. She *should* be running. Fast. All the way to employment at the National Trust.

Quentin kissed her again and she let him. Her brain failed her, weak in comparison to the power of this kiss.

But it was foolish.

Lord, help me!

She pulled away, managing a steadying breath. "Quentin." She'd meant to summon a touch of caution, even rebuke. He was, after all, her employer. She didn't have to search long to find a list of reasons this shouldn't be happening. Instead her tone had been more a plea, like a portion of the entreaty left over from her prayer.

He was still too close, and she took a step backward but ran into the table. She placed her hands behind her, gripping the edge of the familiar, marred top as if it were her only alternative to holding him. At the moment it was.

He closed the gap between them, and Rebecca had no place to go, so she raised one hand to his chest, forestalling him. "No."

He stopped. Though he didn't step back, he didn't follow through with what she fully expected would have been another kiss.

His brows lifted. "No?"

"I'm too confused to sort out what just happened. It's late. We're both tired, perhaps too tired to behave properly."

"I agree I might not be behaving properly, but I don't see any reason to be confused. You were the other half of what I must say was a most enjoyable kiss. What's to be confused about two consenting adults?"

A laugh came out that sounded a bit higher strung than she wished. "Where shall I start? Shall I remind you that I'm the granddaughter to the valet who served your grandfather? A valet's granddaughter isn't exactly a suitable follow-up to Lady Caroline Norleigh."

He grinned. "That's hardly a convincing argument, Rebecca. Come now, class differences in today's day and age?"

"Not to you—but to your mother?"

"She's bound to wake up in the twenty-first century sooner or later."

Rebecca's brain spun inside her head, twirling a dance set off by his words, his kiss, the look in his eye. Still, there was one obstacle she couldn't ignore. "We're not just two consenting adults. There's a third party involved."

Now his brows fell to a frown. "You—you're involved with someone else?"

She nodded. "Yes, very much so."

He looked as though he might say something but held back. Instead, his gaze dropped and he rubbed the back of his neck. "Sounds serious."

"It is."

"I didn't know. I'm sorry. Do I . . . am I acquainted with him?"

"I thought you were. I thought your father introduced Him to you some time ago."

When Quentin looked perplexed, Rebecca knew she couldn't stall any longer. "It's God, Quentin. I may work for you, but I serve Him."

"Ah," he said. "And you believe God wouldn't want you involved with me?"

She shook her head. "It isn't you. It's that we want different things. I want to serve Him, and you . . ."

". . . don't? Is that what you think?"

"Do you? I don't really know, Quentin. I know so little of you except what I've learned through your family history."

He sighed, ran a hand through his hair, and looked at her again. "You define the rules, Rebecca. I'll abide by them."

"Rules for a relationship we shouldn't risk? Perhaps the best thing would be to forget this ever happened. Safest, you know?"

"Safe, as in boring. As in missed opportunity."

She shook her head. "No, as in two lives still intact."

10

Forgive me, Cosima, but I feel an alarming desire to host a good, old-fashioned temper tantrum, and I fear it is only here, in one of my private letters to you, that I shall find a safe place to reveal such inappropriate behavior. Mr. Truebody is a conundrum. I have learned already that he is difficult to please, having rewritten more than a few perfectly fine reports submitted to his office. Today he was beyond simply difficult; he was impossible. He arrived at Escott Manor to imply I am incompetent, as proven by having involved the constable over the matter of Katie MacFarland's arrival.

"Escott Manor Hospital for the Mentally Infirm is under my jurisdiction, Miss Hamilton," said Mr. Truebody. Berrie found his voice especially grating today, its nasal tone harsher than ever. "My jurisdiction alone. Mr. Flegge has no responsibility—or I should say, no *obligation*—to spend his time searching for a family of one who obviously belongs exactly where she was left."

"It's true Katie MacFarland was abandoned, Mr. Truebody,"

Berrie said, "but evidently not by her entire family. There is a brother—"

"Precisely why you should have brought this to my attention. To go beyond my office is inexcusable."

"I felt we should lose no time in trying to find Katie's family, and with you away, the constable seemed the next obvious choice. We've also asked Duff Habgood to search for her family as he spreads the word about our school."

One of Mr. Truebody's razorlike brows rose, leaving the other aimed downward. "Yes, you mentioned that plan, and I agreed to allow this man one month before he will be expected to return and fulfill the duties for which he's been hired. I trust you made that clear to him, whether or not he's succeeded in either of these two missions you've bestowed upon him?"

Berrie nodded. "Yes. One month—that was the agreement."

Mr. Truebody stood. He was a good deal taller than Berrie, narrow in face and shoulder. They were in the smallest sitting room on the main floor. It was meant to be a pleasant room, but at the moment it felt like a closet to which she'd been taken for reprimand.

Mr. Truebody unexpectedly smiled. "You are young and inexperienced, Miss Hamilton, a fact of which I must remind myself. You'll have learned this lesson from now on?"

Condescension was nearly as difficult to receive as correction. "I have just one question, Mr. Truebody. If we are not to go beyond your office for any of our emergencies, will you be notifying the fire brigade should we have need of such services, or in that special circumstance should I be expected to use my own judgment and call upon them myself?"

For the barest moment she was afraid he'd seen through her veiled cynicism, though she'd tried her best to offer the question innocently.

He patted her shoulder. "I trust you will send two messengers in the event of such a tragedy. One to me, and the other for what help can be had."

She nodded, then watched him go, although such a suggestion was one she had no intention of following. Spare a hand that could yield a bucket, just to notify Mr. Truebody? The idea was pure folly.

In the next few weeks, Berrie was grateful to have only limited contact with Mr. Truebody. As students began arriving and inspectors and surveyors came to ensure everything was in order, Mr. Truebody spent whatever time he could spare tied up with them.

Berrie's days became as carefully planned as those of the students. She firmly believed the body and the mind were closely intertwined, and in that vein, days began by invigorating the bodies so the mind might follow suit. Students, staff, and attendants marched in military order, a talent easily picked up by everyone. Berrie had no doubt their little troop would send a shudder across the shoulder of any true soldier, but when they all managed to head the same direction, she found the sight lovely.

Katie, though an excellent marcher, proved in general as much trouble as help. Her penchant for talking aside, she revealed an interest, however no ability, in cooking. Katie appeared fascinated by the idea of making bread, and yet the moment flour touched her skin, she forgot all intention to bake. Each time Berrie attempted to help Katie with the task, she seemed at first averse to the touch of flour and then consumed by it, until she poured the flour onto her forearms and face. Evidently the texture chafed and delighted her at once, although Berrie couldn't begin to understand how.

She had taken to locking the flour away, a measure they no doubt would have had to do anyway, sooner or later.

Daisy volunteered to act as morning and evening attendant to the few girls in residence among the fifteen new students, promising to maintain most of her housekeeping tasks as well. To Berrie's surprise, Daisy invited Katie to the girls' dormitory, a change Katie accepted after only a single night in the bedroom that was soon needed for staff anyway. Evidently the empty bed plagued her at night. There were no empty mattresses in the girls' dormitory, since every extra bed had been moved into the boys' room on the opposite end.

Despite Katie's contentment, she continued to trouble Berrie. Even as it delighted Berrie that Katie often succeeded in her apprenticeship role, Berrie beseeched the Lord's guidance for Katie's brother. Perhaps he was beside himself with worry. She fervently prayed that they might locate him soon and that he could be persuaded to allow Katie to stay. If he were able and willing to fund her tuition, so much the better.

Berrie quickly learned to pray with open eyes, watching the students nearby during their daily chapel times. Such things as keeping her head piously bowed and with a commanded silence all around for prayer proved impossible when surrounded by muttering students in constant need of a watchful eye. After every meal and at the close of chapel time, Berrie asked the Lord to bring Duff home from a successful mission, not only with news of Katie's family but to have listened to the direction the Lord would take him on his other task.

Berrie's eye often went to Daisy during the prayers. The girl could not seem to pray except with turmoil.

"If you please, God and saints above—Lord, help me." Daisy's whispered words came once again today as Berrie said, "Amen" during their evening chapel time in the dining room.

Berrie eyed Daisy curiously. "Is there anything I can help you with, Daisy?" she asked gently.

"Me, miss?" The breathless words came quickly, alarm in her eyes.

"Yes. I wonder if something's troubling you and if I might help. Or if I'm not equipped, perhaps direct you to find a way for someone else to help."

"Oh, miss!" Tears tumbled down Daisy's freckled cheeks and she made no attempt to hide or brush them away.

Berrie stood from her seat at the table to pull the girl into a comforting embrace. "It's all right, Daisy. Whatever's troubling you, we'll make it right. What is it?"

She gasped. "Oh, I daren't say!" Tears fell freely from watery eyes.

Mrs. Cotgrave, who sat with a student on each side just as Berrie and Daisy had, cleared her throat. "You might take Daisy to the hall for your discussion, Miss Berrie," she quietly suggested. "Tears are as contagious as the sniffles in a room such as ours."

"Oh no, ma'am," Daisy said, taking her handkerchief and wiping her face. "I'm right, quick as that."

She sniffed once and produced a smile. Perhaps the few students who noticed the interchange might have believed it an honest one.

"If you want to talk about anything, you've only to come to me," Berrie said. "You know that, don't you?"

Daisy nodded, then reclaimed her seat and turned her attention to the girl beside her. Although she appeared finished with the topic, Berrie glanced at Mrs. Cotgrave again, who appeared every bit as puzzled.

It was difficult to be bothered by Daisy, even if she was inscrutable. She was kind to everyone, hardworking, and apart from prayer time, usually cheerful. If Berrie could draw one complaint, it was that she tried too hard to do a good job.

One thing was certain: Berrie must learn what was at the bottom of Daisy's prayerful distress. She knew the girl was Catholic, but it didn't seem to be a difference in theology. Berrie really didn't know the girl well enough to assume that was the only reason for the obvious ache in her prayers.

Oh, to have the wisdom of the Lord, to know how to respond when the staff became as difficult to understand as those she was trying to serve.

11

Beneath the rumble of an afternoon thunderstorm, Rebecca zipped the larger of the two pieces of luggage. She pulled it off the bed and placed it near the door to her suite, then looked around. Her tour jackets could remain. Many of the books on the shelf were hers, but those too could stay for now.

She would be back. She just wouldn't be living here any longer.

Lightning drew her glance out the window. Her heart had transformed to a whirligig since Quentin had kissed her last night, but logic smashed the memory each time it reappeared in her mind. Leaving was without a doubt the only thing to do. She could certainly handle her position as a day job instead of living under the same roof as Quentin.

She picked up her purse, gripped a suitcase in each hand, then slipped the smaller of the two beneath her arm in order to pick up the envelope she'd left on her bedside desk. She could slip it under his door, but he might be there at this time of the day and spot it immediately. That wouldn't do. She hoped to be gone before he knew she'd left.

She would leave it with Helen. As awkward as it might be to let the housekeeper and her husband know Rebecca was moving to the village, it must be done. Today.

On the ground floor, she left her luggage near the veranda

door and found Helen in the kitchen, the first place Rebecca searched.

"Hello, Helen," Rebecca said. "I've come to ask a favor of you."

Helen looked up from the vegetables she was chopping. "Happy to help."

"I'd like you to give this letter to Quentin after I've left. There's no hurry. You can give it to him at dinner if you like."

"Going somewhere, miss?"

"Actually I'll be staying in town," Rebecca said in as casual a tone as she could muster. "I'll still be working here, performing all of my normal duties. I'll simply be staying in town, probably for the summer." *Or for however long Quentin is in residence.*

"You—you're leaving the Hall?"

"Only temporarily, and only for the evenings and nights. I'll return each morning and be in my office at the usual time."

"But that doesn't seem very efficient, miss, not with that lovely room of yours upstairs. Is there something wrong with the room?"

"No, no. It's just a temporary measure, Helen, nothing to worry about."

Rebecca turned away then, because if she didn't she might be expected to explain in more detail, and that she wouldn't do. She hurried from the kitchen, through the ballroom, and to the veranda, the quickest route to the garage.

The rain was cold; thick and heavy drops bounced off her hair and shoulders as she crossed the yard. She might have waited for a reprieve in the weather but feared Helen would deliver the note too quickly. And if Quentin knew, she was fairly certain he'd try to talk her out of it—a task she didn't doubt could be easily accomplished.

The hatchback of her mini was so small she could barely fit the two suitcases into the folded backseat. She'd forgotten to remove a box of books she'd been given by her father recently, and her second suitcase wouldn't fit until she shifted the box to the front. With a bit of adjustment she finally manipulated the suitcase inside, closed the door, then slid into the driver's seat. At last she backed out of the garage only to skid to a halt. Something—or someone—was coming up behind the car, and they'd nearly collided.

Quentin.

She rolled down the window.

"What are you doing?" He looked more alarmed than surprised.

She pulled the car back under cover of the garage, next to Quentin's Maserati. But she didn't get out, even when he opened the door.

"Did Helen give you my letter?" she asked. "It explained everything."

He wiped the side of his face with one equally wet forearm, then pulled her envelope from his pocket. It sagged in front of her, dampened by the rain.

"I only glanced at it. Helen said you're moving to the village."

"Yes, that's right."

"Why? Didn't I prove last night that I'm capable of being the gentleman? It's not as if I followed you to your room."

Oh yes, he had. In her mind, at any rate. Stiffening, she averted her gaze from his confused one. "There is no reason I can't come and go like the rest of the staff."

"Rebecca—"

She shook her head, drawing a hand from the steering wheel to hold up a palm against his protest. "Please don't say anything except that you approve."

Quentin let go of the car door, raising both hands. "Well, I don't approve. Not at all. I thought you would at least let us explore the possibility of a relationship, Rebecca. One where you define the rules. Remember?"

She nodded. "Then this is the first one: we cannot possibly stay under the same roof."

"Because of what people would say if they knew we've become . . . friendly?"

"No. I don't care much about gossip."

He appeared momentarily pleased, then frowned. "You're worried that I would take advantage of living under the same roof?"

Rebecca couldn't help releasing a smile, small though it was. If she let him know the extent of the joy she'd felt since the moment he kissed her, there would be no enforcing a single rule. Still, she had to tell him the truth. "No, Quentin. It's that I trust myself so little."

He started toward her but she held up a hand again, and to her relief he stopped. "I couldn't sleep a bit last night," she confessed. She paused, looking past him to the puddles on the gravel just outside. It was then she saw that he wasn't wearing any shoes, just white cotton socks turned gray from the rain and mud. She wondered if his feet were cold. Even as she told herself to stay put, she wanted to jump from the car and into his arms. She gripped the steering wheel again. "This will never work, you know."

He folded his arms. "I didn't sleep much either, but I came up with an entirely different opinion. I see every reason to proceed."

She shook her head. "I wonder if you see only one reason, and it's clouding all the reasons to stop."

Quentin laughed. "Because I want you? Yes, that is one of the reasons. Not the only one." He reached down, gently tugging one of her hands from the wheel. "Can we go inside? discuss this? Helen is making dinner. Let's eat together."

She shook her head. "Dinner is an hour away. You cannot change my mind, you know. I'm going."

He tugged again. "But not right now. Wait until after we've

eaten. Let's see if we can't come up with another solution. You haven't commuted to work since you started this job. I see no reason to have you doing so now."

Rebecca stood at last, knowing the moment she did he would pull her close and every resolve she held was in danger of being lost. She let him kiss her once, tasting leftover rain on his lips, the faint, familiar scent of his pine soap blending with the outdoor air.

She pulled away when he tried to kiss her again. "This is why, Quentin," she said breathlessly. "I should be driving down that lane this very moment, and instead I'm here kissing you."

"And it's exactly where we both want to be."

He would have kissed her again, but she put both hands on his chest, shaking her head. "You're proving my point precisely, Quentin. Let me go, or drive me to the inn. Now."

Slowly, he slid his hands from around her waist, momentarily tilting his head forward in an acquiescent salute. "There," he said. "Now come inside."

Quentin started to move, but his eye must have been caught by the suitcases stuffed in the back. "You really were serious, weren't you?" He opened the door wider, reaching into the backseat.

His movement distracted her from responding. Instead, she asked, "What are you doing?"

"Bringing in your luggage."

Rebecca leaned on the door, but he stopped it from closing. "I said I would come in to discuss my moving out, Quentin. I didn't say I was staying."

He let her shut the door, sending a half smile at the same time. "You'll make me or poor William Risdon come back out in the rain for this later, when I can take it now?"

"I'm not staying, Quentin."

He leaned closer, so close she thought he might kiss her

again. He stopped short. "Yes, Rebecca, you are. One way or another."

"If I didn't know better, Quentin," she whispered, "I'd say a woman should be downright frightened by words like those."

He leaned against the side of the car, folding his arms again. Perhaps he was chilled after all, standing there in wet socks. "It's a good thing you know me well enough, then. What I meant was that if anyone must move out, it should be me. I come and go anyway, and the cottage is only a few miles up the road." He touched the side of her face, pulling back the strand of hair that persistently fell on her face. "My father made the trip often between here and there before my parents married."

"What will you tell your mother? She thinks you'll be staying here the summer. You told her the other night about the bird wanting your company."

He winked. "Maybe I'll bring him to the cottage with me." She laughed.

"I plan to tell her, though."

"About . . . the bird?"

He shook his head. "You know what I mean. That you and I will be seeing each other."

"No, Quentin. We have to talk first. This isn't a good idea, not any of it."

He leaned closer again. "I'm going to kiss you now, Rebecca. And when I do, if you can keep yourself from kissing me back, maybe I'll believe you."

He started to move, so she took a step back, admitting defeat with the shake of her head. "All right, I concede there is something . . . strong between us. But I'm convinced it won't work, and until you can convince me otherwise I really think we ought to keep this between ourselves."

"Too late. Helen likely suspects something's up by the way I flew after you."

Rebecca looked down once again at his soaked feet. "We'll have to tell her this isn't something we want the rest of the staff knowing about."

He opened the car door again to retrieve her luggage. This time she didn't stop him.

"Secrets are hard to keep, Rebecca. Especially if anyone spots me following you around. And don't tell me they won't notice something," he added standing in front of her with both pieces of luggage, "even if you ban me from the Hall."

"It could come to that."

"No, Rebecca, it won't. We'll close the place down before that happens."

She didn't doubt he meant it.

12

I must say, Cosima, the days here in Ireland disappear faster than any day I have spent at home. (And I must admit, far more satisfactorily than waiting for a suitor to leave a calling card, whom I should only drive away with my bayonet tongue anyway.) I know not whether to call myself a student or teacher, as I am learning so much. I watch the staff teach simple carpentry, basket weaving, even cobbling. My own classes have evolved from language to an arts class of some sort, as we try to identify familiar objects and colors through my pictures and then let the children try to create their own. It is exhilarating! Katie is a surprisingly gifted artist. I will ask her to draw something specifically for you and send it with the next post.

It is late each day when I write my letters to you. I have taken up the habit of walking the circumference of the manor house after everyone is abed, just to be sure all is well. I do so love the night air and welcome the quiet *after a long day of hooting, whooping, squalling, and babbling (charming though some of those sounds can be!). With my exhaustion comes a sense of accomplishment. I know we have much to do, so much ahead of us, but the days end in peace. I am about to take my walk now.*

Cosima, I fully intended to settle in for the night after my stroll, perhaps adding a word or two more to this letter, but was interrupted. Because of that interruption, I am fully awake with more than enough energy to tell you what just took place. I cannot believe it!

"Miss Berrie? I——I wish to speak to you, if I might."

Berrie heard the scratch at the door accompanied by the whispered words. Opening the door, she saw Daisy dressed to go out. No hat, just gloves and a cloak, carrying a small reticule.

"Daisy? It's late. Are you going somewhere?"

She nodded. Her round face, so youthful with its endowment of freckles, showed the same turmoil she'd revealed at each prayer time.

"I——I've a secret, miss. Only I don't know how to tell ye."

Berrie offered a smile, hoping the gesture might help. "Surely you know me well enough to guess you've nothing to fear by telling me anything."

The girl closed her eyes as if to shut off valves for ready tears.

Berrie touched the girl's gloved hands, finding them every bit as stiff as they appeared to be, holding so hard to that little bag. "Whatever it is, Daisy, you must let it out."

Daisy opened her eyes and grabbed Berrie's hand, the reticule still in between. "You must come with me tonight, miss. You'll find out then what I've been about."

It was nearly midnight, an easy time for fear. But that fear was quickly drowned by curiosity. "Where do you want to take me?"

"Not far, I promise you."

"All right, Daisy, I'll come with you. Only give me a moment to put on my shoes."

"Yes, miss. I'll be late, but I don't care. He'll wait."

Berrie's heart plummeted. If there was one thing she feared, it was scandal. "He?"

"You'll see, miss. Only we must hurry."

Before long, ignoring every sensible thought including the one urging her to tell someone they were leaving, Berrie followed Daisy from the house.

"You must tell me where we're going, Daisy," she said as they passed the stable. "I can handle a horse and cart without Jobbin's help if we're to go any distance." No need to wake the stableman; the fewer who knew of their midnight folly, the better. "If you'll hold the horse steady, I'm almost certain I can handle the rigging."

"We're only going down the lane, miss, to meet someone."

"Whom?"

"I don't know his name, or sure and I would tell you. It may even be someone different from last time."

Berrie put a cautioning hand to Daisy's arm, and the girl stopped, not without a frown. "We're already late, miss." She started walking again and Berrie had no choice but to follow.

"And we'll be later still if you don't tell me what this is about. You're meeting a man? For what purpose?"

"Goodness, not for anything unsavory, miss. I just hand him a letter, and he takes it, is all."

"What kind of letter?"

Daisy patted her reticule. "One like is in my pouch, right here. For Katie's sister."

Berrie stopped altogether, but when Daisy kept stride, Berrie had to trot to catch up. "Katie's sister? Do you know who she is?" Berrie pulled Daisy to a stop. The girl refused to look up from the dark ground. "You know Katie's family? You've known all along?"

Daisy nodded.

"And the letter? What's this about?"

"I send a message every fortnight as to Katie's well-being. Miss MacFarland pays me to keep my eye on her." She looked at Berrie at last. "She wanted to be rid of Katie, but she wants her safe, true and enough."

"Does her brother know about any of this?"

"No, indeed!" She clutched her reticule to her heart, backing away. "If he knew, he'd have me exiled to the other side of the earth, that's for certain. And he can do it, too, him with all those barristers and educated fancy people he meets with. Why, he even has the ship to put me on!" She let the reticule dangle from its strap, freeing both hands to take hold of Berrie's arms. "You mustn't tell him, miss, or there's sure to be trouble. I wasn't going to let you know; I tried to keep it to meself, only each and every time you prayed about it, I felt the Spirit upon me so heavy as to be unbearable."

"But, Daisy! From what Katie has said of him, her brother must be out of his mind with worry. What about how he feels? Surely he'll be grateful to you for bringing Katie home or at least for the knowledge that she's well."

"That's Innis MacFarland's job; she said so herself. She said she would make it so he didn't worry."

"And you trust her to do that? She's set up a lace of lies, all to get rid of her own sweet sister."

"Aye, sweet; and trouble, too. Especially when a particular suitor can't abide by such a sister."

Berrie recoiled from the words. "In any case she's Katie's sister, whether she likes it or not. Let me have the letter."

Daisy fished past the drawstring and produced a folded sheet. It didn't even have an envelope. Berrie turned around and headed back to the manor house.

"But we have to meet the messenger, miss. We're late already. If he doesn't get one, who knows what'll happen?"

"Perhaps this Innis will be worried enough to come and see for herself how her sister fares. Just as well."

"Or she'll tell her brother all manner of tales and have him come down upon us!"

Berrie turned abruptly. "Why are you so afraid of this brother? Have you met him?"

"Not so as he'd remember me, miss. I used to be the house-maid for their neighboring landholder. That's how Miss MacFarland and I met."

"I see. She needed to hire someone Katie wouldn't know, is that it?"

Daisy nodded. "She would have blurted out my connection to her family in no time, had she been aware of one. Sure and enough, she has no way of holding back a thought, even if it's for her own benefit."

"And you think it's to her benefit that she stay here rather than at home with her brother and sister?"

"Of course, miss, or I never would have agreed to the plot."

"Why? It sounds as if it's for Innis MacFarland's benefit rather than Katie's. She wanted to be rid of an inconvenient sister, one who embarrasses her in front of her suitors, or something along such lines."

"Oh, you've figured it well enough, miss. Only, Katie wanted to go. She may not be a teacher full and true here, but she feels more useful than she's felt a day in her life back at home. She's bright enough to know that much."

Berrie looked at the door to the manor house, then turned back to Daisy, weighing what to do. *Lord, help me!*

"You've successfully shifted the dilemma to me, Daisy," Berrie said, her own brief prayer an echo of those she'd heard Daisy say. "But we must do the right thing. We must contact Katie's brother, and if Katie is truly better off here than at home, it'll be our job to convince him of that."

Daisy's eyes widened. "Tell him he's been wrong to keep her home all her life?"

Berrie nodded. "If he truly loves her, as Katie obviously believes, he'll realize what's best for her." She took another step toward the manor house. "In any case, it isn't our decision. We're not Katie's keepers, at least not the ones God gave her to. We must let them decide."

Berrie opened the door and let Daisy in first, glancing back once just in case the messenger had spotted them. There was no one in sight.

She would write a new note, but not one for Innis MacFarland through some anonymous messenger. Rather this one would go with the first light of dawn—directly to Katie's brother.

13

Inside the Hall, after Rebecca let Quentin take her luggage back upstairs, he disappeared to change into dry clothes. They agreed to meet in the library.

She sipped the hot tea Helen had supplied, letting the soothing aroma and warmth ease her animated insides. Helen had left the beverage without a word, without a single question, though Rebecca could guess she had plenty.

A moment later Quentin appeared at the threshold, looking comfortable in fresh cotton slacks, a blue shirt that matched the color of his eyes, and no doubt dry socks inside his brown leather shoes.

She held her cup in front of her, a first line of defense. He came to stand before her, touched her arm, kissed her cheek.

"We need to talk, Quentin, but first I want to thank you for honoring my wish to live under separate roofs. It means very much to me."

Quentin sat. "I respect that you want to honor God in all you do, and it wouldn't do my case much good if I disregarded things that are important to you, now would it? You've chosen what you believe and want your life to reflect that. It's one of the things I most admire about you. Especially since I believe what you believe."

"Do you, Quentin? Really?"

"I shouldn't blame you for being skeptical. I've spent more time in my mother's company than my father's, so you must think I go as she does. I don't."

Rebecca put aside her tea, taking the seat near him. "I'd like to hear the reasons you think this might work, Quentin, and then I'll tell you all of the reasons it won't. Let's see whose list is longer."

"Length isn't always the determining factor," he said. "Weight—now that's something altogether vital." He studied her a moment, a light in his blue eyes that she'd never seen before. Intimate, honest, intent, they aimed past her eyes and heart, directly into her soul. "When I read Cosima's journal, it confirmed to me that certain people are meant to be together. If our faith is similar, Rebecca, why shouldn't we explore a future together?"

"Your mother will object to anything between us, Quentin. You must know that."

"It doesn't matter."

"Oh, but it does. You're all she has left; she won't want you to be alienated from her." Rebecca picked up her tea again.

He frowned. "And so you think I should do her bidding? marry some witless snob?"

"Of course not." She grinned. "Not a witless one, anyway."

He didn't seem to catch her slight attempt at humor. "I'll admit my mother will be somewhat of a challenge, but not a barricade to my happiness. She'll come round, eventually."

Rebecca held his gaze, knowing there was another question she must ask but uncertain how to bring up the subject. If only she'd had more time to rehearse this sort of thing . . . but before last night, discussing a relationship with Quentin Hollinworth was the last thing she'd expected to do.

"I doubt Lady Caroline was witless." She whispered the words. Part of her knew the foolishness of bringing up such a thing, yet she was unable to hold herself back.

He took a sip of his tea, then leaned forward. This time he did not reach for her. "I expected to talk about former relationships at some point, Rebecca. I didn't know it would be so soon."

"I . . . don't mean to pry," she said, "but it seems to me Lady Caroline would be a better match for you than I."

He looked at her with what appeared to be a mix of amusement and perhaps consternation. "I once overheard you tell Helen Risdon not to pay attention to tabloid newspaper reports. Have you fallen victim to them yourself?"

Never in her life would she reveal the stash of them in her desk.

"Caroline and I had much in common a few years ago," he said. "That didn't seem to be true after a while."

"What happened to change that?"

"I don't really know. After my father and brother died, it seemed obvious Caroline and I weren't as well suited as everyone believed. When I began questioning things like God and the Bible and where my father and brother might be, she wasn't the least bit interested. She humored me by accompanying me to church now and then, but she has a sort of blindness when it comes to anything beyond right here, right now. Going to church is a matter of patriotism, nothing personal. Her future only goes as far as this world can take her. Even my mother has more faith, believe it or not."

"How sad," Rebecca said. "But you know your mother only encapsulates the problem between us, Quentin. I've no interest in your social set. You go about London and at the cottage in a circle I could never be part of. Photographers clicking shots here and there, never a thought to myself." She shuddered. "I don't know how you tolerate it."

"You realize you have more in common with my mother in that statement than you realize?"

She shook her head. "Oh, I'll grant you she might not want

newsmen snooping round her parties, but whether she likes it or not, that's the circle she very much wants to be part of. She's aristocratic through and through. Set apart in this king- dom of man where only a small number of the population really belong."

"A snob."

Affirmation came with the silence.

"But your circle, Rebecca—now that's another story. No snobs to be found there?"

"My circle? I wasn't aware I was in one."

"I may hold a Cambridge degree equivalent to yours, Rebecca, but you're the one with the prestige. If my circle is full of social snobs, yours is full of intellectual ones."

She stared at him, stunned. "Do you see me that way?"

"No. But of our two circles, yours is the harder to penetrate."

"That's hardly true, since all one has to do is go to school. We can't very well try being born into the aristocracy."

"You have the wrong blood, so you're forever separate; is that it?"

"Isn't it obvious?"

"You have quite an old-fashioned view of things, Rebecca. You and my mother are more alike than either of you realizes. I can name any number of my mother's friends who've chosen to marry someone outside aristocracy."

"Perhaps so, but they've wanted to join that circle; I don't."

"Now who's the snob?"

"Call it what you like. You see the problem, don't you?" Even as Rebecca spoke she was wounded by his words. How could he think such a thing, anyway? She'd never considered herself a snob of any kind, least of all an intellectual one.

He set aside his tea to take hold of her hands. "Have I hurt your feelings? I didn't mean to. I only thought to counter some of the negatives I thought you would be listing. Let's go back to the positives, shall we? We've already proven we can get along—we've worked well together for three years."

"Not exactly side by side," she reminded him, thinking that in those three years he'd probably spent less than six months beneath this roof. A month in the summer each year, a month over the holidays.

"So what do we have going for us? You cannot call your faith different from mine, though I'll admit I have some learning to do. Some relearning, I'll call it. I also respect you and I'll take it for granted that you do the same for me, since we've gotten along so well in three years of doing business together. Common faith, respect, mutual attraction. That must be more than many marriages have these days, at least ones I've observed. You cannot pass up an opportunity to explore this."

"I can if I truly believe the outcome will only hurt us in the end. And honestly, Quentin, I cannot imagine any other result."

He moved closer, his knee brushing against hers. "Rebecca, what do you feel?"

Something positive took hold inside Rebecca, weightier than all her cautions combined. Faith would have been their only real obstacle, but if Quentin had responded to the call of God upon his life, there would be no stopping their future.

"I feel . . . hope," she told him, "whether I want to or not."

He leaned closer, and so did she, to meet in a kiss. If this was true, nothing could stop them now.

14

There are days I am too busy to eat, even though I may spend a good deal of time at the dining table. When helping another at mealtime, it is difficult to take a bite for myself. The dinner hour here, Cosima, would have my mother shaking her head in consternation. Noisy, messy, often accompanied by trauma of one sort or another, especially by those most sensitive to sounds, smells, tastes, and textures. I have thoroughly accustomed myself to seeing food go in, then come right back out. Forgive the image, but I am now able to speak of the most extraordinary things. I doubt I shall ever be able to sit at Dowager Merit's polite table again, for fear of either assisting the person next to me or speaking lovingly yet honestly of my students.

Perhaps this gives you an idea of our mealtime here, the precise time of day we should never hope for a visitor. . . .

"Look what you've done!"

The cry, louder than the rest of the noise, came from Katie

MacFarland. She sat between Annabel, who rocked in place though she sat on a stiff chair, and Tessie, who hummed, even with food in her mouth. As the two girls who could help themselves the most, they had been assigned as Katie's "charges."

One of them must have tipped her glass, judging from the splatter in front of them. Berrie moved closer to sop it up with her serviette.

Katie stared down at the dark spots on her apron. Trivial to Berrie, to Katie it was anything but.

"Katie," Berrie said calmly, "take off your apron. You'll see your dress is perfectly fine beneath."

The young woman seemed incapable of movement, staring at the droplets as though they were her own blood. Berrie had seen Katie act this way before and knew in a moment it would pass. And so she waited.

Commotion broke out at the opposite end of the table, pulling Berrie's gaze. "He stole my bread! He stole my bread!" That cry was quickly followed by a boy bursting into tears.

Despite Mrs. Cotgrave's being there in an instant, the tears sent a ripple of upheaval through the room. Moans, wails, and whimpers bubbled from one corner to the other, a noise great enough to forestall whatever calm Katie might have been about to reclaim.

"Time to separate them," Mrs. Cotgrave called over the hubbub.

The words seemed, at best, incongruous to the melee around them, though Berrie agreed. She took the two boys at her side, one sobbing and the other holding his hands over his ears, groaning. "We'll finish our lunch in the foyer, shall we, boys?"

Even as they walked Berrie could smell something new, something that often accompanied an emotional trauma. One of the boys hadn't made it to the lavatory.

No sooner had she determined who would need cleaning

than a new noise erupted, this one not from the dining hall.
A crash echoed from the manor entrance, as if the door had
burst open and hit the wall behind. An unfamiliar voice, strong
and male, bellowed down the empty hall. Berrie recognized no
words, only the emotion: anger.

Katie's shriek, delayed but not forgotten, erupted at that
moment. Loud, clear as her voice always was, it echoed above
all other discord.

Mrs. Cotgrave rushed from the dining room, and Berrie
hastened to follow. She stopped only to leave one whimpering
twelve-year-old with an attendant, taking with her the one who
needed a cleaning. His keening grew in volume.

"Katie!" The stranger's voice was nearer, a touch of desperation
lending it more urgency than its loudness. "Katie MacFarland!"

"See here—" Mrs. Cotgtrave started out strong and strident,
echoing down the hall, but stopped abruptly. "No need to be
shouting down the halls, is there . . . sir?"

Berrie saw the stranger for the first time. No doubt fear took
the gumption from Mrs. Cotgrave. Berrie felt an inkling of it
herself in the intruder's large, dark, Gaelic ruggedness. Had he
called for Katie?

Surely he was Katie's protector, sent by the English-fighting
Irishman who thought women should work at home with babies
at their feet. Blue eyes scanned the front hall like lightning bolts
and stopped upon her. In those eyes she saw what appeared to
be a mix of as much fury as worry. But the blue was somehow
familiar. And worry? She knew her first moment of uncertainty.
Had this man been sent by the brother . . . or was he the brother
himself? *God help them all.*

"Where is she?"

"And you, I assume, have been sent by the MacFarland family?" Berrie asked. Granite stiffened her spine, determined not to
have him guess the depth of her trepidation.

"Where is she?" He stepped forward, his body as well as his words demanding an answer. He looked past her, and his nose twitched, undoubtedly receiving the scent from the boy beside her. She knew this intruder couldn't see more than the dim recess of the hall leading to the dining room. The boy beside Berrie cried louder. "And will you stop that racket?"

Yet another step brought the man close enough to fill Berrie's entire line of vision, and the granite holding up her spine crumbled. She retreated, pulling the boy who was now howling nearer. She wanted to tell him where Katie was, but her voice seemed to have fled. Mrs. Cotgrave moved beside her and took the boy from Berrie's protective embrace.

"This way, my boy," Mrs. Cotgrave said, her voice once again her own as she guided him away.

"Simon, is that you?"

Katie's voice rose above the din from the dining room. In the twinkling of an eye, the man went from irate to eager. Pushing past Berrie, he rushed toward Katie's just-emerging shadow, stopping within a hair's breadth of her. His arms went out, then fell back to his side. Berrie sensed that he would have clutched Katie to himself but knew what Berrie had learned: She didn't like to be touched. By flour *or* humans. Not even by her brother, who this man must surely be.

"Katie! Are you well?"

"Can you help me with my apron? I don't want to wear it anymore." She turned around, saying over her shoulder, "It's noisy here."

Berrie rushed down the hall toward them. The noise in the dining room was just beginning to ease with Daisy and Charles taking their charges to the kitchen. Soon all that remained were four boys resuming their meal, a single attendant with them, and Katie's two female students, both of whom had stopped crying and were now eating as if nothing had ever been amiss.

With her wet apron removed, Katie was smiling. "These are Annabel and Tessie, my two students." No one acknowledged the introduction. Annabel kept rocking and eating; Tessie, humming and staring.

"Katie, I've been worried about you." The man's voice was unsteady even as he stood behind her when she took a seat to finish her lunch. "Why did you leave without telling me where you went?"

"Our sister said she would tell you about my job, that you would be happy because I am working, like you. Aren't you?"

"I don't know." He still held the soiled apron as Katie looked down to inspect her unsullied lap. He appeared uncertain what to do with the damp garment, and Berrie found her wits at last, holding out a hand to take it from him.

"Perhaps we can sit in the visiting room," Berrie suggested, after a silent prayer of gratitude that the mayhem had ended. Ned, the sole male attendant left in the room, would be all right now that the meal was almost at an end. Mrs. Cotgrave was bound to return at any moment.

Berrie led Katie and her brother to the room where families said their good-byes to the students they left behind. Even in so short a time, Berrie had seen a wide range of emotions from the students, from indifference to abject terror, heartfelt grief to a simple, happy wave. She had no idea how either this man or Katie would behave or if this was to be a good-bye between the two of them or between her and Katie.

Once inside the parlor, Katie stood near the fireplace and smiled. Without looking Berrie's way, the man spoke over his shoulder. "I'd like to be alone with my sister if you don't mind."

Berrie looked at Katie, hesitant to instantly do the man's bidding.

"Miss Berrie is my friend, Simon," Katie said. "She's from England, but she isn't a tyrant at all. She doesn't try to push me down or take anything from me, not food or anything I brought along. Are you sure the English are so horrible, Simon? I tried to hate her when she told me she was from England, but it was too late because she was already my friend. I only found out she was from England a few days ago. Mrs. Cotgrave is from there too, and even though she's not very pretty, she's been nice to me too."

"I'm glad, Katie." Then he shot a cursory glance Berrie's way. "Will you leave us, then?"

"Of course."

She moved toward the door and Katie spoke. "You shouldn't send her away, Simon. She's my friend."

As Berrie closed the door behind her, she heard Simon say, "I'm glad. Now I want you to tell me the truth, just as I always tell you. Has anyone hurt you while you've been away?"

Berrie closed the door. She didn't need to listen any longer. Katie never told a lie.

15

Rebecca watched from the corner of the gallery. It was a long, rather narrow room, full of family portraits and a sampling of artwork from Renaissance to Impressionism, the obscure to the famous. Famous works included paintings by Rubens and Monet, and English works by Gainsborough and Hogarth—a collection of those artists rivaled only by the museum at Cambridge.

It wasn't the artwork that kept her eye this afternoon; rather, it was Quentin, greeting a group of tourists who had just finished the house and garden tour. They'd come from the golden parlor, where Edward VII, still known at the time as the Prince of Wales, had come to pay respects when Peter Hamilton had died in 1900, publicly acknowledging Peter's donation to the advancement of science through his many fossil donations to the London museum. The tour finished in the gallery, where they were just now.

In the past two weeks Quentin had taken up the surprising recreation of mingling with those who visited Hollinworth Hall. Rebecca enjoyed the tours as never before, seeing Quentin take pleasure in them too. If it was his hope to prove to her he had less of his mother and more of his father in him, that ploy was entirely successful.

Although Quentin had moved to the cottage two weeks ago, his mother was not there when he'd arrived, having left for a friend's villa in Spain. With her gone and Quentin content to join Rebecca in the quiet country life the Hall offered, it was easy to forget the society he was part of. Dwindling fast were her worries that any outside influence could keep them apart. Every morning he greeted her with a smile, and every evening he kissed her good night until her head spun. Every moment spent in his company added to the hope he'd ignited, amassing an inventory of fuel that could last a lifetime.

Quentin seemed to enjoy extending the time visitors stayed at the Hall. He laughed with older tourists about the nicknames some of his forebears held. The first Hollinworth who'd married the last of the Hamiltons was tall and thin and called Piper because he reminded everyone of a pipefish, or so the story went. Another was called No-Beacon Bill because during the war he'd been the one to make sure household lights couldn't be seen by the occasional German bomber. He'd purchased black blinds for the entire village and made after-dark rounds himself—without a beacon to light his way.

Quentin told stories with something Rebecca couldn't possibly expect to emulate: the authority of a family member whose favorite tales had been passed down from one generation to the next.

Rebecca approached him as the others exited, and he slipped an arm about her shoulders. She couldn't help being thankful the bus would take away the last of the camera-carrying guests. She wasn't ready for pictures yet.

"Tomorrow we meet your American cousin," Rebecca reminded him. The last two weeks had flown by.

He pulled her closer, kissing her ear. "I'd forgotten. There is a world out there, isn't there? One not restricted to a two-hour tour."

She trembled at his kiss. "I haven't finished transcribing Berrie's letters yet."

He kissed her again. "You can e-mail them to my cousin when they're ready."

Part of her heard their conversation. A greater part was aware only of his kiss.

Reluctantly, Rebecca pulled herself away, gazing at the portraits representing three centuries of his lineage. "What would they say if they could look down upon us now, Quentin? Most of them were served by one relative of mine or another."

"They can't very well tell us, now can they? My guess is if they could see us together and had half a heart, they'd tell me to keep kissing you."

He moved to do just that, and Rebecca meant to pull away again, to keep a rein on how they spent their time. It was too easy to be swept away.

"Hold there, sir! You'll miss the bus, duck."

Helen's voice penetrated the haze enveloping Rebecca, who turned to the sudden commotion from the hall leading into the gallery. There stood Helen, a look of alarm growing on her face as she pointed to a man snapping a series of pictures. The shutter of the camera was pointed directly toward Rebecca in Quentin's arms.

In an instant Rebecca freed herself. The reporter shot off, Quentin on his heels. The two collided at the door leading from the gallery, Quentin landing atop the man's outstretched arm as he strove to keep his camera from reach. If ever there was cause to believe in the innate nobility of the man, she didn't doubt Quentin now, though she doubted seeing him wrestling a reporter would cause anyone except her to think such a thing. Quentin twisted the camera from the wiry man and in moments had an electronic cartridge in his hand.

"If you'd prefer not to be arrested, you'll take what's left of your camera and leave," Quentin said, only slightly out of breath and agilely returning to his feet.

The man reclaimed his digital camera, now empty of its photo card. It looked like any tourist's. He inspected it for damage, then eyed the card Quentin held in his hand.

"I have a week's worth of work on that."

"I'll have it scanned and anything offensive removed before returning it. Which paper?"

The man told him that and his name, shuffling to his feet. He was gone before Quentin was back at Rebecca's side.

She would never have expected the grandson of a viscount, nephew to the Earl of Eastwater, son to Lady Elise Hollinworth, to go to such trouble. But he had. For her.

16

I must confess, Cosima, that in those first few moments after meeting Simon MacFarland, I wondered if their family might share your so-called curse. Not that he seemed feebleminded, or that Katie doesn't have an excellent vocabulary. I wondered if he might be just a bit unstable, not only from his actions but his inability to meet my gaze. However, the moment after rejoining them, I knew I was wrong. He studied me with such scrutiny I knew he at least did not share Katie's penchant to avoid looking into my eyes. I tried so hard to remember he had been frantic with worry and to excuse his forceful behavior because of that.

"Miss . . . Berrie?"

Berrie looked at him, wondering what he saw as he looked at her so closely for the first time. Someone who'd taken advantage of his sister, forcing Katie to work when she would be better off in his home? Or would he give her the benefit of the doubt and let Berrie, and even Katie, help him form an opinion?

She held out her hand. "My name is Beryl Hamilton, and I am

the headmistress here at Escott Manor. I assume you haven't been sent by Simon MacFarland but are indeed him?"

He nodded.

"And so you received my note?"

"This morning."

"I'm unfamiliar with much of Ireland, Mr. MacFarland. Daisy, the housemaid who was hired by your other sister, said your home was north of Dublin. How far have you come, then?"

"I came by my fastest horse. Less than three hours' ride." He stepped closer. His size alone would have intimidated her, even without the scowl on his face. "Do you have any idea how frantic a family can be, not knowing what's become of one of its own?"

The accusation was clear. "I can imagine it's quite a horrid feeling, Mr. MacFarland. I am truly grieved that your sister chose to deceive you as to Katie's whereabouts."

If he had hoped to ascribe any of the blame to Berrie, he must have abandoned that plan upon hearing her words. His broad shoulders, covered in a black broadcloth jacket that seemed to stretch beyond the width for which it was sewn, slumped to a better fit. "I apologize for her behavior, Miss Hamilton. Innis's act was unforgivable, and I imagine you were also affected by her thoughtlessness."

"We're happy to have Katie stay, Mr. MacFarland, only there are proper procedures for all of our students."

"She won't be staying in this bedlam. My carriage will be here shortly."

Berrie grazed her fingertips to palms, resisting a full clench. She would not be offended by his choice of words. He had, after all, come upon one of the more uproarious scenes even she had witnessed since they'd started the school. "I understand if you'd rather take Katie home; however, I'd hardly term it *bedlam* here."

He eyed her for the second time with such probing intensity she knew a moment of discomfort. "All the more reason for me to take her home, if you're so immune to what this place is. What

I came upon in there——" he cocked his head toward the door——"was bedlam, pure and simple. I'll not leave my sister to such a place as this——a stinking pit."

"Granted," Berrie said with one nod, recalling all too vividly the scent he was greeted with, "it was a bit noisy, but if you'll revisit the dining room . . ."

He was already approaching Katie. Berrie narrowed her eyes. Never in her life had she been treated with such outright disrespect.

"We'll be going home now, Katie-sis."

Upon those words Katie's head shot up. She smiled. "Oh, I like it when you call me that, Simon. Why don't you call me that more often? When I was littler you used to call me that all the time."

"Our carriage will be here soon, and we'll be going home."

Katie shook her head. "No, Simon. I work here, and to work here you must live here. I take care of others day and night."

"You needn't work, Katie. You have a home with me."

"But only Miss MacFarland is there all the time, and she doesn't like me."

"Innis is getting married, Katie," Simon said, "so you needn't worry about annoying her any longer. In just a few weeks she'll be living in her own home."

"Oh." The single word carried neither approval nor surprise. "But, Simon, you're not at home very much, so I prefer to live here anyway, because I like to work."

Simon neared his sister. "We'll talk about this at home."

Katie was shaking her head before he'd said more than a few words. "We can talk here." She looked at Berrie. "Will you tell him, Miss Berrie, how I have certain jobs? how I take care of Annabel and Tessie? I'm teaching Annabel to write and Tessie to sing. She already knows how to hum. Besides, I cannot leave, or there will be an empty bed in our room."

"You must do as your brother says, Katie," Berrie told her. She wanted to sound kind, even encouraging, yet this man made it difficult to lend him much support, even if he was doing the right thing. The legal thing, at any rate. "Remember when you first came, we talked about the papers we all need to stay here? If your brother doesn't wish to sign the papers, you cannot stay."

Katie stood face-to-face with her brother, but Berrie could see Katie didn't look him in the eye either. "You'll sign the papers, won't you, Simon?"

Berrie fully expected Katie to go on, because she hardly ever spoke in single sentences, but she stopped, as if even she knew the importance of that one question.

Those shoulders on the tall Irishman had lost their breadth but now stretched again with a deep sigh. "I thought you were happy at home, Katie."

"I'm happy here." Her tone indicated she'd kept to her policy of telling the truth.

Berrie saw his struggle. So far, she'd seen only families who thought of Escott Manor as an answer to prayer, a haven for their child, a respite for the families themselves, if only for a year or two. What must this brother be thinking, knowing nothing of her, of this school, of what they hoped to achieve?

"Mr. MacFarland," she said gently, "perhaps Katie and I might tell you what it's like here, so when you have your discussion—whether it's here or at home—the answer will be easier."

"For whom?" he asked coldly. "Me or Katie?"

"I hope for both." Then another thought struck her. If he'd been riding all morning, he was probably hungry. Every man she'd grown up with was grumpy when hungry. "Would you like something to eat? Our food is simple, but we have enough."

"No," he said, adding, "I've no wish to stay, and less than that do I want to revisit that dining hall."

"You came upon us at a challenging moment. I assure you not

all of our meals are as unruly as the one you witnessed. By way of explanation I can only offer that our school has recently opened, and we're all adjusting to—"

"Miss Hamilton," he cut in, "I have neither the time nor the desire to listen to excuses. My carriage will be here shortly, and I'd like my sister to be ready. I assume Innis thought to send necessities—clothes and such. Why don't you see they're ready for transport?"

Berrie stood still, staring at the man in front of her. Granted, he was handsome, but that was the only gift God had given him. "Do you know, Mr. MacFarland, you are the most impolite person I've ever met? I have been slapped, kicked, even spat upon by various students in this past week, but not one of those offenses compares to your rudeness."

He appeared unfazed by the insult, although he did meet her gaze again. "Best to pack her bag now, then, so our paths will separate all the quicker."

"Are you arguing, Simon?" Katie asked. She turned to Berrie. "Do you not like him, Miss Berrie? He's my brother. He's a good man. I don't know why he doesn't sound nice right now, but he's always nice to me, even after I've got into trouble. Do you think you might learn to like him somehow, so we can all be friends?"

"I don't think we'll have that opportunity, Katie." Berrie's gaze still rested on Simon. He stared back, as if in a contest as to who might look away first.

He did, and when he turned to his sister, his gaze measurably softened. Berrie wondered at this man who could in one instant be so ill-mannered and in the next, the affectionate brother.

"Will you show me where you've lived these past weeks, Katie-sis?"

Katie nodded, heading toward the door. She looked so hopeful perhaps the girl believed he only wanted a tour and that she would be staying. But Berrie was certain he would pack Katie's bags himself if he thought it was the only way to have her ready by the time their carriage arrived.

Berrie followed. "You should know something about us before you decide Katie's future," she said as she kept pace beside him. It was two flights up to the girls' dormitory, and Berrie intended to use every step to plead Katie's cause. "Escott Manor is a private asylum, a place where children are safe and challenged to learn. We answer to the Lunacy Commission, of course; they have classified us as a hospital because of the residential nature, and so we are. We have one nurse who lives among us and a visiting physician who sees the children every day. We're an open and transparent community. Nothing is hidden. I can assure you Katie has been treated well here and is welcome to stay."

"I've no reason to doubt you, yet you must understand my position too. I am the eldest in my family, responsible for both of my sisters' well-being. The Almighty gives us into the families we have. Who are we to redraw such a thing? Not Innis, not Katie herself—nor your asylum, Miss Hamilton."

Berrie bristled again. "If this is a responsibility you do not take lightly, Mr. MacFarland, how is it that you lost your sister for nearly a full month?" The jab was well aimed; from his profile she saw the immediate draw of his brows. Guilt filled her. It was not her role to chastise him for what a devious sister had done. "Perhaps," she added, "Katie's being here is God's way of helping you with your responsibilities. It seems your work takes you from home often, which might be why Katie didn't mind leaving."

"Simon is an MP," Katie said without looking back from two steps ahead.

Berrie's gaze flew back to Simon's. "You're a member of Parliament?"

"Elected to the House of Commons." He said it without pride, rather matter-of-factly.

Berrie recalled the foolish notions she'd had of him fighting the English as Katie once indicated. Had she really worried he was a member of one secret Irish society or another, waiting to ambush anyone with the blood of the suppressive English running through their veins?

With some consternation, she realized if Katie had only told her sooner that her brother was an MP, Berrie could have written to her own brother at the House of Lords to see if there might be an Irish chair holder in the adjacent house by the name of Simon MacFarland.

"As Katie said, she helps many of the students who stay here. Their language skills aren't nearly as developed as Katie's, and she has extraordinary patience with them. She has also exhibited a wonderful skill in drawing. If you'd like to see some of the class-rooms, they're on this floor."

But Katie was already heading up to her dormitory. "I sleep upstairs, Simon." She glanced toward Berrie. "My brother said he wants to see where I've been living, so I can start there, can't I? To show him how I start my day? Then we can go outside, where we do our drills, and then to the dining room, and then the classrooms."

"I don't think your brother—"

Simon stopped short without warning and Berrie nearly bumped into him. "Drills?"

She could see he disapproved without the slightest knowledge of their version of such a military term, or why they did them. "Yes, drills: walking, exercise, letting fresh air fill the lungs. A healthy body helps the mind, Mr. MacFarland."

"Does it, indeed? Or perhaps physical exhaustion quiets the mouth."

"Interesting that you should jump to such a conclusion. Do you presume everyone to be as mean-spirited as yourself?"

"Hardly. I know human nature, Miss Hamilton, and judge others according to that."

Katie stopped, perhaps because they were no longer follow-ing. She looked down at them from several steps above. "You're arguing again? Arguing is for people who don't like one another. How could I like two people who don't like each other? It doesn't make sense, because I only like a certain kind of person. I would understand, Miss Berrie, if you didn't like my sister. I don't like her either. But this is my brother. You should like him."

She started to ascend again, then stopped. "Did you call my brother a spirit? I know God is a spirit, so we can't see Him. And did you call him mean? He's not; he's a good man. Not a spirit, not mean."

Berrie momentarily pursed her lips. "Yes, Katie, I'm sure you're right."

It was a good thing Katie didn't look for lies, or she certainly would have spotted that one.

17

Helen must have summoned Quentin before telling Rebecca
of the approaching black taxi down the long lane. Quentin was
already standing at the base of the stairs. His gaze engulfed her,
and she felt a rush of blood rise and fall. For a moment she imagined this was how it would be if this were their home, not as
business partner and owner but as husband and wife.

"Helen will have tea on the veranda, so we'll finish there, all
right?" Quentin asked, taking her hand in his as she stepped off
the bottom stair. "Let's go outside and greet them."

Rebecca followed, wondering if he was as eager as he
appeared. Or maybe he was just happy for the same reason she
woke these days with a smile so readily available. From the portico, Rebecca saw that the visiting man was already out of the
taxi, coming around to the other side to assist his wife, who was
helping a little girl from the backseat.

The man was tall, nearly as tall as Quentin. And handsome,
not in the distinguished way Quentin sported his own good
looks but rather American-looking, with thick, dark hair meeting a wide forehead and accompanied by a perfect smile. The
woman just emerging was tall and slender as well, with hair
the color of autumn hay. Before either of them looked her way,
Rebecca saw the man and woman exchange a glance. Maybe it
was the excitement of travel or of being at Hollinworth Hall.

There was a mirror of emotion there, a connection. Marriage hadn't dulled this relationship.

"Lovely to meet you at last, Dana." Rebecca stepped forward, feeling as though they'd done more than exchange a few e-mails. It must be their shared link to the Hamilton family; Rebecca felt they were already friends.

"Rebecca?"

She nodded, stiffening when Dana Walker gave her an impulsive hug. Americans were so demonstrative. Still, Rebecca found she didn't mind the brief embrace.

Dana introduced her husband as Aidan Walker and their daughter as Padgett. Rebecca guessed the child to be four or five at most. She was starkly blonde, unlike either of her parents.

"Padgett." Quentin repeated the name after introducing himself, bending low to shake a hand that disappeared into his large palm. "Now that is a name one doesn't hear every day, at least here in the UK."

She nodded. "My birth mother gave it to me. Mommy said she was going to name me Emma instead, but when she and Daddy brought me home they didn't want to confuse me. So I'm still Padgett."

Dana put a hand on her daughter's blonde head. "She loves to tell that story, even though she was too young to remember. We adopted Padgett when she was nine months old."

Adopted. That made sense. Thus . . . no genetic "curse"?

"Welcome to Hollinworth Hall," Quentin said, standing to his full height again. He turned back to the front door, preparing to lead the way inside.

A mild cry from Dana stopped them all. "I've left my purse in the cab!" She flagged down the driver, who'd just taken off. The black cab skidded to a halt. A moment later Dana disappeared into the backseat and came out with a rather large leather bag and a folded newspaper. "We saw this paper at the train depot with both of you on the society page." Laughing, she added, "Aidan and I have been wondering all the way here if we're dressed well enough to be in the company of such celebrities."

Rebecca's blood stopped altogether, even though her heart still pumped. She watched Quentin reach for the paper, an amused smile on his face. He unfolded it, and immediately she saw two color pictures: one of him laughing with the group of tourists visiting just the day before and another of her standing in the background. Thankfully there was no miraculously recreated shot of them in each other's arms, and she was grateful once again that Quentin had confiscated the reporter's photo card. Perhaps the reporter had paid for pictures taken by legitimate tourists.

Quentin held the paper at an angle for both of them to read. To her dismay, the headline and adjoining paragraph made the more intimate photo unnecessary.

Who's Joining Whose Ranks?

Quentin Hollinworth, heir to the Hollinworth fortune, son of Lady Elise Hollinworth, nephew to Lord Edward, Earl of Eastwater, and great-grandson to the deceased viscount Hamilton, was ranked among the top ten most eligible bachelors in last year's lineup after his breakup from longtime love interest Lady Caroline Norleigh. However, his name on that list may well be in jeopardy again. Quentin Hollinworth is purported to be joining ranks with his commercial manager. . . .

Now the blood raced through her veins. No wonder the telephone had been ringing nearly nonstop until she quit answering this morning, people wishing to book more tours than were available. She'd finally let the auto-response pick up for her.

Now it was all too clear. Tourists wanted to see not only Quentin but *her*—fawning upon him!

"I was so excited to see that," Dana said. "Made me feel . . ."

Rebecca barely heard her. There must have been something in Rebecca's expression, because the enthusiasm behind Dana's words gradually faded to a finish.

". . . famous, too. Is something . . . wrong?"

Rebecca knew she should answer, assure this visitor everything was perfectly fine. That was the polite thing to do, what she expected herself to do. But as she stared at the newspaper, she didn't seem to have an assuring word to call upon.

"No, no, nothing's wrong," Quentin said. His voice sounded so calm and friendly Rebecca knew he thought the report trivial. Perhaps it was, to him. He was accustomed to being in the news. "Let's go inside, shall we? You came for a tour, and we've been looking forward to giving you one." He stepped over the threshold of the wide-open doors, and the familiar echo of footsteps along the multistoried foyer was enough to remind Rebecca she not only had a job to do but had been anticipating this visit for weeks.

"Reporters don't usually bother with us here at the Hall," she said by way of explanation. Leaving it at that, she commanded her friendliest tour-guide smile and waved an invitation to look around the impressive foyer. "As your cousin Quentin said, welcome to Hollinworth Hall. Although after reading Cosima's journal, you might wish it were still called Hamilton Hall."

Dana, holding her husband's arm, nodded as she looked around with clear excitement in her eyes. "It's so incredible to me that Cosima actually lived here. I've pictured it nearly correctly, at least from the outside. And here—with the staircase in the center and the tall ceilings."

"Then let's put off all the usual polite talk about how your travel went and so forth and just start the tour," Quentin invited. "You'll want to see the ballroom and upstairs. I'm not sure which bedrooms belonged to whom, although Rebecca's the family-history expert, aren't you, darling?"

Rebecca nodded, smiling past his endearment. She wanted to enjoy the term as she did when they were alone, but on the heels of learning his celebrity status was already threatening to take hold of her life, she wasn't sure she should welcome it as her heart was so obviously willing to do. "I know which room was Berrie's, another where Cosima gave birth to her children, and of course the room Peter and Cosima would have shared. It's in the wing that's been closed off for years except for Quentin's suite."

They started in the gallery, where Quentin's American cousin could see the same portraits that brought alive so many of Quentin's forebears for Rebecca. The gallery was full of masters from the seventeenth to the twentieth century, but Rebecca barely touched on that history. Instead, she introduced each of the Hamiltons, stopping in front of Cosima.

Padgett pointed. "That's your grandmother, Mommy?"

"Uh-huh. What do you think?"

"She's pretty, like you." Padgett turned to Rebecca. "You're pretty too. I like your curly hair. Mommy makes mine curly sometimes, but I don't like to sit still for her to do it. How do you sit still so long to make all those curls?"

"That's the way God made it," Rebecca admitted. When Padgett's eyes widened, Rebecca resisted adding the truth about how hard her curls were to tame sometimes.

Dana wandered to the portrait of Beryl Hamilton. "You know, I think you favor Berrie," Dana said to Quentin. "I think you have her eyes."

"I've thought so too," Rebecca said, smiling when Quentin shot her a surprised glance. She let her smile linger, wishing there weren't tabloid photographers or mothers entrenched in their own significance to get in their way. He did have the most appealing eyes—eyes she could look into for the rest of her life.

"Amazing how genetics work, isn't it?" said Aidan. "That some things have survived all these years. Like blue eyes and fragile X."

"Fragile X," Quentin echoed. "Is that the name for the curse mentioned in Cosima's journal?"

"My cousin has fragile X," said Padgett. "That's why Mommy and Daddy 'dopted me. Right, Mommy?"

Dana frowned. "Where did you hear that, Padge? Daddy and I adopted you because we wanted to love *you*."

"I heard you talking to Daddy. You said it's a good thing you 'dopted me or you'd have someone just like Ben." She turned her own wide blue eyes to Rebecca.

Rebecca saw Dana's cheeks go pink, no doubt the way Rebecca's had when she'd first seen the newspaper. "That's what you meant by something from Cosima's journal having ramifications today. What's fragile X?"

"It's a genetic disorder that often causes mental retardation," Aidan explained. "It was passed on through Cosima's family. Both Dana and her sister, Talie, are unaffected carriers. One of Talie's children—Padgett's cousin Ben—is pretty severely affected."

"Oh, I'm so sorry," Rebecca said. "How did you find out what it was?"

Dana spoke up. "Through a blood test. Like Aidan said, both my sister and I learned that we're carriers."

"Goodness," Quentin whispered. He reached for Rebecca's hand. "Any reason I should have myself tested as a possible carrier?"

"I doubt it. Unless there have been others in your line with intellectual challenges?"

"Not to my knowledge, though I've been accused of being somewhat dull witted on more than one occasion. Mainly by my mother, actually."

Rebecca laughed with the others, silently thinking he was probably only half joking.

"The full syndrome did show up at least once between Cosima's son Kipp, who must have been a carrier, and my father, another carrier," Dana explained. "You might have a blood test just to eliminate any worries, but I think it would have been evident somewhere along the way in so many generations."

Quentin slipped his arm around Rebecca. "I don't mind a blood test. Might be a good idea anyway."

"They used to require blood tests in America before anyone got married, but most states don't any more," Aidan said. "Do they do that here?"

Rebecca shook her head, brushing away a hint of unease not only over the topic but over Quentin's easy way of revealing their personal relationship. Since this morning's headlines, no doubt all of England saw her and Quentin as an item; no use trying to hide it now. Did she really want to, anyway?

"You mentioned that Quentin has Berrie's eyes," Rebecca said to Dana. "We have some letters from Berrie to Cosima that we thought might interest you. A series of them, actually, from when she ran a school in Ireland."

"Oooh!" Dana sighed and grabbed her husband's hand as she faced Rebecca. "Aidan will tell you I've been running all over Ireland since we arrived, trying to find such a place. We thought from Cosima's journal Berrie may have found a way to follow through with her plans to start a school for handicapped kids. Do you have some information on that?"

"Berrie did open a school," Quentin said, "along with a woman named Mrs. Cotgrave or some such name; isn't that right, Rebecca?"

She nodded. "I'd be happy to e-mail you the letters as I transcribe them."

"Great! I have an appointment with a woman whose family worked at a place called Sparrow Hill during the right time period. Do Berrie's letters mention that it was called that?"

Rebecca shook her head. "I haven't read all the letters, but I don't recall that name."

"I'd love to see them."

"We'll pull them out after tea," Rebecca said. "You'll like the box they were stored in; it's really beautiful."

During the garden tour, Dana was disappointed the gazebo was no longer there, although Quentin had a rough idea where it probably had stood. They finished at the cuddle farm, where Padgett fed the goats, held the rabbits, and petted the lambs.

By the time they shared tea on the veranda, Rebecca felt as though she'd known the Walker family far longer than just a couple of hours.

"Cosima's journal is a prized possession in our family," Dana said as Rebecca pulled out Berrie's letter box. "If you ever come to the States, you'll have to visit us and we'll show you the original."

"Perhaps we will." Quentin looked up from his tea to send a smile Rebecca's way, a smile that seemed to make everyone except the two of them disappear.

Dana looked at the box with the same sort of awe Rebecca had felt when it was first discovered. "I wonder if these letters will prove the same thing Cosima's journal did—that eras may change, but people don't. Not really. When I read the journal, I thought I would have been every bit as afraid of marriage as she was."

Aidan laughed. "You were." He caught Rebecca's eye. "We were dating at the time, and she tried to send me packing when she learned she was a carrier for fragile X."

"And yet here you are, happily married," Quentin said. "Hmm . . . Sounds like obstacles can be overcome if you set your mind straight."

He was looking at Rebecca steadily, and for the second time since his American relatives had arrived, Rebecca felt herself blush.

"And speaking of things like journals and letters," Quentin continued, "the Seabrooke name mentioned in Cosima's journal—the valet who used to make sure the secret room in the London town house was kept up—was none other than Rebecca's great-great-great-grandfather."

Dana's eyes sparkled. "You're kidding!"

Rebecca shook her head.

"And now here you are, marrying one of the Hamilton descendants. A valet's granddaughter." She sighed, adding, "How romantic."

"Dating, at any rate," Rebecca said, another rush of awkwardness descending upon her.

Quentin let go of her hand to slip his arm around her shoulders. "One of us is afraid of marriage too, Dana." He smiled her way. "I'll let you guess which."

Rebecca glanced at Quentin even as both Dana and Aidan laughed with him. A few weeks ago she had been nothing more than his commercial manager. Even joking about marriage seemed more than a bit premature in Rebecca's opinion.

Definitely premature.

18

Simon MacFarland's opinion of Escott Manor Hospital for the Mentally Infirm was in no way altered by his sister's near-constant praise of the place. I could see that in the set of his jaw, the grim line of his dark brows.

I was convinced, Cosima, that he would take Katie away. As little as I wished to spend another moment in her brother's company, I found the notion of her leaving surprisingly regrettable. Yes, she was a student for whom, to date, we received no financial support. And her burdens do outweigh the help she brings. I do not deny it. Yet there is something about her that reminds me of myself. Perhaps it is her unflinching belief that she is where she ought to be, despite all of the challenges.

I wanted to change her brother's mind, but I knew the idea was doomed from the start. Bedlam—that was all he saw.

"So you see, Simon," said Katie, "if I don't stay here, there will be an empty bed. A bed has no purpose if there isn't someone to sleep in it at night. And what would Tessie and Annabel do without me? They would look to see my empty bed each night, and it would keep them awake. Someone needs to sleep in that bed, and since it has been mine all of this time, it should be me. So I cannot leave."

"Where is your satchel, Katie?"

"Under my bed. I have two. It was hard to pack everything I wanted to bring inside only two satchels, but Miss MacFarland did it. I think if she were ever to work, she could be a fine maid. She folded my dresses with hardly a wrinkle. I wouldn't want her to be my maid. I miss Sophy. Is she well? Do you suppose she might come here to live and help me? She's always been my maid, not Miss MacFarland's. I've wondered what Sophy has been doing all these weeks since I've been gone. Whom is she taking care of?"

"She'll be happy to see you when you come home," Simon said, bending on his knee to retrieve the two satchels.

"But won't you bring her here? We'll need another bed, then. Do you think we can find another bed, Miss Berrie? There was another bed here the first time I saw this room. Can we bring it back? Sophy slept close by at home so if I thought of anything I needed in the night she would help me. Now we'll be in the same room along with Daisy and Annabel and Tessie. Perhaps we might bring Sophy's bed from home. That would solve everything."

As Katie chattered, Berrie watched Simon open drawers in the dresser nearby, doors on the chiffonier. He turned to Berrie, having put nothing in either satchel.

"I don't know which garments are hers. You'll have to pack her things or find someone else to do it. Now."

Before Berrie could say a word, Katie moved to stand before her brother. "After I rise in the morning, I set my bedclothes all by myself. That's one thing Sophy won't have to help me with anymore, because I've learned how to do it. Then, after we dress, we go outside for drills. I'll show you where."

She turned, obviously expecting him to follow. Berrie watched, making no attempt to either pack Katie's bag or go along.

"Aren't you coming, Simon? We have a grassy lawn, and that's where we march in straight lines. Miss Berrie says my line is always best. I like to walk; it's good for me. Outside I can see all kinds of trees down the hill and some cottages in the distance and a lake. I think the lake is like the water near our house, isn't it? I cannot go in or I might not be able to breathe. Are you coming now, Simon?"

Instead of answering, Simon stared at Berrie. "Are you going to gather her things, or will I be taking Katie without them? She tends to be fond of certain items, so it would be best if we had your cooperation, but I'll take her without them."

Berrie knew she had to capitulate; even she knew that the law was on his side, and she wasn't an MP. "I'll send Daisy to gather Katie's things."

Simon nodded once. To his credit he didn't gloat over the obvious victory. He followed Katie back downstairs.

"The classrooms are this way, Katie," Berrie reminded her on the middle floor.

"But we don't go to the classrooms until after breakfast and chapel time, Miss Berrie. I want to show Simon exactly how my day is, so when he's at home and I'm here, he'll know what I'll be doing."

Berrie eyed Simon, who remained silent. Would he let his sister think she was staying? Berrie wouldn't have it. If she knew anything about Katie, it was that she valued truth above all things.

"But, Katie," she said gently, "you'll be at home with your brother, so he'll know what you're doing there. You won't be living here anymore."

"Not live here?" Katie looked toward her brother. "I'm staying here, aren't I, Simon? So I can work? I have a job, just like you."

"I'd miss you too much if you didn't come home, Katie-sis. You belong at home."

"If you would miss me, you can live here. There is a room for families; I've seen it. You can live in that room."

"No, Katie, I cannot live here. I have work to do at home. You must come with me."

Katie shook her head. "I have a job." She turned around as if to go somewhere but turned again, obviously uncertain. "I live here now, because I have a job."

Then, on the bottom stair and at her brother's feet, she plopped down in a pile of yellow gingham and white petticoats. She stared straight ahead, unmoving.

Berrie hadn't seen Katie sit so unexpectedly, although she imagined by the exasperation on his face that Simon must have. "Katie, I know you don't like to be touched, but I'll pick you up if you don't walk on your own."

"I want to stay here. I have a job." She folded her arms, determination in her stare.

Berrie's attention was drawn to one of the classrooms nearby. The door was open, and a squeal of delight sounded from inside the room. Berrie recognized that laugh. Jens O'Banyon laughed almost as often as he hugged—at times inappropriately—but she preferred that to the ready shouts and tears of some of the others.

Berrie considered Simon MacFarland again. How could he claim to be his sister's protector when he wouldn't consider allowing her at least one other option besides living under his roof?

"Mr. MacFarland," she said, pleased when her tone matched her intention to placate, "it's clear you want what's best for your sister. All the families who entrust their loved one to us feel as you do. They have an advantage over you, of course, because they've visited us and know what we hope to accomplish."

He eyed her, appearing weary and only vaguely interested. "And what is that, Miss Hamilton? Do you really hope to teach those who come here? From what I saw, the best you might do is keep them fed and perhaps safe. But teach them?" He shook his head.

"Will you come with me?" Berrie asked. "Please?"

Simon stared so long she thought he would say no. Then, just as she was about to give up and walk past Katie to find Daisy, he nodded.

Pulse quickening, she hurried toward the classroom, afraid he might change his mind if she didn't move swiftly.

Unlike the dining hall, the arts room was nearly silent. Jens worked on a basket with Ned's help. Another boy was nearby, separating willow branch sallows from reeds they would need to form the baskets. Jens weaved by hand, although Berrie knew he could be trusted with one of the duller knives they used for tighter baskets. Only those made by Katie could be called symmetrical, as she was the only one who could achieve such a skill.

Two boys at another table had paper and chalk, immersed in drawing. Mrs. Cotgrave sat at the other end of that table, going through pictures with Tessie, Annabel, and Reece, a boy whose features were different from everyone's except Theo's, who sat off to himself with paper and ink. They were gentle in spirit, and she was surprised they didn't come from the same family as they looked so much alike with their slanted eyes, thick tongue and lower lip, and flat, wide nose.

Berrie went to a chest in the corner, where they locked the supplies from too-eager students. From it she pulled one basket, one picture, one perfectly folded serviette.

"This is what I wanted to show you, Mr. MacFarland." She held up the round basket, its tight, symmetrical weave the unimaginable goal of nearly every student and some of the staff, including Berrie herself. She lacked the time to master the art, but Katie had taken to it almost immediately. "Katie made this, and it's our best example. We have another downstairs, and we use it for collecting flowers from the garden."

He stared at it, though he didn't accept it when she held it his way. She turned back to the trunk. "And this—" she held up the serviette—"is another example. Katie sits on one side of the table, two students on the other. She teaches them to fold, and no one does it as neatly."

She placed the cloth inside the basket and set it aside. She'd saved the best for last. A chalk drawing of the garden outside, complete with a weathered stone bench overlooking an imaginary site of light and color in the distant sky. Heaven, or so Katie said. Though she'd chosen only her favorite colors—blue, green, and yellow—the grass was appropriately colored, the flowers detailed if not varied. Heaven was a mix of all three, blended gently.

"Katie's?"

She nodded.

Simon looked to his sister, who had followed them into the room and had taken a seat next to the basket weaver. The boy was letting her work on it with him. Surely Simon could tell which row of the basket Katie had assisted with; it was finer and tighter than all the rest.

"I knew she liked to draw," he said quietly.

"We planned to hang this above her bed," Berrie said. "It's her favorite, but we must have a frame for it first. Some of the other children have asked her to draw something for them, too."

He continued to eye his sister, who spoke quietly to the boy next to her. Her fingers slipped nimbly through the stiff reeds, making something usable out of his less accomplished effort.

"For two weeks I had no idea where she was." Simon's voice was hoarse, unexpectedly soft. "I didn't know if she'd been abducted or hurt . . . or . . ." He stopped as abruptly as he'd begun, clearing his throat, standing straighter than he had a moment ago.

"I'm sorry," Berrie whispered. She could defend herself, tell him the lengths she'd gone to trying to find Katie's home, but she didn't think it would make a difference. It wouldn't erase the worry he'd carried all those days.

He shifted his gaze from his sister to Berrie, studying her as if seeing her for the first time. Or perhaps believing her for the first time. "I can't simply leave her. She's my sister."

Berrie watched Katie, knowing without a doubt what his sister would choose if only he would allow her to. And there was only one way to bring that about. She might regret it, but Berrie knew the option she must offer.

"Mr. MacFarland, we have a family room, where the relatives of our students are welcome to stay for a day or two. If you truly want to listen to Katie, you might consider staying. Judge us for yourself. See how we are, how she is here."

He issued a half smile that was almost appealing. "You would put up with me for a few days?"

She nodded. "For Katie."

He watched his sister again, finally letting out a breath. "For Katie then."

19

A light tap at her bedroom door forced Rebecca to open one eye and see the time on the clock next to her bed. Six in the morning.

She sat bolt upright. No. Surely he wouldn't come here at such an hour? She needed at least a half hour to calm her curls so she didn't look like some sort of American Barbie doll left in the toy box too long.

Popping out of bed, grabbing her robe from a nearby chair, she called through the door panels. "Yes?"

"It's Helen, miss."

Relief poured through her, followed quickly by worry. Was something wrong that she would come to her door at such an odd hour? Rebecca pulled open the door. There Helen stood, apron in place as if she'd been taken straight from the kitchen and transplanted at Rebecca's door.

Rebecca didn't have to look far to see the cause of the anxiety on the older woman's face. Behind Helen stood a taller, slimmer shadow, dressed in white from the top of her white-blonde head to the tip of her pristine Italian shoes.

"Lady Elise?"

She swept past Helen, who looked uncertain what to do, fretfulness stuck on her face. Rebecca wanted to comfort her, assure her nothing was amiss, but couldn't summon such false words. Instead, she turned to Elise, who was scrutinizing her room.

"Can I . . . help you with something?"

"You certainly can. You can stop this nonsense with my son. Today."

"I beg your pardon?"

Her gaze stopped roaming and aimed at Rebecca like two arrows. "You're denying that you're seeing my son? When the newspapers are full of headlines about the two of you?"

"You've spoken to Quentin, then?"

"I came straight from the airport, where I saw one report after another about Quentin being involved with his commercial manager. I assumed he would be here."

Rebecca lifted her chin. "He moved back to your cottage over three weeks ago."

Elise's eyes narrowed. "I can assume, then, that the newspaper has presumed and presented something that isn't true?"

"Not . . . exactly."

"What does that mean? Are you involved with my son, or not?"

Rebecca gripped the belt on her robe. "I'm not sure your definition of *involved* is the same as mine if you expected him to be in my room without the benefit of marriage."

"Marriage! You won't connive your way into marriage. I'll make sure of that."

Rebecca took a step closer, willing herself to pray something she didn't want to utter, even silently. *Help me to be kind, right now, right here.*

"Lady Elise—" her tone was gentler than she thought possible—"I fail to see why you're here. It seems you would have been upset to find Quentin here, and yet now you're upset that he isn't. I hardly know what to say."

"Say that you won't see my son again, now or ever."

"I cannot promise that, either personally or professionally, since I work here."

"Not anymore."

With that, she swept out of the room, a faintly stale scent of what must have been last night's perfume the only evidence of her visit.

20

One of the things I miss most about my home in England, aside from family of course, is my maid. I am in complete agreement with Katie on this. Women's clothes simply are not made for dressing oneself. I cannot tell you, Cosima, how many times I have gone into Mrs. Cotgrave's room in the morning to ask her to button one thing or tie another, and every day to check the back of my hair. Somehow she manages to dress completely on her own, never needing the reciprocation that would make me feel blessedly equal.

This morning I hardly had time to worry about my appearance. I fully expect each morning to bring one crisis or another, either real or imagined. However I did not expect the imagined kind to be coming from the family bedroom. . . .

"Argh! Get out!" The same angry tone as yesterday, though not so loud. "Out! Out you go!"

Berrie pulled open her bedroom door, her eye immediately

drawn to another open door down the hall. From it emerged a half-dressed, tousled Simon MacFarland, leading by the wrist a fully dressed, fourteen-year-old Eóin. Simon, shirtless and shoeless, appeared every bit as bad tempered as he had the moment Berrie first saw him.

She caught his attention and the frown he'd directed Eóin's way now turned fiercer upon her. "You might do well to put a lock on that door," he growled. "Unless it's your intention to have everyone in the place personally awakened to someone sitting on the foot of their bed?"

Berrie tried but wasn't sure she succeeded in hiding an amused smile. Eóin was their silent wanderer, particularly in the earliest morning hour. "A closed door is usually deterrent enough, so we're judicious in our locks. Such things aren't practical in a place one might figure out how to lock but not *unlock*." Then as she took Eóin's hand to lead him downstairs, she said over her shoulder, "We'll be outside in ten minutes for drills. As it's one of Katie's favorite times, you might want to be there."

The grass was damp and slippery from an overnight rain, and the morning sun made the unabsorbed droplets glisten like a crop of freshly grown diamonds. As usual, their little army consisted of four rows of five, including Berrie, Mrs. Cotgrave, and the attendants. Mrs. Cotgrave had tried using a whistle to start their march but gave it up after the first few days as it proved too troublesome a noise for a couple of the children. A clap of the hands was loud enough, and now that most of them knew what was expected of them, they followed without trouble. Not exactly in step, though they made a respectable marching sound with only a few of the boys picking up their feet and pounding them like soldiers. The rest followed along with less dexterity and less noise.

Katie's line consisted of the two girls and Jens and Eóin, easily the best marchers among them. She must not have expected her brother to be their audience today, because Berrie noticed him a full five minutes before Katie did. When Katie spotted him, she stopped abruptly to wave, and to Berrie's dismay Tessie crashed into Katie from behind. Like a train derailment, Annabel and then the boys each failed to stop in time. They all went down in their turn, and then Burt, the student leading the line next to them, stopped as well. Only his stop was more mischievous, since he crouched as he'd been taught in leapfrog. The boy behind him had no warning and thus began another series of tumbles.

Wet but undaunted, Berrie and Mrs. Cotgrave managed to reform the lines and their army marched on, finishing with their usual morning exercises.

"Did you see us march, Simon? And bend? Do you know we can even march in the rain? Then we must all wear those awful coats to keep us dry, and I don't like them. But if I must wear the tarp to march, I will." Katie's voice was as exhilarated as her bright eyes and pink cheeks. After twenty minutes of marching; ten minutes of hopping, bending, and stretching; and two minutes of deep breathing of fresh outdoor air to end the routine, most of the faces were flushed with health.

Simon nodded, his expression impassive.

"Will you come with me, Simon? Breakfast is next. Before that, can I show you my garden? I have potatoes, and I don't want them to stink. Do you remember, Simon, how you told me the potatoes were bad and so many people died and the English didn't help? How can I tell if they'll stink? I have something else too. Tomatoes! They're big red berries, and I'm growing them. They're not ready yet, but Mrs. Cotgrave said the flowers are where tomatoes will grow."

She was already walking off, and Simon followed. It was out of the routine that Katie seemed to enjoy adhering to as much as any of the other students, but excitement over her brother's presence must have taken precedence.

When Katie arrived in the dining hall, her brother still in tow, the room was as quiet as could be expected. Tessie hummed as usual, and a few of the boys muttered or alternately screeched and yowled. Interspersed reminders not to fill one's mouth, admonitions to eat more slowly, and promptings to use a serviette soon mingled with Katie's chatter. It was a peaceful breakfast as meals went, one that made Berrie proud. For the most part, students even remembered to eat with utensils.

When she gave a prayer of thanks at the end of the meal, she included her heartfelt, if silent, addition that the meal had gone so well.

Berrie watched Simon follow Katie from the dining hall on their way to the first classroom. There she would not only practice her letters but help other students. Berrie could well imagine what Simon would see through Katie's day: academics first, color and number recognition, some coin identification, followed by crafts and singing. Before lunch, all levels met in the dining hall for chapel time. Afternoons were called workshop classes, where those in the upper levels took turns choosing, weighing, and selling imitated practical items, such as wooden fruit or other food items, then practiced payment and giving change. Other levels learned domestic chores, where Katie always volunteered for the kitchen. As long as she was kept from the flour, she enjoyed helping to prepare dinner. For boys, the workshops included boot cleaning, simple carpentry, or farm work.

Teatime brought leisure, another favorite hour of everyone's day, including Berrie's. Some were able to play at cricket, while others took supervised walks, sat on the swing suspended from one of the taller trees, listened to a book being read, or on occasion took a trip to the village in Jobbin's wagon.

Without a single outburst for the day so far, Berrie offered another prayer of thanksgiving. Whatever Simon MacFarland decided, at least it wouldn't be based on the worst the manor had to offer.

Berrie found her way to the small library that had once been an office for Cosima's father. As she took her seat behind the desk, she noticed a fat envelope resting in the center. On it was written simply *Escott Manor.* There was no stamp, which meant it had been delivered by private courier. Why hadn't this been brought to her upon delivery, and how long had it been here?

Tearing it open, she was momentarily confused by the official look of the letter. Items received from Mr. Truebody or various committees she'd dealt with so far always included the manor's full name as part of the address. This appeared to be from a solicitor on behalf of one Finola O'Shea. The name was unfamiliar.

Berrie scanned the letter and the thick pages that followed, soon spotting other names: Rowena O'Shea née Kennesey, Mary Escott née Kennesey . . .

Finola O'Shea was related somehow to Escott Manor?

Berrie read the last paragraph, her heart sinking lower with each word.

> . . . therefore by Irish inheritance custom, due to the aforementioned, proven fact that Rowena O'Shea née Kennesey should rightfully have inherited 50 percent of the Escott Manor holdings, we charge the current landholders, Mary and Charles Escott, with due payment of half the property or value of Escott Manor. Rowena O'Shea's unfortunate death should in no way

prevent her loving child from being awarded what was rightfully hers these decades since.

Berrie let the paper float to her desktop, seeing it flutter away from her unsteady hands. *Half* of Escott Manor . . . belonged to someone else?

21

Rebecca hung up the phone. She'd called Quentin's mobile but received no answer. He was likely still asleep, as she should have been. Hopefully he would awaken and notice the message before his mother came to his door in the same manner she'd arrived at Rebecca's.

She showered and dressed, then forced the curls of her hair once more to order. Outwardly she would present herself unfazed by her early morning visitor. Inwardly a weight had settled in the pit of her stomach and wasn't budging.

She wished he'd answered her call, though she told herself he knew his own mother far better than she did and probably wouldn't be taken unawares, as she'd been.

The weight at the bottom of Rebecca's stomach wasn't worry over Quentin abandoning their relationship because of his mother. What troubled her was the knowledge that someone important to Quentin, someone who should become important to Rebecca, didn't approve of them as a couple. True, her father had once told her she didn't need everyone's approval, adding with a grin she only needed his and God's. But it seemed obvious to her that life went easier when those in close relation could give their blessing unconditionally. She had little hope to gain Elise's.

Rebecca went to her office, where a list of e-mails and a stack of Berrie Hamilton's letters awaited her. She hadn't delved very deep when there was a firm knock at the door.

Before she could answer, Quentin stood before her. His hair was tousled, but he was immaculately dressed in a stark white cotton shirt and khaki trousers.

"She admitted she was here," he said, taking a seat on the opposite side of Rebecca's desk. No greeting, no invitation to share one of Helen's delicious breakfasts. Instead he was studying her closely. "Are you . . . all right?"

She smiled. "Of course. Why wouldn't I be?"

He lifted his hands and they landed with a thud on his lap. "Oh, I don't know, Rebecca. Perhaps because for the past three weeks you've been waiting for a blitzkrieg, and there she was, at the foot of your bed this morning."

She laughed. "Yes. And yet here I am. Still intact." She held his gaze. "And still, I trust, with a job?"

He moaned, standing and coming around the desk to pull her up into his arms. "Consider this your home, Rebecca. Not even my mother has the power to change that."

Quentin kissed her, then whispered, "I thought I'd find you with your bags packed again."

"I wouldn't leave without a discussion first."

He tilted his head. "You've changed your mode of operation?"

Rebecca shook her head. "That was before we'd established any sort of relationship, a necessary setup. But now . . . we're invested in one another, Quentin. Your mother's disapproval is still on the outside. Time will tell if we let it in." She paused, then added, "I won't abandon things unless it's mutual—or not without an explanation. I trust you to do the same."

"Agreed. Let's seal that, shall we? With a kiss?"

She offered no protest.

He smiled. "Ready for one of Helen's breakfasts?" he asked. "This morning's drama left me hungry."

She nodded, pausing only long enough to click Print on her computer. "Yes, and we'll take this with us. An e-mail from Dana. I think she's learned something about Berrie's school."

She read the note aloud as they walked to the kitchen.

"'Greetings!

I'm excited to share that I've met a woman by the name of Lorna Kettle, whose great-great-grandmother actually worked at the Escott Manor school. I don't yet know what this has to do with a school by the name of Sparrow Hill. Only thing is: Escott Manor was open for just a year! I have access to all kinds of old records, and I've even seen Royboy Escott's file, so I know without a doubt I have the correct school.

Have Berrie's letters revealed why the school was only for such a short time?

I'm hoping to copy the records I've found, and when I return to England I'll bring with me what I have.

Until then,
Dana'"

Rebecca looked at Quentin with a frown. "Berrie's school was only open for a year? How odd, for all her hopes and dreams."

"Perhaps the letters will tell why."

"I plan to spend the day transcribing them. Care to help?"

She'd only been half serious, but Quentin nodded and added with a grin, "I suppose you don't know I consider myself one of the fastest keyboarders in England."

"Oh, really?"

"Absolutely. I'll challenge you to a transcription race after breakfast. You'll see then who's the fastest under this roof."

22

I used to tease Christabelle unmercifully for her penchant to worry. As the old proverb goes, she will fret the possibility of the little old man falling out of the moon. I think I may even have chastised you a time or two, my dearest Cosima, for all the worry you brought to your marriage, even now as you await the birth of another child. I do pray for you all every day. You know I am concerned, yet God has given me the sweetest peace about the child you carry, just as He gave me peace about your son. I pray He gives that peace to you as well.

I only wish He would give me that peace for my school! Every challenge we meet brings anxiety, when I know I should trust Him instead. Worry, I have learned, seems to be a virus. Once caught, it is nearly impossible to cure. Maybe we both need to guard ourselves against it, but apparently neither of us knows how to counsel the other in doing such a thing.

Upon reading the letter that threatened the very

*mission I was created to accomplish, I immediately sent
for Mrs. Cotgrave. She, better than anyone, understands
the vision and shares my belief that the idea for the
school came from no less than God Himself—first to
you, Cosima, and then to the rest of us. So how can a
woman such as Finola O'Shea and her solicitor threaten
that vision?*

"I shall have to contact Mr. and Mrs. Escott, of course," Berrie said to Mrs. Cotgrave after she'd read the document.

Mrs. Cotgrave didn't look up from the papers. "That'll take some time, won't it, though? Your last letter from them said they were about to embark to Africa. Quite likely they're gone by now."

Berrie closed her eyes. "Yes, I'd forgotten. My brother, then. He'll know what to do. But that will take time as well. He may have to come here, and I doubt he'll want to either leave Cosima or have her travel in her condition, at least until after the baby is born."

"We might contact Mr. Truebody," Mrs. Cotgrave suggested. "Perhaps he has a name of someone who might help."

"I was trying not to involve him." Berrie sighed. "We probably have no choice. Only what sort of help can we afford?" She frowned. "I hate to ask my father for more funds, yet I don't see any way round it."

Mrs. Cotgrave smiled. "God will show us the way, Miss Berrie. He's brought us here for a purpose and isn't going to abandon us now."

A surge of hope filled her. She needed to hear those words. But worry wasn't easily conquered, not with so much weighing on a possible loss. "This will undoubtedly be a legal battle—and a moral one as well. If this Finola O'Shea truly has a claim to half this property, what's the right thing to do?"

"Then another thing we might do is meet this woman, wouldn't you say? See what motivates her to do such a thing— the principle of what's rightly hers or greed." Mrs. Cotgrave's smile reappeared. "If all goes miraculously well, we might persuade her to join our list of benefactors."

Laughter escaped Berrie, though she wasn't amused. "Now that *would* be a miracle, Mrs. Cotgrave. A miracle indeed."

With a prayer, Berrie set out for a walk to Mr. Truebody's office. It was a modest, two-story, Tudor-style home and office all in one, located just outside the center of town. An inviting placard hung outside the door: Tobias Truebody, Justice of the Peace. She wished she believed he might be of some help.

Mr. Truebody read through the letter, frowning. He didn't seem surprised she brought with her a problem that needed to be addressed.

"As you know, we don't offer solicitor services in this office, Miss Hamilton." His gaze never left the letter. "I was afraid something might come up along these lines, having so many women involved in the transfer of property." He'd proven more than once his skepticism over one of her gender running Escott Manor, even if she and Mrs. Cotgrave did answer to him, a board of guardians, officers of health, and the Lunacy Commission—men all.

Berrie ignored the irritation his words inspired. "You might point me in the direction of finding someone, Mr. Truebody— someone who might not charge an exorbitant fee, since we cannot afford to pay very much, as you know."

He nodded. "Yes, I'm well aware of the costly nature of your institution." He raised his gaze to meet hers, his slate eyes void of everything except severity. "You realize this could be the end of your hospital, don't you? Before it's even begun to bud?"

Berrie's patience was tried to its end. She snatched from

his hand the letter, which came away without trouble. "Thank you for your time, Mr. Truebody. As you know, my family is not without influence. I will take this matter to them. If we have any need of—" She stopped herself from the direction her words had taken her. Berrie had yet to decipher what services he provided that she welcomed. He kept a rein on their money, was a zealous clerk to their paperwork, stern mouthpiece for the rules. "If we can think of any way you might be of assistance, we'll contact you immediately."

Then she left his office without caring about the possible repercussions of insulting a man who thought himself more necessary than he was.

23

Rebecca honked the horn, seeing Dana and Padgett emerge from the train onto the platform.

"Here I am!" Rebecca called, staying by the car.

Dana and Padgett rushed to her side, passing through the hustle of the busy Northamptonshire station as tourists and travelers embarked. Padgett threw herself at Rebecca in a fierce hug and Rebecca bent to give her a proper one before embracing Dana. One meeting and a few dozen e-mails, and they were nearly family.

"I can't tell you how grateful we are to be invited to stay at the Hall," Dana said. "Aidan didn't like the idea of us staying at an inn on our own, even in a friendly village like yours."

"Quentin was glad to extend the offer, and I'm so pleased to have your company."

They turned to her car, and Rebecca noticed for the first time that Dana gripped a large suitcase and Padgett pulled what looked like a haversack on wheels. Rebecca frowned, having forgotten about luggage when she'd offered in her e-mail to pick them up. Rebecca had emptied the car of everything unnecessary and could accommodate Dana in the front seat, Padgett and her bag in the back. Dana's large suitcase was the challenge.

"We'll have to tie the bigger case on top and pray the rain holds off until we get to the Hall," she said, reaching beneath the passenger seat to retrieve a rope. "Ready?"

Dana looked skeptical. "Maybe we can find someone to help. My bag is full of papers—copies of the Escott Manor records. It weighs a ton."

Rebecca tested the bag, agreeing it was indeed heavy. But she'd never been one to rely on too much help. "You've been married too long, Dana," she said with a chuckle. "We can do it ourselves. Come along."

Between the two of them, they awkwardly lifted the luggage despite laughter sapping some of their strength. Rebecca tied the piece in place, confident her knot-tying abilities hadn't been lost since her days at the university when she'd toted every belonging she'd owned on a roof just like this one.

"Now we race the rain!" Rebecca hopped behind the wheel just as Dana and Padgett got in.

Thankfully for the clothes and especially for the papers inside Dana's luggage, they made it to the Hall before the first raindrop fell from heavy skies. After settling the Walkers into a suite of adjoining rooms on the same wing as Rebecca's bedroom, they shared a lunch Helen presented, chatting over tales of Ireland and America and England. Padgett was the kind of child who made motherhood especially appealing with her frequent giggle, her polite manners, and her wide blue eyes. When Rebecca told her there were often schoolchildren visiting the Hall, the child's interest was piqued.

"I'm going to school when we get home," said Padgett. "I'm big enough now. Mommy says I'll like school. I already know how to write my name. And I can count, too, all the way to ten. And I can tell the time on a real clock. Mommy says I do it right twice a day. Is it 9:30 yet? That's the time I get it right."

"Not yet," Dana said with a grin. "You've missed it for this morning, and I think you may be sleeping by that time tonight."

"But I'll be sleeping here, right, Mommy?"

"That's right. In the room Rebecca showed you, right next to mine."

"And where does your cousin Quentin sleep, Mommy? This is his house, isn't that right?"

"Quentin is living down the road in the next village at another house a bit like this," Rebecca explained. She looked at Dana. "His mother's side of the family brought another estate to the family line, and she prefers that home to this. Quentin is staying there when he isn't in the city."

Dana smiled. "Aidan was sorry he couldn't get away from his responsibilities and see Quentin again. I think they enjoyed meeting one another. Will he be here for dinner?"

"His mother asked him to accompany her to a charity event in the city tonight, and there are meetings with the board of the recipients this afternoon, so he won't be here until tomorrow. He would have been with me at the station to meet you otherwise."

"Oh, that would have been fun," Dana said with a grin. "We'd have had to strap him to the roof, too, but at least he could have lifted the bag up there for us."

Rebecca laughed, thankful yet again for Dana's company. Maybe she'd lived too long in the isolation of country life.

"So will we be meeting his mother anytime soon, then?"

"I'm not sure," Rebecca said slowly. "Perhaps." Rebecca eyed Padgett, who was now pulling the crust from the remains of her sandwich. "We have a new lamb as of a month ago, Padgett. And do you know what it's missing?"

She shook her head.

"A name. Would you like to choose one for her?"

She nodded, eyes widening again. "Can I see her first, so I know what she looks like?"

Rebecca looked out the window from the breakfast room, where they'd shared lunch. "The rain has stopped again. I think it might be nice to walk down to the barn."

They made their way to the cuddle farm, passing gardeners at work and, in the distance, one of the land agents surveying a crop of wheat.

"Is that Hollinworth land too?" Dana asked, pointing to the field below.

"Yes, they own two thousand acres. Not huge by American standards, I'm sure. Respectable by English. Most is leased, as it has been for about two hundred years."

Dana sighed. "Things are certainly different here. History doesn't seem so long ago."

Rebecca asked the keeper to bring out the new lamb, and Padgett was officially introduced to the nameless little one. They laughed over possibilities, names Rebecca had never heard of, evidently from one American cartoon or another.

At last Padgett held up her index finger. "Mommy! We should give her the name you were going to give me. How about Emma?"

Dana nodded. "I've always liked that name. It would be nice to give it some use, wouldn't it?"

"Can we, Rebecca?" Padgett asked. "Name her Emma?"

"Emma it is. I'll have the stable keeper make a sign as soon as he can, so everyone who visits will know who she is."

"Yippee!" Padgett said, bending low once again and talking to the furry creature as she followed it along the paddock.

Rebecca watched with pleasure. "She's a lovely child," she said to Dana.

"Thank you. We're blessed to have her." She cleared her throat to say something, stopped, then started again. "There is something I've been wanting to clarify." They were far enough from Padgett so she wouldn't hear, engaged as she was. "About what Padgett said when we were here before. About her cousin Ben being the reason we adopted her."

"No need to explain anything to me, Dana," Rebecca said. "I didn't make any judgments from the comment."

"I did," Dana said, adding with a grimace, "of myself. I must have said what she heard, only for the life of me I can't recall saying it. Even Aidan vaguely remembers me saying it. It's true we didn't want to risk bringing another child with a disability into this world, but when we filled out the adoption papers, we said we'd be willing to take a child with a disability. We've had some experience because of Ben, and it seemed like the right thing to do. Not add a new little one with difficulties—rescue one instead."

"But Padgett seems fine."

"She is. Now. When we adopted her, we thought she suffered from partial fetal alcohol syndrome because of her mother's life-style. Padgett was behind developmentally, malnourished. The birth mother insisted she hadn't been drinking during her pregnancy, but no one believed her because of Padgett's lethargy. The woman was telling the truth, though, because once Padgett began getting proper attention and nutrition, she flourished. And now, she really is perfect."

Rebecca wondered at the sadness behind Dana's words. "What every mother prays for," Rebecca said gently.

Dana nodded. "I *am* glad, but it didn't come without guilt."

"Whatever for? You've changed her life forever, for the good."

"Yes, I know. But my sister . . . She has the child I might have had if Aidan and I hadn't been careful not to get pregnant. Every day, my sister, Talie, faces challenges I might have had too. Her son's delays, the frustrations, the pain of knowing he will never be able to take care of himself. That's why I couldn't believe I'd actually said the words Padgett heard, making it sound like I didn't want a child like Ben and so I adopted her. It didn't start out that way . . . but I'm relieved enough to feel guilty." She faced Rebecca squarely. "Selfish, isn't it, to want a perfect child?"

Rebecca gave a little laugh. "Selfish? Because you're relieved God has blessed you with a healthy child?" She shook her head. "I don't think He meant for us to feel guilty over the blessings He sends our way. Look at all Quentin has. Should he feel guilty for having been born healthy to a family with all this? He did have a blood test, by the way, though the physician took one look at his pedigree and insisted something like fragile X couldn't have hidden so long."

"Any results yet?"

"Still waiting." Rebecca looked around, inviting Dana to do the same by pointing to the manor house. "You might easily have been born in his place instead."

Now it was Dana's turn to laugh, and Padgett joined them with the lamb in her arms, who squirmed free within moments. She was indeed a blessing; Rebecca could see that without having to study them very hard.

Padgett was the kind of blessing Rebecca wouldn't let herself dream about in the last few years. She'd chosen the reclusive country life over a bustling city one. She hadn't let herself think about marrying, having children.

Until now.

24

I know there will be little, if any, forthcoming help from Mr. Truebody regarding our lawsuit. Why is it, Cosima, that men begrudge women performing a task—even one they have left woefully untended?

Upon leaving Mr. Truebody's office, I took my leisure in returning to the manor, stopping at the church in town. I enjoy going there, and as I walked, the doors would not let me pass by. I stayed longer than I realized, and it was well past dark by the time I arrived back.

When I approached the manor house in the dim moonlight, I noticed the MacFarland carriage was still here. Katie had been granted another night with us. Which meant, of course, that her brother was still present as well.

Mrs. Cotgrave was halfway across the lawn before we were close enough to speak. I am sure had I not seen the outright worry upon her face over my late arrival I should *have guessed it anyway from the moment she walked forth to greet me. . . .*

"It's late, Miss Berrie. I fear it couldn't have gone well."

"I stopped at the church to pray. It'll take God's help, since I'm sure Mr. Truebody will provide little assistance." The two women fell in step toward the front door of the manor house. "Are things well this evening?" Berrie hoped any fusses were kept to a minimum while Simon MacFarland was still there. Goodness, she hoped he left soon. Without Katie.

"Well enough." She smiled. "Eóin snuck into the family bedroom and left a little something for our guest there. You know how he loves to move things about."

"What was it?" She recalled a pair of shoes he'd left in her room. Mrs. Cotgrave hadn't been so fortunate; to her, Eóin had delivered a dead mouse.

"Only a pot, a pan, and a spoon. All laid out as neatly as could be, awaiting Katie's brother on the bed. Mr. MacFarland returned them to the kitchen just a little while ago, then tucked himself in without a word."

"He's said nothing about whether he'll be taking Katie away?"

Mrs. Cotgrave shook her head as they entered the parlor and each took her favorite seat. "He did wonder where you'd gone off to, as he told me he wanted a word with you. Perhaps he's made his decision."

"And where did you tell him I'd been?"

"On an errand. He's quite the nosy one, asking what sort of errand as if he has a right to know our comings and goings."

The thought of Simon MacFarland allowed every concern to rush back to Berrie's mind, and she withdrew the letter from the pouch in which she'd carried it.

"You must contact this Finola O'Shea through her solicitor,"

Mrs. Cotgrave said. "Invite her here. Very likely she has no idea Escott Manor is now a school."

"Let's pray it makes a difference and she won't demand we all leave."

"Now, there, Miss Berrie. It's in God's hands. You've just spent time in prayer over this, as have I. And the Lord hasn't told me we're to close our door because of this letter. Has He told you that?"

Berrie shook her head, smiling. Movement beyond Mrs. Cotgrave caught Berrie's eye. A moment later Katie stood in full view, dressed in her cotton nightgown without a wrap or slippers. A frown marred her large forehead.

"We're to close the school, Miss Berrie? Because of a letter? We cannot do that. It's our home."

Berric stood but not before Katie turned on her bare heel and rushed from the room. Berrie moved to follow.

"I'll go," Mrs. Cotgrave said, passing Berrie without trouble. "I've put the kettle on; you should have a cup of tea, and then to bed with you."

Instead of retaking her seat, as inviting as it was, Berrie went to the kitchen in search of tea. She took a seat at the wide worktable, where bowls, clean and ready for morning porridge, waited in neat stacks. Nothing in this kitchen reminded her of home, not the aged stove nor the plain but serviceable dishware. And yet she thought of her family just then, wondering if she would return to them sooner than she'd expected.

Over a cup, Berrie bent her head in prayer. She closed each day with a plea on behalf of one student or another, each in their turn. Tonight all of the children were on her mind. The school had only just begun to help them and their families. What would become of them if this letter proved to be a real problem?

She wasn't sure what disturbed her prayer, since she heard nothing. She lifted her head, and there stood Simon MacFarland.

White shirt, black trousers, his thick hair tumbling onto his forehead. Appealing to behold. It irritated Berrie that she should even notice such a thing with so much on her mind—and when the man in question had so brash an interior.

Sitting straighter, she wished she could greet him cordially but found it beyond her. If he'd come to tell her he would be taking Katie home with him, she didn't want to hear it. Not tonight. He'd had a chance to judge their school for two days, longer than many parents had taken. If he found her school and staff lacking, perhaps the letter meant something she didn't want to believe: that she wasn't here under God's mission after all, and the school was doomed for failure. She was a failure. Before she'd really begun.

"Katie came to my room a moment ago."

"I'm sorry. I thought Mrs. Cotgrave—"

"Yes, she was quick on Katie's heel. Mrs. Cotgrave saw her safely to bed."

Berrie received the news with a nod. Then, seeing he showed no indication of leaving, she realized she would have to face his decision tonight whether she liked it or not. She raised a weary gaze to him. "Have you decided Katie's future, Mr. MacFarland?"

"I thought I had," he said, nearing the table and taking a seat.

It briefly crossed her mind she should offer him tea, but she simply sat. Waiting.

"Katie was upset just now. She said the school would have to close its doors." Simon met Berrie's steady gaze, and she strove to hide her regret that he knew of the situation. "Mrs. Cotgrave wasn't very enlightening. Why should you be closing your doors?"

Too many thoughts warred in her mind already to try deciphering whether or not it was wise to share her burden with him. He hardly needed more reason to take Katie away. His elegant carriage awaited.

"I've received a letter claiming half of Escott Manor by legal inheritance, which was evidently overlooked within the last score of years. It says 50 percent belongs to relatives of the Irish woman we thought owned it outright."

"But Escott is an English name. I thought this was all owned by an Englishman?"

"Through marriage. The woman who originally inherited the manor is Irish. Kennesey. She evidently had a sister whose descendants claim she should have inherited half."

"There used to be a law regarding such things. First imposed by the English, Miss Hamilton." His tone was as hard as the look in his eye. "Divide and conquer—that was the goal, so eventually there would be no great Irish landholders left."

"I'm sure you'd like to blame me personally for a law created long before I was born, Mr. MacFarland." Even as Berrie spoke, she was glad he didn't know that her brother, father, grandfather, and other such forebears were at least partially responsible for the laws of England this man obviously detested. She was too tired to defend all of them along with herself and her school.

"May I see the letter?"

Momentarily confused, she didn't comply. When he reached for the document resting before her, she belatedly took it up, handing it to him. He stood, placing himself in the immediate spill of the single sconce's light.

"I'm not familiar with MacTaggert, the solicitor." He studied the pages. "But I'm sure I can find out more about him. In any case, this is likely nothing to worry about. What has become Irish custom is one thing. English law, which as you know we're all subject to, is another. That no longer requires the equal splitting of property."

"So in this case *English* law will protect the right of the school?" It was the first hopeful thought she'd had since opening that dreadful envelope.

"Yes, Miss Hamilton. Like most of life, one can find something redemptive in the vilest creation."

She had the faintest notion he was purposely trying to peeve her, but she held her tongue. She couldn't afford to refuse assistance, regardless of whence it came.

Simon scrutinized the letter again. "A sufficiently subjugating letter, preferably on the letterhead of an MP, will likely put this matter to rest."

Berrie bit her tongue once more. Standing before her was no doubt just the MP to affect an appropriately dominating tone.

25

Rebecca sat at her desk with Dana across from her. Four-year-old Padgett was soundly sleeping in the room that adjoined Dana's down the hall. It wasn't late, but an afternoon of flower collecting, croquet, and another visit to the cuddle farm had worn the child out.

Dana waded through the stack of thick brown envelopes she'd brought with her. "Most of the copies are legible," she said, "although I've only had time to read a little so far. The woman I spoke to said when she was little, her grandmother gave these records to her, telling her how so many of the women in their family worked in hospitals of one kind or another."

"Was she a nurse?"

Dana shook her head. "A teacher for kids with developmental delays. She said these records helped her choose her profession. I have to admit I was a bit uncomfortable around her at first. Back home we're always so afraid to say anything impolite, and there sat Mrs. Kettle, categorizing various students from these records as idiots and imbeciles and lunatics as easily as she'd name blue eyes or brown. Until she explained they were nineteenth-century legal terms, I found myself thinking how relieved I was my sister didn't have to bring her son to a teacher who used such words."

"My degree is in history, but I admit I don't know much

about infirmaries or asylums from the Victorian age," Rebecca said. "My father is the true expert on the time period."

"Mrs. Kettle told me that people thought the feebleminded were a result of environment and lack of education, so with a sort of Victorian philanthropy, they thought they could fix the problem. When they figured out biology might have a part in it, something not to be changed . . . an act of God, well . . . they left their high ideals behind. Maybe that had something to do with the school closing."

"The date matches Berrie's early letters," Rebecca said, looking over the sheet in her hand. Each word fit into what appeared to be a handmade chart, with its horizontal and vertical lines every bit as straight as a computer-generated report. The letters were tall and steady, uniform in size. Remembering Berrie's letters, Rebecca assumed the neatness could be attributed to Mr. Truebody.

"I've only read a few of the files, starting with *E* for Escott because I wanted to make sure I had the correct school. Here," Dana said, searching through another file, "these are the ones I've read. Roy Escott's records are there, confirming everything."

Rebecca scanned the list. Edwards, Eppingham, *Escott.*

She pulled that sheet from the rest.

Candidate: Roy Escott, aged fifteen
   Doctor's observation: Non compos mentis
      Gift relatives: Cosima Escott Hamilton (sister);
Peter Hamilton (brother-in-law)

Rebecca raised her gaze to Dana's. "*Non compos mentis* . . ." She knew what it meant; it simply seemed jarring to find it on a file.

Dana's face clouded with sadness. "Idiot."

Rebecca reached for Dana's hand, squeezing it once. "Legal term, Dana; remember that. And he wasn't your nephew."

"But just like him," Dana whispered. She sucked in a breath, brushed away a tear. "I'm so silly, aren't I? I don't know why I've been so emotional lately. Yes, Royboy was termed a legal idiot, as determined by what was called at the time a Lunacy Commission. Mrs. Kettle defined it for me: idiots were set apart from lunatics in that lunatics once had a mind to lose, while idiots were born without one. Words, just words."

Rebecca squeezed her hand again. "It's a relative you see on the page, but one long dead and not harmed by such terms, even were he alive. He wouldn't know what it meant."

"Maybe not. But those who loved him definitely would."

Rebecca glanced down at the pages again. "I see Cosima and Peter Hamilton were named as 'gift relatives' for Royboy."

"Every candidate needed two respectable persons who pledged to cover his expenses and also take the patient back once the term was finished. Rules—every school has them, even today."

"Is there anything in this box of school records explaining why Escott Manor was open only a short time?"

"No, not that I know of, but I haven't read every word yet. Everything I've seen is dated between 1852 and 1853, mostly limited to patient progress and treatments. I think some of the treatments are still used today, like rewards with a favorite food, calming with music, and learning language with pictures. My sister has shown me some of the things the therapists do with Ben, and it sounds similar."

Rebecca read the data pertaining to Royboy.

> *Previous abode: Escott Manor*
> *Prior treatment: Escott Manor*
> *Suicidal? No*
> *Duration of attack: Life*

How simple the words seemed on paper. How endless it probably was in reality.

The report also listed things he had learned to do:

Count; eat with fork; recite letters (though not read); hold urine and feces except when agitated; undress (note: not dress) unattended.

Concerns: Limited speech, overly trusting, lack of discernment in all areas of life. To be kept away from books due to penchant for ripping bindings.

Royboy's records, Rebecca noticed, were more scant than others. She thumbed through ledger sheets, seeing instructions for one student to be kept away from knives or sharp instruments, another who spilled water when possible, upset chairs, threw items into the fire.

Goodness, but it must have been hard to run such a place, especially when fires were used for cooking, light, and heat in an often dreary, chilly climate.

Yet another page revealed someone who set fire to his bed. Blood pounded in her temples. Is that why the school closed? Maybe a patient had set it on fire. How awful that would have been for Cosima if it were true, having lost other members of her family to fire already.

Compassion filled Rebecca. She fanned the pages, noting one stark similarity on nearly every ledger, no matter the name.

Duration of attack: Life

A life sentence of intellectual challenge. Mental retardation. Idiocy.

She thought of Padgett, sleeping so close at hand. Rebecca eyed Dana, who was reading some of the letters Rebecca had transcribed.

Rebecca didn't believe Dana at all selfish for wanting what

every woman wanted: a healthy child. Was asking for the norm too much to ask?

If it was, then Rebecca was also asking too much. All she wanted was to love Quentin and hope for a future with him. The "norm."

26

I have been so busy I have not been able to write, but
I wanted to tell you about the day I watched Simon
MacFarland's carriage take him away. He had given
in to letting Katie stay, agreeing to a full year with the
promise of his frequent visits. Unscheduled visits, he
warned me.

When he told me he would be leaving, saying he
would do his best to dispel our legal trouble, he also
offered unwanted advice that entirely negated any shred
of gratitude that might have stirred within me. Only now
can I write of it without seething inside.

"I do this for Katie," he said, "not because I believe this
place will make one bit of difference in the lives of any
so-called student. It is little wonder the Commission
terms you a hospital rather than a school. Nothing can
be learned by those you have here, and you should do well
to accept your task as impossible." How I wanted to fight
him, to prove him wrong. Already his sister had learned

to make a basket. Beyond that, she is achieving something vastly more significant: independence.

But she was not the kind of student he referred to. He spoke of those who cannot make anything (baskets, pictures, folded serviettes), either before they arrived or to this day. Perhaps he is right, and they never shall.

Yet should I call what we offer apart from that a failure? At the very least, we are able to give the families relief and the children themselves a place where, at least for a time, someone is devoted to their care. Is that not enough?

Since that day I wished he had not gone, if only to argue the point.

When I returned to my desk that day, I found a note directed to the Bank of England, signed by Simon MacFarland and entrusted to me, for the exchange of an amount that far exceeded the tentative agreement for Katie's stay of one year.

I began this letter early this morning before drills and have returned to share happy news with you. Duff has returned, telling me our school is well received and several new families will be visiting us soon. He was relieved to learn about Katie's family, as his investigation led him in circles. He had come across a family MacFarland early on, but Innis MacFarland had sent him *immediately away, denying she had ever heard of Katie and promising arrest if he stepped foot on her property again.*

I am quite glad I shall never have to meet Innis MacFarland.

But it is nice to have Duff here. Just today, as we were going over the list of prospective families who might be sending us students, we were interrupted by something I had forgotten to worry about. . . .

"Miss Berrie," a voice whispered from the open door of Berrie's office, where Berrie sat with Duff across from her.

Berrie looked up to see Decla peeking around the edge of the white, six-panel door. Her eyes were wider than normal.

"There is a woman here." Decla turned to look over her shoulder. "She must have come in on her own. I saw her poking her head in the doors on this floor, not saying a word."

Berrie exchanged a look with Duff, who stood from a chair that was made small beneath him. She was reminded of Simon MacFarland as Duff stood at full height. What was it about Irishmen that they grew so tall and strong?

Berrie stood as well, curious. "Show us where she is, Decla."

The servant led the way down the hall, past the dining room and the blue parlor they often used for chapel time, toward the open door to the smaller parlor where families said their private good-byes. There stood a woman, her back to Berrie and Duff, a poke-style bonnet hiding her face as she peered inside the room.

"May I help you?" Berrie said.

The woman's shoulders jerked forward; then she turned to face them. Berrie noticed the woman was not as young as her meager height might have suggested. She was obviously fully grown at just under five feet tall. Her hair was the color of dark honey, and the eyes that met Berrie's were grayish green, set on a face of pure white skin. Petite, like a doll.

"I was remembering the room," the woman said. "It's the only one I recognize."

"You've been here before?" Berrie asked.

The woman nodded, stepping forward, one hand extended. "My name is Finola O'Shea, and I visited here as a child. Before my mother died."

Berrie felt her brows shoot up even as she warded off a burst of panic. "You are Finola O'Shea?"

The woman nodded. "I am. My apologies for an unannounced arrival, but upon learning the manor house has been converted for public use, I couldn't resist a visit."

Berrie's wariness mixed with a touch of guilt for not having followed her instinct to invite the woman who, at least until recently, thought she deserved half of this very estate. Hadn't both Berrie and Mrs. Cotgrave believed the problem posed by Finola O'Shea's original contact might not have been just legal but moral as well?

"Welcome to Escott Manor, Miss O'Shea," Berrie said. "I am Beryl Hamilton, headmistress here. And this is Duff Habgood, our senior attendant. We can give you a tour if you like."

She nodded. "Yes, I would like that."

Berrie hesitated. "You do know what kind of school we are, don't you?"

The woman nodded again, and though she stiffened, her height didn't grow by much. "For the infirm. I'm well aware of the inspiration behind this school. I am a descendant of the Kennesey family, true and sure. I had two brothers afflicted by feeble-mindedness, and had they not died, they very likely might have become students here."

Berrie knew about Finola's mother. Cosima had told Berrie of the tragedy, how her aunt Rowena had taken two of her sons and her two nephews as well to the cottage in the forest and set it afire. Only Royboy had escaped.

"Your cousin is here," Berrie said gently. "Royboy."

Finola's gaze met Berrie's. Her hazel eyes flooded with dampness and she looked away, holding out a gloved hand to the fireplace nearby.

"Do you know," she said with a hesitant smile, "I used to think this fireplace massive? Now I see it's quite a normal size, since I'm nearly as tall as its mantel."

Berrie glanced at Duff, whose mouth went crooked at the petite woman's observation. The top of her head barely reached the bottom of the mantelshelf.

"I'm afraid you might not recognize many other rooms," Berrie said, looking around as well. "This is the only one we've left as it was. Other rooms have been converted for various uses, and what objects the Escotts didn't ship to England with them when they moved have been sold and replaced with more practical items for the kind of students we house."

"In truth, I was so young when last I visited, I'm surprised I remembered this room."

A moment of silence followed, as Berrie could think of little else but the near disaster of having to give half of the estate to this very woman. While she'd been assured that matter was settled legally, she wasn't at all sure Finola O'Shea believed it so.

"Miss Berrie—" Duff's voice was low, respectful as always— "is it me you're wantin' to start the tour?"

"Oh!" How foolish to have forgotten her own invitation. Maybe that would be best, to have Duff give the tour while Berrie went in search of Mrs. Cotgrave. Best to have her know of this visitor as soon as possible. "Yes, Duff, that would be helpful. Please come to the dining room when you're finished. We'll have tea."

They left the small parlor, Berrie heading for the kitchen while Duff led Miss O'Shea up the stairs to the classrooms.

Berrie requested tea to be served in the dining room, then went in search of Mrs. Cotgrave. They couldn't easily be spared from the students at the same time, so Berrie only told her about the visitor, not requesting she join them but asking her to pray for a good outcome of the visit.

The tea was set before Duff and Miss O'Shea returned. When they entered, Berrie was glad to see a smile on Finola O'Shea's face.

"I certainly admire what you're doing here, Miss Hamilton."

"Thank you," Berrie said to her. "We've tried to make the school a home for all of us, staff and students alike."

"And it shows."

Berrie offered tea while Duff stood awkwardly back. She knew he had countless duties to attend, not the least of which was to acquaint himself with the new students he would be responsible for. And yet he seemed reluctant to go, when just this morning in her office he'd been eager to start his day and establish a routine like the rest of them.

"Duff, would you care to join us?"

He nodded, taking a step closer, but Miss O'Shea raised a hand. "If you don't mind, Miss Hamilton, there's a matter I'd like to discuss privately with you."

Berrie looked at Duff, whose cheeks turned a pleasant shade of pink, a sharp contrast to his dark hair. Before she could say a word, he bowed to both of them and exited the room.

Berrie poured tea for Miss O'Shea, unable to conquer the trepidation growing in her breast. Did this woman still believe she deserved half of the estate? Berrie had the law on her side, but was it right? Maybe this woman thought the decision unfair.

"I came to apologize, Miss Hamilton."

The words were extraordinary but—far more than that—welcome. "And why is that, Miss O'Shea?"

"Please, call me Finola. The apology is for a recent legal proceeding initiated by one Mr. MacTaggert, a friend of my brother's. My older brother is the one who initiated the attempt to claim an inheritance."

"I wasn't aware you had a brother," Berrie said. Only Finola O'Shea had been listed as the possible recipient of any inheritance to be gained.

"Yes, I do. He did it on my behalf, for my future." She glanced over her shoulder. "I am destitute, you see, with no home and no place to go."

"I suppose that is why your brother named only you as possible beneficiary." Berrie frowned. "Was that the extent of help he could offer? A suit? Why don't you stay with him until you marry and establish a home of your own?"

Finola looked over her shoulder again. "'Tis married I am already—or was—to a man who abandoned me and left me with nothin', not even his name. After the annulment, he made it clear I was no longer entitled to it, legally or otherwise."

A wave of sympathy washed over Berrie. "I'm sorry." Then she frowned anew. "But I still don't understand why your brother isn't of more help than to simply hire a solicitor to try any means to gain funds."

Finola shook her head. "He thought it worth a try. Once I knew what he was about, I begged him to stop, but Mr. MacTaggert had already sent the letter. Not that it did any good, as he received a note stating no funds would be forthcomin'. From no less than an MP! And that's when I discovered the manor was now a school, so I came to see about it for myself."

"That doesn't explain why your brother cannot help you now that you have no other options. Surely he won't bar you from your home, the home you both grew up in?"

Finola smiled, though her eyes looked ready to spill tears. "He already has."

In a single instant Berrie thought of the silly arguments she'd had with both of her brothers over the years, not a single one serious enough to banish anyone. "But why?"

"He fears the curse," she whispered. "I have it, same as me mum. He's afraid I may be . . . like my mother. Alike as to be unsafe. 'Tis why my husband abandoned me—because of Conall, my own sweet son. Me husband paid for an annulment, so he's free to marry someone else." Tears fell freely now. "I don't know what that makes my son. Feebleminded as well as a bastard?"

"Surely not," Berrie said. "Where is your son now?"

"In Dublin, with my friend Nessa O'Donnell. I cannot impose on her for long, or sure and enough her own husband will toss her out along with my son."

"How old is your son?"

"Four years and a bit."

Berrie touched the woman's trembling hand, this woman who was none other than Cosima's cousin. Berrie must do something, and not only for Cosima's sake. Hadn't Christ Himself said when you help the least of My brethren, you help Me?

27

Rebecca watched Quentin lift Padgett onto the horse in front of him. She fit easily on the blanket that extended beyond the smooth English saddle.

The day was fine for riding, a gentle breeze moving air that might otherwise have been too warm for either man or beast. Beneath the cloudless sky the grass was greener, the hedges deeper, the wheat fields golden.

"We'll only trot around a bit where your mum can see, all right?"

Padgett nodded enthusiastically beneath the black, sturdy helmet, squealing with delight when the spirited mare took off. A chestnut Kisber half-bred, the horse was lovely and strong, and Quentin, an assured rider.

"I can see why you care for him," Dana said at Rebecca's side. "He's about as adorable as they come."

Rebecca grinned but could think of nothing to say. Nothing that wouldn't mark her silly and in love.

"How long have you been dating?"

"Not very long. Around the time we first heard from you, as a matter of fact. I actually connect the two, for some reason."

"From the Hall's Web site, I guess you're an expert on planning weddings. Will that be coming in handy any time soon? For you and Quentin?"

Rebecca admired the easy way Dana asked such a question, as if it were an obvious inquiry based on the way Rebecca and Quentin behaved. "You're living up to your country's bold reputation."

Dana's clear blue eyes held nothing but affectionate interest. "My sister calls me nosy. As I always remind her, I learned it from her. And you didn't answer my question."

"Yes, I know." Rebecca grinned, thinking she should leave it at that but for some reason didn't mind talking. Maybe it was the easy friendship that had sprung up between them . . . or maybe there was comfort in confiding in someone whose home was across a big ocean, far away from English society pages. "It's a bit soon to be contemplating marriage. Still, we're not exactly teenagers. We should know by now what we're looking for in a mate."

"You sound like I did before I met Aidan." Dana sighed. "When I was single I just wished I could wake up married without having to go through all of the dating trauma."

"Now there's a lovely dream. I shall start hoping that myself, since it seems to have worked for you."

"But now is the best time, really. All that excitement of getting to know someone you really want to know. You'll have great memories when you're married."

"Yes, if I knew we were headed that way. There are complications, though."

Dana's gaze went to Quentin, who held the powerful horse to a slow walk around the grassy paddock. "We might not have aristocracy in America, but we do have snobs. It seems like the newspaper was trying to paint Quentin as one. I don't see him that way at all, and I doubt you do, either, or you wouldn't be dating him."

"He's anything but."

Dana turned to the direction of the Hall, her gaze lingering there. "Tell me about a wedding here, Rebecca." She grinned.

"Better yet, tell me about how you would plan *your* wedding here."

Rebecca fell into the temptation too easily, sharing plans as detailed as which flower garden she would choose to supply her ceremony and what music would be played. Dana joined in, telling Rebecca she'd been a part of so many American weddings she could certainly think of an addition or two. And she did, suggesting instead of table numbers for a seating arrangement Rebecca might use favorite forebears' names in honor of their memory. Rebecca laughed over which table Dana might sit at—Cosima's or No-Beacon Bill's, who sounded like someone she would have enjoyed knowing.

Their conversation ended with Padgett's call for Dana to watch, and Dana withdrew a camera from her pocket. Padgett's smiles were easy to capture.

Soon they went inside, where Dana led Padgett upstairs for a bath. Rebecca followed Quentin to the library.

"You seem to have struck up quite a close friendship with my cousin and her daughter. All that whispering and laughing."

Rebecca smiled, though she had no intention of admitting the content of their conversation. "Guilty as charged. She's delightful, and so is her daughter."

This being their first moment alone since his return, it wasn't long before Quentin pulled Rebecca into his arms.

"How was your fund-raiser last night?" she asked. "Successful, I hope."

"Fine."

"That's all? Just fine?"

He seemed to stiffen to the tip of his fingers, but she couldn't imagine why. Unless his mother had used his time away to try convincing him to her way of thinking. Rebecca sent up a quick plea for wisdom. *Press and pry, or wait and trust?*

"Did you know Helen and William Risdon will be on holiday

for the next two weeks?" she asked. "Normally it wouldn't be a problem. We have only one function scheduled—a wedding next Saturday morning—and we'll use the same cooks and servers for the banquet after, so they won't be missed for that. They'll be back well before the Featherby judges are scheduled next month. If you don't mind, I'll be using the kitchen so Dana and Padgett don't starve while they're visiting."

He caressed her cheek. "I can bring someone in if you like."

She shook her head. "No, I don't mind. Dana isn't very hard to please, and she tells me Padgett has lived on peanut butter and jelly for nearly a year. If she can survive on that, I think I can manage."

"I can help," he said. "With the peanut butter and jelly at any rate."

Rebecca laughed. "Perhaps we might add that to the tour. Watch the nephew of the Earl of Eastwater prepare his world-renowned peanut butter and jelly sandwich."

She would have left the circle of his arms to take a seat on the nearby sofa, but he held her firm. "Do you know, Rebecca, I missed you yesterday. Would you have come if I'd asked?"

She eyed him curiously. He seemed so serious. "I needed to be here for Dana and Padgett."

He shook his head. "No, if there were nothing in the way, would you have left this safe little world of yours and come to the city, fed the media sharks, played my partner at a high society function?"

"That depends," she said with a grin. "Who was the beneficiary of this charity event?"

He gave her a slow smile. "Barnardo's."

"Then by all means, yes."

She enjoyed his embrace, glad he was reluctant to let her go. "Quentin, it's still true I don't like the idea of living under the shutter of a reporter's camera. But I must tell you, if it's the price to be paid for being with you, I'm willing to pay it."

His smile widened, only to be lost in a kiss.

28

My dearest Cosima,

It pains me to see how your cousin Finola has been mistreated. She still mourns the life that is lost to her with a husband and home. And her son is delightful. He must be very much like Royboy was at his age. He cannot talk but will sit still far longer than most of our other students. We read to him and show him pictures and sing to him, and he is generally very happy.

Finola, I fear, has some adjusting to do. She was so grateful when we opened our doors to her son. We expected she might want to start anew somewhere, perhaps in Dublin, where she might find a job. But she would not leave her son and unfortunately quickly proved she is unfit for most positions (not unlike myself, I admit, before I was called to the vision of this school). She does, however, possess a fine skill for needlework and could likely find a position in such a field if she put her mind

*to it. For now, she is doing our mending, and we hope to
have her help in other areas as time goes on.*

*Simon MacFarland, our unexpected legal champion,
returned for his first unscheduled visit. It was blatantly
clear that he had forgotten how important keeping to a
routine is for everyone, including Katie. He wanted to
take her into the village, but she refused to leave.*

*I feel quite cheated that he has left twice now without
giving me the opportunity to prove him wrong about this
school—and me. Last night on my walk around the
manor, I thought of all sorts of things I might say
to convince him, but without him here it was all for
naught.*

Berrie clapped her hands with the music, along with many of the
students. In the week since Duff had returned, he'd become a
favorite among most of the children, and not only for his music.
He found the humor in each student and elicited a laugh more
often than anyone else on staff. A word, a tickle, a tousled hairline, a funny grimace for those who didn't understand many
things but somehow possessed the ability to decipher a jest. Duff
was the one who made sure laughter became part of the daily
routine.

He seemed to have taken to Finola's Conall most of all. When
he walked with the four-year-old on his shoulders, the two of
them cast a long shadow, one that was becoming familiar when
Duff wasn't teaching in the workroom.

It was late in the evening, and Duff played the tune he always
closed with, a favorite lullaby. Berrie's gaze roamed the room as

she sang along, unable to miss where Duff's own gaze fell most often. Upon Finola O'Shea.

So far, Finola didn't seem interested, perhaps thinking another marriage out of the question. If she had more children, they would likely be similar to Conall. Berrie knew well enough the fears Cosima had of marriage and children and assumed Finola felt the same way, and with far more cause.

Berrie couldn't ignore mixed feelings regarding Duff's obvious interest in Finola. Envy had no part in it, though she couldn't deny it would be nice to have a man look at her in such a way. Not since Lord Welby had expressed an interest in Berrie had she been the object of anyone's interest, and his interest had too quickly waned when she'd begun talking about having a purpose in life that might not be satisfied by marriage, children, and an endless social circle.

Rather, Berrie wondered how it would affect the school if a match were made between two members of the staff. She'd been warned any impropriety among the staff would be more than frowned upon by the Lunacy Commission. She understood that; the trust of the parents was not something they could afford to lose.

And so she wondered if she should worry when Duff carried Conall to his bed, the one he shared with his mother in the shrouded corner of the girls' dormitory upstairs. Surely there was no privacy to be found in this place, but even so innocent a favor might be viewed improper if anyone noticed the way Duff looked at Finola.

Berrie sighed, trying to let go of her concerns. Here she was again, imagining every troubling possibility, even ones that didn't exist.

29

Rebecca removed the fried sausages from the pan. She'd mastered cooking by the age of twelve, after taking on kitchen duties when her mother's lingering illness deprived her of the energy to do household duties. Rebecca's father made the task lighter with his open praise of her accomplishments. Following the example he set, they'd both kept busy through their worries, letting the illness dictate their day: treatments and homecare, plus fulfilling the responsibilities Rebecca's mother left behind. It was less painful to be distracted by work than to watch her grow weaker, and keeping busy helped ease the grief of losing her when she died a year later. Rebecca was the avid student and housekeeper while her father was the breadwinner and single parent. Busyness hadn't taken the place of her mother, but it had dulled the pain.

No doubt Quentin was setting out dishes and cutlery in the garden room with Padgett's assistance. Dana had offered to help with the finishing touches on the meal but had unexpectedly disappeared into the lavatory the moment they returned from church.

When Dana entered the kitchen moments later, she had a pale tint and didn't seem to welcome the scent of Rebecca's cooking.

"Everything all right?" Rebecca asked, taking the last sausage from the pan. She knew her skills wouldn't match Helen's or any

chef's of Lady Elise's, but she hadn't burned anything and the
sausage was fresh.

Dana nodded. "Better than a few minutes ago. I'm sorry I wasn't
any help."

"Not to worry. The fruit was ready, Quentin took in the juice,
and here are the roly-polies now."

"Roly-polies?"

"Padgett's idea." Rebecca handed the plate of melon to
Dana. It was less fragrant than the sausage and pancakes, and
she thought it better to take those in herself. "We're ready."

They found the others in the bright garden room, the table
prepared, but Quentin and Padgett near the bird rather than
waiting at their places.

"Mommy!" Padgett called as they entered. "This is Winston.
Did you know he's even older than you are? Quentin says Winston is old enough to be my grandfather."

"You can help me feed him after we eat," Quentin invited.

"What does he eat?"

"Nuts, right out of your hand."

Quentin led her to the table, where they all took seats except
Quentin, who went to the tea trolley to retrieve the pitcher of
chilled orange juice. Then, once seated, he bowed his head.

Rebecca loved hearing him pray. If she'd ever doubted his
faith, she abandoned such notions the moment she first heard
him pray. She'd asked him why he hadn't prayed that night when
his mother came to dinner, and he'd apologized for that, admitting some habits were only now beginning to form.

"There is a fair in the village this afternoon," Quentin said.
"I thought we'd visit there, if you'd like."

"Sounds like fun," Dana said.

"It will be," Rebecca confirmed, looking Padgett's way.
"You'll get to taste apple snow and fairy cakes."

"What's that?"

"To put it less charmingly," Quentin said, "apples with custard and cupcakes. Not on the same plate, of course. You'll like it better than bubble and squeak, is my guess."

"And what's *that*?" This time it was Dana asking.

"Beef and mash—that's mashed potatoes—with cabbage and onion."

"Hmm . . . I may have to pass along with Padgett on that one."

They chatted about which other sights Dana and Padgett should see, and Rebecca was glad to note Dana's coloring improve as she ate. Whatever had ailed her this morning after church was obviously gone. Still, as excited as Dana was to see more of England, she wasn't willing to abandon the purpose for which she'd come. She insisted they plan their mornings to continue the transcription of Berrie's letters and see where the school records might fit.

Barely finished with her meal, Rebecca heard the echo of clipped footsteps, followed a moment later by a familiar voice calling Quentin's name.

He took up his napkin, wiped unnecessarily at his mouth, then excused himself. Rebecca aimed a carefully manufactured smile Dana's way.

"Quentin's mother has arrived for a visit."

"Oh, good!" Dana said. "I get to meet her at last."

Rebecca nodded, wondering how long it would take to see Dana's eagerness turn sour. *Lord, help me bite not only my tongue but my thoughts, too.*

Elise's voice reached them before she and Quentin did. "You really ought to hire someone to watch over this place, Quentin. No one answered the door, and I walked right in. Didn't you hear me knock?"

"No, Mum. Come in; have some lunch with us."

"It's a bit early for that. I have lunch waiting for me at home. And if by 'us' you mean that commercial manager again, I'll not be sharing another meal with the staff. And in that same room with that awful bird."

Rebecca felt rather than saw Dana's gaze shoot to her, but she didn't look up.

"You know, Mum, that was incredibly rude." Quentin's voice was friendly, as if he'd complimented rather than chastised her.

They arrived in the garden room then, and as Elise stopped across the threshold, the bird squawked the only greeting—and a grating one at that. Rebecca knew there was no etiquette requiring her to stand. She did so anyway, anticipating the need for another chair if Elise decided to stay. Without Helen or William there, Rebecca was prepared to fill the role of servant.

"What's this?"

"You already know Rebecca, Mum. These other two lovely ladies are my American cousins Dana Walker and her daughter, Padgett."

Elise was stunning as ever, dressed in a white linen suit and a feathered hat, with shoes and matching handbag undoubtedly of expensive design. Just now she looked down at Dana with anything but a warm English welcome.

"An American cousin, Quentin? I don't think that's possible, considering neither your father nor I have any American siblings."

He laughed. "Yes, well, I'm not sure how many times removed we might be, but we share the same great-great-great-grandparents, Cosima and Peter Hamilton. That makes us cousins of a sort, don't you think?"

"And you came all the way from America to meet my son?" Elise's gaze grazed Padgett. "With a child, no less?"

Dana stood too, perhaps because Rebecca had. Only Padgett remained seated, though rather than eating, she stacked the roly-poly slices in the middle of her plate.

Dana held out a hand. "With my husband, who's in Ireland at the moment. He's been hired as consultant to a project in County

Kilkenny. Padgett and I are visiting Quentin and Rebecca for a week or so."

"How nice." Lady Elise eyed Padgett. "Just make sure your little one doesn't break anything."

"Of course."

"Padgett has been an angel since she's been here," Quentin said, returning to his place at the table. "Now, please, everyone sit, and Mum, take my chair for the moment while I fetch another."

"I won't be staying. Where is Helen or William? No one answered the door, and there's no one here to bring another setting if I did decide to stay."

"Helen and William are on holiday, Lady Elise," Rebecca offered. "But there is plenty if you'd like to take a seat."

"Why in heaven's name are you eating before noon?"

"We've just come from church, where all our stomachs took turns growling. Rebecca put something together right away."

"So now you have her cooking, Quentin? I thought managing the Hall was her full-time job?"

"Actually we're sharing the cooking while Helen is gone. My turn will be dinner. You're welcome to come if you don't mind being a guinea pig. Though I have my doubts about anyone wanting to be a pig of any sort until my cooking skill can be proven. What do you think, Padgett? Will you be eating more of my cooking than you have of Rebecca's?"

"Will you make peanut butter and jelly sandwiches?"

"How about that as our fallback? I was thinking of roasting something. I'm partial to tenderloin with a lemon pepper seasoning."

"Sounds wonderful," Dana said.

Padgett's edible tower fell, and she looked up at Elise. Rebecca saw her tilt her head. The child looked fascinated.

"Can I pet your hat?"

Elise stared at the child as though she'd spoken an undecipherable language.

In the awkward absence of a reply, Dana reached across the table for her daughter's hand. "I don't think anyone wants someone touching their clothing, hats or otherwise. Are you finished with your brunch?"

Padgett nodded a hopeful nod and seemed to be surprised by the question with so much left on her plate.

"Then let's go outside for a walk, okay?"

Padgett eagerly abandoned her seat, going only as far as Quentin's side. "Quentin said he'd help me feed Winston when we finished eating."

"I did indeed," he replied, and as if the bird recognized his name, he screeched again.

They went to the cage, where Winston fluttered his wings as Quentin opened the door.

"Can I get you some tea, at least, Lady Elise?" asked Rebecca.

"No, I came to fetch Quentin. He was gone before I had a chance to let him know guests are arriving this afternoon and I'd like him to be there."

"Sorry, Mum, but I have plans already." He held his hand over Padgett's small one as she offered a nut to the bird. "That's right. He'll take it now."

And so the bird did, as gently as if he recognized a child when he saw one. Padgett ran to her mother's side. "Oh! Mommy, did you see? He took it right from my hand."

"Yes, I did. Was it fun?"

Padgett nodded, then looked at Elise again. "Why weren't you at church with Quentin and Rebecca?"

Perhaps Elise had a sort of selective hearing, because she appeared not to have registered Padgett's inquiry.

"Mum, Padgett asked you a question," Quentin said, closing the cage door.

She looked at Padgett with surprise. "Yes? What is it?"

"Why didn't we sit with you when we were at church? We always sit with my grandma."

"I wasn't there," Elise answered.

"Don't you go to church?"

Dana hugged her daughter close. "We don't really need to ask something like that, honey. Not everyone goes; we talked about that before."

But Padgett still eyed Lady Elise. "Can I ask you a different question, then?"

Elise looked down at her again. "What is it?"

"What does God look like?"

She raised one sculpted eyebrow. "And why is it you think I would know such a thing? Do you suppose I'm so old that I was there when He created everything?"

Padgett shook her head. "No, Mommy said that happened such a long time ago nobody's alive from then. Mommy also says we go to church to learn more about God. Since you don't have to go anymore, that must mean you know all about Him. So I wonder, what does He look like?"

Quentin burst into laughter, but he was the only one to do so despite Rebecca's temptation.

"I haven't the faintest idea, little girl. And you're a bit outspoken for one so young."

"Yes, you're right," Dana said. "I think we'll take our walk now."

"Perhaps I'll join you." Rebecca followed Dana toward the door.

"See there, Mum, you've successfully cleared the room. Don't you think you could learn to be more cordial so people don't flee the moment you speak?"

He was still cajoling, in the next moment inviting her to feed the bird as Rebecca followed Dana out of earshot.

Outside, Rebecca walked alongside Dana as Padgett ran ahead toward the cuddle farm.

"Wow," whispered Dana, "you do have some obstacles ahead, don't you? With her as a prospective mother-in-law?"

Rebecca grimaced. "Quentin is trying to help me look on the bright side." She sighed. "At least I won't have to wonder what she's thinking."

She glanced back at the windows facing them, wishing she shared Quentin's positive attitude. She might one day be tolerated by Lady Elise, but Rebecca wasn't at all sure that was enough.

30

Did I once say, Cosima, that I never shied from a fight? How godly is that, I wonder? I am the worst kind of sinner, one who not only does the deed but revels in it afterward.

God forgive me, but that man brings out the worst in me. . . .

Berrie finished morning exercises with the students and let Mrs. Cotgrave lead the way back inside. Someone had dropped a scarf during the march, and Berrie went to retrieve it. She was in no hurry today. Simon had arrived during morning drills, and Berrie decided to let Katie, and perhaps Mrs. Cotgrave, offer greetings. Even as she realized her first thought was to keep her distance from him, she wondered at the ease with which she silently called him Simon. With Katie so often referring to her brother by his given name, it was difficult for Berrie not to think of him that way.

Since those first two brief visits, he'd returned a couple times more, never speaking to Berrie, keeping to Katie's routine. Berrie had voiced surprise at his last early morning arrival, and that was the only time he'd spoken to her, letting her know he was staying at the Quail's Stop Inn. No doubt being awakened by Eóin those weeks ago made the inn more appealing.

Simon had probably noticed their new students, all boys. Maybe once he realized more and more parents were trusting her and her staff with their children, he would finally trust them enough to leave Katie for more than a week at a time.

Berrie found her way inside, where she would conduct her first class of the day. Royboy and a new student by the name of Grady sat on one end of a table in what had become the third classroom. Katie, with Tessie and Annabel, sat on the other. Simon was there too, though he didn't take a seat. He lurked in the corner, one shoulder to the wall.

Berrie took up a stack of pictures she'd drawn. The children knew the routine. She handed the collection to Katie for her to lead the process of language through identification. All complied except Royboy, who watched the others and occasionally blew air through tight lips to make a noise somewhat between a whistle and a sputter. They went through the calendar, the weather, the names of familiar items she'd drawn.

Soon Katie had gone through all of the papers, and Berrie had the students stand. The slightest change, even an expected one, brought with it noises from every corner, and it took a moment for her to reclaim their attention. At last she had two students walk toward one another as if passing on the street in order to properly address each other. Even Royboy's "How do you do" was clear and well-timed today. Berrie glanced at Simon, who watched in silence, wondering if he still thought the school a failure.

The task near completion, she approached the front of the classroom, where only Katie and Grady were yet to greet one another. Grady was a large boy for being only fourteen, the tallest of their students. They walked toward each other, but no sooner had Katie issued her friendly greeting than Grady shoved her to the floor.

Berrie stepped forward. "No, Grady!" she said firmly, passing him to assist Katie to her feet. She barely saw two shadows approach, one from each margin of her vision, before Grady rammed her. Gasping for breath, she scrambled to regain her feet, seeing Simon already headed for Grady. He wrapped two strong arms around the boy from behind, rendering him immobile.

"Let go of him!" Berrie demanded, seeing Grady's eyes fill with panic at the strong hold from someone he didn't know and couldn't see.

"I will not. This boy should be in shackles."

Cries soon erupted from Annabel at the table, followed quickly by a howl from Royboy. Katie, now on her feet, babbled to her brother about Grady being naughty and how he ought not to have any dessert tonight.

Berrie stood directly in front of Grady, who looked as frightened as a two-year-old, the approximate age at which he functioned. Though she looked at him, she didn't put her face in his line of vision. Instead she spoke from the periphery of his vision. "It's all right, Grady. You're fine now; he's only making you steady. Listen to me. Stop struggling, and you can take a seat. All right? We'll sit down now."

His struggle only increased and Berrie could see Simon wasn't about to let him go. "Katie," Berrie said gently, "will you go and get Mr. Duff, please? You'll find him in the workroom, where the boys make shoes. Get him now, Katie."

"Mr. MacFarland," Berrie continued after Katie left, not surprised that her own voice sounded placating, "please bring Grady back to his seat and help him to sit down."

"You needn't speak to me like I'm one of them," Simon said, dragging Grady back to his chair. He let the boy sit, keeping both hands on him, one on each of Grady's shoulders. "He's a danger to you and the others and shouldn't be here."

Berrie stiffened. "If you don't mind, we won't discuss this here." She looked at Grady, who tried unsuccessfully to shrug off Simon's hands. "Grady, you must stay in your seat until Mr. Duff arrives. Do you understand?"

The boy only shook his shoulders again, another attempt to be free of Simon's touch. He tried to stand, but Simon held him down.

The others in the class still made their various noises, Tessie, the only one among them who was relatively quiet, humming as usual. If Berrie knew Grady better, she would know how to calm him, but he'd only arrived a few days ago. Duff would know what to do with him since he spent more time with him, and then she could take Royboy out to the hall, where he could better regain his calm. The others would find peace in their seats once the quiet around them was reestablished.

If only Simon MacFarland wouldn't get in the way.

A moment later, Duff arrived with Katie lagging behind. Berrie had no idea what Katie had said to Duff to bring him so quickly, but it must have caused some concern. "Are you all right?" he said quietly.

Berrie nodded. Never in this life would she admit anything was wrong while Katie's brother was in the room. "Can you take Grady for a walk?" Glancing outside and seeing the rain, Berrie added, "Downstairs to the parlor and back might help, maybe a turn around the foyer."

Once Grady was gone, Berrie found a stack of blank papers. Already Royboy was quieter, and she determined he didn't need the customary walk in the hall to regain his calm. She asked Katie to help the others practice their penmanship, a task that for someone like Royboy was little more than scribbling. But the girls were more accomplished and it was something they all enjoyed. Soon the room was right again, and Berrie went to the door. She knew Simon watched her every move. She didn't have to look his way to invite him to follow her outside the room.

She left the door ajar so that she could hear the students and faced Simon. "I'll thank you not to interfere again, Mr. MacFarland."

"Interfere? I put a stop to him and you call it interference?"

"I was quite fine and so was Katie. We were merely taken by surprise."

"Surprise, is it, when you sailed through the air? You or Katie might have hit your head on the table or landed hard enough to break a bone. When I decided to leave Katie here, it was with the understanding you interviewed prospective students and no one dangerous would be allowed under this roof."

"And so we do. Grady is larger than some and perhaps a bit more rambunctious, but he's not malicious. He's new here and will learn—"

"Spare me your attempts to dismiss what just happened. You don't know the boy any better than I do, and I say he's a danger to anyone around him. It was foolish of you to have him in a classroom without a male attendant nearby."

Berrie's lips tightened. She met his irate stare with one of her own. It hardly mattered that his suggestion might make sense; she wanted no part of him. "I'll thank you not to run my school. And don't ever touch one of my students again."

His brows lifted. "What would you have had me do, stand by so he could toss you out the window?"

"He didn't and wouldn't have."

Simon shook his head. "No use to argue that point since neither one of us really knows what he might have done had I not restrained him." If he was daunted in the least by her outrage, he didn't show it. He took a step closer so that he loomed taller than ever. "You'll not let him attend a class without a male

197

attendant nearby if you want to keep this precious school of yours open."

Late that night, Berrie rubbed her eyes and glanced at the clock she kept on the corner of her desk. Past eleven. She really must go to bed; morning came quickly in this school. She prayed tomorrow would not see another dispute with Simon. After their morning argument she'd avoided him the rest of the day.

She stood with a last glance at the papers before extinguishing the lamp. She'd vowed to be involved at every level of this school, from admissions and teaching to the feeding and personal care of every student. No one had been more amazed than herself upon her pronouncement, realizing from her research that the work would entail cleaning up after other human beings in the most personal manner. Even her mother had been surprised, who must have thought what Berrie once believed of herself: she had too weak a stomach for real work.

But she'd proven everyone wrong, including herself. Her only worry now was that she couldn't be as involved as she wanted to be. There was simply too much work at each level to dabble in all of them. Even now she was teaching only one class instead of the three she had started out with. Paperwork could consume a day all by itself, even with the help of a clerk twice a week.

Closing the door, she took the key from her pocket and locked the office. She walked to the foyer, where she intended to end her day in the usual way with a walk around the grounds. It was exactly what she needed tonight—fresh air and then to bed.

A light from the family parlor caught her eye. Surely no one had left a lamp lit? With their wanderers, such a thing could be dangerous. Only the high sconces on the walls, where most children could not reach, were left alight after everyone was in bed.

But as she approached the parlor's open door, she heard Finola's voice.

" . . . 'Twas my own father who determined my weddin' day. He wanted to see it done before he died, and sure and enough, two days after the ceremony my da' was gone. Yes, the whole village downed a pint that day—in his honor." She must have seen Berrie's shadow, for she turned that way. "Oh! I didn't see you there, Berrie. Have a seat."

Berrie looked with some surprise, having half expected to find her talking to Duff, who sometimes followed Finola like a dog after its master. But he rarely made it past ten o'clock, as his days were full enough to demand rest.

Instead, looking stiff and uncomfortable, sat Simon. He had a book in his hand and sat near one of the two lighted lamps. Quite the homey scene, if only he didn't have that pained look on his face. She wondered if he'd had it before she walked into the room.

She shook her head. "No, I was only curious about the light. I'll be retiring for the night shortly."

Simon set the book aside and stood. He bowed briefly Finola's way. "Yes, I agree the hour is late, and so I shall be off as well. Good evening to you, Miss O'Shea." Then he turned to Berrie. "I wonder if you might see me to the door, Miss Hamilton?"

Dread crept up her spine. She didn't want to hear whatever he had to say. Had he used the day to figure out how he would see the school closed?

Without a word, she turned and led the way to the door. She braced herself for another argument, wishing for only one thing: the energy to sustain her side.

"I stayed in order to apologize, Miss Hamilton."

Berrie raised a widened gaze his way. "I beg your pardon?"

He rubbed his palms together once, a frown saying he didn't wish to repeat himself. "I want to apologize for my words this morning . . . about closing this school. I should never have said such a thing, and I assure you it's not my intention."

Too amazed to speak, Berrie stared.

Simon looked at her solemnly. "I was concerned about that student—Grady, I believe is his name—and still am. However, you've taken sufficient safety measures in other matters up to this point, and if you'll agree he needs closer attention than other students, I'm sure any future problems will be avoided."

She folded her arms. Had he really sought her out to apologize? She might be too eager to jump to the worst conclusion when it came to Simon MacFarland. She really ought to learn to control her tongue around this man. "Thank you." She didn't trust herself with more than that.

He put a hand on the door, pulling it open. "I'll be leaving now and probably won't return for a fortnight or so. I've said my good-byes to Katie, so she won't expect me in the morning." He moved to leave, stopping halfway through the doorway. "You really ought to do something about the length of your day, Miss Hamilton."

Then he left, pulling the door closed behind him before she had a chance to speak. Not that she had a word to say. If the admonition had been spoken in reproach for keeping him waiting so long, she might have bitten out a suitable retaliation. The odd part of it was that his tone had been surprisingly gentle, similar to the one he usually reserved for Katie.

Such an observation was enough to leave her speechless.

31

Rebecca clicked on the light and sat behind her desk, glancing
at the clock. It was ridiculously late to start working; the sun
had set hours ago. She'd been delinquent this summer. She was
behind in her e-mail correspondence, hadn't opened her mail
since yesterday, and had yet to meet with the marketing firm
about new brochures. That, thankfully, had been put on hold
until they knew the outcome of the Featherby decision.

But she'd enjoyed being the tour guide for Dana and Padgett
and couldn't think of putting off transcribing old letters or reading hospital records. More than a week had flown by. She'd spent
today in Cambridge with Quentin, Dana, and Padgett. The four
of them had become a quasi family, missing only Aidan, who
seemed to be there in spirit considering how often Dana spoke
of him.

A long white envelope caught her eye, and she wondered
whether her father had sent yet another offer from the National
Trust. However there was no return address, though she noted
from the cancelled stamp that it had been among the mail she'd
picked up today. She slit open the envelope but instead of a letter
pulled out a newspaper article, dated just yesterday. The picture
wasn't very clear—a couple sitting at a small, white table on a
veranda. The man wore a white shirt and dark slacks—Quentin,
she saw with a longer look. And he wasn't alone.

Quentin and Lady Caroline Norleigh seemed comfortably ensconced over an outdoor meal, so comfortably that Lady Caroline was wearing a peignoir of some kind rather than the designer clothing she normally sported in so many photographs of her.

Another Adieu? Or has this bachelor already quit his brief affair with commercial manager Rebecca Seabrooke and returned to his own kind, Lady Caroline Norleigh? The couple appeared together briefly at a fund-raiser for Barnardo's recently. It appears Lady Caroline is once again houseguest at Endicott Cottage, home not only to Lady Elise Hollinworth but as of this summer to her son, Quentin Hollinworth, as well. Is he there to strike up an old flame whilst his new love interest waits just a stone's throw away at Hollinworth Hall? Impossible to guess why he abandoned the Hall to her, unless of course he knew Lady Caroline would soon be waiting for him at the cottage. Ah, the aristocracy! They never stop supplying us with entertainment.

Rebecca forced herself to read the short article again, to look at the photograph. Numbness covered her as she studied the picture, a ready defense against the pain that was there, waiting to take hold if she let it. It wasn't a good shot by any means, rather grainy. It had obviously been taken from some distance and had lost its quality when blown up to identify the subjects. But as much as Rebecca wished otherwise, there was no doubt who they were.

With a wince she swallowed an unsuspected lump in her throat. Was this how it would be—having to learn the status of her relationship with Quentin from the newspaper instead of from Quentin himself? She'd spent the bulk of every day with him for the past week and a half. He'd left just a little while ago. All these days without a word of being in touch with Lady Caroline again.

Was she at the cottage now, greeting him after his day away? Rebecca dropped the article as if burned.

The door of her office opened, and for one disoriented moment she thought it might be him, there to tell her everything. But of course it was Dana, having put Padgett to bed.

"What's the matter?" Dana asked as she took her seat on the opposite side of the desk.

Rebecca regretted the company just then, wishing she were alone to more easily hide her pain, hide the embarrassment of a public rejection. She'd been comfortable by herself these past three years; she was used to that. Refusing to cave in to the tears that seemed ready to gather, she issued a half smile that was anything but happy. Then, realizing she could share what she felt without falling apart, Rebecca handed Dana the article.

"Oh," Dana whispered after reading the page.

Rebecca felt her lower lip tremble and clamped it down. "And I thought all I should worry about was a rather grumpy Lady Elise."

"This doesn't mean anything," Dana said. "What kind of picture is this, anyway? It looks like it was tampered with somehow."

"Probably taken from a helicopter," Rebecca said. "They fly over the property every once in a while, looking for stories."

"So there. It's a made-up story. They're on the same veranda. His mother is probably there, too, only they blotted her out."

"It doesn't matter."

"What do you mean?"

"He didn't tell me." Amazingly, her voice didn't sound nearly as frantic as she felt. She couldn't meet Dana's eye. Sympathy would make Rebecca crack. "She's there, staying with them. He should have told me."

Dana set aside the newspaper. "Yes, he should have. But maybe he didn't want you jumping to the conclusion you're jumping to right now."

"I'm sure he didn't," Rebecca said. "Not until the right time, after he's chosen between the two of us."

"That's jumping to conclusions, Rebecca. Maybe her being there is no big deal and he didn't think it was important enough to mention."

Rebecca found a laugh, albeit a desperately uneven one. "Perhaps you can't tell how lovely she is from that photo. Here." She yanked open the drawer on the bottom right, the one she never opened except when she knew she was alone, under what suddenly seemed a guise of her role as Hollinworth family recorder. Her job description had never included keeping a scrapbook of family doings; that had been her idea. Now it seemed clear why. And all those years she thought she'd been over her crush on Quentin.

"You'll get a better idea of her from these," Rebecca said bitterly. "Here they are at Leo Endicott's wedding—the future Earl of Eastwater, Quentin's cousin. See how striking she is? I think she fits right in, don't you?" She rifled through more pages. "And here, at Ascot. And another—a garden party his mother held, where the photographer risked all but his life just to get that shot of them kissing."

Tears were hot in her eyes, but Rebecca ignored them. Dana wasn't looking at any of the photographs; rather, she was looking at Rebecca.

Rebecca leaned back in her chair, exhausted from her brief but quietly intense upheaval. "It's pathetic, isn't it? That I've kept these?"

Dana shook her head. "I'd probably have done the same if Aidan was ever in the news. Thank goodness he's not."

Rebecca let her gaze fall on the pages in front of her. "I'll take them to the bin. It's what I should have done long ago."

She gathered them up, a modest but embarrassing handful.

"You've missed one," Dana said, taking up the newest addition.

"No, I didn't."

"You're keeping this one?"

Rebecca nodded. "These clippings reminded me Quentin was beyond my reach. I might not need these old ones anymore, but I think I'll have to keep that one for the time being . . . to remind me he's still out of my reach."

The phone rang just then. Rebecca made no effort to set aside the papers and answer it.

"Do you want me to get it?" Dana asked, reaching for it.

"No." Rebecca's firm voice stalled Dana, for which Rebecca was grateful. The phone rang on. "It's Quentin. He's the only one who calls this number so late."

"I think you should talk to him, Rebecca. You should tell him about the newspaper. Tell him how it made you feel. Ask him what's up."

Instead of acknowledging, Rebecca gripped the newspapers and made her way to the outside trash—far from her office, where she wouldn't be able to retrieve them.

32

Did I mention, Cosima, how we gather in the evenings, all of us in our temporary little family, to bring what calm we can to the end of the day? We did so as usual tonight, only a fog had gathered outside so thick we knew it would be dangerous to take anyone out of doors. And so we went to the blue parlor for our family time, where we sing songs or tell tales or share something we are proud of. Katie did not expect it, but I brought one of her pictures to show everyone. It is an extraordinary example of her skill, and I am enclosing it with this letter so you may see it as well.

As you can see it is a lovely bird resting on a nest. Do you not find the strokes of the penciled wing make you believe, if you only tried to touch the little fellow, he might take flight?

Katie's brother, Simon, was with us tonight. I tell you, Cosima, the man is an enigma. I never know if he is pleased his sister is here or ready to take her away. Even

*after this evening, the first time we have been in one
another's company and managed to tolerate each other
for more than a few moments without resorting to an
argument.*

"Tell Miss Berrie about your travels, Simon. Please? About your travels?"

He didn't want to, Berrie could tell instantly by the shrouding of his eyes, the slight droop to the side of his mouth. In that same instant she resisted her own disappointment. It was silly to want to hear about *his* travels, this man she couldn't help but detest. Still, the innocently cast question reminded Berrie of the times she'd asked her own brothers the same thing. Of Peter, who went to places like Gibraltar and Egypt, even as far away as China. And Nathan, who went to America and India and Africa, who was in Africa still, writing home from time to time of all his adventures. How many hours could she have listened to them, living such explorations? She'd had a mere taste of it on the sole voyage she'd taken, her trip across the Irish Sea—a heady taste, one that led her here to her life's work. A taste she thought had satisfied her because it led her to the work she loved—work that was far more important than dreams of sea voyages afar.

Still, it might have been nice to hear another tale.

"Please, Simon? What did you see?"

Berrie looked up, afraid for one awful moment she'd uttered those words herself. Thankfully she saw him looking at his sister instead, a reluctant grin on his sculpted face.

"I saw the sun set with nothing but water between our ship and the sky, as far as I could see."

"And what did you taste?"

"Coconuts in Africa, olives in Spain, grapes in Italy."

"And what did you smell?"

Berrie watched the two of them, seeing it was some sort of game they were both familiar with. But to Berrie it was a hint of transport, the only glimpse she was bound to have of the rest of the world she'd only read about.

"My ship took me to Corsica, where the shores smelled like evergreens. I hiked in the hills, fell asleep on the bracken growing under the trees, ate roasted wild pigs that had fed on island chestnuts. Then we sailed to other islands, to Minorca and Sicily and Crete and others—too many to recall. I saw castles where they locked important people away and dogs that could take care of little children, the sun setting and making the sky and the water and everything around me look purple. And do you know what I learned?"

Katie shook her head, still smiling.

"That families everywhere are very much like ours. Sisters and brothers who take care of each other, even though they live so far away. Do you know what they thought when I told them I was from Ireland?"

"What?"

"That we live in a very strange and wonderful place, just the way we think of them living in a strange and wonderful place."

She giggled, repeating the phrase that she lived in a strange and wonderful place. Berrie let her gaze linger on Simon, unaware they'd exchanged smiles until it was done. The British Empire—a strange and wonderful place.

Maybe it was.

33

Rebecca stirred her tea at the kitchen table. It was impossible to be in this room, with its tall shelves and efficient appliances ready for nearly any size crowd, without thinking of the first time Quentin had kissed her.

She barely consumed half of her tea, but it was the only thing her stomach could tolerate. It was early; she'd awakened hours ago after very little sleep. She knew Padgett was awake; she'd heard her playing with her doll in what had become a favorite spot—at the top of the stairs on the oval Persian rug. From there she could see anyone coming from bedroom or office and at the same time listen to anything that happened below as far away as the kitchen. Dana was likely awake as well, though she hadn't come down for breakfast yet.

Rebecca left her tea at the kitchen table. Even if she couldn't eat, Dana and Padgett must. Whatever malady Dana suffered these days, eating seemed to help.

Taking a pan from the cupboard and ingredients from the tall refrigerator, Rebecca planned to scramble some eggs and serve them over toast, a simple yet filling meal. If she could tolerate the smell with her own knotted stomach, the meal would pass in peace. They made fine friends, she and Dana, both of them suffering nausea from one source or another. Only Rebecca knew the source of hers.

Quentin would come. He did every day, had done so ever since he'd moved out the day after he'd kissed her at this very kitchen table. She stared at the spot, reliving that moment yet again. What had it meant to him?

Dana didn't look any better than Rebecca felt when she came into the kitchen. Her obvious discomfort drove Rebecca's self-pity away. "Sit," she commanded. "I have tea, eggs, and toast ready."

"Just the tea and toast, I think," Dana said.

Rebecca set out the food, taking a seat opposite. "Have you ever been bothered by this kind of nausea before, Dana?"

Dana shook her head, sipping her tea, taking a bit of the toast.

"Dana," Rebecca said gently, "do you know why you've been so sick lately?"

A sigh escaped, almost a cry. Dana nodded. "I've been trying not to think about it, but it can only be one thing. I remember these symptoms; my sister had them twice. And nine months later, a baby each time."

Rebecca knew the normal congratulations weren't what Dana wanted. "You should see a doctor, or at least take a pregnancy test. I can run to the chemist for you."

Confusion emerged through the concern on Dana's face. "The chemist?"

Rebecca nodded. "You know, for the test. To see if you're pregnant."

Dana nodded. "You mean the drugstore."

Rebecca grinned. "Same thing. I'll go right away."

Dana grabbed her hand. "But Quentin is bound to be here any minute. You should be here, talk to him about that picture."

Rebecca shook her head. "I'm brilliant when it comes to delay tactics."

"It won't do any good; you'll have to talk to him."

"I will."

"Do you want me to say anything if he gets here before you get back?"

Rebecca shook her head. "I don't want you worrying about anything for my sake, Dana. You've got enough to keep your mind occupied."

Dana's eyes welled with tears. "I want to think about you and Quentin instead. I want to help. It's better than worrying about having a baby—one who'd belong in Berrie's school if it hadn't closed all those years ago."

Rebecca hugged her. "Don't think it, Dana. It could be wonderful, you know. Giving Padgett a little brother or sister. Having a baby with a man you love so much."

Dana clung to her. "Months of worry, waiting to see if everything's all right. I did that with Talie; I don't want to do it myself."

Rebecca pulled away to look steadily into Dana's eyes. "We all manage to get through what God allows, right? He equips us for it."

Dana nodded but didn't look convinced.

"I'll be back in a few minutes. In the meantime, eat. You'll feel better."

Rebecca hurried out the door.

At the nearest Boots the Chemist shop, Rebecca hadn't the faintest idea which brand was most reliable for the price. She studied a few packages, finally deciding to ask the dispensing chemist which test would prove most reliable. Twenty minutes and six pounds, fifty pence later, she had the clerk putting the test in a bag, and she made her way out the door.

Where she promptly bumped into a camera-toting young man, who stepped out of her way just long enough to snap her photograph.

34

I must tell you a secret, Cosima. Forgive me for starting this letter without the usual formalities of sharing my day, but I find myself unable to think properly just now. In your most recent letter, you said Peter would advise me to steer clear of Simon, advice I heed only too well. My brother has Simon pegged right in that he is so staunchly Irish he might be willing to go to extraordinary measures to see Irish independence. And believe me, I want nothing to do with him on a personal level. Truly.

For the past two months, I thought we were managing one another's company quite well. Last time he visited, just two weeks ago, I shared with you how I enjoyed hearing of his travels. I was relieved to think we might learn to tolerate one another, since he sees Katie so often it is a matter of necessity that her brother and I learn to be cordial. Granted, we generally spend little time in conversation because Katie tends to dominate that, but something happened tonight that I must confess I will *have difficulty forgetting. I hope that by telling you, I might put it into proper perspective. I went outside for my nightly walk, thinking Simon had already returned to the inn where he stays during his visits. It was a clear, starry night, and I walked with a prayer until I heard a noise behind me. I turned, and there he was. . . .*

"Mr. MacFarland?"

"Yes, it is I."

"I didn't expect anyone to be outside. I was startled."

"Forgive me."

It was such an odd place to be, on the side of the manor, where no door or garden or indeed anything of interest was to be found. "Were you searching for something?" The question was absurd, especially considering the dark of night, but Berrie was too curious not to inquire the reason for his unexpected appearance.

Simon hesitated only a moment, looked away, then back to behold her gaze. "Yes, actually. You."

Surprise filled her that he would seek her company without Katie by her side.

"I happened to see you leave, and I wondered where you might be off to at such an hour."

His lack of trust was as evident as the stars in the sky. "It seems obvious, Mr. MacFarland, that your visits continue not only to see your sister but to check on me, to see if I might be caught in some infraction so you may say 'Aha! I knew you were the nefarious kind, and I shall quite justifiably take my sister away.'"

He received the accusation solemnly, without denial. "What *are* you doing out here?"

"I walk the circumference of the manor each night, Mr. MacFarland. To see that all's well."

His gaze still held hers as if determining either the veracity or the worthiness of such an admission. "Perhaps you should hire a night watchman. Or at least, it seems to me, such a task would be better off to one of your male attendants. That tall one—Duff, I believe you call him—he seems eager to do your bidding."

How could she admit her nightly walk wasn't just a service to the school but rather a way of rejuvenating herself? When it wasn't raining, this was a nightly ritual she anticipated the moment the sun began sinking in the sky. To be alone with no roof between her and God, to breathe in the fresh air that smelled wondrously different at night than it did during their morning drills, to see the stars in all their glorious blue. To pray.

"Yes, I'm sure you're right." Not that Berrie had any intention of asking Duff to assume such a duty. She resumed her walk.

As if detecting her lie and unwilling to let it—or her—pass, Simon touched her arm to stop her. The contact was effective. She turned to him expectantly.

"It isn't safe to be alone in the dark."

"Our nearest tenant is a good deal down the hill, a family of five quite content to live their life without snooping around our school. A solitary place seldom brings trouble." The worst she feared was a tree root she'd tripped on a few times in the dark.

"The remoteness doesn't make it safe, particularly such a large manor house. And beside the human predator, there are other things that make the night unsafe. Bats, rodents, who knows if there may be a wild dog nearby." He grinned, something Berrie had rarely seen directed her way. She stared at his mouth, unable to glance away. "And you know, don't you, about all the troubles a leprechaun can bring? Who would know you even needed help, out here alone in the dark?"

She reined in her gaze, redirecting it forward. "Do you often try to inspire fear in others?"

"I'm pointing out things you should have already taken into consideration and therefore asked your Mr. Duff to do this for you."

She was caught by the way he'd said "your Mr. Duff." Was that Simon's reason for searching her out, then? Had he suspected she might be coming out to a rendezvous with Duff? How convenient a scandal would be: disgrace her and make it easy to close the school altogether.

"Thank you for your concern, Mr. MacFarland, but I assure you I'm not alone when I walk at night. My God is my shield and my protector."

"I hardly think it fair for foolish behavior to stir a busy God into extra duty, do you?"

She wasn't sure where to start on the various misguided thoughts behind that statement. "Not that I see my behavior as foolish; however, you can hardly put *God* and *busy* in conjunction with one another or you make Him something less than He is, don't you?"

"True. But in my recollection of theology, there is also an admonition not to test Him. Why purposely force His protection when it's far more logical to have a night watchman or assign this task to one of the male attendants?"

"I like doing it myself!" Berrie hadn't meant to admit the truth, though it occurred to her if she had done so sooner, this conversation wouldn't have gone on or taken such an exasperated undercurrent. "I like the night air, the stars and the moon, the shadows and the sounds. So I won't be assigning the task to someone else, if you must know."

She moved forward again but another touch to her arm forestalled her. She turned, startled because his touch was so gentle she wasn't sure his intention was to give her pause or not.

"I'm sorry," he said.

Confusion drew her brows. "For . . . what?"

"My perceived mistrust of you, following you, interrupting you, irritating you. I believe my offenses—real or at least perceived by you as such—came in that order."

She let out a small smile. "I believe so."

"Apology accepted, then?"

She nodded. She would have walked on, returning the way she'd come, back to the front of the manor and inside, but something held her in place.

"Sometimes when you look at me," he said, his voice low, "I see the deepest mistrust. I wonder if you believe my sole desire is to cast you in the worst of light. I followed you only out of concern, Miss Hamilton. Nothing more."

How true he'd read her, how accurately observed.

"Even now," he whispered, "you don't believe me."

"No, I suppose I don't," she said, taking a step to pass him. He took the smallest step in her path, and suddenly he was far closer than she expected. Then, without warning, he shifted to stand fully in front of her and bent closer so that his face was level with hers. She stood still, knowing she should back away if he did not. She didn't move.

"I don't think anything malicious of you," he whispered. "In fact, I . . ."

He did not finish his statement, and Berrie couldn't imagine how to do it for him. Instead, she stared at his face, so clear in the moonlight, as if it were the first time she saw him and there were some unseen force pulling her gaze into his. She ought to move away, and yet there she stood, studying and being studied. The exchange couldn't have lasted more than a moment and yet it seemed far longer.

Simon started to step away, and Berrie rushed to do the

same. She couldn't want to be so near him; this was the man who always brought out the worst in her.

She started to walk away, but she felt his hand fall gently back to her elbow. If he'd moved away it had only been temporary, because here he was again, too close . . . and yet not close enough. An extraordinary thought crossed her mind as she saw him look at her face, his gaze lingering on her lips. For the barest moment, he was contemplating a kiss. She should look away, step back. But she didn't.

Then his lips were upon hers in a kind of kiss she'd received only once in her life—from Lord Welby back in England. The man who had once said he wanted to speak to her father, then never did.

But this was Simon MacFarland kissing her, and what was more stunning than that, she wasn't doing a thing to stop him. Instead, her arms went about his neck, her lips pressed into his with equal exploration and intention.

The look upon his face when he lifted his mouth from hers made her guess he was as astonished by the kiss as she.

He stiffened, then took a full step back. "That was quite . . . unexpected. I must ask your forgiveness again. I've no excuse. I don't even—"

He cut himself off once more, and aside from completely agreeing that the kiss was unexpected, Berrie wanted to hear his finished statement. "You don't even like me?"

Simon shook his head. "I was going to say I don't even believe a man should kiss a woman unless they're wed or about to be." He cleared his throat. "If that is what you expect of someone who's just taken such liberties with you, I assure you I am willing to do the honorable thing and seek your company with the possibility of . . . marriage."

That his voice sounded positively ill upon that final word wasn't lost on Berrie. Her fists clenched at her sides. "What an *honorable* proposal, Mr. MacFarland. Let me assure you of two things. First, I intend never to marry. And second, even if I were open to such a thing, I assure *you* I would never receive the attentions of someone who fairly strangles upon the thought of me as his wife."

If he was stiff before, he was more so now. "You'll forgive me, won't you, for having a certain kind of wife in mind? A sort you obviously could never be. I don't need someone who is madly in love, blind to my faults, but I would prefer a woman who at the very least respects and honors my thoughts and opinions."

"Perhaps then you might take your charming proposal to someone who can be that for you. It's been my observation that when you respect and honor someone, they might do the same in return."

She started to turn away, noticing he didn't move to follow. So be it. She didn't need him to escort her back to the front door.

"If your intention is to argue, Miss Hamilton, I can think of various other topics than one as serious as marriage. Your loyalty to England, for one. Your work schedule for another. The fact that you've left your family and your home even suggests there might be some reason to have run away from them, and I cannot help but wonder why. There are no doubt other topics that might inspire an argument between us."

"Undoubtedly. Your complete disregard for manners being on top of a great, long list of your offenses." Setting such a list aside, her gaze narrowed as she stared at him. "Bringing up my loyalty to England in hopes of arguing it away from me would be like attempting to argue me out of being a woman. I am what I am— an Englishwoman. As for my reasons for leaving my home and family, I assure you there was no flight involved. I am fully supported by my loving parents, two successful brothers, and a sister and sister-in-law, all of whom mean more to me than anyone. You obviously have no idea that someone could be called of God to do something and be willing to sacrifice the comforts of home to answer such a calling. Which would bring me to another item on my list: your definition of God is so alien to me as to wonder if you have any faith at all, sir. If so, it is a faith completely and utterly foreign to me."

"My faith, if anything, is far more practical than yours. I've no fanciful notions of a God who wants to be involved in my life. As for sacrificing, that I have done more than you can imagine. A life of my own, for one, while I devote myself to my country, which needs too much of me. Beside that, I have two sisters, neither of whom seem to want my protection but need it nonetheless."

She rolled her eyes. "Perhaps they don't. I cannot speak for Innis, though you did say she is about to be wed, but as for Katie, she is safe and happy here."

Simon folded his arms in obvious skepticism. "Can you honestly stand here and tell me she has a job in your school, as you've let her believe? That she isn't just one more student for you?"

Berrie kept her gaze level with his. "I believe with every part of me that in time Katie will be more help than harm here. Eventually she truly will be the example for other students in most if not all areas we're trying to teach."

"Eventually." The word sounded just short of scoffing.

"Maybe God designed Katie for exactly what she's doing—patiently helping others try to figure out language and baskets and folded serviettes. She can't do that cloistered away in your home." She wanted to turn away at last, go back inside, and let him go to the inn, but in his silence she wondered if her words had made any impact at all.

Finally he spoke. "You are advocating a future for Katie, something I've never been able to envision for her except to keep her safe." His tone had taken an unexpected turn, one of consideration rather than conviction.

"Everyone has a future," she whispered, "but wouldn't Katie's be better if she were allowed more than just safety? Why not think about all the things she can do instead of all the things she can't?"

Simon almost smiled. She saw a glimpse of something similar in the corner of his mouth. "Since the moment I met you, Miss Hamilton, you've never ceased to give me something to think about. To be honest, I hadn't imagined Katie staying here more than the year I agreed to."

Berrie was surprised he admitted that he'd been lacking in any way regarding his sister. Acknowledging a fault in himself— that was one thing she'd been convinced Simon MacFarland would never do.

But that was no more astonishing than his kiss had been, and the memory of it made her heart beat beyond her control. He ought to leave, and right away, so she could try erasing the memory altogether.

35

All the way from the village, Rebecca feared speeding through tunnels in a paparazzi car chase like the one that killed Princess Di, even though there were no tunnels or underpasses between the chemist shop and the Hall. Rebecca's fears were made more ridiculous since she never allowed herself to exceed the speed limit. And yet how dare he follow her? There he was in her rearview mirror.

But if the reporter had any intention of taking more snapshots, he gave it up once she turned onto the private property of Hollinworth Hall.

She pulled her mini beside Quentin's car, its presence giving away his arrival. She did not emerge from behind the wheel. Sitting immobile inside, she clutched the wheel, eyeing the package she'd bought.

Had she seen the man in the chemist shop? Perhaps. Certainly there had been a few customers there while she surveyed the pregnancy tests. Surely he knew what she'd purchased, and the logical assumption would be that she'd bought it for herself. How long would it be before all of London was reading not only about Quentin Hollinworth's dual love life but that one of the women he was seeing had bought such a thing?

If only she'd had the sense to take Dana with her, let Dana

buy the item. But there would have been no doing that; poor Dana had been especially pale this morning.

Rebecca considered the possibilities, looking at herself in the rearview mirror. Perhaps the reporter didn't know who she was. She slapped her forehead. Of course he knew.

A tap at the window jarred her from her misery. Quentin was there, bending down to peer through the window with a smile, albeit a puzzled one.

She emerged on the other side, eyeing him over the roof of her mini.

"I didn't see you come out of the Hall." Her voice sounded as strained as she felt.

"I didn't. I was in my car about to go in when I saw you arrive. Is everything all right?"

"No." Rebecca would have preferred time to calm her senses but forged ahead anyway. "I just had my picture taken by someone I'm almost certain was a reporter."

He came around to her side of the car. "I'm afraid that's something you'll have to get used to, darling."

He took her into his arms, and for a moment she let him. She needed his comfort. Then she remembered his embrace *wasn't* comforting. Not when visions of Lady Caroline in a peignoir replayed in her mind. Rebecca pulled away, took a step back. Instead of telling him the truth, all of it, she held up the bag in her hand. "I was buying a pregnancy kit, Quentin. How soon do you suppose that will be reported?"

"A what?" He looked first amazed, then once again puzzled. "Why were you buying such a thing?"

"For Dana. Not that I should be telling you that; her husband doesn't even know yet. You know what that reporter will say, what he'll tell the entire reading world. What people will think."

He smiled calmly. "You once told me you didn't care much what people think."

"I do when they're misconstruing *facts* . . . and when one of the readers might be my father! What will he think when he reads such a thing?"

Quentin put his hands on her shoulders, but the attempt to steady her failed. "We'll tell him the truth, the sooner the better, before he reads about it. It's the only way. In fact—" his tone grew quieter, slower—"there's something else about this whole media mess you ought to know. I only found out about it last night myself. I tried calling you. You must have been asleep already."

She shook her head. "I heard your call. I didn't answer it."

His brows drew together. "Why ever not?"

She didn't answer. Instead, she asked, "What were you going to tell me?" She meant to let him tell her but couldn't hold back. "A little detail you forgot to mention—about Lady Caroline being your houseguest again?"

"Yes—I mean, no, not at all. She's not my houseguest; she's my mother's. And you knew? For how long?"

"Someone sent me a clipping. I must have received it by yesterday's post, but I only opened it last night. Just before your call."

"And so you decided not to talk to me? Didn't you want to ask me about it?"

Rebecca tried to walk past him, not ask even now. The garage was narrow on this side, and with him in the way she couldn't get by. He stood firmly in place.

"A friend of mine from London telephoned and said something about the article, and I knew nothing of it. I would have told you sooner if I'd known."

"If you'd known what, exactly? That I was bound to find out anyway that you and Lady Caroline are once again sharing the same roof? You knew long before that story became public."

She hated this argument, hated her words and the jealous, spiteful tone behind them. Life had been so much easier before admitting her feelings for him. Why had she ever done such a thing?

Quentin seemed to take the pause the same way she had, with a distasteful assessment of what was happening. Their first argument.

"You have a right to be angry," he said quietly. "I should have told you my mother invited her to stay at the cottage days ago when she first arrived. It's my mother's attempt to put us back together. Caroline is the sister of an earl, like Mum herself, and therefore Caroline . . . measures up. It's all a ploy—one I had nothing to do with."

She sighed. "Oh, Quentin, that doesn't surprise me at all. But I needed you to tell me that . . . from the beginning."

"You already don't like my mother. If I'd told you, it would have only made it worse. And it means nothing to me, having her there."

Rebecca studied him. "You're standing here telling me you felt nothing at all when she came to the breakfast table in her peignoir? Forgive me, Quentin, I find that hard to believe."

"All right, I'm a man, but I have complete control over my actions. What's in my head matters most, Rebecca. And I don't want her. I want you."

He reached for her again but she held up her free hand, the other one still clutching Dana's kit. "She's right for you, Quentin. Your mother is convinced of that and so is the newspaper. They said you'd gone back to 'one of your own.'"

"Surely you don't believe everything you read in the paper. They're about to bring out a false report on that little purchase in your hand."

She felt a smile tug at her lips, unbidden yet there. She wanted to cling to her cautions, put him at arm's length both physically and figuratively, but when his lips came down on hers, she hadn't an ounce of resistance.

Ignoring wariness wasn't like her; at the moment, however, she hadn't the faintest idea what to do except return his kiss.

36

Your letter is full of the most wondrous news, Cosima. I have not only a nephew but now a niece as well! I especially enjoyed your description of her and hearing of the peace the Lord God has given you regarding her. I am sure you are correct in that she has nothing of that so-called curse, just like her older brother. Certainly you recall what Royboy was like as a baby, and you would know if either of your children had similar traits. What joy! I shall continue to welcome each and every letter as you get to know this newest member of our family.

The plans God has for our lives continue to surprise me, Cosima. He has given me the greatest passion for the success of this school; I guard it as an eagle guards its nest. Lately, though, I have discovered a battle in me, and even though I have Simon MacFarland to blame (yet again!), this is a most unexpected turn for me.

I am sure he has forgotten entirely that he not only kissed me but proposed marriage, such as it was. A fact

I wish I could forget. We argue every time we speak. I should continue to detest him, should I not?

But sometimes I miss dreaming about a husband, even as I tell myself I could never have enough time in the day for my work and a family. Still, pouring myself into my work of late has left me with the feeling that something is missing. I remind myself this is my family now, and the children temporarily mine. So will you pray for me, my friend?

Having Simon continue to visit so often is no help. I have succeeded in ignoring him with each visit until last night. We were outside again, thankfully not alone this time. . . .

The evening was clear and one of the other attendants had lit a fire in a round pit he'd dug a few weeks ago, marking it off with white rocks so the students wouldn't venture too close. Duff sat on the stump of a tree with his fiddle in hand, while most of the others sat on the felled log, piles of hay, or blankets. Katie had invited Berrie to sit next to her on a blanket, and Simon sat on Katie's other side.

"I noticed something today," Katie said to Berrie while the others sang. Katie had a clear voice and was the best singer among the students. But she had a smile on her face just now that was nothing short of sparkling, so it was difficult to wish her back to singing or the smile would be missed.

"What did you notice, Katie?" Berrie asked. Katie often said the most surprising things, simple yet profound in her way. As when she'd noticed the birds around the manor before she'd

drawn her first image of them. Berrie had tried to identify some
of the specific varieties since her brother Peter had tried teaching her such a thing from the youngest age. Katie took to the
old custom of calling any small bird a sparrow. She said God
must love the little sparrows, because He not only made a lot
of them—many more than bigger birds—and gave them more
colors and songs, but He'd also given them more courage. She'd
never seen a big bird go after another bird many times its size,
although she'd seen more than one sparrow go after a crow that
came near its nest.

Katie directed her smile Berrie's way. "You know that I notice
things, Miss Berrie, don't you? And the things I notice are often
missed by others?"

"Yes, Katie, that's true."

"Today I noticed something about you."

Berrie glanced beyond Katie to her brother, hoping he wasn't
listening. Katie's observations might very well be honest and true
but weren't always flattering. Of Mrs. Cotgrave's mole, Katie had
noted it grew a hair in its very center.

"And it was about Simon, too."

If Simon hadn't been listening before, he was now. He turned
his gaze Katie's way, saying nothing.

"I noticed, Miss Berrie, that you and my brother, Simon, are
very much alike."

Berrie couldn't hide her surprise at Katie's words but decided
her reaction wasn't any less than Simon's. His brows were lifted
higher than hers must have been.

"Why do you think that, Katie?" Simon asked.

"One thing is because you both work all the time. Do you know
Miss Berrie does a lot of work in her office, Simon? Just like you do
at home or when you go to London. And another thing is you both
tell others what to do. This is good when you're telling me what to
do, but I think that's why you sometimes argue, because you're both

231

used to having others do as you say. And another thing is you always leave your dried apricots on your plates after dinner, so that means you both don't like dried apricots. And the last thing is you both have the same look on your face sometimes, like you know when one is going to tell the other to do something and you don't like that because this is your job, to tell others what to do. So that's why I think you're both very much alike."

Berrie glanced from Simon to the others, grateful Duff hadn't stopped playing and few beyond them had heard Katie's words. Having anything in common with someone who not only detested her but this school was ridiculous.

"That's very interesting, Katie," Simon said.

He didn't sound irritated in the least. Rather he smiled as he spoke, which was odd indeed.

"I've noticed a difference, too." Katie frowned and her large forehead wrinkled. "One that shouldn't really be there."

Berrie exchanged a glance with Simon, noting he didn't encourage Katie to continue any more than she did.

"It's this," Katie said. "It's God. Miss Berrie prays all the time, Simon. The way you used to. Do you remember how you taught me about God? that He is like the air? And I thought of something else He's like. Words. Did you know you can't see words? We can write letters, but they're just pictures of sounds. They aren't something you can hold in your hand. And time. Yesterday is something you can't touch or hold, either, but we know it's real because we remember what we did. So God is like you said, like air, and He's like words and yesterday, too. Since you told me this, I don't understand why you don't pray anymore. Has God gone away from you but not from me and Miss Berrie? Why would He do that?"

Simon looked away, staring into the light of the fire instead of at anyone else. On his face was a frown, one of the first Berrie had seen not inspired by her or her school.

"He hasn't gone away, Katie," Simon said at last, in a voice so low Berrie knew only she and Katie could hear.

Katie smiled broadly, the opposite of her brother's continued frown. "Then you don't have any differences at all, you and Miss Berrie. Isn't that nice?"

Duff had ended the last song and Mrs. Cotgrave was already herding students inside. Berrie stayed behind as the others walked ahead, shaking out the blanket and taking time to fold it more carefully than necessary. It was true she thought Katie's brother as interesting as he was annoying, but surely she hadn't said or done anything to indicate to Katie that she *wanted* to have something in common with her brother?

She'd given up on the idea of marriage years ago, perhaps as long ago as her first season out, in London. She knew why she'd received nary a single offer, and it was because any time a man looked at her with interest she'd quickly grilled him on too many topics. Faith, foremost, then politics and education, child rearing and social ills, the punitive system and foreign policy. She couldn't help herself; those were the topics that appealed to her most when her father and brother sat down to the table. She refused to behave as though she knew nothing of such things when she had an opinion on it all.

But each and every man she'd met that first year, and then the second, seemed to want only the body of a wife and not the mind. Even Lord Welby.

She watched Simon walking with his sister. He couldn't be younger than she was, perhaps even a year or two older. Why wasn't he wed already?

Berrie stopped such a surprising line of thinking, all caused by Katie's simple observation. It didn't matter if she was right. The Lord didn't have marriage in mind for Berrie; she was sure of that. He had more important things for her to devote herself to than marriage and family. This was her family now, all of the children other parents had entrusted to the school. Nothing was going to change that.

Besides, even if she had misunderstood and the Lord God did want her wed someday, she was certain it wouldn't be to a man with whom every conversation escalated to an argument.

Berrie slowly returned to the manor, knowing she wouldn't walk tonight. Not when she recalled the last time she'd done so when Simon was still there. She glanced back to see Duff tending the dying fire. A further glance took in the surrounding area, and she frowned. Finola stood at the edge of the firelight, watching Duff dousing the last of the flames.

Maybe Berrie would take her walk, after all, and ask Finola to join her. No sense allowing an opportunity for something unseemly—whether or not she need worry about such a thing.

37

Rebecca sat on the bed with Padgett, each of them holding a small plastic pony. She tried to follow Padgett's imaginative story line of ponies rescuing a lamb named Emma who'd fallen into a ravine, but Rebecca's mind was on Dana in the lavatory. She'd learned the pregnancy test was best taken first thing in the morning, and so they'd spent yesterday in desperate distraction. A train ride to Stratford-upon-Avon, an outdoor performance of Hamlet that Padgett had slept through. Lazy lunch, late shopping.

Though Quentin had wanted to come, he let Rebecca talk him out of it. She told him it was only because Dana needed a friend, refuting the look she saw on his face that silently accused her of hanging on to her unease about Lady Caroline. Rebecca believed his assurances and told him so. Still, while she worried with Dana, Rebecca wondered where he spent the day, if Lady Caroline had been part of it—by his choice or his mother's. By last night she thought if jealousy was to be partner in this relationship, maybe God wasn't its designer after all.

Rebecca glanced at her watch. Dana had been in there more than five minutes. Rebecca heard nothing from behind the lavatory door, no indication of what Dana might be facing. She wanted to call through the door but couldn't imagine how hurrying things along might help. And so she participated while Padgett's pony rescued the little lamb.

At last the doorknob twisted and Rebecca's gaze flew to the doorway. Dana did not step into the bedroom; instead she stood just inside the lavatory, beyond Rebecca's vision. Padgett, caught up in her play, seemed not to notice.

Rebecca trotted her pony to the make-believe barn, tugging gently on one of Padgett's braids. They were coming undone from having been slept in and would need Dana's attention before long. "I think this pony needs some breakfast. How about you?"

"Not hungry," she said, then went on with the story.

Rebecca slid from the bed, facing Dana. "Well?"

Her face was anemic, but her skin had been that shade nearly every morning since they'd arrived, color returning only after a meal. There was one difference. Her eyes were streaked with red. "It's positive."

A swirl of confusion rose in Rebecca; what should be a joyful moment for Dana, learning she was pregnant, was something altogether different for her. Rebecca stepped closer, grabbing Dana's hand. "Okay. So now you know for sure." She glanced over her shoulder to Padgett, who was still oblivious, then turned back to Dana. "Are you going to call Aidan?"

Dana's eyes widened—not in eagerness, rather in horror. She took a step back. "Will you take Padgett downstairs? give her breakfast?"

Rebecca nodded. "I'll have tea and toast ready for you. Herbal, no caffeine. And a glass of milk, maybe oatmeal, and a banana . . ." She knew she was rambling, that the words weren't any comfort, but they were noise, and silence seemed worse.

After breakfast, Padgett took her ponies outside, and Rebecca watched her through the window. She played well by herself, bringing her imagination wherever she went.

An hour later, Dana entered the kitchen. Her hair was wet from a shower, her face still pale and her eyes puffy, nose red, giveaways for tears. Rebecca sliced banana, ready to add it to the oatmeal she'd made. She wanted to say something, call upon some heavenly wisdom that would ease Dana's fears of the future, fears for the tiny life growing inside her.

But Rebecca knew better than to offer empty hope. She'd learned not to do such a thing when her mother became ill, not to listen when others tried infusing her with their own hollow promises. All the months she'd spent hoping her mother would get better had only made accepting her death harder. Hope had become the enemy, at least for a while.

It wasn't until her father had confronted her and demanded to know if she would have preferred never having known her mother, having been spared the pain but also the pleasure of her as a mother, that Rebecca began to accept the adage about life being a miracle, no matter how long it lasted. She realized then that hope was sometimes found only in an eternal perspective.

"Did you call Aidan?"

Dana stiffened. "No."

Rebecca said nothing.

"I want to finish going through the school records," Dana said. "I think I'll do that before I help transcribe any more of Berrie's letters, if you don't mind."

"All right," Rebecca said gently. "But are you sure that's best? The records are a bit—"

"Too realistic?" Her voice sounded oddly inflexible, defying Rebecca to say otherwise.

"I thought you agreed Berrie's letters are more interesting, not so clinical."

"Don't think the records are telling me something I don't already know." Dana stared straight ahead, sounding hard. Not the kind of voice she'd heard from Dana so far, even while she'd been so worried.

"Maybe," Rebecca began gently, "you know too much already.

Whatever happens with this baby cannot possibly include every-thing going through your mind right now."

Dana still stared ahead and Rebecca had no idea if her words were welcomed or resented, whether they were received as one of those hollow-hope offerings. She'd been too busy and isolated out here in the country for the past three years. She hadn't been a friend—a good friend—to anyone since university days. She wasn't sure she knew how anymore.

"Eat," Rebecca prompted. "You always feel better with some-thing in your stomach."

Dana accepted the warm oatmeal. She didn't finish it but ate enough that the hue of her skin no longer matched the pasty color of the bowl contents.

"Rebecca," Dana said after she emptied the remnants of her meal in the trash, "would you mind walking Padgett down to the farm while I go through the rest of the records this morning? I'd like to get through as much as I can without her interrupting every five minutes."

Rebecca nodded even though she wanted to refuse. Dana's mood was somber enough; reading those records wouldn't do much to improve that.

But Rebecca kept Padgett on the farm for hours, feeding the animals, letting Padgett ride the pony, holding Emma, who was getting too fast and agile to allow such a thing for long.

Rebecca watched, wondering what was ahead for this little girl. Big sister to a handicapped sibling? Even that might be better than being alone, as Rebecca had been. Her mother's health had never been good, and her father told her it was a miracle she'd been able to carry Rebecca full-term. Having more children had always been out of the question. Maybe having a special-needs sibling would come with difficulties all its own, although she supposed any relationship had its share of that. Wouldn't Padgett be better off with someone else to love in her life? Or would this new one only be a burden, as Dana must fear?

Before being in contact with Dana, before reading Cosima's journal, Rebecca hadn't thought much about such children. School groups always seemed to bring students on the gifted end, with mainly bright, well-behaved children. Only rarely had anyone arrived at the Hall with a child possessing any sort of intellectual disability.

Even when Quentin had waited for the fragile X blood test results, Rebecca hadn't really delved into the idea of having a child with cognitive challenges. She'd believed the doctors, and they'd been right. Quentin's results had come back negative. As Dana had predicted, there was no fragile X in Quentin's line.

Rebecca didn't begrudge Dana her fears; she wasn't even sure she could comfort her, since lately she hadn't been able to overcome many of her own fears about life-changing decisions. She did know she would be Dana's friend and support her in any way she could.

Rebecca wouldn't offer empty hope, but maybe it wouldn't hurt to offer a reminder about the eternal one. That much she could offer with trust.

Near lunchtime Rebecca took Padgett back to the kitchen, hoping Dana had called Aidan by now. He not only had a right to know, he was probably the only one who could really help her get through this.

Rebecca let Padgett spread a piece of bread with jam, which wobbled its way from knife to table, a bit of it splashing coincidentally onto the bread. Rebecca laughed and helped, grateful for one thing: at least her mind wasn't on herself. It was silly to dwell on Caroline Norleigh.

While Rebecca finished making sandwiches for Dana and herself, she sent Padgett to the office for her mother. Even if she wasn't finished with those records, she needed to eat.

"Mommy's not there," Padgett said, staring up at Rebecca with wide blue eyes that weren't in the least worried, trusting Rebecca would know where next to look for her missing mother.

"Did you check in her bedroom?"

Padgett shook her head.

"Let's go have a look, shall we? Maybe she needed to use the toilet."

"The baffroom," Padgett corrected.

Taking the child's hand, Rebecca nodded, adding a smile though she wanted to jump to any number of worries. It was too quiet for someone to be in the lavatory; she could hear water running from any room in the Hall. Upstairs the quiet was more definite. She wasn't surprised to find both Dana's and Padgett's rooms empty.

"I suppose she went for a walk, then," Rebecca said, leading the way downstairs again. "Let's go look."

They went out the front door. If Dana had exited the back and headed anywhere near the farm, they would have easily spotted her. Rebecca wondered what Padgett must think, whether she found it odd her mother had chosen to go outside but not in their direction.

"There she is!"

Rebecca followed Padgett's path straight to the pond, where Dana sat on the bench nearby. It offered a peaceful view of the water and the countryside beyond the Hollinworth land. Rebecca didn't often come this way, preferring the view from the back.

"It's lunchtime, Mommy." Padgett crawled up to her mother's lap. "How come you're out here all by yourself?"

"I just needed to think awhile." Dana gave her daughter a smile. "Let's go have lunch, okay?"

She stood, carrying Padgett in her arms. Rebecca stepped forward, reaching for the child. "Mind if I carry you, Padge?"

Though the child nodded, reaching for Rebecca, Dana didn't

let go. "If anything were to go wrong because of me carrying her, it would have happened already."

Something in the way she said it made Rebecca wonder if Dana almost hoped something might end this pregnancy. Rebecca chastised the thought; no sense reading something that might not be there, especially a thought as unfair to Dana as that.

"Everything okay?" Rebecca asked, once Padgett resigned herself to staying in her mother's arms, resting her head on Dana's shoulder.

"Oh, couldn't be better." There was that tone again. "I'm making a list of all the things I might want to worry about in the future. I certainly have enough material."

"You mad, Mommy?" Padgett asked. She might not be able to understand the words, but she understood the same tone Rebecca heard.

"No." Dana offered another smile, this one a little tighter, narrower. "Just a little sad. It's okay to feel that way sometimes."

"Okay, just so you're not mad." Padgett grinned. "I hope you won't be sad much longer. 'Cause that makes me sad."

Dana leaned closer to Padgett, rubbing her daughter's nose with her own. "You know what? You just made me feel better. Give me a kissie."

Padgett kissed her mother's cheek, then squirmed to the ground and raced ahead, reaching the door first.

"Before you ask, no, I didn't call Aidan." Dana stopped, turning to Rebecca.

The transformation was amazing; in one instant she'd convinced Padgett she was fine, almost convincing Rebecca as well. But she wasn't. The look on her face now proved it. Rebecca said nothing.

"How am I going to tell him, Rebecca? I can't even think about it without being terrified."

"I don't know Aidan very well, Dana, but I do know he loves you. His reaction might be better than you think."

She folded her arms. "I'm not worried about his reaction. He'll remind me there's a fifty-fifty chance of everything being fine, be the first one to tell me everything will be all right. He might even be able to convince himself of that."

"And he might be right."

"Please! I don't need two optimists around me."

They heard Padgett's call to hurry up, that she was hungry, and they resumed the path to the front door.

Rebecca wished she could do more than offer a place of refuge, a home that wasn't even her own. She wished she knew how to offer hope that was more immediate than eternity, more tangible than a distant future, more secure than either one of them felt.

But she didn't know how.

38

My dear Cosima,

I hate to begin with bad news, but this regards your cousin Finola and her son, Conall. Not to worry about either one's health, however. It is a legal matter. Since Conall is so young, our license does not extend to students his age. The Commission says we cannot keep him, even though his mother is here with us. It is a problem even Simon MacFarland cannot fix, and so Finola will have to leave us. And go where, we cannot guess. Perhaps her brother will have a change of heart, though I doubt that, given the fact he has not visited or contacted her since she arrived and so I cannot help believing he doesn't miss her in the least.

She has already packed, telling us she will go back to her friend in Dublin, where she shall prepare to beg her brother to take her back in. . . .

"I hardly know what to say," Berrie told Finola, who stood at the door with her two bags filled, Conall at her side.

Surprisingly enough, Duff was nowhere to be seen. Jobbin waited outside in the misty rain to drive Finola into town, where she would await a coach to Dublin.

"There's nothin' to be said," Finola replied. She handed her bags to Jobbin, who put them in the back of the wagon. He would be damp by the time they arrived at their destination, since the driver was subject to the weather, but at least Finola and Conall would be more comfortable beneath the canvas top that stretched along the rear. "I've come to expect bad news at my doorstep; it's happened from my childhood. Nessa will understand. She's an O'Brien by birth, and they've always known to expect the worst." She smiled wistfully as she climbed into the wagon. "My friend has welcomed me before, my Nessa O'Brien O'Donnell." The singsong name carried affectionately on Finola's lips, and Katie repeated it even as she handed Finola her son. Neither Katie nor Conall appeared to notice Finola's sadness. "There's naught to be done for me, at least until my wee one's not so wee anymore."

"His twelfth birthday seems far off," Berrie said. "But we'll always have a cot for him. And you, too, Finola."

She nodded, eyes downcast, perhaps to hide a tear. She left then, and Berrie watched the wagon rumble down the rutted lane.

Duff never came, not with so much as a wave.

39

Rebecca gazed at the night sky and thought of van Gogh's *Starry Night*, the way a few clouds swirled around stars bright enough to shine through. She closed her eyes, breathing in the scent of roses from the garden first planted by Hamilton gardeners, maintained for almost two hundred years now. For a moment, with stars above, roses at her feet, and the man she could so easily love standing beside her, Rebecca imagined life to be nearly perfect, even if it wasn't supposed to be.

"God has them all named, you know," Quentin whispered.

"What?"

"The stars."

Rebecca smiled, leaning closer, putting her head on his shoulder. It was late and Dana and Padgett had retired for the evening, giving Rebecca and Quentin time alone.

"Yes, I know. Amazing, isn't it? That He gave us so many beautiful things?"

Quentin turned her to face him and stared at her with a smile that said the beauty he saw was in her. "Yes, it is." He kissed her, then added with his lips still pressed to hers, "Amazing."

Rebecca delighted in his kiss, his words, the look in his eyes. "It's easy to think life is simple sometimes," she said. "That all we have to do is enjoy the gifts we've been given."

"It should be. Why isn't it?"

"I suppose if it really were that simple we'd forget all about the Giver." She glanced back to the veranda door, thinking of Dana. "I know Dana is questioning why God allowed this pregnancy after all she did to prevent it. She's trying to believe He's forgotten all about her, I think. Blaming Him for letting this slip by without notice, like some kind of mistake."

"She'll be all right," Quentin said.

"At the moment she needs a friend." Rebecca gave him a half smile. "Which means you and I won't have much time together, at least until she decides to let Aidan in on this."

"I've never pretended to understand the workings of the female mind," Quentin said with a grin, "but it seems to me she should have called him by now."

"I agree. We all adjust to our challenges in our own ways, I suppose."

"And your challenges, Rebecca?" he asked, stroking her cheek gently. "How are you adjusting to . . . us?"

She smiled slowly. "Now there's a challenge."

He didn't smile, and she wondered if he'd missed her teasing tone. "Your father took the news rather well about the pregnancy kit story. Is the press still haunting you?"

"No, I think I've learned my lesson. Never do anything in public that can be misunderstood by those who watch—and realize there will always be someone watching. Which might mean I spend the rest of my life cloistered away." Then, having heard her own words, she added abruptly, "The rest of the time we're together, at any rate."

Quentin frowned. "Do you foresee a limit on that time?"

"I don't know."

He held her close, pressing her head back on his shoulder. "That's not the answer I was looking for, Rebecca."

She knew that. She saw it on his face the moment she'd uttered the words. But what else could she have said? Left her former statement at that? That she hoped she would be with him the rest of her life, adjusting to whatever that meant?

Maybe she was old-fashioned, but she wanted him to be the first to hint that marriage was their mutual goal.

40

I know I just posted a letter to you yesterday and you will be surprised to receive another from me so soon, but I must write again already. It seems I cannot keep this to myself, even though that might be best. I can tell no other person here, not even Mrs. Cotgrave. My main concern has always been for the integrity of this school, and that is why I should say not a word. Yet here I am.

One infraction I might be able to explain, were I unfortunate enough to have someone know about that kiss. It was so unexpected—by both of us, I am sure—it could be termed almost an accident.

But tonight? Oh, Cosima, forgive me for babbling. I really must find a way to bar that man from these doors, and were it not for Katie welcoming him as she does, I would demand that very thing. He has confounded me again! After tonight, I vow I shall never, ever walk the grounds while that man is under this roof. . . .

"I really don't need an escort, considering I've been doing this without one for half a year."

Simon did not respond, did not even look at Berrie.

She waited, wondering if stretching out such an awkward, silent moment would be enough to change his mind. He did not budge. The night air was chilly without a shawl, so she couldn't wait much longer.

"You really needn't waste your time, Mr. MacFarland," she said as she began walking.

He fell in step beside her. "If I sat in the parlor reading a book and something were to happen out here—something I could have prevented—then which would be the waste of time? My reading or my being out here?"

Instead of answering, she asked, "Do you take on the role of protector for everyone around you or only for those you find particularly helpless?"

"The answer to the first part of that question is no, and as to the second, I find you about as helpless as a porcupine."

"While I find your comparison of me to a bristly little piglike rodent amusing, it's clear you think I can take care of myself. So why must you follow anyway?"

"As I said, if anything were to happen, I would feel guilty." At a glance, she thought she saw a grin as he continued speaking. "And since you seem to think I'd rather have you more uncomfortable than myself, you ought to know I intend to follow you until you're safely back inside anyway."

"It's far more likely I should get hurt during the duties of my day than alone out here," she muttered.

"If you pretend I'm not here, Miss Hamilton, you might enjoy yourself more."

She cast another quick glance. She could do that. They rounded the first corner and she slowed her pace. There was nothing enjoyable in rushing. Nor, though, was there any comfort to be found in his company. She couldn't enjoy herself as usual, find solace in the quiet, pray, or contemplate what she'd learned that day. Impossible.

Berrie came to the far end of the manor. There was a tree root she'd tripped on more than once in the dark. She should warn him; it was the polite thing to do. It was the right thing to do.

Another step, then another, but still she kept silent. A stumble would serve him right, with his self-imposed role of guardian. Besides, he'd told her to pretend he wasn't there.

They turned the corner, and as they neared the familiar spot, her guilt multiplied. She could not, after all, refrain from warning him. "There is a—"

"I thought you were going to ignore me."

Very well. However she couldn't seem to hold her tongue entirely. "You know, Mr. MacFarland, if you could ever hold a civil conversation you might actually find the sort of woman you're looking for. Someone who honors your thoughts and opinions, I think was how you phrased it."

Simon stopped so abruptly she thought he'd tripped as she'd done at least a dozen times before. But she was confused; they weren't upon the spot, and he was still standing straight. "What is it? Why have you stopped?"

"I'm stunned you recalled my words. I thought you instantly cast aside anything I've said."

Berrie resumed her walk. She shouldn't have acknowledged his pause anyway. Doing so proved she was hardly ignoring him. Looking at the ground instead of ahead, she saw no sign of the protruding root.

"I am capable," he said.

"Of what?" She continued walking, picking up her pace so she could throw the words over her shoulder.

He kept in step beside her. "Of carrying on a civil conversation. I thought I'd proven that, but perhaps you're right. We have yet to prove it when we're alone, haven't we? We should make an attempt. For Katie's sake, of course."

She kept walking, looking at him. "For Katie's or for yours? It's obvious you still mistrust me and my school. You've been forced to spend much of your off-season investigating what happens here instead of enjoying the comforts of home, and soon you'll no doubt be headed back to London—"

Words suddenly abandoned her in a twist of pain, her ankle held immobile by a trapped foot. Then her foot fell free and she lurched forward, only to be caught up in Simon's arms. His steady hold prevented what surely would have been a fall.

She looked up at him, awash with relief and gratitude. And guilt. Was that the stumble she'd meant for him by her silence? Served her right.

"Thank you." His hands remained on her elbows. He still stood far too close.

"There now," he said softly, "I wasn't wasting my time after all, was I?"

Then, not at all like the last time they were out under the moon, this time Berrie knew his lips were going to descend upon hers. He kissed her every bit as thoroughly as he had the last time, and everything stopped as she let him. Thinking ceased, breathing ended. Everything but her heart was still.

"It could be," Simon said, still holding her close, "this is why I followed you out here."

She looked up at him, amazingly content to be held even though part of her knew she shouldn't. This was hardly proper behavior, especially for a woman bent on never marrying. "But you don't like me. You don't even trust me with your sister."

Simon shook his head. "That's not true. Has it ever occurred to you, Berrie, that I might come round as often as I do not only to see Katie? that she may be right about how alike we are? If ever we decided to fight on the same side, together we could be one formidable opponent."

"But we have yet to find anything we could fight together. Are you telling me you enjoy our nearly constant bickering?"

"I am. And what's more, I suspect you do too."

She pulled away, shaking her head. Even as she guessed he didn't believe her denial, she had no words to back up the empty gesture. Instead, she took a step, testing the foot that had been caught by the traitorous tree root a moment ago. It was a bit sore when pressed but entirely usable.

"How is it?" he asked. Berrie instantly found she liked the solicitous tone he normally used on Katie; it made Berrie want to hear it more often.

"Tender but functional, I think."

Simon held out an arm. "Let me help, then. I can carry you back if you like."

The idea appealed to her almost as much as it shocked her, but the source of that shock seemed unclear—whether it was the prospect of him lifting her or that the image of it in her mind didn't seem unpleasant. "No, I'm fine, really."

"You realize, I hope, that I don't go about kissing every woman I walk with."

Desperate not to limp, Berrie walked slower than she had before. Such a pace hampered her attempt to get back inside, to hide, to be alone and sort out her conflicting thoughts.

Simon took her arm, and she didn't pull away. Leaning into him took away some of the pain from her ankle as she walked. "I know no such thing, Mr. MacFarland. Perhaps you kiss every woman you meet, since it's blatantly obvious you don't like me and yet you've kissed me not once but twice."

"It isn't true that I don't like you. I actually admire you greatly." He lifted his free hand to sweep in the direction of the manor. "Look at all you've done, how you've helped so many others. How could you not stir the deepest admiration in anyone who meets you?"

"But you think me a failure! How can you admire me?"

He shook his head. "I think your task impossible. There's a difference."

"I don't see a difference." She tried to walk faster and failed. "How can I be anything except a failure if what I attempt to do is impossible?"

"The lives of the students here won't change to any great degree once they're back home. I've lived with my sister too long to think otherwise. But you are making a difference in their lives for the present. I believe that's admirable."

Berrie stopped, clutching his arm not solely for balance. "We're not here to give only respite. We *are* here to change lives. Even if we give them just one talent they will have for the rest of their lives, we won't have failed them. Will we?"

She hadn't meant to ask that question aloud. Yet he didn't give a quick, crushing reply, which was what she feared.

He smiled. "No, Berrie. You won't have failed."

They rounded the last corner of the manor, and with the door in sight, Berrie's hobble quickened.

"I realize you want to be free of my company," he said, still holding her arm, "but you shouldn't rush on that ankle."

It would be futile to deny the truth, so she said nothing. Nor did she slow her pace. Only at the door did she let him take her hand, stopping her altogether.

"We should talk. With civility," he added with a grin, bringing her hand to his lips. "Because like each other or not, Miss Beryl Hamilton, there is something between us I don't think either one of us can ignore."

41

For five days—three days beyond the date Dana was to have returned to Ireland—Rebecca watched Dana do nothing except read and then reread the files from a school that was over 150 years old. Treatments may have changed, Dana admitted, but not the basic, underlying behaviors. Dana told Rebecca one of the things her sister, Talie, worried about most was her son's future. School records revealed a slice of that future: the struggles and failures, the successes so minor they couldn't possibly matter. *Fold serviette: task accomplished in 149 days.* Repeated at every meal for almost half a year, the student had finally picked up the simple skill of folding a table napkin. Some never accomplished even that.

When Rebecca suggested Dana set aside the records for a while and concentrate on Berrie's letters instead, or better yet, take a day to enjoy more sights, Dana had looked at her as if Rebecca did not understand and never would.

Quentin offered to help cheer Dana, but Dana didn't want to visit with anyone, though she couldn't deny him the use of his own home. Both urged her to talk to Aidan, who called every day. Their conversations were short and businesslike, since Dana made no attempt at privacy when he called. The only one who seemed oblivious to Dana's growing depression was Padgett. She could create a convincing smile on Dana's face, but it disappeared when Padgett went to bed or was otherwise occupied.

Dana sought solitude, but Rebecca couldn't in good conscience leave Dana with the records taking hold of her. So the two of them sat in Rebecca's office together, Rebecca trying to coax Dana to another diversion, but rarely succeeding.

For those five days while Rebecca necessarily chose Dana's company over Quentin's, the subject of Lady Caroline never emerged. In Rebecca's mind the other woman came up often. Rebecca wondered if this time apart was testing her, teaching her that jealousy is a selfish, ultimately self-destructive force, one she wanted nothing to do with. It was also a test for Quentin, intricately enmeshed with Rebecca's own: by allowing him the freedom of time, did he find himself lured back to Caroline's company? It was too easy, with Lady Elise happy to provide the opportunity.

While careful not to offer false hope to Dana, Rebecca didn't allow it for herself, either. She hoped for a future with Quentin but didn't count it as certain.

"You have a visitor, Miss Rebecca," said Helen after tapping lightly on Rebecca's office door. It was good to have Helen and William back, and not only because Rebecca didn't have to cook anymore.

Rebecca eyed the older woman, wondering if she imagined a frown, while at the same time trying to guess who might be calling. She didn't have any appointments this week, by her own design. "Who is it, Helen?"

"She's waiting in the downstairs parlor. Caroline Norleigh."

Rebecca's gaze went to Dana's, whose brows rose with the first hint of interest in days. Confusion quickly took the place of Rebecca's surprise. Quentin was in London, having phoned her on his way earlier that morning. He said he was on an errand but would return that afternoon. If Lady Caroline were expecting to see him, she'd come to the wrong place.

But that didn't explain why she'd asked Helen to announce her as Rebecca's visitor.

"Do you want to see her alone, or do you want some friendly company?" Dana asked. There was a hint of a smile on her face, confirming what Rebecca had long believed. Getting outside one's own trouble was one of the first steps toward well-being. She should be glad for that, even if Dana was stepping out of her own and into Rebecca's.

She couldn't refuse, though her visitor might interpret the extra company as unexpected reinforcements on the opposing team. "I'd like that."

They went down the stairs to the parlor, where Rebecca saw the tall, willowy shadow of Lady Caroline Norleigh. She didn't have to move to reveal the natural grace she possessed; her posture did it for her. Her clothes enhanced the look: impeccable, tailored. And her hair—so thick and yet calm, the stuff of Rebecca's dreams.

Though they entered together and stopped just inside the doorway, Rebecca felt Lady Caroline's gaze travel then rest on her. The visitor stepped forward, hand outstretched. A smile completed her lovely features, confident she was welcome.

Rebecca shook the woman's cool, slender hand, unable to resist returning the required smile. Beauty inspired that, even from a rival.

"I'm afraid Quentin isn't here," Rebecca said. "He's gone—"

"To London; yes, I know." She never stopped smiling. There was something in that smile, so familiar from the society page, that suddenly seemed as two-dimensional as the photos. But Rebecca rejected the thought, afraid she was assigning fault where none existed. "I came to see you, Rebecca. I hope you don't mind."

"Not at all, though I'm a bit surprised since we've never met."

"And yet we know each other."

Rebecca wasn't sure how to respond to that, and so she turned her attention to Dana, beside her. "You'll be happy to meet Quentin's cousin. Dana Martin Walker, from America."

Lady Caroline offered the same friendly handshake, and Dana returned the smile, even though such a gesture had been so rare from her lately.

"It's actually quite wonderful that you're here as well, Dana." How easily she spoke, as if the three of them were chums of many years. "As it says, where two or more are gathered . . ." She turned to the two sofas in the center of the room, each facing the other, giving Rebecca a chance to exchange bewildered glances with Dana.

Rebecca could tell Dana recognized the phrase from the Bible too. A strange source for Lady Caroline Norleigh, who Quentin reported was not a woman of faith, and never a hint in copious newsprint disputed Quentin's claim.

"'It,' Lady Caroline?" Rebecca asked, following to the sofa where the other woman offered a seat with an elegant palm.

"Why, what else but the Bible, the Word of God? It says where two or three are gathered, He shall be there in the midst."

Rebecca hadn't planned to sit and have a friendly chat—or prayer—with Lady Caroline Norleigh, but just then the couch behind her scooped her up, holding her securely where a moment ago she feared her knees couldn't do the job for which they'd been created.

Dana took the seat next to her more intentionally. "Quentin hasn't mentioned you," Dana said, "but I happened to see a news photograph of you with Quentin recently. I didn't realize that you were a woman of faith. I suppose Quentin told you about Rebecca's deeply held beliefs."

Rebecca listened to Dana's easy tone of voice. She sounded just as kind as she always did, sadness set aside. Rebecca was grateful for that; she wasn't sure she could trust her own voice just yet. Lady Caroline . . . had discovered faith? Wasn't that the one thing Quentin had found lacking in her? If that were no longer the case . . . then what?

"Actually it was Quentin's mother who mentioned Rebecca to me." Caroline took a seat and leaned forward, looking at Rebecca intently. "You must have guessed by now why I know of you. It's in all the papers, how Quentin spends his days with you, his nights with me." She smiled again, a smaller version of the welcoming one, perhaps a touch of embarrassment thrown in.

Rebecca's pulse sped even as her senses tried bombarding her with worry. She *knew* Quentin's faith was real. There was no need for the abashed look on Lady Caroline's face; sharing a roof didn't mean they were sharing a bed, no matter what the news reports—or the lady in question—wanted to intimate.

"He hasn't stopped speaking to me about his newfound faith," Lady Caroline continued, "and it's awakened something in me. Faith isn't something I normally talk about, but since we seem to be connected whether we want to be or not, I thought I could share such private thoughts. Do you mind?"

"Of course not," Rebecca whispered. "It's . . . lovely that Quentin has inspired you."

"Yes, isn't it? Of course I have a lot to learn, but then so does Q. He's so pleased I've recognized the value of faith. It's especially important because we have such a long history together."

"Q?"

Another abashed little smile. "Quentin. I call him Q sometimes."

Rebecca stared, wondering what to say that wouldn't dishonor her own faith, Quentin's, or God Himself. She'd purposely avoided the society pages since the pregnancy kit episode, thinking the papers were after sales more often than a quest for truth. Would they have warned her? Would they have revealed, somehow, this private faith she spoke of? But words continued to abandon her.

"Do you mind if I play the brash American and ask you something really personal, Lady Caroline?" asked Dana.

Rebecca was grateful Dana filled the silence as Rebecca couldn't hope to do. Lady Caroline looked at Dana, the newsprint smile still in place. "Not at all."

"I was under the impression that whatever sort of relationship you had with my cousin Quentin was over some time ago."

Lady Caroline laughed. "Q and I will always be connected; we live in such a small world."

"I supposed that's true, since Quentin's mother invited you to live at the cottage."

Another laugh, one Rebecca couldn't hope to match convincingly. "I've actually left as of this morning. That's another reason I've stopped by, since the Hall was on my way. As I drove by, I said, 'Why not?' Why not stop in and introduce myself, let you know I won't be at the cottage anymore, and why. Perhaps now the silly reporters will leave us be."

While that was a welcome thought, something else was on Rebecca's mind. "And does Quentin know?" she asked softly. "About your moving out, I mean?"

"Yes, we discussed it last night." Lady Caroline laughed again. "He offered me his London flat."

42

I know my brother insists everyone should fulfill each claim or promise that one makes, but honestly, Cosima, I started the day thinking this is not always wise. Simon was here again, and upon seeing him this morning, he said he hoped I would agree to meet him in the family parlor tonight so we could see about that "civil" conversation we agreed to attempt. All day the prospect distracted me, so by this evening I had worked myself into feeling quite shy about the whole thing. Imagine that. Me, shy. I knew I needed to work myself out of that emotion, the quicker the better.

Berrie stood by the fireplace, looking at anything except the man in front of her. She could tell from the periphery of her vision he was every bit as uncomfortable as she was, if she could judge such a thing by the rigid set of his shoulders and the wary way he watched her.

She hadn't felt so unsettled since immediately following her debut ball, when the first of a line of beaus came calling, all of whom found one reason or another to cast her aside. She simply didn't have the temperament to sustain a man's interest. That was hardly necessary now; all she had to do was carry on a simple, polite conversation, not try to convince this man she could play the role of a demure society wife.

"Shall we sit?" Simon invited.

She nodded, taking a seat on the edge of Mrs. Cotgrave's favorite chair. The Wolsey was a lounging chair, but Berrie had no intention of relaxing. She wished it were time for tea, but they'd just finished dessert with the staff and students, and it would be odd indeed to order something from the kitchen just now. Not that she would be able to eat anything, but stirring a spoon might have taken away some of her nervousness.

"I asked Mrs. Cotgrave to see that we're not disturbed," Simon said, taking a seat opposite her. "She entirely agrees that your hours are too long and you ought to take time in the day to sit without someone demanding something of you."

He must have no idea this conversation demanded far more of her than sitting with the children did. "I have a brother who is an MP, Mr. MacFarland. I work no harder than he does. When he's in session, he often arrives home late at night, as I'm sure you do when necessary." A muscle in her back pinched, but she refused to sit at ease.

"Which is perhaps one of the reasons sessions only last a season, not the entire year. And my name, as you know, is Simon."

He'd added that last statement with a softer voice, and her gaze shifted to his. "Before we attempt to have a polite conversation, I have a rather obvious question."

He lifted an inviting brow.

"How do you suppose two people who've barely exchanged a word beyond those in anger will accomplish such a thing? You've as much as said you hate everything English, you don't approve of my work, and more important than either of those facts, our faith seems to be in opposition."

He shook his head. "I obviously don't hate everything English, or I would not be an MP, and I would assuredly not allow Katie to stay in an English-funded school. As for not approving of your work, I thought I made it clear that I admire what you're doing here. I understand you're not looking to cure any of your students or teach them out of their maladies. You accept reality, and I admire you for it."

"You believe that what I do is a trifling matter. This is what I've been called to do. It's the reason I intend never to marry."

"Never?"

"Never."

If he thought their attempt at amiable conversation might be a step toward anything more personal than being able to tolerate each other's company for Katie's sake, he might have shrugged off the effort, stood, and immediately departed. He did none of that. Instead, he offered such a confidently charming smile Berrie was tempted to smile in return.

"Never," he repeated slowly, "is a very strong commitment, Berrie. A long one, too, for someone as young as yourself."

"Yes," she said, her certitude matching his doubt. "You didn't mention our faith. I take it you agree we have a vast difference there, and it is one of the things we should avoid discussing. Along with English law, I assume, despite your position as an MP. Anything else?"

"You miss the point, Berrie. We know we have differences, but that shouldn't make us feel as though we can't achieve a worthwhile discussion about such things. Perhaps we might learn something from each other."

Now it was her turn to doubt his words. "I think we've proven already we can't keep a civil tongue when we're on those topics."

"Perhaps eventually we'll start listening to one another."

No sense trying to avoid at least one topic, then. "I'm ready to listen now, about your faith at least." Berrie was satisfied to see his smile dim. Maybe the task at hand would prove impossible and she could get back to work.

"You've never heard me denounce faith in God."

"How generous of you not to deny His existence," she said. "But were we to discuss our faith with anything less than a difference of opinion, I think you would need to go a bit further than that."

"I don't speak of my faith," he told her.

Something in his tone or manner warned her to leave it at that. Certainly he would prefer if she did. Yet she couldn't. "Katie seems to think you haven't any faith at all."

Simon looked briefly toward the open door. If he was stalling, weighing whether or not to speak about something he would rather not, it was working.

"My faith is still there, even though I've tried to be rid of it. Ultimately, though, I find I'm with the apostle Peter, who asked to whom then shall I go, if not the Lord?"

"Why did you want to be rid of it?"

"My parents died within a year of each other, both suddenly. My father had an accident in our factory. I'll spare you the details, but suffice it to say 'twas not an easy task to watch him die of his injuries. Shortly after that my mother grew sick. Some sort of cancer, the physician told us. She seemed to want to be with God instead of us and was gone in a matter of months. Katie and Innis needed our mother's guidance. Guidance I can't provide. God left us without help."

Simon stopped as if surprised by his own words or maybe the hard tone behind them. He had the same sort of look on his face as when he'd kissed her that first time.

She might not admit she'd welcomed that kiss or the one that followed, but Berrie did welcome his words now, admitting he wasn't without faith. His words proved he wasn't as invulnerable as he wanted everyone to believe. "But God brought Katie here. Perhaps He's sending you the guidance you need, only on His timetable."

"You could be right," he said slowly. "Although the way Katie arrived here didn't seem to be by the hand of God."

She smiled. "No, but nothing happens He isn't aware of."

"And what about you, Berrie?" he asked. "Your faith has never wavered?"

She laughed. "Plenty of times. Not so much in God or His involvement in my life but in the choices He's led me to. I was raised in a family that taught me to sing, to host successful galas, to be able to speak to the Queen and every rank beneath her. My parents are both wonderful people, faithful to God and each other. And yet they only let me be served rather than serve others. When God put the vision of this school in my heart, I knew it would take a servant's heart . . . and I wasn't sure I possessed one." As she heard her own words, she marveled at how easily the truth fell from her lips.

"You believe now that you possess a servant's heart, don't you?"

Berrie nodded slowly, thinking of the tasks she did every day that she never could have done without the strength and assurance of knowing God had placed her where she was.

He leaned forward, an emphatic prelude to his words. "Then your school is a success on every level. For you, the families, the students themselves."

"I'm not sure I expected to hear such a statement from you, Mr. MacFarland." Then, holding his gaze, she added, "Simon."

He welcomed her use of his given name with a smile.

"What of other topics we shouldn't discuss?" she asked, wishing her voice hadn't sounded so breathless. She'd forgotten to breathe for a moment. "Politics, for one. Shall we venture there?"

His smile disappeared and she wondered at herself. Had that

been her purpose—to cancel the sense of companionship that had been sprouting? No wonder she'd pushed every beau in London away; she knew how to fling words like cannonballs.

"I will admit something to you, Berrie, that only occurred to me since meeting you."

She waited.

"I almost accomplished hating the English, because of what happened when the potatoes grew foul those years. Ships that my factory built carried goods outside this country—wheat and barley and livestock—that could have fed the mouths that went hungry for lack of a potato."

The force behind Simon's words made her wonder if he had indeed accomplished that hatred for everything English. Perhaps he wondered it too, because he glowered rather than gazed at her, until in a moment that softened.

"I'm sorry." His smile reappeared through the frown. "I still struggle, as you can see, to remember individuals do not always represent the whole. Precisely why God must have wanted us to meet. I need someone to remind me of that."

"But why would He bring someone whom you can barely tolerate? I should think He would have given you someone you would welcome."

Since he'd moved to the edge of his seat and leaned forward, and she'd chosen to sit on the edge of the Wolsey, they were already closer than necessary. He barely had to reach to take her hands in his. "Do you wish to convince me I cannot tolerate you, Berrie, even when I've admitted more than once I admire you? I'll not accept that all we have in common is an interest in kissing. You are brave, intelligent, hardworking, and above all, stubborn. As Katie observed, you're very much like me."

Berrie looked down at their hands. Something was changing here too quickly for her to sort. She should pull away. Instead her fingers wrapped tighter around his. "I'm not sure two people as opinionated as we are have business attempting even so much as a friendship."

He freed one of her hands, allowing his own to touch her face, to stroke her cheek from the bottom of her ear along her jaw to just beneath her mouth. "Since I've met you," he said, "you've never been far from my mind. I don't want you to be."

He was going to kiss her; she knew he was, and more than that, she wanted him to. But she couldn't let him. That was one area in which they'd already established an affinity, one she couldn't allow. She raised a hand, shifting farther back in the Wolsey but leaving one hand in his. "I told you—I'm not planning to be wed. Not ever."

He frowned. "I don't believe you mean that."

She lifted her free hand to draw his attention to the room and beyond, to all it represented. "I have work. Important work. I don't see how I can be married and work at the same time."

"I realize whatever I say to that will do little for my cause to woo you. If I agree that your work is important, which I believe is true, then you'll have won any argument against marriage. If I say it isn't important, you'll have nothing to do with me." He smiled slowly. "But what if I tell you I planned for you to say that and I've come up with a solution?"

She lifted one brow.

"We have two options, only one of which I think you'll be interested in, but I'll propose both anyway. One would be for you to hire more help and give most of the responsibility to Mrs. Cotgrave, who is obviously well qualified—"

He cut himself off at her frown. She didn't have to speak.

"And the other option would be for us to have a very unconventional marriage." Simon stopped again, his smile broader. "Did you note, Berrie, that I said the word *marriage* without—what did you call it?—without strangulation."

She tried to laugh but could barely breathe. "Well done." Though brief, the words sounded raspy.

"Why couldn't we be married and both of us work? People in Ireland do it all the time."

She wanted to object, to stand, to leave, and started to do so, but her hand wouldn't leave his. "I'm sure they live under the same roof, those farmers and weavers and washerwomen." Not a very strong objection; she knew she could do better than that.

"I admit it wouldn't be ideal, since somehow I have a hard time envisioning you following me about in my career, and I cannot feasibly continue to stay here with you. But my ship-building business in Dublin nearly runs itself. It was necessary to hire the appropriate people once my father died, and it's gone very well, though I'm away for extended periods. My work in Parliament is something else; there will be times I'm away for months on end."

Berrie stood, winning the battle to break contact with him. She faced the fireplace instead of Simon. The stone mantelshelf felt cool beneath her heated palms. "I'm the headmistress here. The only headmistresses I know of are either spinsters, as I plan to be, or widows, like Mrs. Cotgrave."

He was behind her too quickly, his hands on her shoulders. "Since I refuse to volunteer making you a widow, we'll have to consider the options I proposed."

She shook her head, something forming in the pit of her stomach she'd never felt before. A battle of the greatest propor-tion, such odds she had no clue how to overcome. She'd been called to be a servant and yet here was someone trying to pull her back, inviting her to live the life she'd convinced herself wasn't for her. A wife, an emissary to him and not to God alone. It couldn't be, even though her heart suddenly yearned for that very thing, if Simon was to be part of such a picture.

She turned to him, unprepared for how close he stood. She

needed to flee, though her feet would not carry her. His lips came down on hers and she wanted to stop him but didn't.

Until a new sound came from the doorway. Gleeful clapping. "Oh, Simon, you're kissing Miss Berrie! Just like Papa used to kiss Mummy. That means only one thing. You're married now!"

Berrie pulled herself from Simon's gentle grasp, unable to look at either him or his sister. She flew past them both, not stopping until she reached the privacy of her room. If there had been a lock, she would have used it.

43

Rebecca stared at the closed door. Lady Caroline was transferring residence from Lady Elise's cottage to Quentin's London flat?

Quentin had called that morning to let her know he was going to London. How much more private was his flat, without having to share his mother's company and the entourage she normally invited to the country cottage.

"Well, that was odd," Dana said to Rebecca. "Why did Lady Caroline come?"

Rebecca tried summoning a smile but couldn't. Oh, to have the ability to command one as contagious as Lady Caroline's, even if it was two-dimensional. "To let me know she's back in Quentin's life and there's nothing separating them now."

"I'm not sure about that. Do you think her faith sounded sincere?"

"She's moving into his flat. If Quentin's interest is reignited, that's all that matters." How logical she sounded, how completely detached from the situation. She knew the anesthetizing shock of the visit would wear off and she must face the possibility of losing a future she'd only begun hoping for. The fear was there already, beginning to seep through like a fog just starting to gather. Despite her hesitation to start seeing Quentin, despite all of her cautions, she'd been unable to prevent imagining life with him. There was no specific line when her imagination of the future had turned to something she counted on, only the realization that the line had already been crossed. Here she was, with nothing to protect herself against its loss.

Lady Caroline was moving into his flat. How long before that was in the papers?

All her life Rebecca had seen God's hand, God's timing. Her father had told her that her own birth had been God's timing, having been conceived when her mother's body was healthy and strong enough to sustain such a challenge. Since then there had been countless other instances. When Rebecca was little, just when she began begging her father for a dog all her own, God had softened his heart, and a neighbor showed up wanting to give a puppy away. And when she was older, Rebecca made a commitment to support a missionary from their church without the faintest idea how she would earn the seventy-five pounds she'd pledged. Within a week she had an afternoon dog-walking job, one that would last through the summer. Payment: seventy-five pounds. Other cases ranged from dramatic to mundane, but always, always they were there. God's timing revealed itself to Rebecca nearly every day.

When Quentin had arrived this past spring, just before Dana arrived as well, it was like God stepping in and giving Rebecca all she'd lacked in the past few years: a future with a man she could love, a friend with whom to share the excitement.

But maybe she'd misread that timing. Had God allowed Dana to arrive when she did, to face her own struggle and need a friend, so the loss Rebecca might face would be put in perspective? Compared to what Dana faced, the loss of a relationship that barely had time to bud was inconsequential.

She walked up the stairs, wanting what Dana had wanted all week: solitude, to keep company only with her worries. But Dana followed her. "You should talk to him, Rebecca. I've been taking up too much of your time lately, but you don't need to babysit me anymore. You need to ask Quentin what's going on."

Rebecca stopped, frigid. "You're a fine one to give that advice, Dana. Every time your husband calls, you tell him you're busy finishing up the records, that you'll come back to him tomorrow. Three tomorrows have passed and here you are."

Dana averted her gaze. For a moment Rebecca regretted her tone, but she stood firm against the guilt. Maybe sometimes friends were supposed to offer a proverbial kick, and it was only now, knowing she would have to face her own insecurities, that she could suggest Dana do the same.

The telephone rang in Rebecca's office and she hurried to take it, if only to avoid the rest of the conversation with Dana. Rebecca picked up the receiver and heard Quentin's voice. Her heart jabbed at her chest.

"I'll be there in a half hour." Quentin's voice sounded different, hesitant, but that didn't surprise her. "There's something you need to know."

She sucked in a breath and stared at the desk in front of her, certain he would tell her about the conversation he'd had with Lady Caroline the night before, about her discovery of faith, how nothing stood in their way now. Rebecca put two fingers to the bridge of her nose, thinking pressure might stop her tears once they were ready to flow.

"I don't want Dana to be blindsided," he was saying, much to her confusion. *Dana?* "I've just come from Heathrow to fetch Aidan. He called last night when you and Dana were out walking, and I talked with him."

Now her gaze flew back to Dana, panicked. Dana stepped farther into the room, a frown emerging on her face.

"Did you tell him . . . ? You know, about the baby?"

Dana's eyes were wider now, filling with the tears Rebecca thought would be in her own eyes a moment ago.

"No. Look, he's sitting right here. He's been worried about Dana, and I don't blame him. I guess I should have told both of you this last night, but Aidan asked me to wait until it was too late for Dana to tell him not to come. Personally, I agreed. I told him I'd pick him up as soon as he could get a flight. It's for the best, Rebecca."

"Yes, yes, I'm sure you're right." She sucked in a breath, still looking at Dana. "I'll tell her Aidan is on his way here with you, right now. And you're right. It is for the best." She hung up a moment later, facing Dana. "Now neither one of us has a way to push off what must be done."

Dana nodded, her face solemn. "For the best, you said." She eyed Rebecca. "Best to get it over with, for me. You're probably right. I know it has to be done. But for you?"

"If this relationship is to be done with . . . the sooner the better, as they say."

She'd meant to sound hard or at least assured. The wobble in the middle betrayed the tender vulnerability amassing inside her.

44

My dear Cosima,

I have nothing with which to compare the moment I realized Simon was sincere in his proposal. Should I have thought of Lord Welby, who danced with me so many times that night of the ball and then asked to speak to my father when I returned from my visit to Ireland with you? No, in retrospect I am glad Lord Welby never announced intentions to my father, as I am sure any marriage between us would have been dull with our inevitable indifference.

I am anything but indifferent to Simon. Do you know, Cosima, that although he has kissed me in a way no gentleman should, I believe him to be one? It is clear if I were back home with no future other than marriage, it would be Simon I would want without doubt.

But my life is different now. I finally let go of my dreams for marriage. Yes, it was a struggle, yet I have accustomed myself to a future as a headmistress, to being

*the servant God intended me to be. How can I be a true
servant and return to life in London or take it up anew in
Dublin, no less than the wife of an MP, along with the
lifestyle that would entail?*

*Oh, Cosima, do you see how that would be turning my
back on what God has called me to do? I could no more
abandon this mission than I could stop breathing.*

*Through my door last night, I told Simon I must have
time. He gave me no more than the evening and the night.
He expects to speak to me this morning after drills.*

I have no idea what I shall say to him. . . .

"It occurred to me after I left," Simon said, watching the others
return to the manor after drills, "that the turn in our discussion last evening might have been a surprise to you. I admit I
entertained the notion of marriage before yesterday, but I hadn't
meant to broach the topic so soon."

Berrie folded her hands together, then let them go. "I appreciate the fact that the first time you mentioned marriage it was
because you believed you'd overstepped propriety, but—"

He shook his head, slowing their step with a touch to her
arm. "That first time I mentioned marriage was the first time I'd
ever said such a word aloud, at least in relation to myself. Last
night was entirely different. I've considered the matter, and I
believe our marriage would bring both of us happiness."

"It was kind of you to share that decision with me," she said,
"though you've presented it as if I have no say in the matter."

He laughed. "Your kiss made it clear you feel the same way."

She stopped, watching the last of the children being led into
the manor house, knowing she should be following. The moment

seemed symbolic of the decision she must make: the school . . . or Simon?

Myriad thoughts battled in her brain, making her heart beat so erratically the blood eddied along its route. She stopped. "I cannot . . . think, Simon."

He stepped closer. "Do you want to marry me?"

Berrie took a step back, knowing his close proximity tainted her already unsteady thought process. There was only one thing to do, and she knew it. Be honest. "I used to hope for everything you offer." She cast him a self-conscious smile, not used to sharing such intimate thoughts. "I wanted to be married, have children, run a household, do all of the social things my parents have always done. But somehow that didn't seem to happen for me. You're not the first person to think I'm difficult. When I saw the need for a school such as this, I knew why. I wasn't meant to be married; I was meant to serve these children and their families instead—children many others don't want to be around."

"It's an honorable goal," Simon said quietly.

She nodded, holding his gaze, seeing his smile dim. "It is honorable," she said, "and one I still want to fulfill. We've only just begun."

He was silent a long moment, looking at everything except her. Reaching a hand to his forearm, she willed him to look at her. At last, he did.

"I don't believe I could be both headmistress and wife if I'm to do either one very well."

He blinked, nodded, and stepped back, letting her hand fall to her side without his arm there to hold it up. "Yes, I can see you would think that." He offered an ineffective smile and a quick glance. "Whatever you do, Berrie, you do with passion—wholeheartedly. Teach, argue. Kiss."

Blood rushed to her cheeks and she could do nothing to stop it. He was right.

"I'll be leaving for London next month," he said quietly.

"Katie is used to my long trips away. She should give you no trouble about that."

The thought that he would be altogether absent sent a wave of unexpected panic through her, though it was undoubtedly best. Could she be his friend, truly his friend? one day hope for him to find someone else to marry, and then watch it happen?

That was one thing she would not do with any passion.

45

Padgett threw herself into her father's arms when he stepped through the door. Aidan twirled her around and kissed her cheek, then asked about the new toy in her hand. She introduced him to her replica of Emma, the fuzzy little lamb that always needed to be rescued.

Rebecca watched, a weight in her heart at seeing the kind of family she wanted. She didn't want to show her need for one, aware of Quentin's eyes on her. Her eyelids went down like twin doors closing off anything from inside or out. Even with what Dana and Aidan faced, whether a healthy or an impaired child on the way, she knew Aidan was committed to the two women in his life already, Dana and Padgett, and would be to this new life too. That commitment was in his eyes, visible through the moment of awkwardness when he settled Padgett back to the floor and faced Dana for the first time in almost three weeks.

"Hey," he said gently, "I missed you."

Rebecca saw Dana try to smile, but the effort was lost when she pressed herself against him, eyes closed, a soft sob escaping.

"Padgett," said Rebecca, "why don't we let your mom and dad say hello on their own for a little while? Would you come with Quentin and me down to the farm?"

"Okay, only I want to show Daddy how I can ride a pony, and he has to meet the real Emma." She turned to her father, who was still holding Dana and showing no sign of letting go. "Do you remember, Daddy? The *real* lamb I named that I told you about on the phone?"

He drew one hand from Dana's back to rumple his daughter's hair. "Yes, I remember, sweetheart. We'll meet you at the cuddle farm in a few minutes, okay?"

Rebecca took Padgett's hand, leading the way. Maybe Rebecca was doing what Dana had done for the past five days, putting off what must be done. Taking care of Padgett was one way of not facing whatever needed to be said between her and Quentin. A small delay, still welcome.

The sky was slightly overcast, a faint fog in the distance that muted hedgerows on the horizon. Rebecca kept her eyes on Padgett, rigidly avoiding contact with Quentin. She did little more than glance his way, catching a smile, a look of contentment.

At the cuddle farm, the lamb approached Padgett as one friend greeting another. Rebecca watched from the gate, aware when Quentin came up beside her, wanting to resist when he slipped an arm about her waist but welcoming it instead.

"Maybe things will get back to normal around here now," he whispered.

"What do you mean?"

He kissed the side of her face just below her temple. "Maybe now you'll be able to spare some time for me."

"The Featherby judges are coming next week," she said, drawing in a quick breath because he kissed her ear and it tickled. His kiss confused her; why had Lady Caroline made a point of telling her about her faith, about Quentin's offer of his flat, if it wasn't because Quentin was once again interested in her?

"Featherby judges!" Quentin moaned. "Now I have to share you with *them*?"

She stepped outside of his reach, walking farther down the

fence towaard Padgett, who was running with Emma. Quentin acted as if nothing was different. "I thought I was the one doing the sharing."

He caught her hand. "Sharing me? Oh no. The judges are in your hands; I haven't helped much in that regard."

She shook her head, facing him squarely. He wasn't dense; she knew that. So was he keeping the truth from her intentionally? "With Caroline Norleigh."

He frowned. "Now it's my turn to ask what you mean."

"She visited here today." Rebecca would have preferred he told her about the conversation they'd had the night before, about his offer for her to live in his London flat, but as usual she couldn't wait. "She told me the two of you had a discussion last night about her faith, among other things."

"Yes, we did. She said she's investigating Christianity, and I encouraged her. That's what you would want me to do, isn't it?"

"Of course." She was supposed to be pleased. Didn't God's Word say the angels in heaven rejoiced each time someone finds true faith? Caroline Norleigh was no exception; maybe the angels were rejoicing this very moment. All Rebecca felt was a weight at the bottom of her stomach because Quentin didn't tell her of his offer for Caroline to move into his flat. "She also said she was moving out of the cottage."

He nodded. "I thought you'd be pleased about that."

Rebecca watched him closely. "She said you offered her your place in London."

Nothing on his face changed. No shade of discomfort appeared on his brow, around his relaxed mouth, in the blue eyes that had been in his family for so many generations. "She doesn't get on well with her mother. It's better when they're living apart. I suppose that's one of the reasons she was so receptive to my mother's invitation to the cottage."

"And so receptive to your offer now?"

"I suppose." Quentin returned her stare. "I'm not staying there, as you know. And it's only temporary. She's planning to find something of her own."

Rebecca wished she had more time to decipher her feelings, the chance to step back and try seeing what was rational and what was not. Here he stood, and even though she could have told him they needed to talk, alone, without watching Padgett or waiting for Dana and Aidan to arrive at any moment, she didn't want to wait.

"You told me the only thing lacking in Caroline was that you were no longer in the same circle—because of your faith. It appears she's joined you."

"Maybe." He took a step closer, and Rebecca took a step back. His mouth tightened. "But even if it's true, nothing has changed between you and me."

Those were almost all the words she'd wanted to hear, but even as she heard them, she saw the disappointment in his eyes that he'd had to utter them. Then nothing further, nothing about other reasons he no longer wanted to see Caroline, other reasons they could no longer be the couple they once were.

"Why is it, Rebecca, that I'm the one trying to persuade this relationship forward? You're always looking for some reason we shouldn't be together, and I'm beginning to wonder why."

"I'm afraid." The words left her lips before she could stop them, the two words that were the most honest, the most vulnerable she'd uttered to him. "I don't want to be, but I am."

"What are you afraid of? I've told you whatever I once felt for Caroline is gone."

She shook her head. "You told me you ended that relationship because you'd changed, God had changed you. Now she has the chance to let God change her. Maybe the reason you ended that relationship no longer exists."

He shook his head too fast, and she knew he wasn't really listening. So she went on. "I've seen my father miss my mother for more than a dozen years, Quentin. He's told me, all these years, that missing her was worth it because of the happiness they had when they were married. But seeing him miss her, knowing he lives with such an ache every day of his life, I'm just not sure the years they had together were worth all that pain."

She hadn't intended to say any of that, hadn't considered revealing such raw emotion before this moment, but listening to herself, she knew it was true. When Quentin tried taking her hand again, she pulled it away, refusing his touch. "You see, don't you, Quentin? I want to love you, but I can't. I won't. Not until I'm sure it'll be worth it if pain is part of the package. And I don't think you can be sure about anyone else—me or anyone in your future—until Lady Caroline is as convinced as you are that she is in your past. Maybe she senses something isn't finished— maybe your mother senses the same thing—because it *isn't*."

His face showed what she feared most: consideration of her idea.

"If she really has found a faith that's compatible with yours," Rebecca said, "you need to find out if that's all that was missing before. I won't have you wondering about her after we've gone further together, or worse, after we're married. You see it, don't you? that you can't go forward until whatever was between you and Caroline is really over?"

He turned away, rubbed a hand over his eyes, looked out. She did too, watching Padgett pet the rabbits inside the cuddle farm fence. She hadn't expected their conversation to take this turn. What she thought, hoped, prayed would happen was that he would assure her nothing had changed between them. He'd done that, only it hadn't ended there.

She might wish it had, but there was no going back.

46

I am sorry I have not written to you of late, Cosima, but I believe you are better off having been spared anything I might have posted. Only my Lord and my God can know the depth of my sin, how selfish I have been, impossibly wishing I could serve a husband and this school. Surely Simon would have but briefly put up with a wife married to him as well as a mission.

Forgive me. I promised myself I would not write to you until I had gained some control over my thoughts and self-pity. It appears I have begun writing again too soon.

But something horrid happened today that I must share with you at once, and ask you to somehow explain to my father and brother. I am sure they will hear of it soon unless a miracle intervenes.

It began yesterday when Eóin's father came for him quite unexpectedly, pulling away his son with the promise we would see no more donations in Eóin's name.

I was rightly concerned, of course, deciding I would

visit the family after an appropriate period of time had passed. Then this morning Tessie's family came for her under similar circumstances.

The only thing they have in common is both families hail from nearby. And then . . .

"A letter for you, Miss Berrie, by special courier. From Mr. Truebody."

Berrie looked up from her desk, accepting the letter from Daisy. The note was brief. A summons, without explanation, demanded her presence that very afternoon.

Berrie frowned. She would have to leave immediately if she was to make it by the appointed hour. She was tempted to jot a note in return, stating countless other obligations she needed to attend. Dropping all of them for an unspecified summons seemed hardly fair. So she found Mrs. Cotgrave in the art room and showed her the letter.

Mrs. Cotgrave's face reflected Berrie's concern. "You mustn't ignore it," Mrs. Cotgrave advised. "It could provide an explanation for Tessie and Eóin."

She'd tried convincing herself that missing their children had been the reason their families had wanted them home. Now she wasn't so certain.

Mrs. Cotgrave volunteered to accompany her. Berrie wanted to agree, but she knew with both of them gone at the same time, the teachers and attendants would have a hard time of classes, dinner, and chapel. Taking little more than a moment to retrieve a shawl, Berrie sent Daisy to Jobbin for the wagon.

Travel to the village went smoothly except for the worry bouncing around inside of Berrie. Everything at the manor had been going well. Two students were to start next week, and even now Duff was in Dublin searching for families in need of their services. Already with sixteen boys and three girls, the manor was getting crowded. Their limit was to have been twenty. With Tessie and Eóin gone, they could take in two more.

Between her worries, thoughts of Simon were never far from Berrie's mind. Would he be concerned, knowing two students had been mysteriously pulled and Mr. Truebody had summoned her? Would Simon, had she accepted his proposal, be at her side?

She imagined him on one of the ships his manufactory had built. Was he, even now, crossing the Irish Sea on his way to London? How long would he be gone? Did he, like her brother Peter, stay in London through the fall until the holidays and then return to Parliament in January through the spring?

An ache in her chest reminded her she missed him.

Berrie arrived at Mr. Truebody's at the appointed time with barely a minute to spare. When she tapped on his outer door, a familiar housemaid answered, showing Berrie to the office. She waited just outside, hoping he wouldn't keep her waiting too long. She fully intended to have Jobbin back with the wagon in plenty of time for the children's regular routine.

After a few minutes she stepped closer to tap on the door, even though the housemaid had already done so to announce her arrival. The sound of muffled voices stopped her hand midair. Mr. Truebody wasn't alone.

Her lips tightened. Had his urgent summons been nothing more than another exercise of his power, requesting she respond immediately even though he was busy tending to other matters? The idea was enough to raise her knuckles once again, intent on using them.

But the door opened, and before her stood Mr. Truebody. She saw immediately his color was unusual; though his cheeks were flushed, the rest of his skin looked sallow, enhanced by a touch of perspiration along what had once been his hairline.

"I believe you know Mr. Flegge."

Surprise sent her gaze the constable's way before Mr. True-body had finished speaking.

"And of course Mr. Denmore and Mr. Axbey."

She nodded; the former an inspector, the latter a surveyor. She knew them to be at Mr. Truebody's beck and call, possessing no mind of their own but one and the same to do his bidding. Perhaps if she'd learned to be as subservient she might not resist Mr. Truebody's rigid attention to detail.

What business could concern all present, she had no idea. Mr. Flegge's inclusion troubled her; why would Mr. Truebody have called him in? She knew well enough that he tenaciously separated the constable's business from his own office of justice of the peace.

Mr. Truebody spoke as he went around to his seat behind the large oak desk that took up most of the room. "We have before us two documents, Miss Hamilton. One—" he held up a sheet with a legal seal at the bottom—"is a lawsuit about to be filed against your institution. The other—" he now held up what appeared to be a newspaper—"is more damning than that. A note to the general public, warning them against the harm children may encounter were they to be admitted to Escott Manor."

For the first time standing in Mr. Truebody's presence, Berrie wished for a chair. Not even during her initial visit, when so much was riding upon his approval, had her limbs felt so weak. "But . . . why?"

"Do you have any idea where one Mr. Duff Habgood is at this very moment?" Mr. Flegge asked. He looked at her as if he enjoyed the secret he held.

Too befuddled to sort endless fears erupting inside, Berrie grasped one thought. She knew where Duff was; she'd sent him herself. "In Dublin. There are so many families living poorly in the city, how much harder it must be for those with children of special circumstance. So I asked him to seek families in need of our . . ." She let her voice dwindle away, as not only had she lost eye contact with the constable who'd asked the question, but all the men were shaking their heads before she'd finished her statement.

"He is indeed in Dublin," said Mr. Truebody, his voice more nasal than ever, "but is in fact the guest of Dublin jail, held on charges of ravishment. The victim was housed in your facility, Miss Hamilton, which, at least according to this report in the *Telegraph*, is evidently a house of impropriety that touches even upon your reputation."

Words refused to form for Berrie, her thoughts were in such a jumble. Duff . . . ravishment? It couldn't be; not sweet Duff. And had she detected a more personal accusation, one that somehow included her?

Mr. Truebody raised a finger to draw back her attention. "As you will recall when the Lunacy Commission first sympathized with your petition to open Escott Manor as a hospital for the infirm, I expressed my concern over having one so young, inexperienced, and unmarried in your position. And now you can see my concerns were entirely valid."

She glanced at the faces around her, all accusatory. All was not lost, as these men seemed to think. It couldn't be.

"Our first concern," continued Mr. Truebody, "is the children. We cannot permit the integrity of those living under the same roof to be in any question."

Did he think for a single moment that wasn't *her* first concern? "I'm sure this is all a horrible misunderstanding. Duff Habgood would never accost anyone; I assure you of that."

"Unfortunately that may not be the case. Regardless, a reputation ruined is damaging to an institution, particularly where children are kept."

Berrie turned to Mr. Flegge. "What can you tell me about this case against Mr. Habgood?"

His lips parted but Mr. Truebody cleared his throat, cutting off whatever the other man might have said.

"Then there is the subject of your own offense." His voice was gratingly nasal now. Berrie wanted to wince at the sound but willed herself perfectly still.

Chin high, she met his gaze. "I assure you I have done nothing to compromise either the school's reputation or my own."

"Is that so? And do you still house a girl by the name of Katie MacFarland?"

"I do."

"And is she indeed the sister of Simon MacFarland, an elected official to the House of Commons? the very man who wrote to me regarding the residency of a woman and her child, that I might consider bending the rules?"

Masses of unknown origin began simultaneously gathering in the pit of Berrie's stomach and at the base of her throat. "Yes."

"According to Miss Katie MacFarland," said Mr. Truebody as he picked up the newspaper report, "you and Mr. MacFarland are married. Yet there has been no such legal ceremony that I am aware of. And in my position—" he eyed her harshly—"I would be aware of such a thing, would I not? Are you, in fact, married to this Simon MacFarland?"

"Of course not!"

"Why is it, then, that his sister reports you and he are—" he picked up the newsprint, adding spectacles to the bridge of his nose—"'sure and truly wed, as they behave just like my beloved Mum and Papa before they went to heaven. Kissing and such'?"

Berrie slapped her palms to her cheeks, feeling them as hot as two coals and surely as red. She wanted to flee but knew that would do nothing to aid her cause.

"Have you, Miss Hamilton, engaged in improper behavior even before a resident?" Mr. Truebody asked.

He waited and she knew she must say something.

Mr. Truebody's stare lingered. "As you know, the population in a facility like yours is highly impressionable. Such behavior, particularly from an unmarried woman such as yourself, is not to be tolerated."

The scrutiny of each man bore down on her and Berrie felt the collective weight until it threatened to overcome her. To swoon just now might prove a blessed delay, but a delay just the same, not an escape. She gulped a breath of air, straightened her shoulders, and met no one's stare. "There has been a misunderstanding."

"Then you were not engaging in improper behavior?" Mr. Truebody asked.

"There was . . . a kiss," she admitted. "Nothing more improper than that." She could hardly tell them it came with a proposal of marriage, not when her refusal would be the equivalent of public humiliation for Simon.

"Need we remind you, Miss Hamilton," said Mr. Truebody, "such behavior is not tolerated in polite society and less so in a hospital where you are responsible for the most vulnerable of children."

"It wasn't a public demonstration," Berrie said, her voice wavering. "It was a misunderstanding on Katie's part. She believes any sign of affection between a man and woman to be a sign of marriage."

"I am a reasonable man, Miss Hamilton, and certainly willing to take into consideration that this quote comes from an inmate," Mr. Truebody stated. "I've taken it upon myself to contact Mr. MacFarland. He is under no obligation to return here, of course, as there is no legal recourse against his actions with you unless you tell the constable here and now that Mr. MacFarland forced his attentions upon you?"

Diverting her gaze to the floor, she shook her head.

Mr. Truebody sighed, straightening the papers on the desk

before him. He looked at them instead of Berrie. "Given the fact that Mr. Habgood has been arrested, whatever happened between you and Mr. MacFarland is the lesser of the two concerns. Yet the Commission must believe you possess the purest virtue. Not only must the Commission believe it but the families of your students must believe it as well. Once lost, a good reputation is hard to regain."

"Surely there is a way to make this right." Her voice was hoarse with the lump still there. "Not only for myself, but surely for Mr. Habgood. Perhaps the victim isn't a victim at all, only under a false impression of having received some sort of improper attention from him. To some of our more sensitive students, even a glance can be an affront."

"The victim was not one of your residents," claimed Mr. Flegge. "She is fully capable of stating irrefutable facts."

If Berrie thought, even for a moment, Tessie had issued the extraordinary claim and that was why her family had come for her, she abandoned it now. "Am I to know the name of this victim?"

Mr. Truebody held up a hand in Mr. Flegge's direction, effectively silencing the other man. "It is known only to those involved in the case, in deference to the dignity of the victim. We have it on the highest authority this woman is of sound mind and will testify to being accosted by one Mr. Duff Habgood. Under the roof of Escott Manor, a so-called haven for the innocent."

"Forgive me for saying so, but will justice protect only the dignity of the victim and not that of Escott Manor, which is also blameless?"

"Blameless, Miss Hamilton? Even were you proven innocent of the personal transgressions alleged in the news report, you've shown yourself to be a poor judge of character in having hired someone capable of such a heinous act. As I warned when you petitioned, scandal must be avoided at all cost."

Mr. Truebody stood now, staring down hard at Berrie. His skin fairly glistened, mesmerizing in its wet pallor. "Which is why I demand that you leave Escott Manor Hospital for the Mentally Infirm until the truth can be ferreted out, both about your misconduct and Mr. Habgood's. Obviously further funding will be pending developments at Mr. Habgood's trial."

"Leave?" The word was barely more than a whisper. Through her haze of misery, another word stood out among the rest. "Pending? If Mr. Habgood is found innocent of such charges, there is still a chance for the school to survive?"

Mr. Truebody removed his spectacles, his long, narrow face smug in his regard of her. "I answer to benefactors, Miss Hamilton, as well as the Lunacy Commission. It will be up to them. Rest assured if Mr. Habgood is found guilty, as everything indicates today, then Escott Manor will indeed be closing its doors."

47

Rebecca watched the taxi pull away from the Hall, taking Aidan and the single bag he'd brought. Padgett waved and cried, but her mother's hug soon dispelled the tears. "We'll be together again in a while, sweetie." Her words, meant as a balm to Padgett, were slow to sink in.

Or maybe it was something else, something even Padgett was somehow sharp enough to discern. Rebecca noted the imprecise promise, wondering how long it would be before Dana was ready to resume the life she'd arrived with in the United Kingdom. For the past two days while Aidan was here, he'd been discreet in his persuasion, mindful that Padgett heard every word. It was clear to Rebecca. He wanted Dana with him.

And it was just as clear Dana wanted the same thing, but she hadn't talked to Rebecca about why she wasn't letting that happen.

As far as Rebecca knew, they hadn't yet told Padgett about the coming addition to their family. There was time, of course. Dana had said she calculated herself to be a couple of months along. Dana did agree to see a physician, and she made an appointment they would keep the next afternoon.

Once the taxi was out of sight, they went back into the Hall. Helen came for Padgett, having promised to let her help bake scones for the afternoon Victorian tea that had been set up weeks ago. One last practice run with the new wardrobe, with the Featherby judges arriving later that week.

"Would you like anything?" Rebecca asked. "Tea? A snack?"

Dana shook her head. She'd been eating better and rarely sick during Aidan's visit, but Rebecca had observed the nausea was never far from an empty stomach.

"I want to talk," Dana said, leading the way into the small front parlor. The weather was fine today, so the tea and the women hosting it would be served on the veranda instead. "And for once I don't want to talk about myself."

Rebecca took a seat. "I'll talk if you do," she warned. "A fair exchange."

Dana shrugged. "You haven't said a word about where Quentin's been hiding these past few days while Aidan was here. Where is he?"

"I expect he's in London."

Dana frowned. "With Lady Caroline?"

Rebecca tried a casual shrug but the movement was tense, spastic. "I don't really know. I won't say he's 'with' her—that's rather unfair to the faith he's shown, isn't it? But yes, with her . . ." She stopped herself, tightness closing her throat; knowing the next word would quiver, she chose to end the sentence instead.

"Did he tell you he'd chosen her? Is that why he left?"

"Not exactly. I'm the one who suggested he should go, decide whether or not that relationship is really over." She lifted a steady gaze to meet Dana's, putting words to what she wanted to feel. "I don't regret it."

"Of course not. You have to know."

Rebecca nodded.

"He'll be back," Dana whispered, the exact words Rebecca wanted to tell herself and refused to do.

She shook away sudden tears and laughed. "Of course he will. This is his home."

"You know what I mean."

"Maybe." Rebecca pulled in a steadying breath. "In any case, I've been thinking about what's next for me. I have to stay through the Featherby visit, of course. After that, I think I will be contacting my father. He's been wanting me to work for him since I graduated, and I think it's time I took him up on that offer."

"What? You—you'll leave the Hall? You can't!"

Rebecca laughed again, more a reflex than genuine amusement. "Of course I can; the Dark Ages are over. I can leave the fiefdom any time I wish."

Dana shook her head. "But one Seabrooke or another has been under this roof for hundreds of years."

Those tears she'd tried shaking away showed up again, stinging. "What else can I do, Dana? Watch him raise a family here?"

Dana looked about to protest, perhaps an assurance that such a thing wouldn't happen, but said nothing instead. Maybe she'd learned by Rebecca's aversion to false promises that she didn't want to hear any either.

"Now," Rebecca said, her voice a little too loud, a little firmer than intended. She successfully warded off the lump. "What about you, Dana? Why didn't you go back to Ireland with your husband?"

"I wanted to," she said softly. "I did. I just couldn't. Not yet. It wasn't him; I told him that. What would I do there except obsess about all this alone? His hours are horrendous. The only way I've been able to hide any of my worries from Padgett is because I've had your help. If it were just her and me all day, every day . . . I won't do that to her. I can't, not until I'm adjusted to this whole idea."

Dana closed her eyes, but tears slipped out anyway, glistening two paths down her smooth cheeks. "I know there's hope, but I don't feel it." She opened her eyes. "He deserves a healthy child, what any other woman except me would have been able to give him."

Rebecca slid from her seat, taking a spot next to Dana and pulling her into a hug. "He has you and he has Padgett, and from what I can see, that's already made him happy. Whatever's ahead will be a further blessing."

"A blessing? I think Cosima called it a curse, and at the moment I agree with her."

She cried then, and Rebecca offered no words, just her shoulder. Tears stung her own eyes for Dana and for herself. This was hope again, proving itself an enemy. Dana for a healthy child, Rebecca for a husband.

Even the Bible acknowledged what Rebecca felt. *Hope deferred makes the heart sick.*

48

Cosima, I cannot express what panic I felt, coupled with shame. How could this be happening? Duff under arrest and my own reputation tainted? No matter to me, but the school must be saved!

I left Mr. Truebody's office desperate to find Duff and learn the truth. His exoneration is the key. Jobbin, bless his heart, took me at once to Dublin. There are three jails in the city and more poverty than I imagined. God was with me, though, as I tried to remind myself throughout this day. At the second public detention hall, I was assured Duff was in its unfortunate residence. I asked to see him and was told visiting hours had passed, and so I must return tomorrow morning.

Tomorrow. Ah, yes, tomorrow I must also end my residence at the school. I plan to take a room at the Quail's Stop Inn until this horrid mix-up is straightened out.

Never have I prayed for guidance so hard. I looked

into the faces of our little ones to say good night, really meaning good-bye. I looked into Katie's guileless eyes; if she had only kept her words to herself at least part of our trouble could have been abated. I cannot blame her; she meant no harm. I can scarcely bear it. Am I failing in the one task our Lord God has assigned to me?

Simon will soon know the school is in danger of collapse, yet I cannot ask him—

I began writing this last night and fell asleep at my desk. The splatter of ink is mixed with my tears. I left early this morning. There was no word from Simon, and so I will not continue to hope in that regard. I wanted to be first in the line of visitors at the Dublin jail. Duff was relieved to see me. . . .

"I feared you'd believe the charges, Miss Berrie," Duff said in the form of a greeting. There was something new in him that Berrie wouldn't have believed could form in so short a time of incarceration. Half his face was covered in days' worth of stubble, but that was not nearly as disconcerting as seeing him in chains. Wrists and ankles both shackled. Berrie drew her gaze from the unsettling sight, finding less comfort in the depths of pain in his eyes.

"I don't believe a word, Duff, only you must tell me what this is about. Mr. Truebody gave me very little information, and the newspaper only says a woman reports you've accosted her. They give no name. Who is it, Duff, claiming something so outrageous?"

His dark eyes, already nearly absent of life, went dimmer still. "Finola."

She drew in a quick breath. "Finola O'Shea? *Why*, Duff?"

He shook his head desperately. "I did nothing! I wanted to care for her and her little one, too, but never once did I touch her or say an untoward word."

With a wide table between them, Berrie knew she couldn't touch him even in comfort, especially with his hands tethered. "I believe you, Duff. Only we must clear this up, or the school's future is at risk. Why should Finola do this?"

"I have no guess!" His face, his voice, the droop of his shoulders all spoke the anguish behind his words. "I—I wanted to love her, but I never touched her. I vow 'tis the truth."

Berrie nodded. "We'll prove it, then, Duff. Somehow. Even now, I've sent a note to my brother and sister-in-law, asking their help."

He was shaking his head. "They want a speedy trial because of my position at the school. 'Twill be over by the time anyone from London can help."

He was undoubtedly right. Berrie stood. "The truth will be heard, Duff. I'll do my best to make sure Finola is the one to tell it. She must be made to explain why she's conjured this lie."

Nothing made sense. If Duff was innocent, as Berrie believed to the depth of her soul, why should Finola bring such a charge? Surely she wouldn't want the school to be endangered; it was her future! Once Conall was old enough, didn't Finola plan to return? There was nothing for her to gain, only a future to lose, in such false accusations.

Berrie must find her. If she'd mentioned the town where she'd once lived, where her brother still resided, Berrie couldn't recall. Even Duff knew only that Finola had come from County Dublin, somewhere north of the city. Cosima might know how to find her cousin, but Berrie had no time to wait for letters to go back and forth between Dublin and London. So she asked Duff the name of the barrister who would be representing him, and the bailiff told her where she could find the lawyer. To Berrie's relief, Jobbin was able to take her there without delay. Unfortunately the lawyer was not found in his office, though a clerk told her he would return in a few hours' time. She asked the clerk, a round-faced, friendly apprentice to the law, if she could learn the whereabouts of someone named in a suit against one of their clients.

Instantly the clerk lost the image of youthful innocence she'd imagined him to possess. He aged before her eyes and grew cold as well, stating even if their lawyer was in his office this moment, he could not divulge such information. He then showed her the way outside, though she could easily have found the door on her own.

This was not to be easy, but Berrie refused to believe the task impossible. The clerk's behavior told her it would be futile to seek the lawyer who'd once represented Finola on her brother's behalf, the one demanding half the estate. Undoubtedly that office would prove as protective of its client as this one had been.

Finola had a friend right here in Dublin. Berrie remembered the name—Nessa O'Brien O'Donnell—and how Finola had fairly sung the rhythm of it. Nessa would surely know how to find Finola, and with a bit of luck, Finola might even still be there, staying with this friend.

But in such a large city, how could someone with as common a name as *O'Donnell* be found? She told Jobbin the challenge. All she knew of the woman was that she must possess some means, for she and Finola had met during Finola's more prosperous childhood at a girls' school on the north side of the city. Jobbin tipped his hat and directed Berrie back to the wagon with the smile of a man who knew what next to do. A Nessa O'Brien O'Donnell of little means would be hard to find in a city like

Dublin. But a Nessa O'Brien O'Donnell with anything higher
than the most modest of respectable homes and from a certain
girls' school? He knew the pubs in both rich and poor neighborhoods, and both were frequented by those who knew their neigh-
bors. The rich ones would be a much narrower search at that. He
estimated they would find Mrs. O'Donnell within two hours'
time.

The search might have been quick for Jobbin, but for Berrie,
waiting in the wagon while he visited one pub after another proved
nearly intolerable. Her mind hopped from worry to worry, especially when she smelled the scent of whiskey on the older man's
breath.

"I have to raise a glass, don't you know," he told her, "otherwise who would trust me with a bit of information, harmless or
otherwise?"

She received the pronouncement tacitly, adding a new prayer
to her long list of others: for Jobbin's safe sobriety. Still, she
looked for a wobble in his step or a slip of the reins when he was
driving the wagon.

Her prayers were answered before she detected any compromise on Jobbin's behavior. After a half dozen pubs in the northern
neighborhoods, he had narrowed down the girls' schools, then
the O'Donnell and O'Brien families. Before long, Jobbin pulled
up before a three-story home in a respectable neighborhood.
Berrie let him help her alight, grateful he appeared at the ready.
The humble Escott Manor wagon wasn't a Hamilton carriage,
but Berrie knew how to hold herself as if it were.

A maid answered the door, and Berrie would have handed
her an announcement card had she not left such habits and pos-
sessions on the other side of the Irish Sea. Instead, Berrie told
the servant her name, asking if Mrs. O'Donnell was at home and
could receive a brief visit. Berrie was told to wait.

Standing inside the front door, Berrie couldn't hear much of what went on beyond the entry alcove. If Finola was indeed here with little Conall at her side, they were either napping or perhaps out of doors in a yard if one was to be found with such a city house as this. Humbler than the London town house Berrie had known all her life, this was still a comfortable place. Dark wood-work graced the hall and stairway to the left, and to the right she saw a parlor furnished with well-upholstered chairs, a settee, and a piano. Every furniture leg in the room, as far as Berrie could see, was draped in a familiarly modest and up-to-date fashion.

The maid returned, leading Berrie into the parlor. "Mrs. O'Donnell will be down shortly, miss," she said. "May I bring in some tea?"

"No, thank you," Berrie said, despite her desire for something warm and soothing. The thought of putting something into her roiling stomach both enticed and revolted her. "I've no wish to be an inconvenience. I shan't stay more than a few moments."

The maid curtsied. "Very well, miss."

The room hosted a variety of bric-a-brac, and for a moment Berrie pictured Conall here, with his unsteady gait, his inability to understand the word *no*, his attraction to shiny items like crys-tal and porcelain. Any number of items would be in danger if he were allowed access.

"Miss Hamilton?"

Berrie turned at the inquiring voice behind her, seeing a woman enter who was about Berrie's own age. She was pretty; her eyes were small, her nose narrow, but her smile demanded all notice. Stark white, straight teeth were the epitome of health.

"I'm told you have a few questions for me, only I don't believe we've had the honor of acquaintance."

"If I am in the correct home, we have a friend in common: Finola O'Shea."

The woman's light brown hair was severely pulled back so her attractive smile showed off those teeth and generous mouth.

"Finny is your friend too? How nice. I've known her nearly all my life. How is it that you know her and yet you and I haven't met?"

"Finola and I are new acquaintances. We have a connection through Escott Manor, where she stayed for a short time. In between visits here, I believe. Is there any chance Finola is still here?"

"Oh no. She asked her brother if she could return home, and he agreed. To be honest, I don't know why Thaddeus agreed to let Finny return. Generosity isn't in his disposition."

"Her brother must have had a change of heart," Berrie said, "about letting Finola stay with him."

Nessa O'Donnell harrumphed. "I take it you've never met Thaddeus?"

Berrie shook her head.

"So like his father it would make you doubt the wisdom of God, having created not one but two such men."

"Her stay with him is only temporary, of course," Berrie said, "until Conall is twelve. Then, if they haven't something else in store, they can return to Escott Manor."

"Ah, yes, Finny told me about that offer from the head-mistress. It's really too bad it didn't work out for them to stay there right along. Conall won't be twelve for another eight years."

Berrie was surprised by the woman's frankness. She must not be aware of the charges Finola was bringing against Duff. Otherwise Berrie was certain the woman would have brought it up the moment Berrie revealed her link to Escott Manor—the very place that employed Finola's alleged attacker. Berrie decided to keep her identity as headmistress to herself. "I was wondering if you could tell me how I might visit Finola?"

She stared at Berrie. "I'm surprised you don't know, if you're friends."

"She knew where to find me, and since her plans were uncertain when she left Escott Manor, she didn't bother to give me a forwarding address yet."

That seemed logical enough, even to Berrie. Mrs. O'Donnell told her where the O'Shea manor house could be found, an hour north of Dublin. On her way out, Berrie knew she must try to ask one more question without alarming the other woman.

"Tell me, Mrs. O'Donnell," Berrie asked, "did Finola ever mention a man by the name of Duff Habgood, one of the men who work at Escott Manor?"

Mrs. O'Donnell shook her head. "Finny hasn't been of any mind to talk about a man, not since her husband annulled their marriage. She vowed never to trust one again, and Finny isn't the kind to go back on a vow, especially to herself. Why do you ask?"

"I thought she and Mr. Habgood were friends," Berrie said and left it at that. She bid Mrs. O'Donnell a good day, then found her way outside, where Jobbin waited with the wagon.

She gave him directions to the O'Shea manor house. They wouldn't arrive until almost dark, but there was little to be done about that. She couldn't wait another day.

Settling back, Berrie mulled over the information she'd received. Finola had gone to the O'Donnell home after leaving Escott Manor. If Duff had supposedly accosted her while she was in residence at the school, and if Finola and Mrs. O'Donnell were the hob-or-nob friends Mrs. O'Donnell seemed to portray, wouldn't Finola have confided in her about an attack? Especially if she were going to make the incident public by bringing action against Duff?

Berrie was more certain than ever no attack had taken place, but even if something improper had happened between Duff and Finola, if it had occurred *after* Finola left the school, might that make a difference? He'd been in Dublin, searching for families in need of their school. Had he come upon Finola by accident, and had she misinterpreted a simple greeting as something more than it was? Duff admitted he'd been enamored of her; perhaps he'd forgotten himself and hugged her upon sight. Maybe Finola was so embittered against men in general, because of the way her husband had treated her, she would take any revenge upon Duff that she could. An innocent substitute for the wrongs her husband had enacted.

Such theories filled Berrie's mind as Jobbin drove the wagon at a brisk pace north of the city. It was more vital than ever that Berrie speak to Finola, to make her see what sort of trouble this caused the school. It endangered Finola's own welfare, not just Duff's, if she still hoped the school would be part of her future.

If Berrie wasn't able to change Finola's mind about this accusation, all might be lost.

49

The telephone rang. Rebecca glanced at the clock. Almost eleven. Only Quentin would—

She scrambled to answer, nearly dropping the receiver from unsteady hands. After issuing a successfully calm greeting, her mind didn't register her sunken heart until moments after realizing the voice on the other end was a woman. Despite her disappointment, the momentary shot of adrenaline had fully awakened her. Rebecca had been at her desk, almost too tired to work a moment ago, but she had a few things to catch up on before the judges' visit day after tomorrow.

"Is Dana there?" the voice said after her hello.

"Dana? Yes, she's here, but I'll have to fetch her; she's retired for the night. This is Rebecca Seabrooke. May I ask who's calling?"

"Oh, Rebecca! We've never directly corresponded. This is Dana's sister, Talie Ingram." A pause, filled by a slight echo on the line. "I'm sorry, it's almost eleven o'clock there, isn't it? I've been so busy I didn't realize how late it must be for you."

"If you'll hold the line, I'll see if she's awake." Rebecca popped up from her chair.

"No, don't."

Rebecca caught back the receiver, her movements still jerky, spurred by emotion that had nothing to do with the call. "Yes, what's that?"

"Don't wake her. In her condition she needs all the rest she can get. I only called to let her know I'm coming. I have a million things to do before my mother gets here to watch the kids. Tell Danes I'll be there tomorrow night by this time, right at the door."

"So you know about the baby?" Rebecca was breathing more naturally now. She sat down again.

"Aidan called a couple of days ago. He's pretty worried about her."

"Yes, so am I."

"I don't know if I'll be any help, but I'm coming to offer whatever support I can. And to see if I can convince her to return to Ireland and to Aidan as soon as possible."

"That's wonderful. Dana told me you went through this sort of pregnancy yourself, not knowing what was ahead."

"Longest months of my life. I'm living proof that the fifty-fifty chance is real, but from what Aidan says it sounds like she thinks it's 100 percent guaranteed she'll have a fragile X child."

"I think that's an accurate assessment."

"You tell that sister of mine every minute she worries is another minute wasted. Oh, forget that. She won't listen to you any more than she'd listen to me. Just tell her I'm coming. One more thing, then I really have to go. This is a little awkward. I hate to ask favors, but Aidan seemed to think it would be all right if I stayed there with you and Dana. Will that be all right—you know, with the owner? I'm not sure cousin-umpteenth-removed counts as family, so I don't want to impose."

"It will be fine," Rebecca said. How easily she offered this roof, when it was entirely possible she wouldn't have much to say about its usage before long.

Talie said good-bye and Rebecca hung up. Dana's sister might not be able to fix anything, but Rebecca guessed she was certainly going to try.

50

*I continue my letter from a very unexpected spot, Cosima
—Jobbin's wagon. You will hardly believe me when I tell
you all I have to say. I can only ask you to pray. How can
the Lord God abandon me, when the school, I am still
convinced, was His plan? Oh, Cosima, is all lost? Have
I truly failed so miserably?*

When Jobbin stopped the wagon, Berrie peered beyond the
canvas only to wish the journey weren't yet over. At first glance
the house appeared little more than a pile of crumbling rocks.
Indeed, the entire fence was more rubble than design, and an
archway leading to the front door looked so precarious that Berrie felt it would be unwise to stand beneath it. Surely Finola
didn't live here with her brother? On the other side of the
dilapidated fence, between the structure and the gate, grew a
garden Berrie's entire family would collectively shudder at upon
sight. Overgrown, weed-infested, a jungle in its thickness so
that no single plant could be deciphered from another, much less
admired. A tree, long dead and devoid of bark, watched over
as a testimony of what was to come to the rest of the neglected
ground beneath it.

"Wait here, miss," said Jobbin, and Berrie was only too happy to oblige. She'd worried Mr. Truebody might not welcome her usage of Jobbin's time or his wagon should Mr. Truebody know, but upon her hesitation Jobbin had assured her it was his own time and his own wagon should the justice of the peace remind him she was no longer his employer. Now she was thankful for him yet again. "I'll make sure we've the right home and be back out here for you quick as that."

She watched him enter through the squeaky gate; it hadn't been closed before and refused to close even with his effort. Sight of him was quickly devoured by the garden, only to reappear again on the other side below the deteriorating arch that once might have bidden a friendly welcome to all who approached the tall wooden door. Still, her heart pounded while he stood beneath the arch and rapped soundly at the door. She was certain that all would crumble at any moment if not for the sturdy vines crawling up between the cracks, green mortar lending the archway its last vestige of strength.

Though she heard his knock all the way to the wagon, no one responded. He waited, tapped again, waited. Then, turning round, he walked back outside the archway, disappearing once again into the thick wild growth. She spotted his balding head and he appeared like an odd sort of featherless bird, one that couldn't fly but could only hop from spot to spot.

He was gone altogether once he rounded the side of the manor, and she settled back in her seat to wait. The day was cool and promised to be cooler still with the setting of the sun. Even if this was the right home, and even if she was able to speak to Finola, it appeared this night would be spent in the wagon. They hadn't passed a single inn nearby, and she had no idea where one might be found. The wagon floor would be the roughest bed she'd ever known, and she'd sleep on the emptiest stomach, but she didn't worry about that. It was Jobbin she thought of. He

would have to sleep under the stars, or under the wagon itself if
stars gave way to rain clouds.

She took the moment of solitude to pray, knowing it would
require no less than God's hand to unveil the truth. She prayed
He aided the search for that very thing.

Before long she heard Jobbin's call, followed by the rumble of
the wagon as it accepted his weight.

"All's well, miss. I'll pull the wagon up and around. Just a
moment we'll be right as ninepence."

The wagon lurched forward, and she peeked out to see
where they went. A lane curved alongside the wasted manor
house, descending to a view of the green Irish landscape more
lovely than even around Escott Manor. Trees too often stood in
the way there. Here she saw a wide expanse of the sun-streaked
horizon, beneath which were endless square pillows of crops
and meadows in various shades of green, each divided by the
trimmed lace of neat hedgerows.

Jobbin soon pulled the wagon to a halt, and Berrie slid to the
other side, where he waited to help her down. Standing on the
footboard, she looked at the home before her. This angle offered
an altogether different view. Neat brick fairly glowed beneath
the orange sunset, with mullioned windows glimmering like so
many eyes taking in the view. The lawn was trimmed here, absent
of flowers or much fauna, but neat nonetheless. Only the edge,
where stones peeked around the corner, hinted at the wither-
ing limb that was attached on the other side. Why it hadn't been
demolished and removed, Berrie couldn't tell.

"I was told the family's not at home but that we can wait
inside," Jobbin said as they walked closer to the open door. The
room proved to be a kitchen with tall hearth, wide wooden table,
wash sink, and shelves lining an entire wall. The scent of baking
bread made Berrie's mouth water even as her stomach twisted.

An older servant introduced herself as Moira and went about

gathering ingredients to serve with tea, though age slowed her progress. She was similar in years to Dowager Merit, Berrie's grandmother, but far more sprightly, smiling as easily as the dowager frowned. She chatted about how good it was for Miss Finola to receive visitors, that she'd been sick of heart since returning home and this would surely brighten her spirit.

Berrie wasn't so sure. She was here to challenge her story, to do nothing less than call Finola a liar and beg her to stop the insanity of a legal battle. She wasn't going to leave until the truth was known.

Berrie should have refused the warm hospitality Moira offered, if only because she knew the servant wouldn't present a sip or crumb if she knew why Berrie was here. However her demanding stomach wouldn't allow a refusal. She watched Moira painstakingly butter bread and press boiled eggs with red tomatoes, making room on a plate of what looked like ginger cake and shortbread waiting nearby. It all looked wonderful to Berrie, but she guessed anything would. She must eat to rid herself of her nervous lightheadedness. But the tea was barely steeped when a boy burst in from the kitchen door, and Moira left the array of food untended on the cook's table to face him.

"They're back! Oh—pardon me, miss," said the boy, dressed in worn brown trousers and a jacket that must have been a castoff from a child of comfortable means some years ago, with its frayed collar and buttons torn from a double-breasted style. He looked at Berrie, then at Moira.

"This is a friend of Miss Finola's, Paddy. Come to visit."

The boy's eyes, nearly as brown as his jacket, went wide. "A visitor? That's good—isn't it, Moira? Good?"

"Of course it is!" Her words encouraged, but the wrinkles on her brow deepened.

Berrie watched the exchange, puzzlement growing. Was it so odd to have a visitor in this part of Ireland? or just to this manor house?

There must have been an entry other than the kitchen or the pile of stones she'd seen before, because moments later Berrie heard a commotion from up the stairs leading to the rest of the manor. She stood, prepared to follow Moira to be announced as Finola's visitor.

"Sit, sit," Moira said, her voice low. "It'll be best if you wait just a moment, and then I'll see about your visit."

Then she left the kitchen, going slowly up the stairs.

Berrie was tempted to follow and announce herself. But when she moved to do so, the boy called Paddy stepped in her way.

"If you're Miss Finola's friend, like you said, it's best to wait here for Moira."

"Why is that?"

He tilted his head. "You don't know Finola very well, do you, miss?"

"Well enough to visit," Berrie said.

"Then maybe it's her brother you don't know well enough."

Berrie contemplated whether to wait or go unannounced, but there was something on the boy's face that made her believe it would be best to follow direction. It wasn't long before the sound of footsteps echoed from the hall up the stairs, and Moira stood there silently, bidding her to come.

"They're in the upstairs parlor," Moira whispered. "Though I was at a loss to tell them your name, miss."

"Didn't Jobbin—my driver—announce my name?"

Moira shrugged. "If he did, I must have forgotten."

Berrie followed the maid, seeing walls in need of paint, floors as worn as the carpets trying to hide them. They passed the arch to a dining room, where stood a long table and only three chairs, no sideboard or wall coverings, not even a screen before the fireplace. At least little Conall would have nothing to tempt him to break, but what of keeping him away from the fire?

Moira stopped before a tall wooden door that creaked on its hinges when she opened it. All Berrie saw in the dimly lit parlor was a piano, a pair of settees, and one lamp table. Two tall windows on the far side let in light, but they were so shrouded in draperies that the effect of sunlight was minimal.

"Cecily! How wonderful to see you," said Finola, stepping forward and grabbing both of Berrie's hands in hers.

Berrie looked about for the bearer of the name Finola addressed. All she saw was a man, presumably Thaddeus, standing beside the piano. He was tall and thin, his face shadowed in the dim light.

Finola squeezed Berrie's hands so tight Berrie wanted to wince and pull away, but Finola's grip was too strong unless Berrie were to make a fuss. Finola's face warned away such a temptation. Her skin, always so pure and flawless, looked colorless except for circles beneath her eyes. Those eyes were anything but weary; even in the limited light, Berrie saw an alertness that looked strangely fearful.

"You've never met my brother, Thaddeus, have you, Cecily?" Her voice was higher pitched than Berrie remembered, and she seemed happier and more animated here than she'd ever been at Escott Manor, where her skin wasn't marred by fatigue and her cheeks had been rosy. "And we've known each other so long, it's a shame, too."

Berrie wanted to demand what was going on, why Finola was behaving so strangely and calling her by another name. But she would wait at least a few moments more. It wasn't only Finola's odd behavior giving her caution. More importantly, there was something decidedly missing from this picture. Where was Conall?

"Thaddeus, this is my friend, Miss Cecily Ferguson. Cec, meet my brother, Thaddeus."

Berrie accepted his hand without the slightest attempt to

right the wrong name. He hardly looked pleased to meet her. His nose protruded sharply with a resting point made for spectacles, the way the bridge jutted out between his brows. And his mouth was too small, his forehead too broad. Katie would say his face was unsymmetrical, and the thought reminded Berrie of why she'd come and all she was fighting for. And why she must be careful not to overlook anything.

"How lovely to meet you, Mr. O'Shea. Both Nessa and Finola have mentioned you, and now at last we meet."

"Have they now?" he asked. "So you know Nessa, too. And am I to believe they spoke highly of me?"

"For as often as they spoke your name," Berrie said honestly, "their opinion of you couldn't have been more clear. I just came from Nessa's. She told me you invited Finola back here, so I thought I would visit since I'd missed Finola's company by only a few days."

"Is that so? You came out here all the way from Nessa's just to see Finola?"

"Of course."

"Then that wagon out there, with the driver waiting for you, is yours?"

Berrie nodded, though her heart went heavy. The ruse was already up, and she knew it. Those who traveled in Nessa's circle wouldn't have such humble transportation, nor would she be traveling the hour distance with no one but the driver as chaperone and protector.

Thaddeus took a step closer, far too close for a gentleman to stand. An intimidating distance, if Berrie were easily intimidated. She forced herself to remain where she was.

But her head still spun from the day's worry and activity and lack of nourishment. "I am a friend of your sister's, Mr. O'Shea, and I'll thank you to allow us time to visit."

There was nothing pleasant in the smirk that might have

been meant as a smile. "My sister and I are very close," Thaddeus said. "She would enjoy sharing your visit with me. Wouldn't you, Finola?"

"I—yes, of course, Thaddeus. Though I'm sure we'll bore you within moments."

"Nonsense. Though it does grow late, and we've just dined with a friend, so we have little to offer by way of repast."

"I'm perfectly content," Berrie said.

Finola grabbed Berrie's hand. "My brother brings up a good point." Her voice was strained, her gaze fixed straight ahead. "It does grow late. I'm so pleased to see you, though, Cecily."

"Yes, as I am to see you."

"You're far from Dublin," Thaddeus said. "You took a great risk coming here without knowing whether or not you would find us at home."

"I'm known for my impetuosity, I'm afraid."

"An impetuous woman is one who learns to live with many regrets. Where, exactly, did you plan to pass the evening if Finola couldn't be found at home?"

"I was quite impressed by your housekeeper—Moira, I believe is her name. I'm sure she would have found accommodations for me."

"Impetuous and trusting," Thaddeus said. "But you'll forgive me if I add, not wise. A woman without a chaperone, depending on the generosity of a servant? Tsk, tsk, you really must be more careful in the future."

They took seats on the two settees, Thaddeus across from the women. Finola still hung on to Berrie, having entwined their arms together.

"I can't help noticing little Conall is absent, Finola. And I so wanted to see him. Where is he?"

Finola's fingers pressed into Berrie's skin, and if her fingernails had been any longer or sharper, she surely would have drawn blood. "At a friend's house," Finola said. "Just for tonight. While Thaddeus and I were dining."

"Yes," Thaddeus said, leaning back, folding one leg over the other. "We don't like to leave him at home. Moira runs the household, but she's getting on in years and doesn't oversee things as meticulously as we'd like. The child is better off under the care of more fastidious staff. You must understand, if you're familiar with Conall and his clumsiness."

Nipping back a defense of Conall's so-called clumsiness, knowing how hard were the simplest tasks for children just like him, she restricted her response to a nod.

"You'll be returning to Nessa's, won't you, Finola?" Berrie asked. "That's partly why I came, to see if I could persuade you to return there with me for at least the duration of my visit."

Thaddeus shook his head, though Berrie was sure Finola had been about to speak. "Finola has agreed to live at home again, and until I am wed, she has agreed to oversee things here. It's a fair exchange, I think, since I am the sole heir but am welcoming her to stay."

It occurred to Berrie that he hadn't made any attempt to equally divide their inheritance, the way his lawsuit had demanded Escott Manor be divided between Cosima and her cousins. Berrie knew she couldn't bring that up without revealing her true identity and so remained silent. Surely there was a reason Finola didn't want her brother to know who Berrie was.

"And how is it, Miss . . . is it 'miss'?"

Berrie nodded.

"Miss Ferguson, then?"

Berrie nodded again, wondering if he expected an invitation for him to call her Cecily as his sister did.

"How is it that you arrived here by such humble transportation?"

"My . . . family had need of the carriage, so I took the market wagon."

"Hmm, extraordinary that they should let you use such a necessary piece of equipment. Not only that, they let you travel without Nessa at least, as chaperone. Why didn't she accompany you?"

"She intended to," Berrie said, hoping she could follow her own path of lies, "but she wasn't feeling well when I left, so I came alone."

"And you left a sick friend to visit Finola? How odd."

Berrie had no answer, only looked from his piercing gaze to Finola's desperate one. She had nothing more to offer, not the truth, no more lies, nothing. It appeared obvious he didn't believe her anyway.

"Why don't you tell me what you're really doing here, Miss Ferguson? If that's even your name?"

She tried to smile. "I'm sure I don't know what you mean."

"I mean that from the moment my sister called you Cecily, the look of shock on your face revealed the first lie. Who are you, and what are you doing here?"

Berrie stiffened, wanting nothing more than to leave—but to take Finola with her. Something wasn't right here, and whatever it was, it held Finola in fear.

"I am nothing more than a friend of your sister's," Berrie answered firmly. "And I'd like to take her and Conall back with me to Nessa's. Tonight. Immediately."

"And as I've already explained, that's impossible. Nessa doesn't want Conall living there, and Finola wouldn't dream of leaving him behind." He eyed his sister. "Would you, Finola?"

"Of course not."

"And besides that, Finola is needed here." Thaddeus looked back at Berrie. "So I'm afraid you've made the trip for nothing. My apologies, but there's nothing to be done for it."

He stood, and it seemed obvious he expected her to take her

leave. Berrie turned to Finola, who was still fastened to her side. Finola slowly withdrew, her eyelids shading her eyes.

Anger coursed through Berrie. Clearly this brother had something over Finola. The fear in the other woman was like a scent, unmistakable. For the first time in her life, Berrie wished she were a man, if only to be able to back up a demand for the truth with physical strength, intimidating enough to get this brother to speak.

Berrie knew one thing: she wasn't leaving without learning what was really going on. What had she to lose? The school was already at risk, her reputation as well. If that was lost already, she had nothing else left.

Such freedom added to her headiness. She sprang to her feet, prepared to launch whatever words it would take to battle this man for the truth.

But her tongue would not obey. Although she stood, it felt as if the blood in her body stayed seated. Her vision went blank, her knees collapsed, followed immediately by the feeling of falling through darkness toward a spinning abyss.

51

"The conversation ended so quickly it didn't occur to me to offer a ride from the station," Rebecca said, standing at the window the following evening. Dana and Padgett sat on the sofa behind her, playing a game of Snakes and Ladders that once belonged to Quentin.

"She'll be fine," Dana said. "One thing about being the oldest child, they're good at pretending they know what they're doing, even if they don't. She'll figure it out."

The telephone rang and Rebecca went to answer. Perhaps it was Talie, calling from the station. If there were no taxis available, Rebecca could be there in her mini in twenty minutes if the fog wasn't too thick. "Hello."

"Rebecca."

The voice didn't belong to Talie at all but to Quentin. Rebecca's blood caught fire in her veins. "Hello." The repeated salutation was silly, though that was all that came to mind.

"I'll be there early tomorrow."

No small talk, no niceties. A warning? The Featherby judges were due for the first tour at ten. Was that why Quentin was coming—the *only* reason? Such questions wouldn't form on her lips. "All right."

"Is everything all right?" His tone was clear and gentle, making her aware of how much she missed him. "Are you all right?"

323

Her eyes closed, she took a calming breath. This was the Quentin she knew. "Yes." She cleared her throat, aware—if only distantly—that both Dana and her daughter were watching. "I almost called you earlier; perhaps I should have."

"Yes?" His voice was surprised or eager, she wasn't sure which.

"Dana's sister is coming to England. Today. Right now, as a matter of fact. She should be here any moment. I hope it's all right for her to stay upstairs for a few days."

He didn't respond immediately, and she wondered if he was disappointed that was all she said. Had he hoped she would have called for some other reason? She wouldn't, though. He must know that.

"It's perfectly fine," he said at last. "Tell her I look forward to meeting her."

"Yes, I will."

Another pause. Rebecca wished she could think of something to say, something funny or light, so he wouldn't know how desperately she missed him, how much she wanted to know his thoughts. She'd never been good at asking such things.

"Tomorrow, then."

"Yes."

And then he hung up.

She didn't have to say anything for Dana to guess the caller had been Quentin. Rebecca could tell that the moment they caught eyes.

Even if she'd had the words to describe how she felt, even if she wanted to share them, even if Padgett wasn't there to hear them all, there wouldn't have been time for such an exchange. The expected taxi lights sparkled down the lane, and both Dana and Padgett were at the door before the vehicle pulled to a stop.

The sisters hugged as though a lifetime had separated them not just an ocean and a few weeks on the calendar. Rebecca would have known without an introduction that this woman was Talie's sister. They both had the same wheat-colored hair, the same slant to their brows. With a squealed greeting, Padgett laughed as her aunt hugged and held her close.

They went inside, where Helen had stayed to serve cocoa and biscuits. It wasn't long before even the sugar couldn't keep Padgett awake. Rebecca volunteered to take her upstairs to bed.

Rebecca lingered over Padgett's bedtime routing, helping her with pajamas, overseeing toothbrushing, reading two stories instead of one. She told Padgett about how God made the sun and the moon and the stars and that He was with them all the time, even when they slept. Padgett wondered if when they went to heaven they could ask God to tuck them in with a blanket that twinkled of stars, but Rebecca told her there wouldn't be any darkness there, and she wasn't sure about sleeping. It might be fun to jump on a blanket of stars anyway, so they might hope for that.

When Rebecca finally stepped outside the child's room, she determined she would stop in the parlor only to say good night, then give the sisters more time alone. She might have only met Talie moments ago, but from what she knew about her through Dana, Rebecca doubted she would wait long before attacking the mission for which she'd come: getting Dana to return to her husband's side.

Passing her office, Rebecca noticed a light from behind the open door.

"Rebecca, come in," Dana called from her usual chair on the opposite side of Rebecca's desk. Talie sat beside her, and the two held various pages Rebecca instantly recognized. From Dana's box of school records.

Rebecca's heart went heavy. So this was how it would be, Dana pulling Talie down over such dour reports?

But Talie smiled. "Dana is trying to convince me the child

she's carrying—and no doubt my own son Ben—has a future just like the ones written about in these records."

Rebecca took her familiar seat behind the desk. From Talie's tone, it didn't sound like the task would be as easy as Dana might hope. "Yes, so she's tried to tell me, too."

"I told her I wanted to see Berrie's letters, and so far she's only shown me these. Maybe you can tell me where Berrie's letters are?"

Rebecca opened a manila file on her desk. "They're here. I've spent the past few weeks transcribing them with Dana's help." And a bit of help from Quentin, too, although she didn't think it necessary to mention him. "Dana was working on it before she decided to concentrate on the school records."

"Mind if I see those?"

Rebecca handed all of the transcribed letters to her. They were nearly complete.

Talie looked through the pages. "I'm not a bit tired, but I'm guessing you both are. Why don't you go to bed? I'd like to stay up and read through some of this. We can talk more tomorrow."

Dana frowned. "You've hardly seen any of the school records." She flipped through a stack.

Talie put a hand over Dana's. "I think I've seen enough of those."

Dana's eyes rounded. "You can't mean you're not going to read the rest of these? I thought you'd want to see them!"

"I can tell what they'll say, just like the IEPs I receive every semester from Ben's school." Talie set aside the file in her hand, not letting go of Dana. "Haven't I always told you Ben looks worse on paper than he does in real life? What do you expect me to see in those pages? All the things those kids couldn't do? That's all it says. It doesn't say anything about what made them laugh, or the twinkle in their eyes when they saw someone familiar. The joy when they finally learned something or the communicating they could do without language. You can't write a report on that, Danes."

Dana leaned closer to her sister. "Don't you get it? 'Duration of attack: *Life*.' Nothing changed in their lives. Nothing's going to change for Ben. Maybe nothing's going to change for my baby."

Talie didn't back away; they were nearly nose to nose. "And that's okay, Danes."

Now Dana leaned back, as if she were the sister who could claim jet lag. She shook her head, eyeing Talie. "I thought you'd get it."

"I *do* get it. Maybe it's you who don't, and maybe our talk shouldn't wait until tomorrow. Maybe you need some sense knocked into you right now."

Dana plopped the records from her lap onto Rebecca's desk, leaning back like a truant student assigned extra classes complete with a lecture she was about to endure. She stared ahead instead of at either her sister or Rebecca.

"You know, Danes," said Talie more gently, "when I first found out about Ben, when I was pregnant just like you are, not know-ing, I did the same thing you're doing. Immersed myself in as much information as I could. I tried to read everything I could get my hands on about fragile X. Do you remember?"

Dana nodded. "Knowledge is power, as they say."

Rebecca guessed she wasn't the only one to hear the hard edge to those words, a phrase that Dana might believe explained her obsession with the old records. But Rebecca couldn't see any power Dana was gaining in gathering how many things might go wrong with the child she was carrying. All Rebecca saw was a chipping away of hope.

Talie touched one of Dana's stiff, folded hands she had pressed to her still-flat middle. "I saw what you see in these records, all the limitations my child would face. It wasn't until Luke stopped read-ing the reports that I realized he was right. It wasn't doing either one of us any good. We knew enough of the basics, and at the time that was all we needed. And now I see that time has a way of clarifying things, so getting an overdose of information that might not even apply was probably the wrong thing to do."

One of Dana's brows crinkled, and her mouth twisted to a snarl. "One of the kids set fire to his bed, but you didn't read that part. Another one wandered away and they didn't find him for two days. Two days, Talie! They found him in the middle of nowhere, eating grass! Do you know what would happen if a child got away in Chicago? He could be hit by a car, get picked up by a maniac, drown in the lake!"

"Those sound like worries any parent might have," Rebecca said. She knew she wouldn't have much to add to this conversation, having so little experience either with children or with the disabled, but the fears Dana listed sounded typical.

"They are," Talie confirmed, "and not just little kids, either. You worry about all of that with Padgett, too."

"She's smart enough to look both ways before crossing a street, not to talk to strangers, not to go swimming unless I'm there. It's different and you know it. There's an end to my worries with Padgett, at least worries like that."

Talie nodded.

"Besides, I have new worries about Padgett, just like you worry about Kipp. They'll still be here after we're gone. Are we supposed to saddle them with the responsibility of taking care of their handicapped siblings? Is that the kind of future you want for Kipp?"

"It might not be the kind of future I would have designed." Talie sighed, looking directly at her sister, eyes steady, brows slightly drawn. "Look, Dana, I'm not going to sugarcoat this, because I live every day with what you fear. Maybe I've made it look too hard to handle. This is the life we were given, me and Luke and Ben and Kipp. We can't change it, but it's made me realize we can do it, we *can* handle it."

"Good for you." Bitterness accompanied Dana's words. "There are some who can't. Remember Rowena? I'd say taking the murder-suicide option isn't handling it. I'll bet she's not the only one who's ever gone that route or considered it."

"She missed out on what God would have had her learn. About community and letting others help her and seeing how someone like Ben relates to others—with innocence and a smile. Even without that, there's something else—something that reminds me every day that God is right smack in the middle of Ben's diagnosis."

Dana didn't reply, even though Talie had set her up for an interested prompting.

"Life is all about servanthood."

The words didn't make an obvious impression on Dana, but they spurred something in Rebecca. Maybe twelve generations of valets, head cooks, housemaids, and ladies' maids had left some remnant in Rebecca's blood. Maybe it was just because that was how she thought of herself when it came to Quentin.

"Don't you remember the annual holiday season sermon our pastor gives, Danes? how servanthood is the key to happiness? If you're lonely during the holidays, serve someone else. If you're brokenhearted, ease somebody else's pain. If you're grieving a lost loved one, help someone who faces the same thing. It's the way God designed us to be, the way Jesus was. Be comforted through comforting others."

Rebecca could see the words had no impact on Dana, although Rebecca, who listened with rapt attention, felt her pulse run faster.

"Every day I get a special reminder that Jesus washed His disciples' feet," Talie continued. "Whenever I change Ben's diapers, I'm reminded that we're supposed to put the needs of others before our own. Ben's condition forces me to do it, but why should I have to be forced? Maybe because between the two of us—me and

Ben—I'm the real slow learner. God put me in a situation that's all about servanthood. Am I supposed to resist it when His example was so much more extraordinary? I should get down on my knees to thank Him for giving me such a clear picture of what He really wants: for us to serve others."

Rebecca savored the words, desiring to ponder them, claim them as part of her life. Maybe being the granddaughter of a valet made it easier for her to accept. She wasn't the only one to be a servant. They were all to be servants. . . .

Her own thoughts scattered as she looked at Dana, seeing nothing had changed. Rather, Dana looked nearer to tears than she had all day.

"Danes, what is it? Do you really doubt you can handle a child like Ben?"

"Of course I do!" Tears transformed her eyes to splotchy pools. "When I thought I could handle someone with a disability, God gave us Padgett, but He made sure she was all right. What has being a parent to her proven, Tal? That I'm fine as long as I have my happy-go-lucky husband and a healthy child." She scrubbed a tear from her cheek. "She's taught me nothing, except that I'm selfish enough to want things easy."

Dana's voice was filled with rage, her fingertips shook with it as she wiped away more tears.

"Aidan is prepared for whatever's ahead," Talie whispered. "He was the one who reminded me he was willing to adopt a handicapped child. He doesn't get why you've changed your mind about that. On the phone he asked me how you could have been willing to adopt someone with special needs and now all of a sudden not be willing to give birth to one?"

A sob ran across Dana's shoulders. "It's why we tried to prevent a pregnancy. Bringing in someone new with a disability wasn't in the plan. Only rescuing someone already here."

"A noble but obsolete line of thinking. God gave you that

baby you're carrying to love and raise to the best of your ability. Same as He gave you Padgett."

Dana moaned. "A fine parent I've been lately, pushing her into Rebecca and Quentin's care so I can wallow in my worries. Maybe Padgett was *my* will all along, not God's. Me pushing that adoption through when all God really meant was for me to have enough time for whatever needy child He's going to send my way."

"Now you're just being ridiculous. There *is* hope this baby will be fine."

"Right now . . . I'm not so sure."

Talie laughed, but it was more an indictment of Dana's statement than any resemblance to enjoyment. "There's always hope, Danes. You know that. So God allows bad things to happen to everyone—that's true, but we're supposed to learn from the bad stuff and grow and comfort others. And always, *always*, know that in the end, the final act is one of hope. This life isn't all there is, you know."

Rebecca sat forward. She hadn't planned to say a word, yet here she was, clearing her throat to jump in again. "When my mother died, I felt like hope had let me down. I'd hoped she would be all right, but she wasn't. My father once told me that the sweetest surrender is to God, after sorrow, when we learn to trust that God's hope is enough."

She hadn't meant to think of Quentin just then, but he came to mind along with Berrie and Cosima and even Talie, from what little she knew of her. "Do you know, Dana, that hope has been my enemy again lately? Maybe it was that way for Cosima, when she hoped for a marriage she thought she had no right to dream of, and for Berrie when she founded her school and nearly lost everything—a marriage she told herself she didn't want, a mission she was sure God designed her for. And your sister. I'm sure she had the same kind of dreams you have for Padgett. It's all about hope. But sometimes we have to bring it to the throne of God and see what He has in store instead of what we expected."

"What if I don't want what He has in store?" Dana's gaze shot from Rebecca to Talie and back to Rebecca. "I suppose that sounds rebellious. That's how I feel. I thought I could handle it if Padgett had limitations all her life; I thought I was prepared for that when I signed those adoption papers. Then she turned out to be fine, no problems at all. I was relieved; I'm still relieved, every day of my life, because I get to dream about all the things she might do someday. No limits."

"She'll still have limits," Rebecca said. "We all do."

"None of us gets to choose everything in life. We get what we get." Talie looked at her sister. "You *should* thank God Padgett is okay. We all do. But just because God let you have one healthy child doesn't mean He didn't make you strong enough to deal with one who isn't."

New tears balanced on the brim of Dana's red eyes, overflowing on each cheek.

"Don't get me wrong," Talie said, leaning forward again, nearly whispering. "I don't want this baby to have a single problem. There's still a possibility he or she won't, you know. Let me bring a little clarity here. I've been living with Ben for a few years now, so maybe I've learned a thing or two. I'll give you the best and worst of it right here, right now. You want to know?"

The smile on Talie's face was hard to resist, and Rebecca found her own smile easier when Dana fell for it as well.

"Okay, the best: *Ben doesn't talk back.* Don't laugh. God gave you Padgett, a pleaser if ever there was one. But there will come a day, because she's only human, when she'll stop doing everything to please her favorite person, Mommy. Maybe she won't even use words to talk back; she'll just go her own way, and there you'll be, left behind to watch her go. It's going to happen. I've never met a parent who hasn't had their child—even the good ones—go through it to some degree. But Ben? His rebellion only goes as far as getting up in the middle of the night. And he doesn't do that to bug me; he just can't sleep."

"And the worst?"

Talie shook her head. "Don't rush me. Think about the best a moment; don't miss its importance. You'll get to live with someone who will remind you every day of what's important: a smile."

"I usually ask for the bad news first, Talie. You can give it to me now."

Talie shook her head, pausing despite her sister's impatience. "Okay. It's the loss of freedom. And I'm afraid it's permanent unless I make some radical changes. Other parents can do so much with kids who can go anywhere. But being Ben's mom, I'm either stuck in the handicapped row—if there is one—hoping he won't make too much noise, or I just stay home. Staying home is easier, more convenient. It's not best. The isolation can become too comfortable, I suppose."

Dana wiped her face one more time, folded her arms tight. "I know how you used to be before, Talie. How you valued privacy, so maybe you're bent toward isolation anyway."

Rebecca eyed Talie, wondering if they had more in common than she knew. How much more isolated could Rebecca have been in the past three years, living out here alone except for Helen and William?

"There's a difference between being isolated and private," Talie said. "I know you like your privacy just as much as I do. Then I got a diagnosis that brought in a bunch of professionals—doctors and specialists, therapists coming and going, not to mention the whole world being able to tell right away that something is wrong with Ben. You can throw privacy right out the window with a diagnosis like that."

You can also throw privacy out the window if you marry someone in the public eye, Rebecca thought.

Talie eyed her sister again. "You're going to be all right, Danes. No matter what. You have Aidan; you have Luke and me. The future is in God's hands. Padgett and Kipp were placed in our families for a reason, you know. God gave them to us as blessings. We shouldn't underestimate what they can live up to—with God's help. And we shouldn't underestimate ourselves. I heard an old saying once, about the verse in Genesis that we're all made in God's image. It's both a blessing and a caution. Knowing we're made in His image reminds us of His love for us and our potential. But we need to be careful, too, and remember that we're only an image. We're not perfect like Him, not one of us. The best we can do is put our lives in His hands like the Bible says. Living sacrifices, you know?"

Rebecca watched Dana nod, knowing the words were what Dana needed to hear. Only Rebecca hadn't realized they were the words she needed to hear, too. When had she taken back the reins in her life? It was time to put them back in God's hands.

Just then the door to her office squeaked. It only did that when it was moved too slowly. Rebecca looked, along with Talie and Dana, to see Padgett standing there clutching Emma, her eyes wider than ever, her face in contrast looking tinier than ever.

"You sad again, Mommy? 'Cause of me? I heard you cry when you said my name."

Dana slipped out of her seat in one fluid movement, scooping up her daughter. "Of course not, honey. Not because of you. I'm okay now."

Rebecca moved out from behind her desk. "I'll take her back to bed, if you like. I can tell her another story." A happy one. A silly, ridiculous one that would be sure to erase all the worries that were far too big for her at the moment.

But Dana shook her head. "No, I'll go to bed too. We'll be fine." She kissed Padgett's cheek. "Won't we?"

Padgett clung to her, nearly dropping the stuffed replica of Emma in the process.

Rebecca watched them go, her heart twisting in worries of her own.

52

I used to regard women who swooned as the greatest actresses, whose only goal was to call attention to themselves. The only exception to that were silly young ones who let their maids cinch their corsets too tightly. Never in my life had I considered someone might faint because of hunger and angst, but I have been entirely convinced.

When I awoke, I was in a bedroom. Moira was there with a fresh cup of tea and what looked like the same sandwich I had almost been offered earlier. . . .

"There you are, now," the hovering servant said with a wrinkly smile. "I'd say you need a bit to eat and more rest, and you'll be fit as ever. Have you ever fainted before, miss?"

Berrie shook her head, still feeling strange. She reached for the tea, taking a sip, then a bite of the sandwich. It could have been made by the Queen's own chef or scraps meant for the poor, and Berrie wouldn't have known the difference. She didn't eat so much for taste as for need; her stomach, and her head, demanded to be fed.

"Just hungry, then, miss?"

She nodded, her mouth too full to speak.

"That's good," said Moira with a laugh. "I was afraid we had a waif on our hands, a miss such as yourself in a bit of a family circumstance, if you know what I mean."

Berrie should have been shocked, but her mind was still in a fog, and the sandwich was beginning to taste good, very good indeed. She finished it as quickly as Royboy might have done with his penchant for stuffing his mouth.

She wished there were another, but only the tea remained. She sipped it, noting a bitter taste of cloves and chamomile. Her stomach demanded more no matter the flavor. She glanced around the room. Like the hall she'd passed on her way to the parlor, this room was in need of fresh paint. But the bed was solid, the mattress and covers beneath her soft. Though the room had no artwork, there were a chiffonier, two lamp tables, a writing desk and chaise longue, far more furniture than the parlor boasted.

"Where is Finola?"

"I'll be sure to tell her all's well. It's late now, and you're tired. She'll see you in the morning."

Berrie set the tea on the tray next to the bed and struggled to rise, moving her legs to the edge. Moira reached out, placing a hand on one of Berrie's shoulders, another to prevent her limbs from reaching the floor.

"Hush now, miss. There's nothing to be done tonight. Besides, I've put a little something in your tea to help you sleep. Nothing to worry over. Now sleep."

"But I must speak to Finola. . . . Really, I must speak to her now."

Even to Berrie, her pleas sounded halfhearted. But inside she railed against the fatigue, the weakness, the confusion. She must find Finola and make her take back her lies, or the school would surely be lost. . . .

Berrie opened her eyes, though even her lids felt heavy. A shard of light came through an opening in the drapes, giving away the morning. Pulling herself up to sit, she noticed Moira sleeping on the chaise. Watching over Berrie . . . or standing guard?

Quietly, Berrie stood, testing her footing. She was groggy but otherwise herself. Nothing a good breakfast couldn't cure. She would find Finola first, no matter how early the hour.

Though the floor creaked once, Moira didn't stir. Her even breathing assured Berrie of her sound sleep. Berrie went to the hall, seeing three other doors: two opposite and one next to hers. Unlike hers, those doors were closed. She went to the near-est and leaned closer to see if she might hear something to give away anyone inside. The last person she wanted to awaken was Thaddeus.

She heard nothing, then went to the second, just across. It too was quiet. From behind the third, she heard the sound of deep snoring, and she prayed such a sound sleeper was Thaddeus.

Berrie tried the other doors. The first was locked; the handle didn't budge. The second door was not locked, but the room proved empty.

Berrie returned to the locked room. Perhaps Finola was there, locked inside? Thinking of yesterday, sensing something she didn't understand might be going on beneath the surface of this dark and run-down home, Berrie was prepared for nearly anything.

She tapped lightly. No response.

"Finola," she whispered. "Finola, are you there?"

Nothing.

Berrie could risk no more noise if she were to stay free of both Thaddeus and Moira. So she went to the stairs, deciding to find

Jobbin and return with him. He might be twice as old as Thaddeus, but if Jobbin and Berrie confronted Thaddeus together, he might be bullied into letting them speak to Finola.

She found her way through the unfamiliar house, glancing out windows to see if a veranda or pathway might give a clue to the nearest door. Archways and thresholds were narrow and tattered with peeling paint, windows in every room hung with fraying drapery. She tried opening one of the tall windows, noting a step leading down to a grassy lawn outside, but the lock was stiff and unusable.

At last she recognized the parlor where she'd fainted and from there found the kitchen downstairs and her way outside. First glance showed no sign of Jobbin or his wagon. She guessed they'd taken shelter in the barn not far off.

The cool morning air refreshed her mind, lending energy to her step. "Jobbin! Are you there?"

The barn walls, like every other surface, were in need of paint, but the structure appeared sturdy enough. She went inside, calling Jobbin's name again. Thankfully she saw his wagon, so she knew he couldn't be far.

"Here, miss," said a voice from one of the stalls. A moment later Jobbin appeared, adjusting the jacket he'd obviously slept in. The strip of graying hair looping the back of his head was splintered with hay.

"Jobbin! We must go inside and see Finola. I don't know what that brother of hers is doing to her, but I'm fairly certain whatever it is cannot be good."

Jobbin scrubbed his scalp with one hand. "You might be right about that, miss. I think that maid tampered with my tea. I never hit hay so hard in all me life, not so many hours after a visit to a pub, that is."

"The same happened to me. Something isn't right here, Jobbin. Only we can't leave without talking to Finola."

"Right. I'll come with you, then."

They walked back to the kitchen entrance, only to be met inside by Moira struggling to hurry down the stairs. "Ah, so the saints are with us still! Blessed be the God of all heaven. We're saved!"

"What is it, Moira?" demanded Berrie. "What is it the Lord God needs to save you from?"

The woman let out a breath of air, less a laugh than a gasp. "Ah, 'tis an expression, nothing more. I was merely afeared you'd gone off without breakfast, and without it you might be risking another faint."

Berrie put her hands on the woman's heaving shoulders, certain the old woman was hiding something. "Moira, you must take me to Finola. I need to speak to her immediately."

Moira smoothed back her hair, straightened her apron, conjured a smile. "Of course, miss, only she's the late sleeper in the family, true enough. Always has been, even as a wee one."

Berrie was certain that was true; Finola had proved it often enough at Escott Manor. "You'll have to wake her, Moira. I must ask her some questions, and it cannot wait. I must return to Dublin, but not without talking to Finola first."

"Now, now, there," said Moira, still breathless though she kept her smile firmly in place. She went to the stove, opened the coal door, and stirred cold ash left from embers of the night before. Picking out the cinders and putting them in a small bucket, she behaved as if nothing were amiss. Finally she took up the nearby coal pail, pouring a portion of the fat, round pieces into the firebox. "We'll have some breakfast, if you please. I can see this man at your side is in need of a bite to eat, and if I recall the way you ate that sandwich last night, you'll need somethin' as well. Soon you'll be filled and happy, so settle in."

Berrie shook her head, stepping past the bustling servant. "I cannot wait, Moira. If you don't rouse Finola, I will."

Moira dropped the coal bucket in a clatter, hastening after Berrie. "Sit and enjoy a bit of food. Come back!"

Berrie might have argued, but a noise distracted her. She heard it from a distance, similar to the wailing she often heard at the school. *Conall?*

"Is Conall here, in this house somewhere? Is Finola with him?"

Moira shook her head. "No, miss. We'll be getting Conall later, where he's spent the night. It's barely past dawn; we cannot collect him until the hour is decent."

Berrie was quiet again, listening. She was sure she'd heard something. It was quiet now. Instead of taking the seat Moira offered, Berrie looked at Jobbin. One nod was enough. He followed her from the room, Moira's protests ignored.

Upstairs, the hall was still quiet except for the snoring from behind the first door. Berrie passed that one, going to the one that was locked. "Can you open that even though it's locked?" Berrie asked Jobbin.

"I'll try," he said, assessing the threshold. "It's an old door, miss, which means an old lock." His gaze went from the closed door to the open one, the room where Berrie had slept. He disappeared into that room a moment, coming back with a fireplace poker, sharp and strong.

"You ought not to be doing this," Moira said, catching up to them after a slower ascent. Even as her face accompanied the warning, her voice was little more than a whisper.

The door pried open beneath Jobbin's ministration with a crack of brittle old wood.

Berrie pushed the door wide, stepping inside. "Finola!" she called, but as the word passed her lips, Berrie saw the room was empty.

"I was certain she was—"

"May I ask what is going on here?"

Berrie turned. Just behind a startled and somewhat worried-looking Jobbin, beyond the frowning Moira, stood the narrow outline of Thaddeus O'Shea, darkly clad in a dressing gown he was just tying round his thin waist. From the dimly lit, empty bedroom, Berrie could barely make out the man's unkind features.

"Where is Finola?" she demanded.

He yawned. "Asleep, I'm sure, at this hour. What is the meaning of breaking my door? I demand an explanation."

"I'd like to speak to Finola."

"You keep saying that, and I keep asking you why you've brought your driver up here to damage my property."

"It appears neither of us will get our answers, Mr. O'Shea, unless you intend telling me where I can find Finola's room. I thought she was in here."

"As you can see, she isn't. She left after your rather convenient fainting spell last night."

"Convenient?"

"Yes. You needed a place to stay; how was I to refuse a woman who swoons to achieve her goal?"

"Did you say Finola left? Where did she go?"

"To our friend's house, who kept Conall while we dined elsewhere yesterday."

Berrie shook her head. "Moira told me Finola is here, only asleep."

Thaddeus's thick brows met in the middle above the shelf that was the top of his nose. A deep frown filled his face, but he didn't deign a glance in the servant's direction. "Moira does not know everything that goes on in this house."

"I will not believe Finola left without seeing me, especially considering my condition."

"Perhaps your friendship isn't as important to her as you believed," he said softly. There was no tenderness in his tone.

Berrie took a step closer, nearer the door, but unavoidably

closer to Thaddeus. "Where is this friend's house, then? I shall see her there."

He laughed. "I think not. I'll not have you disturb any of our friends at this hour so that you may break down one of their doors as well. I think it best you find your way home to Dublin, Miss Ferguson. If that's your name."

"Why should you doubt it?"

He needed to take only one small step closer, his face directly in front of hers, so that she smelled the foulness of his breath. "You are an Englishwoman, not Irish. Neither Nessa nor Finola have had cause to befriend many Englishwomen. But I don't care who you are or why you've come. I know only that you will leave or I will have the constable take you away."

"For what reason?" she asked. "I've done nothing wrong."

"Damage to another's property constitutes a crime in this county." Thaddeus pointed to the door Jobbin had pried open at her urging. "Leave or I shall have you arrested."

Berrie narrowed her gaze. "I don't know why you seem to be holding Finola here against her will, but I intend to find out."

Then she walked past him and Jobbin followed close behind. They went back to the kitchen, Moira following slowly but stopping at the threshold without a word.

Jobbin went to the barn to hitch the wagon, and Berrie waited outside, watching the manor house. She must find Finola somehow. The young woman had clearly been frightened the evening before. Why else hide Berrie's identity, except fear? Was she afraid to let her brother know Berrie was the headmistress of the school they were suing? At the moment, nothing made sense.

A pounding round the other side of the manor drew Berrie's attention. She turned to see how Jobbin was faring with the wagon, but he wasn't finished. Curious about the pounding, she walked up the lane that led to the dilapidated wing. The noise was louder from there.

She spotted a lone horse, not tethered, sweating as if it had been ridden hard and long despite the early hour. From where she stood, Berrie couldn't see past the tall weeds and shrubs growing wild on this side of the grounds. The pounding, however, surely came from this side. Who would be unwise enough to stand beneath that archway and make such a fuss? She walked closer, parting the tall greenery.

"Simon!"

He turned, standing directly beneath the precarious arch. When their gaze met with only overgrown weeds in between, he jumped from the porch and rushed to her side. His arms went around her, and she let hers do the same.

"You—you're all right?" he asked, holding her eyes with his.

Berrie nodded. "Yes . . . no! Oh, Simon, the school! Do you know?"

"Yes, I know. I came as soon as I heard. I went to the school, and they told me you were looking for Finola, to find out about this case against your attendant. Have you spoken to her?"

She shook her head, pulling away to look at the crumbling manor. "She lives here with her brother, but something odd and a little frightening is going on in there. He wouldn't let me speak to her alone, and I'm sure he was the one who made sure I didn't try to see her during the night, while he was asleep."

Simon frowned. "How did he manage that?"

"His housekeeper put something in my tea and Jobbin's as well. Something to make us sleep."

"You're certain you're all right?"

She nodded, in that instant realizing not only his concern but her own amazement that he'd come. She wanted to pull him close, kiss him, thank him. There was, however, no time for any of that.

"How is it that you're here? I thought you might be on your way to London."

"I was, but the courier from Mr. Truebody found me before my ship sailed."

"And you came to find me?"

"I tracked you here—though I think neither Mrs. Cotgrave nor Nessa O'Donnell appreciated the hour."

Berrie had so many thoughts she couldn't possibly sort through them: why he'd come, what he thought of their unfortunate report in the news, how he might be of help—if he wanted to help. But she could ask none of that. She wanted only to let him hold her, as he was doing just then.

A noise from the other side of the door drew her attention.

"Did you hear that?" she asked.

He nodded. "And it's high time someone answered my knock, don't you think? Though I can't imagine what the inside must look like if this door and garden are any indication."

She shook her head. "This side of the manor doesn't seem to be used anymore. Jobbin and I came here yesterday, and he knocked but no one acknowledged us until we went round the other side. You'd never know the two sides were attached. One side habitable, this side . . ."

Berrie stopped, listening. Whatever she'd heard was gone now. This side of the manor appeared as silent and deserted as it had the day before. Or was it? Could what she'd heard earlier have come from behind these crumbling walls?

She dismissed the thought. It couldn't be. No one would dare enter such a ramshackle place. The newer addition was old and worn down enough; this side was ancient and dangerous. Surely no one would willingly . . .

No, not willingly. But otherwise? Pulling herself from Simon, she ran beneath the archway, pounding on the door much as he had done moments ago. He was at her side before she'd made much noise, pulling her wrist.

"Come away from here, Berrie," he cautioned. "I was so frantic to find you I didn't notice this whole place looks about ready to fall in."

"But—" She stopped, hearing another noise. Pounding . . . from inside. Berrie threw herself at the door, no longer satisfied with ineffectual knocking. She would push in the door; surely one so decrepit would open more easily than the one Jobbin had broken upstairs.

"Berrie!" Simon lifted her off her feet before she could pummel the door yet again, just as pebbles and mortar showered them from above like hail in a spring storm.

She sputtered clay dust from her face. "No, Simon. I think Finola is in there! I heard something earlier, something like Conall. I think her brother's locked them inside."

Simon shook his head, frowning. "Why in the world would someone—?"

"I don't know! I only know he's hiding them."

She squirmed free, throwing herself at the door yet again. A voice from beyond the weeds stopped her from attacking the door once more.

"Miss Ferguson!" Paddy's voice came through the dense shrubbery, followed by the rustling of foliage, and finally the boy himself skidded to a halt not three arms' lengths away. "He's heard ye, miss! And he's comin' round for sure. You'd best be off!"

Simon put a steady hand on the boy's heaving shoulder. "Who's coming, young man? And who's Miss Ferguson?"

"Mr. O'Shea is coming! A meaner man you don't want to know."

Berrie thrust herself against the door again and more pebbles fell into her hair, but she didn't care. "Finola! Are you there? Conall!" She pounded again, tried the handle. It budged!

"I am here, Berrie!" The call came from directly beyond the wooden door. "Conall's here too. The door is wedged."

Simon came up beside Berrie. "Stand back, Berrie. The foundation is tilted." He leaned closer to the door. "Stand back, Finola!" Then he kicked not the door but the frame surrounding it, dashing inside as it burst open and the precarious outer archway collapsed at Berrie's feet.

"Simon!" He'd disappeared in a veil of gray, and she heard crying—Conall's. Through the cloud, she saw the door on its side and darkness beyond that.

"We're here," Simon called. "Don't come any closer, Berrie. The whole place is about to fall."

Berrie stepped closer. "I can't see you!"

"We're sheltered by a beam just inside. I'm going to push Finola through first, and she'll have Conall in her arms. Take him from her, but don't step on the porch foundation. Do you hear me?"

"I hear you!"

"Of course we'll offer all the aid we can," said another voice, "like this!"

She saw rather than heard Thaddeus's approach, then felt two rough hands on her shoulders, pushing her at the half-fallen wall that had once been the front entrance to the crumbling manor house. She wasn't sure what hit her first—the stones he'd pushed her toward or the ones that fell from above. It all seemed to happen at once.

With an irrational thought, she wondered if it mattered. But just as quickly, she realized it didn't, before all went black.

53

The sun rose on activity already begun throughout the Hall. Staff arrived to see about their various tour segments, from maids dressed in Victorian attire to certain part-time tour guides who, Rebecca suspected, were frustrated actors and actresses who loved dressing and playing the part of nineteenth-century nobility.

Before going to bed last night, Rebecca had told Talie about the day's activities, apologizing that her hands would be full while dealing with a full tour day that included the long-awaited visit from the Featherby judging committee. Rebecca invited Talie to join one of the tours or sleep in as long as she liked; she was sure Dana and Padgett would keep Talie busy if she didn't join a tour.

Despite all the distractions, Rebecca was sure of one thing: the Hall was as ready as it could be for the judges' arrival. Her personal life might be headed for ruin, but she knew how to run an estate. She would ignore the thoughts infesting the small parts of her mind, that Quentin's arrival might bring support for the Featherby but also a good-bye. Attention to that fear would have to wait.

With a last glance at the mirror to check the tailored black suit that had cost her more than she liked to recall and a final tuck to the forever wayward strand of hair, she left her suite telling herself nothing would spoil this day's work. Nothing.

No sooner had she stepped into the hall than a cry from the playroom stabbed Rebecca's manufactured confidence. Rebecca rushed forward, met by a ghostly white Dana.

"She isn't here, either! Padgett's gone!"

54

Surely it cannot be good to lose consciousness twice within a twenty-four hour period. I can honestly tell you, Cosima, it is possible to survive. I still have mortar dust in my hair despite a good washing here in the comfort of the Quail's Stop Inn. The proprietor was kind enough to lend his wife's personal bath, but the back of my head was so tender I could not scrub very well.

Your cousin Finola is here with me, and I must tell you I underestimated her. She is as fierce a protector as any I have seen. Conall, I assure you, shall never be in need so long as his mother is here to care for him. When I roused, having been pulled from the rubble by Simon, I was not quite sure whether I was dreaming or not. There, beyond Simon's shoulder, was Finola, struggling to her feet. She set Conall aside. He was babbling, unhurt, and blissfully unafraid.

Whether she would have found the courage had not Simon, Jobbin, and I been nearby, I cannot say. But

there she was, making a weapon of her body, nearly
succeeding in knocking over her wiry though much taller
brother. . . .

Simon must have seen the horror on Berrie's face. He turned
from bending over her to face Finola, who rammed her brother
and reached up with small, ineffectual hands to wrap around his
throat.

"You could have killed us—like Mama! You're just like her."

Simon pulled Finola from Thaddeus, more for her safety, Berrie guessed, than her brother's. Simon's interference moved her
beyond reach.

"If you don't want to be arrested for the attempt of murder,"
Simon said, standing well within the reach of Thaddeus's fist, "I
suggest you have the wreckage of this manor either removed or
made safe."

They were of similar height, but Thaddeus was considerably
slighter, frail in comparison to Simon. Surely one hit from Simon
would fell the other man.

"You'd best listen to him, Thaddeus," Finola said, now like
a hummingbird, flitting around her brother. "This is Simon
MacFarland, and he's an MP. Sure and enough he can have you
arrested—and he ought to—for putting me and Conall in that
room." She turned from them to Berrie, rushing to her side and
helping her to her feet. "He forced me to make those charges
against poor Duff, thinking if the school closed, the estate would
be sold and we could get half the inheritance. Duff didn't do a
thing except be nice to me."

Berrie let go of Finola's hand, grabbing her arms. "You'll
come with me then, and tell the justice of the peace and the constable? drop the charges against Duff?"

Finola nodded just as tears began clearing a trail through the dust on her face. "I suppose I'll be in some trouble for lying." She turned away, going to her son and taking him up in her arms.

Berrie looked at Simon. "Is she?"

Instead of addressing either Berrie or Finola, Simon cast a somber look at Thaddeus. "Not as much trouble as is about to land at the foot of your brother. Come on." He took Berrie's hand, then touched Finola's elbow. "Jobbin, I was told you've been taking Berrie around in your wagon. Do you have it ready?"

55

"What are you saying?" Rebecca asked, confused. She followed Dana into her empty room. "Where is she?"

Rebecca heard someone behind her and saw Talie, looking every bit as concerned as Dana.

"I thought she was in with Talie, but she wasn't. I checked in the kitchen, then in every room up here. She's gone—with her toy Emma."

Rebecca shook her head. "No, no, she must be here some-where. We'll all look for her. You two get dressed and meet me in the kitchen. I'll ask Helen and William if they've seen her."

Dana was already throwing on a long-sleeve shirt over the T-shirt she slept in, exchanging cotton sleep pants for a pair of jeans from a nearby chair. She followed Rebecca from the room.

Talie grabbed Dana's hand. "We'll find her, Danes. Don't get all stressed. She's here, probably somewhere in the house. It's big enough to get lost in. I'll get dressed too and meet you downstairs."

Rebecca didn't have to look at Dana's face to know the words wouldn't have brought comfort. Padgett had been exploring this house for over a month now; she wasn't likely to get lost anymore.

As they walked steadily down the stairs, Rebecca saw imme-diately that Padgett's favorite spot at the top of the stairs showed no sign of her—no toys, no empty bowl from cereal she might have served herself before anyone else was awake.

Dana had looked in all of the other favorite spots: the playroom, where Quentin's and his brother's toys had been left for future generations; the library, where a shelf of children's books had drawn Padgett more than once; the media room, where a large-screen television had been installed, complete with a selection of children's movies Dana had brought along; the garden room, where she often passed time with Winston.

"Helen was already in the kitchen when I went downstairs," Dana was saying. "She hasn't seen her."

"Do you know how long she might have been gone?"

Dana's eyes shut tight. "I didn't sleep all night, until this morning around five. Then I must have slept so soundly I didn't hear a thing. She was gone when I woke up—about seven forty-five."

Rebecca glanced at her watch; it was half past eight. Full staff was due any minute with the tours to begin at ten. "We'll soon have all the help we need to search every inch of this place, Dana."

They went to the kitchen, where Helen was putting scones made from one of Cosima Escott's favorite recipes into the oven. She turned with brows lifted. Obviously reading the answer to her unspoken question on their faces, she took off her apron and turned back to the oven only long enough to turn it off. "I'll get William."

Rebecca and Dana split up, searching every room on the first floor, calling Padgett's name. Making her way to the foyer, Rebecca glanced out one of the windows, seeing several of the tour participants gathering on the portico with Rebecca's education manager. If Padgett wasn't found in the next few minutes, she would begin recruiting searchers.

Rebecca found the old servants' staircase in the hallway

leading from the ballroom. It was one place Rebecca had never shown Padgett. It was dark inside, used these days for cleaning supplies.

"Padgett? Are you in here?"

She looked behind hanging dustcoats and up the straight staircase. No Padgett.

"That's an odd place to look for someone," said a familiar voice from the hall.

Rebecca stepped into the light, seeing a perplexed look on Quentin's face. He was dressed for the importance of the day: a dark blue Italian suit, crisp white shirt, tie daubed with blue, a platinum pin holding it in place.

"Good morning," he greeted.

Rebecca had no words, not even the ones she'd contemplated saying the moment she saw him again. "Padgett's missing."

He frowned. "What?"

"Dana woke a little while ago, and Padgett's bed was empty."

"She has to be here somewhere. I suppose you checked the playroom first?"

Rebecca nodded. "Last night she overheard us talking. Dana was quite upset. I think—"

"This is all my fault, isn't it?"

The words came from behind the open staircase door, which Quentin gently closed. Dana's face was wet with a new supply of tears, her eyes puffy, her skin a mix of ash white and feverish red.

"Of course not, Dana," Rebecca said, stepping closer. "I was going to say she might have been upset and perhaps is hiding, that's all."

"Or run off!" she cried. "Who knows where she could be if she left the house?"

Rebecca exchanged a glance with Quentin. If she had left the house, there would be only one place she'd go.

"The cuddle farm," Quentin said before Rebecca could.

They fairly raced to the ballroom veranda exit, the fastest way from the house in the direction of the farm. Rebecca heard a call behind them from Talie, but no one stopped, and she saw Talie dart onto their path.

The full staff was already there, no doubt readying things for the Featherby tours.

"Chad, has Padgett been here already this morning? Maybe to see Emma?"

"I was just going to check Emma and her family," he said as he walked, not seeming to notice the urgency behind Quentin's inquiry or the uncommonness of having visitors to his barn at this time of the morning. "Saw to the cow, fed the horses and the chickens, but haven't seen to the lambs yet."

He opened the back barn door that led to the paddock area, the small pasture where the lambs and goats grazed and slept.

Rebecca scanned the area. No Padgett. "There's Emma's mama," she said, pointing to the familiar, pleasantly plump ewe. Emma was old enough for her own adventures but often stayed close to her mother anyway.

Emma was nowhere to be seen.

The bleating of a goat off to the side of the paddock called attention. His horns were stuck in the gate.

"Now that's peculiar," said Chad from behind them. "Excuse me, will you? Got to keep that one from letting loose and into the garden, today of all days, isn't that right, Miss Seabrooke, Mr. Hollinworth?"

Quentin followed, and so did Rebecca. Talie and Dana went back into the barn. Rebecca heard them call Padgett's name.

"What's odd about the goat's getting caught, Chad?" Quentin asked, while he looked over the animals.

"He's our scoundrel," Chad said, grabbing one horn and unlatching the gate, freeing the struggling animal without letting him behind the confines of the paddock. "Has a taste for ferns and'll nibble 'em flat."The goat stumbled off and shook his head. "Strange he was caught that way. He must've gotten the top latch undone somehow. See here?"

Rebecca gauged the height of the latches. The lower one was well within reach of Padgett, but the upper? She probably couldn't reach it, the way the ground dipped away from the fence. Rebecca exchanged a glance with Quentin. He seemed to be thinking as she did: Padgett could have come this way, climbed the fence to unlatch the top, but then been unable to fasten the top latch from the other side, where the grading was steeper.

"Emma's not here," called Dana from the barn.

Quentin waved her forward. "She went this way." He turned to Chad. "I want you to tell the entire staff we're searching for Padgett, and this takes precedence over the tours today. Everyone is to lend a hand searching. Everyone and everywhere, mind you—even the Featherby judges themselves if they get here before we find Padgett. Understand?"

"Yes, sir," said Chad.

"I have my mobile phone and you're to call me if she's found."

Chad nodded again, and his pace was quicker back to the barn.

Quentin led Rebecca, Dana, and Talie outside the paddock. "Let's split up, but not beyond sight of one another."

The three fanned out, looking ahead at the wheat field, the wooded glen, the fallow field, and the numerous hedgerows along the rolling countryside. Ponds and lakes dotted the landscape, but Rebecca couldn't bring herself to ask if Padgett could swim.

They passed the cottage the land agent used as his office. Rebecca saw Quentin head there. If Padgett had come this way, perhaps she'd been attracted to the house with its gingerbread-style roof.

Watching Quentin traipse across the uneven land in his

expensive shoes and tailored suit made one thought stand out in Rebecca's anxiety-ridden mind—one she would contemplate later, once they had Padgett safely back in her mother's arms. Quentin Hollinworth was as much a servant as she was, or he wouldn't be out looking the same way the rest of them were.

The office must have been empty based on the lack of response Quentin received from his knock.

"Everybody's praying, right?" Quentin called as they resumed their search. With only a short distance between them, Rebecca had no trouble hearing the words she welcomed almost as much as any others. A reminder of the One who was really in control, who knew exactly where Padgett was this moment.

Just then Rebecca heard the chime of Quentin's mobile phone. Hope flared.

"Yes, Chad? . . . What's that?" Quentin's voice hinted the same hope he must be holding. "Oh." Hope abandoned them all in that single, deflated word. "No, that's fine. Tell her it's silly to wait; I'll not be available the rest of the day."

Rebecca kept walking, praying. Each of them took turns calling Padgett's name. Rebecca listened as she'd never listened before. She prayed for Padgett's call in return or Emma's bleat.

"Here! Look at this." Dana rushed a few feet ahead, bending low to pick up something from the trimmed meadow grass. Rebecca recognized the toy immediately.

"It's Padgett's toy Emma!"

"At least we know we're heading in the right direction," Quentin said.

"Wait," called Talie from Dana's other side. "Did you hear that?"

All four stopped. Rebecca heard nothing, but a moment later Dana dashed forward, racing beyond Talie.

"Padgett! Padgett, can you hear me?"

Rebecca saw Dana scale a rise and nearly disappear in a dip in the ground. Sprinting after her, Rebecca saw what she expected: the other side green and blue with a pond reflecting the wide blue sky.

And there, lying on the bank, was Padgett beside Emma.

The lamb struggled to its feet, bleating at the sight of rushing oncomers, although tethered to a rope and unable to go far. Padgett lifted her head at the lamb's warning, and to Rebecca's first glance she looked groggy.

"Oh, hi, Mommy," she said, rubbing her eyes.

Dana pulled her into her arms, and the tether connecting her to the lamb dropped, but the lamb stayed nearby.

"Is that all you have to say, young lady?" Dana said through her tears. "Why are you so far from Rebecca's? Why did you leave without telling me?"

"I just went out to think, same as you did, Mommy. Only I couldn't find that lake you liked for your thinking time. Emma led me to this one, and then I lost my—oh! You found Little Emma." She grabbed the stuffed animal from her mother's hand.

"You were looking for the lake outside the front of the Hall?" Dana moaned, cuddling her daughter closer. "You only needed to go to the front . . ." She didn't finish her sentence, kissing Padgett again. "Padgett, don't you ever, ever do that again. Never leave without telling me, so I know where you are, okay?"

"Okay. But I wonder about something. You know how you went to sit next to the pond to think 'cause you were sad? I was doing that because I was sad for you, because you were crying all night, only I didn't know what I was supposed to think about. So I just said that prayer Rebecca says about God making everything. Is that okay?"

Dana laughed first, and Rebecca, Quentin, and Talie joined in. It was a balm to frayed nerves.

"You, young lady," said Quentin firmly once the laughter

dwindled, "need to think about something else right now: how to make your mommy never worry again. Can you do that?"

"Okay. She wasn't supposed to worry now."

"And how would you have gotten back home, Padgett?" her aunt Talie asked. "Do you know which way goes back to the Hall?"

She shrugged one shoulder. "I don't, but I thought maybe Emma would. She always knows how to find her mommy back at the farm, so I thought she would lead me back. That's why I took her on the leash, so she wouldn't go too fast and leave me behind."

Quentin took up Emma's rope leash, and the lamb did indeed lead the way back to the Hall while he called Chad on the mobile to let them know Padgett had been found. The staff was to resume "Featherby mode," as he called it with a grin.

The judges were due any minute if they weren't there already.

Rebecca's relief and gratitude over finding Padgett was too soon replaced. The judges awaited . . . and so did Quentin's decision about where he wanted to be—here or in his London flat.

56

Mr. Truebody was shocked to learn of the O'Shea plot to close our doors. I will not say that he went so far as to admit he should never have given up hope, but I will say this: when Simon MacFarland is in the room, the embodiment of true power in this country (so stark a contrast to our justice of the peace), Mr. Truebody is a man nearly tolerable. He assured me he would do all he could to calm residual fears of both parents and benefactors alike and see if the Commission might approve Finola's residence with us (an option he never bothered to broach to this point!). He also offered a bit of advice. . . .

"It is commendable that Mr. MacFarland has accompanied you here today, Miss Hamilton," said Mr. Truebody. "He has not only expressed his own confidence in having you run Escott Manor but has taken full responsibility for the reports in the papers regarding his sister's misunderstanding. I have only one thing to add."

Berrie waited, not daring to glance Simon's way. It had been humiliating enough to stand in this office with him at her side, listening to him explain that a kiss had indeed taken place. He went on to tell Mr. Truebody that the kiss was not at all scandalous, given that it had been accompanied by a proposal of marriage, albeit that proposal had been flatly refused for the sake of the school that was now endangered.

"You ought to have accepted that proposal, young lady," continued Mr. Truebody. "If you truly want to save the institution, then let me assure you it should be run by a married woman rather than a maiden such as yourself. It would offer much greater security to the benefactors. I can safely vouch for this office that if you were under the safekeeping of a man, a man to whom you are first responsible, I am certain such benefactors would be assured of the highest quality of leadership and protection from any further scandal."

Myriad protests went through her mind, a demand as to what made a man better fit to oversee her school, but she knew this was neither the time nor the place. Besides, she had already seen Simon humble enough to publicly admit he'd been refused; she didn't need to announce to one and all she refused to need him, or any man, to help her in this mission.

Instead, she imagined what a demure young lady would say. "Thank you, Mr. Truebody. I'm sure you're right."

"Then this session is at an end. I trust Mr. Duff Habgood is already on his way back to Escott Manor since you first went to the constable's office with Miss O'Shea. He is welcome to remain in the employment of the hospital, Miss Hamilton, but under the circumstances it would be best if he resided outside manor grounds, especially if we are to gain the Commission's approval for Miss O'Shea to return. Until memories fade."

"And myself?" Berrie asked.

"You may resume your role. If there is any change, I will summon you here and give counsel. You will, in turn, inform me if your status as an unmarried woman changes?"

Berrie grew warm, sparing no more than a glance at Mr. Truebody, who wasn't eyeing her but rather looked at Simon beside her.

She was sure her step was a bit quicker on the way out than it had been on the way in. Simon stayed at her side, opening doors when necessary, taking her hand to help her board his carriage outside.

"So your school is saved," he said, sitting across from her.

She couldn't help smiling. The past two days had been little more than a blur of misery. "Yes, thanks in no small part to you."

"Me? It was you, Berrie." He held her gaze a moment, then shifted to look out the window. "I would say you proved quite thoroughly that you don't need anyone, despite what Mr. Truebody wants to believe."

Berrie looked down at her hands, glad they were covered in gloves. Despite the cool weather, her palms were moist. If she was honest, she would blurt the truth, that she'd missed him and regretted her refusal. How could she admit that now? He would think she did so only to follow the advice of Mr. Truebody and thus ensure the survival of the school.

"It would never work, you know," she whispered, more to herself than to him.

"What wouldn't?"

She looked at Simon, swallowing away the lump in her throat, forcing down the fear of making an utter fool of herself. If she was to speak to him honestly, it must begin now. "You would think I married you only to save the school, or at least my place in it."

"And . . . would you? Marry me, that is?"

Berrie let her gaze float out the window, too afraid he would see something she wasn't ready to reveal just yet. "Are you asking me under those circumstances? That I marry you to secure my position?"

He laughed so easily she knew he felt none of her uncertainty. "No, Berrie, I most definitely am not."

His words only added to her confusion but no less than when he slid from his seat to settle beside her. He took one of her hands.

"If you were to marry me, Berrie, it would not be a marriage by arrangement or convenience. It would *not* be in name only, nor for the sake of your school, your position, your reputation, or your future. It would be a marriage in the fullest sense, where we shared the same breakfast, tea, and dinner table, the same washbasin." He leaned closer so that he was whispering in her ear. "The same bed."

The heat beneath her gloves spread throughout the rest of her. She looked at him, knowing she couldn't hide that his insinuation was neither frightening nor unappealing. Still, she had to bring up thoughts that should surface better sooner than later. "And share the same arguments?"

"Fight the same fights," Simon corrected, "on the same side for a change."

"But what of my duties? And yours? I didn't refuse you because I didn't want to be married to you, Simon. I refused because I wanted to spare us both the frustration that will come if either one is torn from what we must do."

He put a hand on each side of her face so that she could look only at him. "I prayed that was true."

"Did you, Simon? Have you been praying for us?"

He nodded. "You believe that school is a mission from God. If that's the case, then how could I hope to wrest you away unless He wanted me to share in some part of that mission? I believe it's possible, Berrie. I have a staff already in place who can take care of some of your paperwork."

She grinned. "You might have mentioned that the first time you proposed, Simon. I'm sure I couldn't have said no to that."

"And judging from Mr. Truebody, any time you have to appear before him, it would undoubtedly be best to have a male voice—a mouthpiece, I admit, but one from whom he would obviously prefer to hear."

The thought of never again appearing alone before Mr. Truebody was heady indeed. Still, Berrie frowned. "Simon, you needn't convince me of my benefit from marrying you. From the time you first kissed me, I've fought against wanting to marry you, and I'm more than ready to give up such a fight. But what possible benefit can I bring to you except the burden of a wife who will speak her mind and split her time between hearth and mission?"

"Don't you recall, Berrie?"

She shook her head.

"I must confess that my words during my first, ill-conceived proposal to you have been burned into my memory—much to my shame. I claimed that I did not need someone who was madly in love or blind to my faults. I merely wanted a woman who respects and honors my thoughts and opinions. I know now that you do. And if you can love me as well, that's all I ask."

"I do, Simon; that I do."

57

The judges arrived precisely on time. The new scripts, new ward-robes, refurbished teaching tools had been in place for over a month and the staff and Hall were ready, only within minutes of the judges' arrival.

Though only one Featherby official was required, there were three today. A director of the program, Eva Wetherhead, explained that Hollinworth Hall had long been one of her favor-ite garden properties, and she didn't want to miss the opportu-nity to visit. She brought with her two judges, one who was in training.

"As you know," said Eva Wetherhead, "our goal is to promote good practices in education, particularly through historical envi-ronments." She turned to the other judges, and Rebecca guessed the one with slightly widened eyes to be the one in training. "Hollinworth Hall is known for its association with those who have a love of learning, as far back as the Viscount Peter Hamil-ton, who was renowned for his contributions to science, to the last viscount, who donated so much time and money to Cam-bridge." She looked at Rebecca, who stood next to Quentin. "Will you both be leading our tour?"

"Yes," said Quentin as smoothly as if they'd been leisurely await-ing their arrival instead of having spent the last hour in such commo-tion. "Miss Seabrooke planned for us to start in the ballroom, then visit the cuddle farm. I believe we'll finish the outside portion on the veranda with the Victorian tea and end the tour in the gallery. Is that right?"

Rebecca nodded even though he didn't need her approval; she might have arranged the tour, but the material she'd used was all his. His home, his farm, his staff. She was reminded she might have been foolish to fall in love with him. If he truly wanted to return to Caroline Norleigh, then their brief exploration of a relationship would leave her not only with a broken heart but also without a job.

Thoughts of working somewhere else were impossible to face, particularly today when everything at the Hall was at its best, from the gardens to the cuddle farm to the workshops in both the smithy and the science hut full of Peter Hamilton's fossils. She couldn't leave here, not when so much of her life, of her family's lives, had been lived out on these grounds. She couldn't leave, and yet she couldn't stay. Not if Quentin was to marry Caroline Norleigh.

They went through the farm, no evidence left of the drama that had played out less than a half hour ago. No one, not a judge nor a member of the tour, would guess the path of worry they'd taken to find Padgett. All was well, and Talie joined them on the tour, a smile on her face.

They went to the science hut, surveyed the gardens—both practical and ornamental—and visited the maze that had been searched such a short time ago in vain. As they reached the veranda, Rebecca noticed almost instantly that one figure didn't belong. Although her suit was probably far more expensive than the replicas of Victorian daywear, Lady Elise's contemporary outfit was a jarring reminder of what era they all belonged to.

"I'll see her," Quentin whispered, "but I'll be back in a moment. Alone."

Quentin excused himself from the tour, and Rebecca

watched him join his mother, leading her inside the Hall. Rebecca kept her gaze on the tour participants, though she wondered what was so urgent that Lady Elise had arrived today.

Rebecca knew the judges would want to mingle with the tour group afterward, particularly the students and their teachers. The education manager was there to assist with the students and the tourists to make sure no questions were left unanswered and the purposes behind each exhibit were clear. Rebecca was eager to use that time to see that the judges were satisfied in their overall assessment.

The gallery seemed dark after the bright sun, so she filled a few moments with stories she'd heard Quentin tell before introducing the great masters, the Hollinworth forebears, the various eras and methods of artwork demonstrated in the collection. And while Rebecca was sure the judges were enjoying themselves, she glanced at Talie more than once, particularly when the portraits of Peter and Cosima Hamilton were introduced. Talie looked as though she were meeting old friends.

Just as the formal portion of the tour ended, Rebecca spotted Quentin coming into the gallery. While she was grateful he'd wanted to participate and it might have been more authentic to have him tell his favorite family tales, the tour had been anything but a failure, even without him. She greeted him with a smile. There were some things that wouldn't be robbed of peace, and the knowledge that she'd done her best for the award was one of them.

"Have I missed the whole thing?" he asked, unnecessarily straightening his tie.

"Not entirely," she said. "They'll want to say good-bye, I'm sure. You can see them off." She looked over his shoulder, wondering if his mother had left.

Quentin leaned closer, speaking into her ear. "If you're looking for my mother, I'm hoping she took my advice at last and left. But be on the lookout for her. Between her call earlier and now this visit, she's said more than once she wanted to speak to you, too."

She had been the one who called? "Why does she wish to see me, I wonder?"

He grinned at her. "Don't worry; I've made her promise to be civil. I did tell her today isn't a good day, but the word *Featherby* means absolutely nothing to her." He left Rebecca, extending a hand to one of the judges. "I apologize again for abandoning the tour earlier. I was called to a family meeting I couldn't ignore."

Miss Wetherhead smiled reassuringly. "You have a treasure here, Mr. Hollinworth. My colleagues and I would like to see the tour buses load and drive off, if you don't mind, and retrace a few steps of the tour. After that we'll have you sign some of our pesky paperwork and be of no further trouble. All right?"

"Yes, of course. The Hall is open for you today as long as you like." He turned to Rebecca. "Rebecca?"

She heard his inquiry but could not look at him. Instead her eye was caught in the direction from which he'd come, looking toward the hall leading into the gallery. There stood Elise Hollinworth, staring directly at Rebecca.

"I—I'll join you in a few moments," she said. There was that voice again, the one she hoped never to hear out of herself. Meekness drenching every word.

If Quentin wanted to speak—and Rebecca guessed he did by the way he looked at her and stayed at her side a moment too long—she didn't give him a chance. She walked past him to his mother. Lady Elise's gaze was on her until Rebecca stood a foot away. Then, without a word, she turned on her heel and led her not to the kitchen, where Helen would be found, nor to the parlor that was open and inviting to all, nor to the dining room that overlooked the Victorian tea still being performed on the veranda and lawn until the last tourist and judge was gone. She went, instead, up the stairs and directly to Rebecca's office.

Once inside, she closed the door behind Rebecca.

Lady Elise stood tall and regal in front of the window Rebecca peered through each day. It was Lady Elise's office all of a sudden, her home, her son. Rebecca the outsider. Elise stood now with her back to the window, watching Rebecca. Perhaps this was an experiment to see how long it took for Rebecca to visibly squirm. She willed herself to be still.

Elise's eyes narrowed, her stare burrowing into Rebecca like radiation. Rebecca knew no one questioned Lady Elise; no one but Lady Elise questioned time spent with her, and no one questioned her thoughts, opinions, or motives. But, while Rebecca had no desire to offer disrespect, neither did she desire to offer the opposite—too much of something not earned.

It was all so simple now. Everything Talie had said about the truest role being found in servanthood. The role Christ chose was servant; how could she think herself above that? So many things were easier to see now.

Suddenly Rebecca smiled, and from somewhere inside she recognized the gesture as the miracle it was. Sincere. "Is there some reason you wanted to speak to me, Lady Elise?"

"My son is not here to see those silly judges you have downstairs. He is here to see you. But you knew that already, didn't you?"

How could Rebecca express what she couldn't understand herself? She couldn't know the future any more than Lady Elise could. Rebecca did know one thing: her faith and Quentin's were real. No decision would be made without much prayer. There was too much inside her to be contained in one facial expression: a little confusion over Lady Elise's summons, a remnant of hope she couldn't rid, hope that the look that seemed so steady in Quentin's eyes that morning couldn't be misread. None of that could she share with Lady Elise.

"Yes," Rebecca whispered. The meekness was taking a backseat to peace. She heard it in her voice.

Lady Elise's perfect countenance cracked. There was a moment of indecision in her eyes. "You welcome me as if for all the world you knew the future, that our futures would be entwined by Quentin. The peace of knowledge—it's all over your face."

Rebecca nodded again. "Yes, because I don't wish to worry about the future so much. God has it in the palm of His hand."

Lady Elise crossed her arms, regarding Rebecca with nothing short of curiosity.

"I don't approve of you," Lady Elise said.

"Yes, I know. I'm sorry."

"But not sorry enough to stay away from him."

Rebecca shook her head. If she were talking to Dana or Talie or any one of her old friends, she would have stepped closer, patted the fretful woman's hand, soothed the worry off of her face. This, however, was Lady Elise. "In the Bible, it talks about how we should honor our father and mother. I want to do that; I want Quentin to do that. But it's not wrong for Quentin and me to be together if he decides to be with me instead of Lady Caroline. The stuff of society pages—that doesn't really mean all that much, does it? Really?"

"Society page!" Elise laughed. "Do you think that's what bothers me? If that was all that concerned me, I'd have thought nothing of him taking any woman as wife." Her icy gaze changed before Rebecca, a slow thaw, though detectable. "This world isn't the one I grew up in, you know. Everywhere I turn it's less unique, less specialized. I turn the corner and an American McDonald's turns up—here, in Spain, in Greece, in Japan. I can buy my favorite perfume online now, did you know? The kind I used to have made in a small factory in France just for me. Now I can stay here and order them to make it and have it delivered to my door. Someday there will be nothing unique anywhere anymore." She looked around the office, then held up a palm. "Even here, what was once a bedroom for the daughter of a viscount is now an office for a commercial manager. It's disappearing. Soon the aristocracy will be another memory of the past. It's already happened."

"I'm sorry, Lady Elise," Rebecca said, insight blooming in her mind, and along with it a measure of compassion. "I imagine you see me as one of those fast-food places, don't you? Taking the place of something special, something unique."

If understanding might have bred comradeship, it couldn't be proven by Lady Elise. She turned her back on Rebecca to look out the window.

"He'll be up here shortly. I can't keep him away from you." Lady Elise glanced back, allowing Rebecca no more than a glimpse at her face. She looked older—not sad, rather resigned. "I won't try anymore. You've won."

Didn't Lady Elise realize where Caroline Norleigh was living? Rebecca hid her unresolved fears, knowing the moment was more about Lady Elise than any future—to-be or not-to-be— between Rebecca and Quentin.

"It wasn't a tug-of-war, with Quentin the rope, you know. Don't we both want him to be happy? I haven't won."

Elise eyed Rebecca again, her face neither warm nor cold but placid, the first time Rebecca had seen it so. "Of my two children, I knew Quentin was most like his father. I kept him by my side as often as I could for as long as I could. My husband already had Robert. But now Quentin has discovered his father in him— his faith, his preferences. Not me or my way of life. He'll be loyal to you; I can guarantee that. My husband always was, to his dying day, despite my failings."

"You seem to be certain that my future with Quentin is guaranteed, Lady Elise, when it's anything but."

Lady Elise started to speak, then closed her mouth. She walked past Rebecca, stopping at the door with a hand on the knob. Her face as she looked across the room was the Lady Elise Rebecca knew, cold and distant. "I won't stand in your way, Rebecca, but I warn you: if you dishonor my son or our name, I'll make sure you regret it the rest of your life."

She was gone then, though Rebecca still felt her presence, her words lingering with what should have been a warning. But they weren't. They were the only kind of blessing Lady Elise knew how to give.

Hope flared again in Rebecca even as she tried cautioning against it. Maybe for some unknown reason Lady Elise no longer stood in their way. . . . Was there anything left between Rebecca and Quentin for it to matter?

Rebecca followed Lady Elise, who went downstairs without a word to the veranda exit rather than passing the knot of people still gathered around the buses waiting to take tourists away. If she went straight to her car, she would be down the lane before the buses pulled out. Rebecca would have joined those outside, but she spotted Talie with Dana and Padgett in the front parlor.

"That was a wonderful tour, Rebecca," said Talie. "Now when I read Cosima's journal again, I'll be able to picture everything more accurately. Even her."

Rebecca was tempted to fall to a chair and join them. They all looked so comfortable sipping iced tea, Dana and Padgett at the piano. The morning had seemed to go on forever, but the day wasn't over yet. She must see the Featherby judges off, and more importantly she hadn't yet spoken to Quentin. Though he had been all smiles for the judges and completely caring during the crisis of chasing down the wandering Padgett, not one word had been exchanged to indicate whether he'd made a decision about where his heart rested. With Rebecca or back with Lady Caroline.

"Do you want some of the tea Helen brought in, or will you wait until the judges are gone?" Dana asked as she played "Chopsticks" with Padgett. "The tea is on the table."

Rebecca barely heard the question. What she heard instead was a tone of voice she'd forgotten could come from Dana. One of interest and, if not tranquility, at least calm without an undercurrent of fear or depression.

"I should go to the judges," she said, still eyeing Dana. "I will in a moment. It's been quite a morning, hasn't it?"

Dana nodded, smiling, echoing the keys Padgett pressed. They'd kept quiet and out of sight since their return, but now that the tour was over, they could make all the noise they wanted.

Instead of taking another step toward the front door, Rebecca stepped closer to the piano. "I haven't had a moment to settle down from this morning's adrenaline overdose. You two seem to have calmed down nicely, though."

Dana stood; Padgett continued to play. Dana stopped in front of Rebecca, placing two steady hands on Rebecca's arms. "As terrible as this morning felt, it taught me something. While you and Talie were off on that tour, I had the most incredible prayer time. Padgett and I both prayed; didn't we, honey?"

She nodded, never missing a note of the simple scale beneath her fingertips.

Talie approached too, a similar smile on her face. "Danes was just telling me about it, Rebecca. I don't think she needs her big sister telling her what to do anymore. Any authority not already ceded to Aidan I've lost to an even higher power."

Dana grinned, dismissing Talie's tease. "When Padgett told me she'd been depending on Emma to lead her home, it occurred to me all the worrying I'd done was needless. Worse, even though I was praying, I wasn't really trusting. Have you ever done that?" She laughed so briefly it sounded almost like a sigh. "Of course you have. You've been doing it all this time about Quentin. Do you know what I learned?"

Rebecca shook her head, unable to deny she'd done exactly as Dana accused.

"God has already given us the strength we need. We just have to get rid of all the layers of doubt covering it up. That's what tests do. I faced what every parent fears most: not knowing where Padgett was. Even if it only lasted an hour, it was the longest hour of my life. And I survived. I think I must be stronger than I thought, because not once during that whole horrible episode did I fall down in a heap and wrap myself into a fetal position, giving up. I made it through, and I think I can make it through whatever's ahead, too."

"All and whatever, as Cosima's journal says," Rebecca whispered, relief whisking through her at Dana's discovery. "So you'll be going to Ireland and joining Aidan soon, I take it?"

Dana nodded. "Tomorrow. Talie's coming, just to keep me company until Aidan finishes his assignment. He said we can go home at the end of next week." She pulled Rebecca close. "If I promise not to make hope an enemy anymore, you have to do that same thing. Remember what your father told you. The greatest hope comes after a surrender."

Rebecca closed her eyes and warded off ready tears, then opened her eyes again.

"The buses are leaving," Talie said from the window.

Dana squeezed Rebecca again. "Find him. Talk to him. You have to know. You said it yourself. The sooner, the better."

Rebecca knew Dana was right. She gave a single nod, then left the room.

He was outside with the judges, and when he caught her eye, he smiled. Instantly her breathing came faster, her pulse quickened. Would he look at her in such a way if he were about to say their relationship should revert to a professional one?

Before she could join him with the judges, Quentin extricated himself from the group and approached her.

"They want to go through their checklist one more time,"

he said. "I actually don't think they want us around for the time being. They asked to meet us in the gallery."

She followed him back into the house. Instead of going in the front entry, where they were sure to be obligated to join Dana and Talie, Quentin led her around the house to the veranda door. It was the shortest route to the gallery. They passed the Victorian tea ladies who lingered in their costumes though the tour had ended; they passed Helen on her way to the kitchen with a tray of soiled Irish china. At last they came to the gallery, their footsteps echoing on the shiny marble floors.

"We could use a few minutes alone, don't you think?" he asked. "There's something we need to discuss."

Rebecca agreed, her heart at once hot and cold, the sensations clashing in her chest and constricting her breathing. "We might want to see the judges off first."

"They said something about walking back to the cuddle farm." He looked around the room at the portraits, the marble busts, the ceramic artwork that represented generations of collectors, of wealth and aristocracy.

Rebecca looked too. It was all so familiar. Would another woman, one like Rebecca without a lofty line of ancestors, feel out of place in such a room? Perhaps. But Rebecca's past was woven through Quentin's, and since hearing the words Talie had spoken the night before, she was thankful for the servanthood her family stood for.

"This seems as good a place as any for our discussion, don't you think?"

Rebecca pulled her gaze from the aristocrats around her to the one in front of her. She nodded. Indeed, this was the perfect place, no matter what the outcome. If Quentin had chosen one of his own kind, perhaps it could be better understood here.

"Do you know why I left, Rebecca?"

The answer was too obvious, but she needed to say it aloud

even though the truth behind the words cut into her heart. "You went to London. To see Lady Caroline."

He shook his head. "I did go to London, and I did see Caroline. That's not, however, why I left." He paused.

She could see him gathering thoughts like so many lost puzzle pieces, something between confusion and eagerness on his face.

"I have another question for you. Do you remember when we were just working together before we admitted any personal feelings for one another?"

One brief nod was enough; that relationship had lasted far longer than the personal one might.

"On occasion you would say things along the line of protecting me, and always, always, your actions followed through."

"Yes, that's my job. To protect the interest and integrity of the family."

Quentin grabbed her hand. "Don't you see? It made you seem the stronger of the two of us. It was part of the reason I hesitated so long to confess my feelings for you. Perhaps why I started seeing Caroline to begin with, when even then I found myself wanting to know you better from the first moment we met. Do you remember when that was?"

"I began working here three years ago—"

He stopped her with another shake of his head. "No. Your father brought you here when you were fifteen and I was sixteen. You came to see the home where so many Seabrookes had invested their lives."

She remembered too well. It was the first time she'd seen him in person, though she'd imagined talking to him many times before that, ever since her father had drawn attention to his picture on the society page. Of him next to his mother at a polo match.

"I think I fell in love with you then, Rebecca, all those years ago. I knew you excelled in every subject at school—my father

mentioned it——that you graduated with far more honors than
I ever tried to achieve. That you were active in your church. In
any event I never forgot you, and when you came here to work,
I was a bit awed, amazed you chose to start a career here instead
of anywhere else. And you excelled here too, of course, as I fully
expected. Still, there was that . . . feeling in the background that
you were not only smarter but stronger than I. It made me feel
less a man. Can you understand that?"

"I never meant to make you feel that way."

He nodded. "Yes, I know. That made it worse."

There was a longer silence this time. Weight mounted in
her chest, compressing her heart, her breathing. Rebecca hadn't
expected this. She'd expected him to tell her his choice, and
even if in the deepest part of her she believed he might choose
her, she had tried to prepare herself otherwise. Only nowhere in
that preparation did he tell her why she'd failed to keep his love.
Perhaps someday the knowledge might be useful, but for the
moment all she wanted to do was flee.

Yet his quiet voice kept her immobile. "The other day, when
you told me you were afraid, it made me realize for the first time
that you weren't immune to all the fears and insecurities the rest
of us are subject to." He gave her a lopsided smile. "One would
think that would have made it easier, putting us on a more level
field. It didn't, and that's why I left."

Must he be so thorough in his explanation? Each word stung.
"Because I was no longer the person you thought?"

"No, because suddenly I saw myself capable of disappointing you, responsible for letting you down someday. Hurting you.
All the time I thought I was safe from doing that to you, because
you had this special ability to read everything around you, expect
what was ahead, be prepared——and therefore spare yourself,
somehow, the unexpected blows the rest of us face. When I realized you were every bit as afraid as I am to go through the pain of

loss, it made me worry I might someday be responsible for doing that to you. So I had to make sure I would never do it."

That he thought of her so unrealistically, put her so high on a pedestal of human understanding, magnified how wrong he was. Had she hidden herself so thoroughly from him that he wasn't able to figure out how little she really knew? Even as she asked herself that, she repeated in her mind the last words he'd spoken. If he thought of her so unrealistically, they only needed the truth to set things straight.

"I don't expect anyone to be perfect—myself or anyone else around me," Rebecca whispered. "Have I really been that intellectual snob you once believed me to be?"

"No, it was I. I was the one with the cloudy vision."

"How do you see me now, then?"

"At the moment, just about as insecure as myself. I'm not sure that's a good thing, but it's comforting at any rate."

"I think all you need is time to realize my many faults. I'm not only insecure, I'm jealous—an especially unattractive trait."

"That's because I've been irresponsible in the way I handled things with Caroline. I shouldn't have allowed my mother to invite her to stay at the cottage, not when I was pursuing a relationship with you. I see now it was inconsiderate at best. And when she left, I never should have offered her my flat. I thought I was being generous, kind even. It was thoughtless. If I'm to convince you I'll never let another woman come between us, it should begin with her. A clean break, one that won't have you—or Caroline, for that matter—wondering if any remnant of that relationship still exists."

"And does it?" Her heartbeat battered her chest, needing the answer.

Quentin shook his head. "No."

"Not even if she's discovered a faith similar to yours?"

"I hope that's true. Maybe some spark of faith is igniting in her, but that's between Caroline and God. In the year I've been away from Caroline, I've gained perspective that's even more accurate than I had when she and I first parted. I see now that we couldn't have gotten on well for long." He grinned. "I also see why my mother likes her so well. They're a bit alike. I've always seen myself living here at the Hall after I marry. If I were to marry Caroline, I fear I'd be repeating what my father did and end up with Winston my only companion." He tried to make light of the comment but in a moment closed his eyes. "I cannot promise not to let you down from time to time or even that I won't die as your mother did, but I will promise you this: the cause will never be because of another woman, past, present, or future. I promise you whatever pain I may cause won't outweigh the happiness I try to bring to your life."

Hot tears gathered, stinging the corners of her eyes. "I couldn't ask for more than that."

He gathered her into his arms, stroking the side of her face where an errant curl had fallen. "I told my mother that I was planning to ask you to marry me today. She won't stand in our way."

"She gave her blessing earlier, I think." Such as it was.

Quentin eyed her. "Did she give my surprise away, then? Let you know my intention before I had the chance?"

"Perhaps if I was more astute I'd have guessed something along those lines, but no."

"Well?"

She raised her brows, perplexed.

"Your answer?" he prompted.

Rebecca laughed. "How can you not know? Of course I'll marry you, Quentin! Oh—on one condition."

His frown returned. "What's that?"

"That you'll let me serve you. It's in my blood, you know. Twelve generations."

"We'll serve each other."

He kissed her then, and Rebecca was grateful for his firm hold; this measure of happiness made her light-headed.

She wasn't sure what noise distracted her or if Quentin had noticed anything at all. She pulled away and his gaze followed hers, turning to the threshold on the other end of the long room. There stood three members of the Featherby committee and another woman Rebecca didn't recognize. She hadn't arrived with the judges earlier.

"Ah, we've been found out again," Quentin said amiably. "This room isn't very good for privacy, is it?"

Taking Rebecca's hand, he pulled her forward. "Forgive us."

Eva Wetherhead nodded with a smile, holding her notebook to her chest. "Nothing to forgive, Mr. Hollinworth. You may live in a national treasure, but it's your home, after all. We're all in your debt for letting us trespass now and then." She glanced down at her notebook. "We only need your signature and to leave this copy with Miss Seabrooke." She handed Rebecca an envelope. "A schedule of when you can expect to hear from us." She smiled warmly. "But I must say, you might want to leave the award banquet date open."

Rebecca felt Quentin's arm slip tighter around her.

"We'll be sure not to plan our wedding on that day, then," he said with a grin.

Three gasps sounded, two from the Featherby judges and a third from the other woman who stepped from behind the judges. She toted a camera, and Rebecca knew instantly she wasn't a late judge but a reporter.

"I can quote you on that, Mr. Hollinworth? You and Rebecca Seabrooke are getting married?"

"As soon as the event can be planned. And with Rebecca's experience, I should think it won't be much trouble at all."

"May I take a picture?"

This was something new, asking permission. As Quentin pulled her closer yet for a pose, Rebecca decided she would find out the reporter's name and ask her about covering a fund-raiser she had in mind to benefit medical research into fragile X syndrome. Events covered on the society page always received the most attention. . . .

My dear, dear Cosima,

As I think back upon my arrival here, how I was so
hopeful and yet ill prepared, how I learned so much about
the truth of God's plan for me, nearly suffered His
mission's loss, and yet learned to worship Him through it,
I can tell you most honestly that my life has never been
richer or happier. I have learned true contentment in
serving others, not the least of which is my husband, who
serves in his way. I am, without doubt, a cloudy image of
the Most Holy, but I believe He is teaching me even
through my flaws. When I thought I might lose the
school, I knew I had learned one thing: that the dream
He gave me would be fulfilled regardless of whether He
used me to do it.

And now I look forward to so much more. We do
have a most unconventional marriage, but to me it is only
unconventional in its passion. Simon and I have learned
how to fight on the same side, mainly for those less
fortunate than we.

Some of the publicity, no matter how unfounded, is
slow to die. Mr. Truebody, in his eagerness to work with
Simon, came to visit and suggested we change the school's
name. And so we have chosen a name in honor of the
picture Katie once drew, which now hangs just inside the

school's door, the first thing one sees upon entry. The sparrow, beloved of God, not forgotten. Simon and I take care of the sparrows together, as God has led us to do. And so we are no longer Escott Manor but Sparrow Hill.

Already we are making plans to open yet another school, closer to Simon's home near Dublin. There is so much need, and now with the Lunacy Commission more than ready to help, we feel confident Mrs. Cotgrave and our staff can take care of Sparrow Hill while we focus on a second school. There is, of course, some benefit in working closer to our home. Do you suppose we might petition Parliament to move here as well so Simon should not have to travel so far? (I hope you are smiling at my whimsy.)

In any case, I plan to travel with him to London from time to time, so you and I will have more time together once I have learned to trust that the school and its new counterpart run well with me there or not. It is a plan I most eagerly await.

Until next time, my dear Cosima. May the God who loves us both never let us forget that His ways are best.

Your loving sister-in-law,

Berrie

Dear Dana,

Congratulations on the birth of your daughter! I received the photo attachment to your e-mail without trouble, and little Riley is adorable. You, too, look incredibly lovely for having given birth only a day before the shot was taken. The progression of photos from then until now shows the joy has only increased in your life, day by day, throughout the past month.

Quentin and I prayed continually as the day of your child's birth drew near. It's interesting that the doctor was able to use cord blood to determine the fragile X status, and we'll continue to pray for His will as Riley grows up knowing she will face a future similar to yours as a carrier. But as you know, the Lord's limits are broad, and His help endless to achieve what He's designed us to do.

In your note you expressed your gratitude for my help in seeing you through a difficult time. Dana, we were there for each other. It was all part of God's perfect timing, you know, that we should be there for one another, holding up one's faith when the other faltered. It's how the body of Christ works.

My wedding date draws near, and I can see proof in your pictures that you'll be fit to travel to be my matron of honor, as we planned the day months ago. I imagine traveling with a nursing baby and Padgett and Aidan (forgive me, did I just lump him in with the children?) will be a challenge, so if there is anything Quentin or I can do to make this more manageable, please let us know. We'll be off on honeymoon to Greece, so Helen and William Risdon will be pleased to have your company here in the Hall for as long as you can manage a visit, your family and Talie and Luke's as well. You must take them round to all the sites you only half saw when Quentin and I tried distracting you in the early days of your pregnancy.

It will be wonderful to see you again, Dana. When I look at my wedding photos years from now, I shall always remember what our friendship has taught me. The greatest hope comes after surrendering, whether that hope is fulfilled in our lifetime or not. So thank you for helping me take a step toward greater wisdom, my friend!

See you soon,
Rebecca

A NOTE FROM THE AUTHOR

Having fragile X syndrome enter my life was the beginning of many new life lessons for me, not the least of which was in the area of servanthood. Now why should learning such an apparently simple thing demand a dramatic, life-changing circumstance? Perhaps because it was something God didn't want me to forget. In Christ, God embodies the heart of a servant, from washing His disciples' feet to shedding His own innocent blood for others who are guilty. Perhaps it should be easy to learn from such an excellent example, but for me it came through serving my handicapped son.

I don't pretend to get it right every day. But I do thank God for teaching me there is dignity in serving, and healing in doing so. When you serve others, as Isaiah put it so eloquently, "your light will break forth like the dawn, and your healing will quickly appear."

If you would like to know more about fragile X syndrome, please visit www.fragilex.org. I pray for the day when fears like Dana's will be made obsolete by a cure.

Maureen Lang

ABOUT THE AUTHOR

Maureen Lang has always had a passion for writing. She wrote her first novel longhand around the age of ten, put the pages into a notebook she had covered with soft deerskin (nothing but the best!), then passed it around the neighborhood to rave reviews. It was so much fun she's been writing ever since.

Eventually Maureen became the recipient of a Golden Heart award from Romance Writers of America, followed by the publication of three secular romance novels. Life took some turns after that, and she gave up writing for fifteen years, until the Lord claimed her to write for Him. Soon she won a Noble Theme award from American Christian Fiction Writers, and a contract followed a year or so later for *Pieces of Silver* (a 2007 Christy Award finalist), followed by its sequel, *Remember Me*.

Maureen lives in the Midwest with her husband, her two sons, and their new puppy, Susie.

Turn the page for an exciting preview from

the
Oak Leaves

*Her family tree yielded
a legacy she never expected. . . .*

MAUREEN LANG

Available now at a bookstore near you.

TYNDALE

1

The dull hum of the garage door sounded. Luke was home. Talie looked up from the books and papers spread across her kitchen table. She might have been tempted to stay up all night reading, but not now. Welcoming her husband home was the only thing she liked about his occasional business trips.

As the door from the garage opened, Talie stood to greet her husband. "Welcome home!"

He moved to put his briefcase in its usual spot, but finding the table covered with the memorabilia Talie had been studying, he settled it on a nearby chair.

"Hey," he said, taking her into his arms and kissing her.

Amazing how even after four years of marriage her heart still twirled at such a thing, especially when he gazed at her afterward. She read nothing but pure love in his lively blue eyes.

"Good to be home." He scanned the adjacent family room.

Talie guessed he was looking for the baby. "I tried to keep Ben awake, but he crashed about twenty minutes ago." She grinned. "You can probably get reacquainted around two in the morning, though."

"Has he been up a lot while I was gone?"

She nodded.

Luke shrugged broad shoulders out of his suit coat. "I'll look in on him when we go up."

"How did everything go on your trip?"

"Better than I expected. They offered me the job."

"They did!" Talie hugged him, then pulled away. "Why didn't you tell me when you called earlier?"

"I wanted to see your face." He kissed her, studying her again afterward. "And it was worth the wait."

Pride for him mushroomed from deep inside, spreading up and out through her smile. Once, before she'd met Luke, before other dreams had taken its place, she'd had a career vision of her own. Going up through the ranks of the education trail, from teacher to department head to curriculum director, from assistant principal to principal and on to superintendent. Now, seeing Luke's dreams going forward, she tasted vicarious living but, amazingly enough, didn't miss those old aspirations for herself. She was living a new kind of dream, one she wouldn't trade for anything.

"Congratulations, Mr. Architectural Engineering Director. When do you start?"

"Right away. I move into my new office tomorrow. They want me to restructure the department, so I'll probably have to hire a couple of new people."

"We'll have to celebrate. Get a babysitter, out to dinner—the works."

Luke loosened his tie and went to the refrigerator. As incredible as he looked in a suit, she knew he far preferred jeans and a T-shirt. He grabbed a Coke. "What went on around here while I was gone?"

"Jennifer down the street is starting a playgroup for the kids in the neighborhood. I'm taking Ben tomorrow."

"Sounds good. How many kids?"

"Five—all of them born last year like Ben."

He took a gulp of soda. "Did you have a good time at your mom's? Get a lot done?"

Talie turned back to the table. "The garbageman is going

to hate her on Tuesday, but the house looks great. I think she'll be ready to list it any day now. Look here. . . ." She held up the family Bible she'd been looking at before he arrived. "This is the treasure we found among all the trash."

"What is it?"

"A Bible that belonged to my dad's grandmother. I have a whole box of things that must have been hers. The letters are wonderful. Letter writing is a lost art now that everyone has e-mail. And look at this. I think it's a journal."

She picked up the smooth, leather-bound book. It was tied closed with a ribbon. "I'm almost afraid to touch it—the binding is cracked. It's all so incredible." Talie sighed, looking at all of the things strewn on the table. "This is like a call back, Luke."

He looked from the journal to her. "Call back?"

She nodded, her heart twisting from missing her dad. "When I was a kid our family would take driving vacations. On that first day we'd get up at three in the morning to miss rush hour traffic around Chicagoland. We'd all fall back asleep, but that's what Dad liked—to drive in the quiet. Sometimes, though, I'd sit up front with him. He used to say I was helping by keeping him company. I knew he didn't really need help. He just wanted me to feel useful."

Unexpected tears welled in her eyes. "He liked it when he could see taillights ahead. Not too close, just up the road." Instead of the kitchen table in disarray she saw a pair of round, red lights gleaming from an invisible dark road ahead. "He used to tell me that was his *call back*. The car ahead called back that the road was still there, free and clear for him to follow."

She blinked, seeing again the items in front of her. "These are like a call back. Seeing what's gone before can help us know what to expect from life. It's especially meaningful when it's your own family history."

Talie returned her attention to the Bible, opening it to the names and dates that went back to the eighteenth century.

"Is your name written in that Bible?" Luke asked.

She scanned the list toward the more recent additions at the end but then shook her head. "No, but my mom's is next to my dad's, with their anniversary date. So many names! For our next baby we can pick a name from the family. Like . . . Josephine or Sarah or Emily. Or here's one I really like: Cosima. We could call her Sima."

"What, no men in your dad's history? Aren't there any boys' names?"

"We already have a boy, silly. We need to hope for a girl next time."

"Fifty-fifty chance of it going either way, honey. Let me see." He took the Bible from her. "Matthew would be good. Or . . . wait. Branduff? Seamus? Sounds like a bunch of Irishmen. I thought your family was German and English."

"The German is from my mother's side. I guess I'll find out more about my dad's family from these names. But something awful must have happened in 1848. Five deaths are listed on the same day."

"Hmm . . . 1848. Ireland had a potato famine around that time, I think."

"That's probably it," Talie said with a nod. "Isn't it amazing that they couldn't feed themselves yet they kept birth records all the way back to the century before?"

Luke smiled. "I'm sure you have quite some family history there."

"And look at this. Dad really did have an Aunt Ellen. Ellen Dana Grayson, his mother's sister. But I'd rather not show this to Dana."

"Why not?"

"Because she's named for the mysterious Aunt Ellen. Her

full name is Ellen Dana, only my mom liked Dana better so we always called her that."

"So why is this aunt mysterious, and what difference does it make if Dana knows about her?"

"Look here." Talie pointed to an entry. *"Ellen Dana Grayson, born 1910, died 1941.* She never married, and she died in a place called Engleside. Sounds like a rest home, but she would've been too young for that. She must have been sick. I don't want Dana knowing she was named for some sick, lonely relative who never got married. You know how Dana is. She already thinks she's an old maid and she's not even thirty yet. She'll think history is bound to repeat itself just because of a name."

Luke shook his head. Talie had seen that look on his face before, the one that said she was being overprotective again. She was willing to concede she wanted the best for her younger sister, but that's how big sisters were *supposed* to be. She wasn't about to shirk her duty, even on a small point like this.

Luke was still studying the names listed in the back of the Bible.

"If I draw a rough draft and put all the names and birth dates in order, could you make a family tree?" she asked. "We could hang it in the study."

"Sure. Just birth dates, though? You're going to avoid anything morbid like when they died, even though that's the most interesting part?"

Talie hesitated.

"It's that date, isn't it?" He was watching her closely. "May 16, 1848."

"I know it's probably nothing more dramatic than the potato famine, but I guess I'd like to find out what happened before we advertise on our walls that five members of my family died on the same day."

"Don't get me wrong, Talie. I love a good mystery. But I don't think something that happened more than a hundred and fifty years ago can make much of a difference in our lives. Now let's go upstairs and peek in on that baby up there. And then—" he set aside the Bible and pulled her into his arms again, nuzzling her neck—"you can welcome me home as if I've been gone a lot longer than a few days."

Talie left their bed, knowing from past experience her movement wouldn't disturb Luke. His steady breathing said it was true again tonight.

She went downstairs to the kitchen table, where she'd left the dilapidated journal. It was old and stiff, the satin ribbon faded.

Touching one of the shamrocks engraved on the front, she untied the ribbon and opened the soft leather cover. The pages proved to be remarkably free of damage despite their apparent age. No water spots, no mold, just clear handwriting on thick paper that had barely yellowed through the years. Maybe it was a good thing her father had been so disinterested in the past; storing the items in the dry darkness of their attic hadn't done the collection any harm.

Talie instantly guessed it to be a personal diary. A stranger's, yes, but someone whose blood had flowed in her father and now flowed in her. She read the first page.

To my son Kipp and his wife, and to their children and children's children in America,

I can think of no better way for you to know me than to share with you my journal from the time in my life that revealed

God's plans for me—plans far different from my own.
This is my legacy to you.

    I assure you each word is true. If you inherit anything
from me, may it be the knowledge that love is stronger than
fear, especially with faith in the One who is love: "Jesus
Christ the same yesterday, and to day, and for ever."

—Cosima Escott Hamilton, 1874

Talie pulled out the Bible and turned to the records pages. *Cosima Escott, born in Ireland in the year of our Lord 1830, to Mary and Charles Escott. Married 1850 to Peter Hamilton.*

Born in Ireland? Talie's father had told her their heritage was English, not Irish. And the names Escott and Hamilton certainly didn't sound Irish. Pressing her finger along the records page, Talie found the year of Cosima's death: 1901. Though she'd died more than a hundred years ago, she'd lived to a ripe old age. Good for her; her years had outnumbered Dad's by almost a half dozen. Not bad for those times.

Strange that Cosima had chosen to write "love is stronger than fear" as her legacy.

Talie slid her finger down the death column again. There it was: May 16, 1848. . . .

Maybe Cosima's pages held the answer.